INN LOVE

FOR

CHRISTMAS

with love

Annie Elliot

Copper Crow Publishing

Published by Copper Crow Publishing
Bella Vista, AR

First paperback edition March 2023
Book design by Copper Crow Publishing

ISBN: 978-1-960985-00-2 (paperback) | ISBN: 978-1-960985-01-9 (hardback)

www.hillarysperry.com

Seasons of Sugar Creek: Winter

One Last Christmas
CYNTHIA GUNDERSON

A Home for Christmas
RIVER FORD

A Christmas Boyfriend Recipe
LISA H. CATMULL

Pining for Christmas
HEATHER TULLIS

A White Christmas Lie
AMEY ZEIGLER

Inn Love for Christmas
ANNIE ELLIS

Inn Love for Christmas

SEASONS OF SUGAR CREEK

ANNIE ELLIS

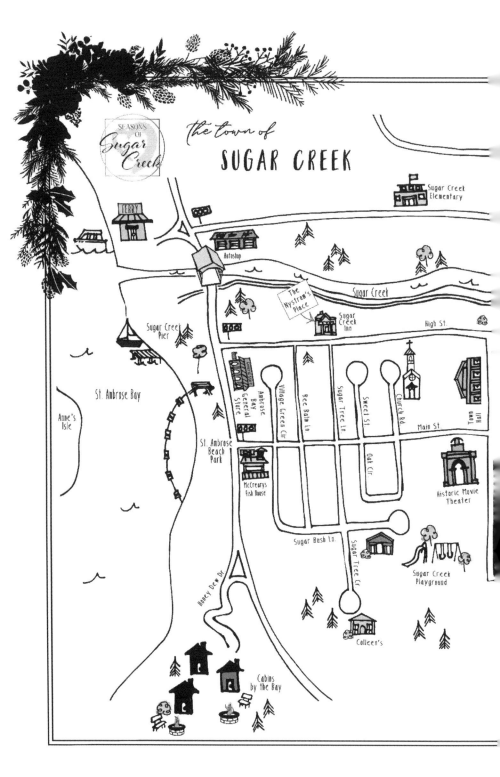

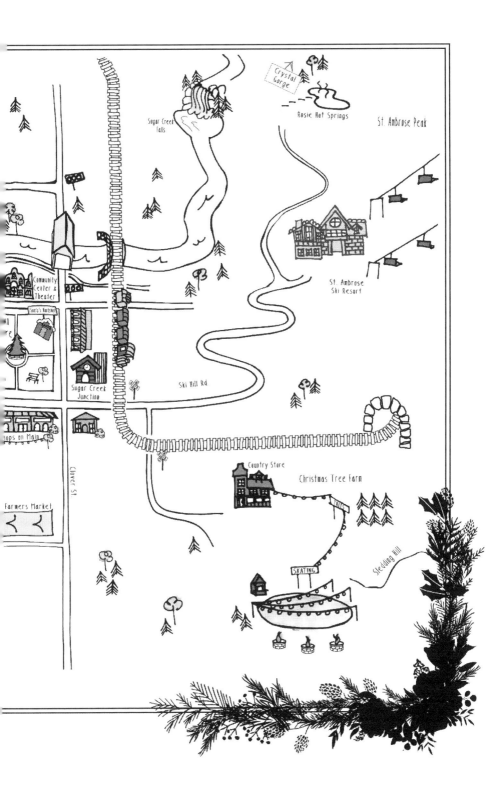

For Grandma Deannie Fish. &
Great Grandma Ingrid Nystrom

Your spirit and heart have blessed my
home with family, love, and unity
since I before I was born.
I am so grateful to have grown up in
a family rich with Swedish heritage
and family tradition.

Chapter 1

Lucy

Most people wish on stars.

They hold their breath as a star shoots across the sky or recite nursery rhymes about starlight. They wish on falling stars, evening stars, and the first star in the night sky.

Anyone can wish upon a star.

I wish on snowflakes.

My mother used to say that each snowflake holds a tiny bit of magic inside, and when the snowflake melts, it releases its magic. If you can catch a perfect snowflake on your skin and make a wish before it melts, your wish will come true.

Not the best thing to tell a kid if you want to keep them from getting frostbite. Since Arkansas tends to have very short winters, it was never much of a problem for me growing up. And on the rare occasion that snowflakes did fall, I'd be outside in my t-shirt and shorts, prancing around, counting the arms of every snowflake and making wishes just in case.

Of all my wishes, only one changed my life.

The year I turned eight, it snowed the day before Christmas Eve. As per usual, I had snuck outside in my summer clothes, dancing and making wishes while my parents argued inside.

I could still hear them fighting when a perfect, tiny snowflake fell on my finger. Maybe I'd been outside too long, and my skin was colder than normal, but I counted every arm of that snowflake without it melting. As I finished, something in the house crashed.

Please, let my parents stop fighting.

The wish burst out of me. I wanted it more than anything. As I blew on the snowflake, warm breath melted the flawless arms into a wish as it dissolved on my skin.

The wish worked. They stopped fighting. Then, the front door slammed, and my dad walked to his car and drove away.

I haven't seen him since.

I cried a lot that Christmas. But my mother soothed my tears, holding me while I told her it was my fault and I'd never make snowflake wishes again. Of course, she made me promise not to let an angry man destroy my love of magic. Snowflake magic may have changed my life, but her magic made it all okay again.

I only got one gift for Christmas that year, a tiny silver snowflake necklace, so I could always make wishes.

I've used all my wishes. After almost twenty years of wishing with my necklace, the magic is all dried up.

It's the only explanation for losing my boyfriend of five years. I wished him into my life and now after the magic is gone, so is he.

Bing! My seatmate jumps, knocking my elbow off the armrest between us as an announcement sounds on the overhead speaker. "Ladies and gentlemen, we're making our final approach into Burlington, Vermont.

Please stow your tray tables, put away all large electronic devices, and return your seats to their full upright position. We'll be landing shortly."

The older woman in the seat next to me grips the armrest. "Oh, my goodness. The landings are the worst. I've always heard the landings are the worst." She's wearing a bright red sweater with a light-up Santa brooch pinned to the lace collar. Christmas trees hang from her ears. I'd have thought I was sitting next to Mrs. Claus if her sweater wasn't printed with an outline of Vermont beneath the quote, *"Sweet as Maple Syrup"*.

"I'm sure we'll be fine. They've done this hundreds of times." I don't know if it's true, but I try to reassure her anyway.

"You're right, I'm sure. It's fine." The anxious woman pats my wrist and casually grips it. Her voice takes on an edge of panic. "Talk to me. Now, please. I need a distraction. Tell me anything. Why are you here?"

"Umm, I'm surprising my boyfriend." *Fingers crossed he's still my boyfriend.*

"That's precious. How long are you staying?" Her eyebrows have taken up residence in her hair line. A permanent expression of surprise quivers on her face as she glances nervously back and forth from my face to the window.

"We're staying till Christmas." I'm not sure if she can even hear me as her holiday fingernails tighten around my wrist.

"What's the occasion?" Would-be Mrs. Claus has closed her eyes, her face taking on a green undertone.

"He's got a family reunion the first week . . ." I check the seat pocket for an air sickness bag while I keep talking, trying to accommodate the anxious woman. It will really put a damper on the trip if she gets sick now. Besides, I'm wearing the sweater Erik bought me. It's fitted and low-cut, and I don't have a secondary get-your-boyfriend-back outfit. "Then we're supposed to spend the rest of the time at a little ski resort in Sugar Creek."

There's a slight wobble as the plane descends below the clouds and she's now gasping and fanning her face. "Oh, my." We descend past marshmallow fluff to where we can see land, and her gaze immediately zips back to mine. "I haven't had a boyfriend in fifty years. How long have you two been dating?"

"Five years." *Five years*, and he tries to break up with me over the phone. Not good enough, Erik.

"Oh, my. And you're staying in Vermont for Christmas? How romantic. Is this engagement time? I bet he brought a ring with him." She's looking much more relaxed.

I laugh bitterly. Everything I've said so far at least has potential to be true, but the idea that I could come home from this trip engaged is too much to even pretend. "Considering the fact that he changed his flight to leave before mine, and he wished me Merry Christmas after his breakup text, I'm thinking a ring's not in my future just yet."

The holiday spirit drains from the almost Mrs. Claus's rosy cheeks, along with all other color. "Oh." She clears her throat. "My."

I look away, leaning against the cold, oval window. Mountains and trees and picturesque villages dot the landscape as we glide toward the airport that will deliver me to my last hope.

The silver snowflake sprawls delicately beneath my fingers. It's habit to play with it and offer random wishes.

Bring Erik back to me. Let us stay together.

All my wishes hurt right now, but they're made, and I watch the snowflake closely as if it might melt away. It doesn't. It still has six perfect arms. As fake as my wishes.

Love is either a gift or a scam. A beautiful, unpredictable moment bringing people together and making them better, or a convenience for the lonely who need a buffer from reality.

At the moment, I'm undecided on which is the truth.

"It's all right, dear," Mrs. Claus mumbles. "True love only has to happen once. You'll find him." Then she turns to the person on her other side and redirects her conversation. "What brings you to Vermont?"

The air over her shoulder turns cold, and I sigh. It's probably for the best. I don't know if I believe in true love, but Erik is as close as it comes for me.

From the time I was eight years old my mother's revolving door of relationships kept a string of men in my life. At first, I thought she was trying to find me a new dad and I took every opportunity to connect, but eventually I stopped even learning their names. As I grew up, I started to recognize this as her version of love. Little did she know, her relationships gave voice to my *unique* dating list. Not a *Find the Perfect Man* list. It's a list for me, to remind myself of the things I can control.

Atop the list: *Don't add to the parade of men in my life.*

But Erik isn't part of the parade. When I met him, he checked boxes all the way through my list . . . mostly. He was supposed to be The One.

I didn't anticipate needing to wish our love back into reality.

My necklace glitters where I haven't entirely worn the finish off. I rub the shiny pendant anyway. If it's possible to have a true love, Erik is going to be mine. I force my skepticism away and think a new wish, for good measure.

Help me find my true love.

This is not a failed relationship. Wish or no wish, I'm going to prove it to him. My anticipation builds as the matchbox homes grow larger in the toy village below. Among white roofs and white yards, snow-kissed trees sport coats of even more white. Columns of smoke rise from the chimneys as the world shifts into life-size surroundings, and all of a sudden, it's real.

I'm here. In Vermont. And I'm going to get my boyfriend back.

"It's perfect." The breathy words have no destination. I'm alone, looking up at the German-style ski lodge above Sugar Creek. Three stories of cream-colored walls rise behind dark wood beams, crisscrossing the eaves. It sprawls along the mountainside, Christmas trees climbing the snowy banks behind it. An array of vibrant skiers zip down the mountain, tiny dots of color leaving wakes of white spray behind them.

The postcard scene of tourists in bright, squishy outerwear is a little surreal. Picking my way across the parking lot to the front doors, I pull my coat tighter. It's freezing. I didn't know I'd need a snowsuit just for walking around.

Once inside, golden walls and natural elements of wood and stone welcome me. *I can do this*, I think, making my way to the front desk.

Find Erik.

Kiss him.

Celebrate Christmas together.

Three simple things. Easy.

"Excuse me? My name is Lucy Sweet. I'm checking in with Erik Nyström. He arrived yesterday, can I get my key?"

The girl at the counter smiles behind square, purple spectacles. "How nice, Erik Nyström, yes. I think he just went to the restaurant. Oh –" The card is already in her hand when she hesitates. I have to stop myself from grabbing the keycard from her. "Are you sure he's expecting you?"

"Of course he is." My hands shake along with my smile as I respond, my eye on the unmoving keycard. "Why wouldn't he be?" Surely he didn't tell everyone that he broke up with me.

"Well, it's just . . . I can see that you were on the reservation, Ms. Sweet, but he left a note saying you weren't coming."

I force a laugh into the awkward silence. "Oh right, that makes sense. 'Cause I wasn't going to be able to. But then I could." My eyebrows have gotten expressive as I sell the narrative, and I take a moment to breathe. "So, I came. I wanted to surprise him, and here I am."

The reception clerk sets the keycard down as she considers me, brow furrowed. "Maybe I should clear this with him first."

"No, really!" I throw my hand out after the card, just short of ripping it from her hand. I give the counter a good-natured pat. "What if I check for you? You said he went to the dining area? I can surprise him there."

The girl nods, looking nervously down the hall.

"Okay, I'm gonna leave my bag here and I'll go talk to him. He can straighten this all out. I don't need a key for that." I swing a pointed finger at her and force a laugh. It's almost as awkward as finger guns.

Don't mind me. Just trying to sneak into my boyfriend's room. I let my fake enthusiasm go and follow the polished-oak signs toward the dining area. Voices and the tangy smell of cooked meat and spices lead me to a room full of tables. Skiers and guests gather around.

The room's vaulted ceilings and wall of windows create a massive space that overlooks the snowy mountains. A fire crackles in the large fireplace. A chandelier of woven tree branches sparkles with tiny lights, as if dozens of fireflies have been called to the fire and then caught in the branches above. It's beautiful.

It doesn't take long to find Erik across the room, standing at a tall table surrounded by other guests. I don't know if they're friends or relatives here for the reunion, but as I cross the room, the brunette talking to him notices me and steps closer till she's touching him. Hesitation weights my intentions, and I pause briefly before tapping Erik's shoulder.

I beam up at him, as he turns, waving me away. "Someone already got our order, thanks—Lucy?" Recognition and confusion taint his grin. "What are you doing here?"

Here's my moment of truth. I lift a shoulder and smile flirtatiously. "This is our vacation, isn't it?" Dropping my voice to avoid questions from the others, I lean in. "And we have a conversation to finish."

His brow creases. Before he gives his excuse to the others at the table. Taking my elbow, Erik walks us a few steps away. "I said everything I needed to yesterday."

"Don't I get a say in this? I'm not ready to break up. Especially not over a text message. We love each other, and I want us to give things another chance." There, that was almost exactly how I'd rehearsed it.

Only, in my head, Erik falls into my arms, kissing me and expressing his gratitude that I haven't given up on him. In reality, his nostrils flare, and he sweeps an arm around my waist, ushering me from the room. He doesn't stop until he's got me boxed into a corner of the hallway.

With one hand on the wall and the other on his hip, he leans over me. His blond hair doesn't fall forward thanks to his favorite pomades, but I can smell his fresh, outdoorsy scent. Tension ripples under his jawline as he shifts toward me, and I can feel the angles of his clean-shaven jaw without touching them. He's really close, but it doesn't look like he's planning to kiss me. "You're not supposed to be here."

"Why not? You broke up with me through a text. It doesn't work that way." My fears reel up, battling with my courage. The two of us together makes sense—I have to make him see that. "Think of all the great times we've had. Just last week, you told me you couldn't imagine life without me. What went wrong from then until now?"

"Nothing went wrong." His voice grumbles low, through clenched teeth. "Your ad campaign got me promoted. I was feeling pretty good." He glances over his shoulder and back in frustration. "But having you as a work partner is very different than having you as a life partner. I want to be with someone that excites me. I love you, but I'm bored, Lucy. This relationship is boring. I appreciate that you think you can save this, but trying to revive a stale relationship with more of the same thing doesn't save it." He hesitates, running a hand through his hair. "What happens when, one day, you or I find someone better? Then we'll be over anyway."

"That's not going to happen." It comes out like an echo, a terrible, painful echo of what I wanted.

"How can you know?"

"Because you're the one I want to be with forever. It's a choice, Erik." Tears and frustration boil inside me. His pride won't allow him to concede, but he knows I'm right. We deserve a chance. "I thought you loved me. Tell me you don't, and I'll leave."

"I don't love you anymore."

My brain stumbles to a stop as Erik's clipped words run in my mind. That's not what was supposed to happen.

Cold shards of anger intensify his blue eyes, staring into mine. I know he loves me. He said he did, just seconds ago. I won't let this man's anger or pride ruin my shot at lifelong romance.

"I don't believe you."

I take his hand. He pulls back, and it's as if a wall drops between us. He looks back toward the restaurant.

"Sometimes love isn't enough."

He turns down the hallway without another word.

"Love is always enough," I whisper, willing him to turn back. Wishing for him to come back to me.

But he doesn't.

I silently curse snowflake wishes and the blind hope that comes with them as Erik rejoins his table without me. Unclasping my necklace, I wrap it between my fingers and squeeze till it hurts. I want to drop it off a ledge or throw it into the mounds of snow outside. But I've worn it almost daily for more than a decade. I drop it in my purse instead.

"Love is enough," I whisper after him. I just have to make Erik see it too.

An hour later, I decide I've officially been scammed, by love and the internet. After being told there were no rooms available at the ski lodge, I went in search of a new place to stay.

Outside the car, the gravel I hold up my phone screen to compare the pretty little hotel in the photo to the dilapidated Pine Tree Cottage where I just booked a room. Anger flares wildly under my carefully contained emotional state. Never has a picture told more lies than this one.

"Ya were gonna stay here?" Gary, my QuickLyft driver, shakes his head. His thick New England accent makes it feel like I'm even further from home, pushing me to the verge of tears. "This place has been abandoned for years."

"Well, they should take down their website, then." My shoulders sink even lower than my spirits as the truth of my situation weighs me down. "I have nowhere to stay."

Gary approaches me from the car, and I fall into his arms, hugging him tightly. "Thank you. You're so nice. I really needed a hug."

"There, there," Gary says awkwardly, head swiveling as if trying to create space between us. "My wife always says tears are made for cleaning the soul."

It's not till Gary clears his throat that I realize he's not hugging me back. In fact, his hand is pinched over the handle of my suitcase, and I quickly connect the dots that he hadn't meant to hug me at all.

As soon as I step away from him, Gary grabs the suitcase with both hands and reloads it in the trunk. "We're gonna go get ya a New Englan' grilled cheese. That'll give ya somethin' to smile about."

When he pulls up in front of J's Burgers, my stomach rumbles a greeting, the smell of buttery carbs flooding the street.

Gary pulls out my luggage, and I offer him a sad smile.

"Thanks," I say as he pulls away from the curb. "Wait! My purse!" I call after him, throwing my arm up and waving to get his attention.

Gary screeches to a stop, and I open the door. Crawling to the opposite side of the backseat, I find it lodged between the cushion and the door. "Why can't anything be easy today?"

I set my phone down and use both hands to yank it free. When the purse finally slips out, I tumble backwards, and my knee hits the floorboards with the sound of ripping fabric. I look down at my torn pants and have to hold back tears. "You've got to be kidding me. This is just the worst day ever."

As he drives away, it's like I'm at the end of my own movie and my last chance just disappeared down the road. Roll credits.

I need to call Shaunda. Reaching for my phone, I find an empty pocket.

"No . . ." I gasp, giving myself a whole-body pat down to find it. "No, no, no! Gary!" I yell, trying to run down the road in my little, heeled boots. I'll never catch him.

My one way to communicate—gone.

I should have guessed this would happen. I'm not that lucky.

Lucy will always be one letter off of lucky. It's something one of my mom's boyfriends told me when I was a teenager. I can't remember his name, but the phrase stuck with me. Today, the distance between me and that *K* feels as big as the mountain I just left my boyfriend on.

Fighting back tears, I roll my shoulders and straighten my spine. I've lost my appetite. Finding a place to sleep tonight is more important than food anyway. Grabbing the handle of my suitcase, I trudge along the slushy sidewalk, toward the end of the block where a massive Christmas tree glimmers. Its ornaments shimmer in the cold sunlight, calling me forward. Strings of unlit lights grace roof lines and windows on every shop along the street, but the scene feels hollow and empty. Even the tree decked in darkened lights is unaware that something's missing.

Transfixed on the grand tree, my gaze tracks all the way up the branches to the top. I'm just like this tree. All day, the decorations think they're good enough, not realizing everyone's looking at them, wishing they were lit up. Not only the tree but the whole town square lies in wait, incomplete without its spark.

I've let my spark dim. Erik watched it go out. He was right, I have become boring. But I have spark. A lot of it. I've just waited too long to turn on the lights.

Chapter 2

Torin

"I'm pretty sure Santa Claus doesn't fix leaks," I growl from the kitchen floor in my red velvet Santa pants and boots.

"Be careful with that suit, Torin. It belonged to my papa."

"Yeah, Ma. That's why I left the coat over there. At the moment, I need the pants." I glance out from under the cabinet as my mother lays a towel over my legs.

"Just in case." She backs away, giving me a stern glare. "You know we've had that Santa suit as long as we've had this Inn."

After immigrating through Ellis Island, Dad's grandparents settled in the maple-filled mountains of Vermont. Great Grandpa Nyström bought his dream plot of land near a creek, with a view of the lake bay. He built a home to last generations, and Great Grandma built family traditions to last just as long. Their first year in Vermont, she sewed a set of red velvet robes trimmed in white fur, for her husband to play Santa Claus at the Sugar Creek town square festivities.

The Nyström men have been playing the jolly old elf ever since, or so the story goes.

Over the years, things expanded to become a full Santa's Workshop event sponsored by the Sugar Creek Inn, though everyone just knows us as the Nyströms. It's expected. And today, because my dad got hurt, I'm wearing an old Santa suit and fixing the old plumbing in an old house.

I lean into the wrench, twisting it around the sink drain. With a pop, the wrench slips off the pipe and I slump against the wall of the cabinet. "I've got to finish this."

"Daddy!" Alice appears in the doorway, the strings of two star-shaped paper lanterns in her fists. "Look at my pretty stars!" Both her pigtails have come undone, leaving her fine golden hair sticking out on the sides of her head.

"Hey, sweetie, where did you get those?" It takes a second to slide out from under the sink without damaging the sacred Santa pants. "Daddy spent the last two days hanging them."

Despite the staples and Christmas lights holding them in place, the roof of the wrap-around porch is apparently short a couple of star lanterns. Alice giggles and twirls, holding the stars out to her sides as they fly around her.

"Oh, *sötnos*," Ma says, calling her by the Swedish term of endearment and taking the lanterns from her hands. She sets them on the counter and taps Alice's forehead. "You are mischievous."

Alice looks at me, scrunching her nose adorably. "Why is Daddy dressed like Santa?"

"Because Gramma's very determined." I wink at my little girl with my arm stretched behind the sink disposer. It's harder to reattach the drain line from this angle, but when Alice is around, she never fails to command every ounce of my attention.

My mother narrows her eyes at me, then bends down to Alice's height. "Your Daddy is dressed up to be Santa's helper. Isn't that nice?"

"Uh-huh." Alice watches me and turns back to my mom. "Gramma?"

"*På Svenska*?" she asks Alice. *In Swedish?*

Even though I only know *en lite grann, a little bit,* of Swedish, my mother has decided it's time to start teaching Alice.

Alice's face squishes in worried concentration before her eyes light up. "*Farmor*?"

My grin swells when she finds the Swedish word for Grandma, but my mother is the one who sweeps her up in a tight snuggle. "*Mycket gott, sötnos.*"

Very good, sweetie. I like the phrase almost as much as Alice, who giggles in my mother's arms.

As I adjust the clamp on the drain line, Alice plays with my mother's apron strings. Her bright green eyes match mine. They're the only feature I can really claim. Her blonde curls and button nose are just like her mother's. When she smiles, Corrine smiles up at me through her.

Teasing Ma with her apron strings, my dad hangs on her shoulder. Ma waves him off. "Go bother Torin, I'm helping my Alice."

"What do you want, *en söt*?" Dad calls Alice by his pet name for her, *sweet one,* trying to sneak her away.

"Why does Daddy need to help Santa?"

My dad's eyes go wide, and he steps back. "Childhood trauma is your territory, *min älskling*?" *My dear.* His sweet nothings don't do much for Ma and she rolls her eyes before speaking to Alice.

"*En söt.* Remember when *Farfar* dressed up as a helper Santa?" She points at my dad to help Alice recognize the word for Grandpa.

Alice nods. "He fell down by the big Christmas tree."

I snort a laugh as I tighten the clamp on the reattached garbage disposal line. "Now I get to do all *Farfar's* chores."

"I sprained my wrist. I'm not useless," Dad says. "I can fix a leaky drain in my sleep."

"We know, *älskling*." Ma turns back to Alice. "Well, because *Farfar* is hurt, your Daddy gets to be one of Santa's helpers."

"We could ask someone else this year," I offer helpfully. "Where did I put the screwdriver?"

"Santa asks our family to be the helpers," my mother says firmly, and my dad puts the screwdriver in my hand. "And today is the first day that Santa gets to come to Sugar Creek and find out all the kids' Christmas wishes, so your Daddy has to go be the helper."

"Is Daddy an elf or Santa?" she asks, swinging her feet over the edge of the counter.

"Neither." I slide out from under the cabinet, stretching as I stand. "But today I'm pretending to be Santa. Is that okay? It's like playing dress up."

Alice gets a big grin on her face. "I like to play dress up too. Can we be princesses tonight?"

"If I get a crown." I kiss my little girl and set her on the floor. "Why don't you go play?"

Alice bounces from the room. We don't need to keep talking Santa with my four-year old.

There's a towel on the counter and I wipe my hands on it, nodding toward the sink. "Try it out, Ma. I think we're good."

She turns on the sink, and I instinctively pull back, flinching against potential water shooting from the pipe joints. Nothing happens, and relief soothes the tightness of my neck and shoulders.

"Thank you, Torin." She turns the water on and off happily.

Drip.

My head snaps to the sound. Drip. Somewhere a joint isn't completely sealed.

"Let me look at that. I'll take care of the problem." Dad leans over the sink, subsequently knocking his sling against the counter. He flinches, hard.

"No," my mother and I say in unison.

"Why not?" he grumbles. "A kitchen sink is easy. I learned to repair plumbing lines in skyscrapers."

"Is that when you built the Empire State Building? Or the Chrysler Building?" I'm not sure I've got the brain space to revisit my dad's questionably accurate stories about his glory days in New York.

"Watch your tone. I didn't build them, I'm not that old, but I've worked on 'em both. There's nothing like walking the scaffolding five hundred feet in the air without a tether."

"Maybe I should call a plumber." Ma looks my dad over, adjusting his sling.

"No. To both of you." I lean back under the sink, searching for the leak. Adding the expense of a repair man to the already tight budget shoots my heartrate up. I haven't talked to them about how bad the finances have gotten since Corrine died, and I'm dreading the conversation. My parents never had a mortgage on this place until my wife's medical bills were due. It's the reason I came home after she died. They refinanced their inn to help me, and now I'm trying to help them.

Trying to lighten the mood, I wink at Ma. "I'm not plumbing a historic building, but I'm doing my best. How will I ever find a woman as great as you if I can't prove I'm as good as Dad?"

"And who are you trying to win over?" She doesn't seem amused. Considering she'd like me to find a romantic partner, it may not have been the best joke. "Mmhmm. Well, your sarcasm isn't going to win you any points."

Dad's face appears next to me. "Is it working? Check the P-trap, it's always—"

"Don't pester him." Ma pulls Dad back by his good arm.

"Ingrid," his voice has gone pleading. "I don't pester. I'm supportive. Trust me, *mitt hjärta*." *My heart.* My dad can even make home repairs flirtatious.

"Let him finish," my mother says, unimpressed.

The pipe is damp along the back of the sink flange. I extract myself from the cabinet again. "I'll stop by the hardware store on my way home. I don't have time to fix it now."

"Oh, it's almost time for Santa's workshop to open. Wally, go get Alice for me," she says. He kisses her cheek before heading to the stairs after Alice.

"Why do you need Alice?" I ask, putting the Santa coat on. It's hot and the fur itches my neck.

"So, you can take her to daycare for a few hours. I have a Sugar Mamas meeting this afternoon, so I booked her a spot at the Happy Play Daycare."

"Daycare?" The word is a rock in my throat. "I thought you'd be keeping her?"

"She'll be fine." Ma hands me the belt and pats my shoulder. "You look very nice. Are you ready? It's time to go meet Blaire at the workshop."

"Blaire?" She lives next door and has taken to ambushing me whenever I go out, whether it's grocery shopping or the playground.

"Yes, she offered to be an elf, isn't that sweet?"

"Or devious." Now, she has an automatic excuse to be with me every day.

"You're being silly. You know that, right?"

"She cornered me last week, talking about a problem with her fireplace for almost two hours while Alice had a playdate at the park."

"Well, you did say your home repair skills would help you find a good woman."

"Blaire is probably ten years older than I am. It's not gonna happen. Besides, Corrine's only been gone two years. I've got time."

"Time," she tsks, "is a selfish sailor. Bringing in the haul only when he's ready and keeping your boat 'til the day is gone, and the fish are stinking."

I look down at my outfit rethinking my agreement to take on Dad's Santa duties. "I know you want me to do this, but I have a lot going on right now." It's only the first of December. It's going to be a long month if I have to be Santa with Blaire every day. "Can't we get one of your Sugar ladies to find someone? Why don't you ask one of their husbands to be Santa?"

Planting her hands on her hips, she falls into her full Swedish accent. "Torin Alik Hugo Walfrid Nyström, our family has a responsibility to this town. We are the Santas. The other *Sugar Mamas* have their own responsibilities. This is ours. You wouldn't let your mother down, would you?"

Never in my life have I wanted to go head-to-head with my mother, especially over Christmas. Only moments ago, she'd seemed all sweet and happy. Now, she's gone fierce. The steel of her spine magnetizes the air and, somehow, she's grown taller during her lecture.

I shrink a little, persisting in my argument. "I work here all day and with my Seattle office all night. I can't. I'm trying to pay back a loan. I'm not retired."

"What do you do? Look at your computer and tap the keys a few times a day. Go be Santa and tap later."

I may be a full foot taller than her, but I've never felt as small as when my sixty-year-old mother puts her hands on her hips and points out my inadequacies.

"I don't just tap keys. I'm a finance manager. You know that. And frankly, I'm lucky to still have a job. When I came home, I told them it was temporary, and it's been two years. I'm sorry Ma, but I've got things to do. I can't."

"Oh, so no Santa for us. *Nej*. Will you be the one to tell Alice that Santa forgot to come to Sugar Creek? And what about Alice and the other children? They want a Santa."

Alice is my weak spot, and she knows it. "Come on, Ma. What if Dad just does it some of the days?"

"If you want him in a cast by New Year's." Sass and guilt are my mother's secret weapons.

"Of course I don't want that." Maybe if I give Dad time to heal, he'll be able to help around here again and things will be less stressful. Not that it will fix the real problems. Things were bad before Dad hurt himself. If Ma wants me to play Santa a few hours a day, I should help her out.

"I'll be home before five," I promise, giving her a quick squeeze and a kiss on the forehead.

Taking Alice into the Happy Play Daycare dressed in full Santa gear wasn't my first mistake, but it was a big one.

I became an instant celebrity the moment I walked through the door. Kids wanted hugs and asked questions about the reindeer or Mrs. Claus. My favorite was the little girl who wanted to confirm her place on the nice list while ensuring her brother got coal.

Finally, back in the car, I shake off the jitters from my preschool preshow. It's three minutes after twelve. Santa's Workshop should be welcoming visitors right now. *The square is only a few blocks away. Relax.*

I'm turning the corner toward Main Street when my phone rings, lighting the screen. The call picks up on speaker and I greet my friend enthusiastically. "Max! You called back."

"Of course, man. I'm Max Crew, your real estate guru."

"You know, I've never heard a more annoying slogan," I grumble as I turn another corner.

"Then you shouldn't have come up with it."

"It was an accident. There's a reason I didn't go into marketing."

"Your parents wanted a finance guy?"

"Well, yeah, pretty much." Pausing at a four way stop, my gut tugs with nostalgia as a young couple pushes a stroller toward town square. I ignore it and pull through the intersection. "Hey, I wondered if you'd had a chance to look at my parent's property analysis."

"Right, cause you're selling. I forgot," he laughs. I don't say anything else, and the line goes quiet. "Wait, you were serious?"

There's a parking spot right behind the little red and gold building where I'll be spending the next four hours. I pull in and thump my head back against the headrest. "Yeah, I was thinking about getting it on the market before Christmas, if my parents agree."

"Oh, dang. I haven't even looked. I'm sorry, I thought you were joking."

I close my eyes. "I wish I was joking. Hey, I've gotta get going. I'm supposed to be Santa today."

"I'd totally tease you about that except that I'm trying to wrap my brain around you selling your place."

It's not quite twelve-ten. I'm already late – a few more minutes won't hurt. "It's my parent's place. And don't reach out to them about it yet, okay? We haven't talked about it. I want to find out some details and see what selling looks like first."

"Aw, man. I'm terrible at keeping secrets." Max drops his voice. "Is it really that bad?"

I nod in the empty car, the question squeezing my chest.

The inn used to pay for itself, but with the refinancing and a business mortgage and high interest rates, our sporadic guests don't cover our expenses. We're not making it.

"It's bad." *I failed them.* "We've got maybe a month or two before things get dicey, but that still gives me time, right?"

"Not much time."

I slam the car door and lean against the frame. There are plenty of visitors already out and about. Thankfully, most of them are hanging out at the firepits and the Main Street shops on the other side of the block. It's quiet here. I try not to let my emotions go crazy.

"I know, but they're in this situation because of me. Two years of trying and, instead of fixing it, we have to sell. I should have things together by now. I should—"

"Hey," Max interrupts my rant. "This is not your fault. You're doing your best. Your wife died, Torin. Nobody expects you to have everything figured out. Corrine was special to all of us."

His comment isn't completely out of the blue, but it still shocks me. I didn't intend to turn Max into my therapist, but my failure at the inn is pulling out a lot of stuff.

"Thanks," I mumble numbly. A wave of missing Corrine washes over me.

"Look, I've got to go. I'm supposed to be out there wrangling a bunch of snowy toddlers already. I'm sure Blaire's tired of waiting."

"Blaire . . . Thomas? You're joking."

"Don't ask." Fielding a few minor jabs, we say goodbye and hang up as I cross the sidewalk and garden at the back of the workshop.

The whole town square is bordered by a sidewalk. Santa's Workshop sits kitty-corner just inside it, facing the large Christmas tree at the center. The miniature plywood building was built by my father, from the displays of elves in the windows, to the gold curls on the bold red walls. It's very Christmas, but it's not perfect. The hinges are old, the supports need to be replaced, and the doorknob is starting to stick. Just like the inn, it's showing its age.

It does the job, though. Designed to go up and down quickly with the town's Christmas decor, it stores the loose decorations and supplies. I try not to think about what it will cost to replace when it finally breaks.

Circling to the front of the building, I find Blaire, waiting in the Santa chair.

"Torin!" She jumps up quickly. "I would have set up already, but I don't have a key. I put the sign out, though." Like a gameshow model, she holds her hand out to the *Santa's Workshop Is Open* sign.

"Thanks," I say, and she grins. "Maybe next time you can wait until I'm here, but I appreciate the effort."

"Oh, of course. That was silly. I was just trying to impress you. You know. Our first day and all." She turns away, flustered.

With Blaire and I working together, it only takes a few minutes to finish set up. Eventually, she positions herself at the head of the line, where a queue of kids is forming.

Blaire lets the first child past the candy cane ropes, and he climbs into my lap. I find out he's three and wants a truck with big wheels. I pose for a picture, give him a candy cane, and repeat.

An hour into the process my phone rings. By a stroke of luck, I've just sent the last kid in line to Blaire for a candy cane. I mime a telephone up to my ear with one hand and sneak out of my chair, heading inside the Santa's Workshop building. It's tiny and doesn't offer much privacy.

When I finally manage to get my phone out, I'm ready to shut the ringing block of metal off completely. Until I recognize the number. The daycare.

"Santa needs a minute," I call to Blaire.

I can just see her through the opening of the door, and she nods as a little boy grabs one of her long braids and pulls it.

"Hello?" The girl on the other end of the line greets me when the line connects. "I'm looking for Mr. Nyström."

"That's me." I turn around, facing the splintered plywood wall. "Can I help you?"

"Uh—" the girl drags the silence out like an old carpet, thin and worn. "You need to come pick up your daughter."

"I can't." I glance behind me at Blaire and the little boy out front. "I'm sorry, I'm working. Is there any other option?"

"Not really." This time there's no hesitation. "Alice is coughing on the other kids and it's scaring them. She needs to go home."

Denial breeds quickly. I knew daycare was a bad idea. "Alice is perfectly healthy."

"I'm aware. I heard the kids talking about her mother. Someone teased her about not having a mom, which was wrong, but Alice responded that her mother died of pneumonia and if she coughs on them, they'll get pneumonia and die too. Now half of the kids think they're going to die. You need to come get your daughter. Have a talk with her before she comes back, too, please . . ." She waits a moment and raises her voice. "Mr. Nyström? Did you hear me?"

"Yes." I blink at the wall, not sure what to do. The daycare is only a few blocks away, but it might as well be Burlington. "Yes, I did. I still can't come right now. Is there anything else I can do? Can I come in an hour?"

There's another shriek in the background of the daycare and a giggle makes me drop my head. I know that giggle. I'd recognize Alice's laughter anywhere.

"Mr. Nyström? I—"

"I'll take care of it," I say. A sound of exasperation slips from my throat in a short breath. "Blaire?"

"I'll get her." Standing behind me, Blaire answers the question I didn't ask.

Turning around, I realize how small the workshop really is. Big enough to hold Santa's chair and decor items in the off season. Not big enough to maneuver around another adult without touching.

Her lips twitch up into a brief smile. "I came in to get candy canes. I didn't mean to eavesdrop, but I'm happy to help."

Taking favors from Blaire seems like the wrong move. "You don't have to do this. I might be able to call—" I draw a complete blank. "Someone —"

I'm sure I look more desperate than ever. I don't have another choice.

"It's fine," Blaire laughs. "Santa can't leave the workshop when he has guests. You can't leave Alice either, so I'll get her."

It's fine. She's just doing a favor. That's all it is. I ignore the sinking pit in my stomach as her hips swing all the way out of the workshop.

Chapter 3

Lucy

When Erik said to pack snow boots, it didn't occur to me that they'd be different from my regular winter boots. But as I walk down the sidewalk over chunks of rock salt and dirty slush, it's become very clear that my faux-suede, moderate-heeled, Florida winter, ankle boots are not real winter boots.

Sidewalks merge with gutters under low mountains of dingy snow. It's not pretty, or picturesque, or anything like the snow globe world I was promised. At the end of the block, the large Christmas tree dominates my view. It's got to be more than twenty feet tall, sitting in a large town square type of area. It isn't far to the tree, but I've already slipped three times crossing this icy gauntlet of a sidewalk.

Why didn't Erik suggest hiking boots? Or tennis shoes, at least?

Probably because people who aren't from Florida understand what snow boots means. Or maybe because he knew he was gonna break up with me, so he didn't care. The thought comes with sniffles and more tears.

I breathe deep and slow like I'm in a frozen yoga class as a couple walks past, holding gloved hands. Thick bundles of bright-colored knit hug the woman's neck. The scarf pairs with a matching hat that has a fist-sized, fur pouf perched on top. She looks decadently warm.

I've never been so jealous of clothing.

For a second, I can feel the heat of the fireplace from the resort. I'm supposed to be there with Erik right now, cuddling by the fire. The thought sends my spirits spiraling.

I just want him back. Out of habit, I reach for the silver snowflake at my neck to make a wish, but it's not there. Right. I've given up on snowflake wishes.

Past the mucky piles of slush, I reach the corner, faced with the overly festive town square. A scene of nutcrackers stands guard over the fire pits and carolers in Santa's village, in addition to the giant tree at its center. I'm in no mood to appreciate the overall feeling of jolliness, and I almost turn back, but I still don't have a place to stay. Praying for a kindhearted soul to let me borrow their phone or give directions to a hotel, I tiptoe across the street.

"Ho, ho, ho!" Santa Claus' laugh startles me as I make my way around the town square.

Nestled in the corner of the snowy venue, a large sign proclaims I've made it to Santa's Workshop. A pair of sentinel nutcrackers flanks the small red structure while a procession of bouncing toddlers waits in an impatient column outside the plywood building. Snow lines the roof in evenly spaced mounds, like frosting on a gingerbread house. Golden swirls painted around the windows give the childlike workshop a magical quality. Without warning, my eyes burn with tears as I remember the days when snowflakes and Christmas wishes held all the magic I'd ever need.

Despite the adults keeping them in check, rowdy boys and girls dance and weave around the ropes and giant nutcrackers. Santa Claus sits on a large throne at the head of the tiny hordes. No elves, assistants, or awkward teens step up to help.

When I'm close enough to hear a little girl offer a plea for a Mini Me doll, I pause. I designed the marketing campaign for the doll she's requesting. It's good to know it works.

The little girl isn't as young as I originally thought, but the doll is her only request and the sweetness of the interaction tugs at my heart. I've been that little girl, sitting on Santa's knee with a simple plea. At heart, I might still be that little girl.

"Billy, get back here!"

The shout draws my attention. A panicked mom reaches out for her son, who is careening toward one of the nutcrackers.

I rush forward, catching the boy only a few paces from knocking the larger-than-life soldier on top of Santa.

"Careful." Trying to soften the reprimand, I smile down at him. Then he jerks out of my grip, knocking me off balance.

In my already treacherous shoes, I stumble, catching my foot on the red carpet in front of Santa's chair and tripping right into Saint Nicholas' red velvet lap.

I look up into Santa Claus' shocked face.

"Are you alright?" Then, correcting his tone, he laughs in a theatrical Santa Claus voice for the kids. "You're a little old for visiting Santa, aren't you?"

Behind his white beard, pale green eyes transition from shock to concern. This man is not a grandpa. I climb quickly out of his lap, and he stands, helping me to my feet.

"I'm so sorry." Glancing at the little boy reunited with his grateful parents, I brush myself off and shake my head. "I was just trying to help."

"I can see that." His cheek bones lift above the beard, his smile crinkling lines at the corner of his eyes.

They're captivating. A crown of peridot green surrounds his pupils, bursting pale lime striations out to a ring of deep moss. A fairy garden of green I can't stop staring at.

I drop my gaze to the ground. Guilt tightens my body from shoulders to toes for even noticing this man's beauty. His very solid biceps are thick under my clenched fingers when my awareness returns.

I let go quickly.

"Well, that's not embarrassing at all." Stepping back, my heel catches a stray spot of ice and I slip.

Fear washes over me. In a wild search for stability, I reach out to grab hold of Santa once again and something snaps as the magical Christmas land blurs to red.

Face planting into Santa Claus' chest wasn't on my Christmas list, but it should have been. I've now fallen into this man twice in two minutes. I can confirm, this Sexy Santa is entirely lacking the traditional milk-and-cookies belly. A blush of heat burns my neck and face.

Peeling myself off his velvet suit, there's something white and fluffy in my hand, but I can't place it. I straighten, fixing my sweater and brushing my hair back blindly. I'm preening, and it annoys me.

I look up to explain, but he takes my arm, quickly walking me toward the exit.

"Let's get you on your way," Sexy Santa says. Keeping his face turned to the building behind us, he lowers his voice. "So, can I have my beard back?" His voice has a deep familiar quality, sounding even less like the holiday icon, now that I've had such an up close and personal exploration of him.

He glances down at me, confusion in those beautiful green eyes. I've taken too long to respond, and I force myself to gather words . . . and thoughts. "I don't—um—I don't know what you're talking about."

Next time, I'll gather thoughts first.

Dark hair peeks out from under his fur-edged hat. Just a hint of stubble covers his square jaw. He looks like he belongs in the mattress ad campaign I'd been working on before I left Florida. We could easily cover 70-80% of the market, luring the entire female population and a good chunk of the not-so-female population to try out any bed he was lounging on.

"My beard. It's a family costume, so I need it back. Please?"

It takes a moment for his question to sink in. He's missing his beard.

"I don't have it." I sound a little defensive, and when he glances down at my hands, I follow his gaze. Sure enough, tucked into my folded arms is a pile of white curls. "Oh!" I hold it out, feeling like a fool for the third or maybe twenty-third time this morning. "I'm so sorry—again."

"Don't worry about it." He laughs, discreetly taking the beard back. His smile crinkles the corner of his eyes, coaxing my own smile forward.

He's easily six inches taller than me, and when he laughs, the smell of peppermint fills the air like he's been sneaking candy canes. Facing away from the kids, he reattaches the long white beard. Or tries.

He pulls the costume piece away, examining the back of the beard.

"Is everything all right?" I ask.

Sexy Santa's green eyes focus on the damage, and his smile transitions to a perceptive frown. "I think it's broken."

"Can I see it?" I know as soon as he hands it to me what's wrong. The elastic snapped. "Shoot."

My worry returns in full force. I feel sick. Sneaking a glance behind me, I point to the workshop. "I might be able to help. Go back there, behind the building. I'll meet you in a second."

He cocks his head as if he's weighing the options, but based on the whining starting up behind me, I don't have time to explain.

"Please? Trust me," I say, steeling myself for an argument, but he nods and leaves. Back with the crowd of children and parents, it takes a sharp whistle to get their attention. But when they all face me, I offer a bright smile. "Hi everyone. Santa is feeding the reindeer, but he wants me to tell you he'll be right back. If you're really good while you wait, Santa will have two candy canes for each of you when he gets here."

There are only a few whimpering children when I leave. I grab my suitcase and hurry after Sexy Santa.

I've got to stop calling him Sexy Santa.

Santa's Workshop backs up to the sidewalk that runs around the edge of the square. The red building is a bold accent to the snow-covered garden plots. Standing near a little archway lined with greenery and ribbons, Sexy Santa completes the holiday decor.

Dang it. Santa! Santa. Not Sexy Santa.

The *very handsome* Santa Claus man completes the holiday decor.

"I hope you have a plan," Sexy Santa says, "because it sounds like you're promising my candy cane supply if I don't make it back quickly."

"Oh, you misheard me. I promised double candy canes, regardless of when you get back."

He leans his head back and groans.

Peppermint tangles in the air between us with something else. Eucalyptus or evergreen . . . something fresh and spicy. It's nice. It reminds me of Erik. Memories fill my head. Erik's scent brings everything from laughter and sunny beaches to arguments in a snowy lodge.

"Hand me the beard." I pull my travel sewing kit out of my bag, as Sexy Santa holds out the damaged costume. Taking it, I put the elastic back in place and start stitching.

"Are you any good at this?" He sounds nervous. "That's a family heirloom."

"I'm good enough, but thanks for the added pressure." Looking up, a laugh almost escapes, but my breath catches. We're almost nose to nose before he pulls back, watching me. Warmth rises through my neck, heating the skin below my jawline. It's a struggle to finish the stitches and tie off my thread, but I finally manage to trim it and hand it back. "Here," I say. "It should be fixed."

He keeps his distance, and the air cools as he looks over my work. "That's perfect, thank you. You may have just saved Christmas."

"Nothing that dramatic."

He holds up the beard. "Pretty close." His eyes drift over me, and fire flares in my gut. "You blush pretty easily, don't you?"

I take a deep breath and release it slowly, focusing on the snow. The very cold, icy snow. I have to relax. I can handle this. Prepared with a calm smile, I look up. "It's not that bad. My mother was the same way."

"So, it's genetic?" He smiles.

My body temperature rises. If he wasn't so good looking, this wouldn't be such a problem. I may have just broken up with my boyfriend but I'm still a fully functioning, grown woman. *Fully functioning,* I think. *That's the problem.*

"You should thank her. It's cute."

I scoff and turn away. "That's the first time anyone's ever told me that." Erik used to point out my flushing skin every time it happened, but it was more of a request to chill out than a compliment.

"I should get back to work." Putting the beard on only partially covers his face. His eyes are still a problem. "How do I look?"

"So good." I breathe. He quirks an eyebrow at me and doesn't even try to hide his grin. I catch myself and adjust my tone. "Good! Good. Great." My inflection changes on every attempt to recover from sounding so besotted. "You're very . . . merry."

He narrows his eyes, like he doesn't believe me. "My beard is crooked, isn't it?"

"A little. Do you care if I fix it?" I reach for the side of his beard, hesitating.

"Please," he says, leaning forward.

It's unexpectedly intimate, and I can't quite fix it. I give up with an awkward apology, and he pulls the beard off, revealing the full force of his smile. Those lips.

My stomach flips.

"Mommy, are they gonna kiss?" A little voice asks behind us.

We were supposed to be hiding from the children, but on the snowy sidewalk surrounding the square, a little girl and her mother walk past in thick coats and hats.

"Of course, honey. They're under the mistletoe." The mother keeps walking, unconcerned with Santa's romantic life.

Mistletoe? I look up in shock. We've moved under the garden arch, and above us is a bundle of white-berried mistletoe.

The girl stares back at us and Sexy Santa pulls his gaze from her to me. "Should we?"

I blink at him. Did he really just ask me that? "Umm, I—"

"It's just a kiss." He bends close, whispering, "A mistletoe kiss."

"Oh—" I shrug, my mouth open in surprise. "Yes—umm, okay. It— umm— it is . . ." *It is mistletoe.* That's what I'm supposed to say. But he's grinning and I've lost my voice. I suddenly feel very dry.

His eyes drop to the movement of my tongue as I lick my lips and he pulls me close. Brushing his lips against mine, there's only the pressure of a brief kiss before I pull back.

The fleeting warmth is shocking. *It's just a kiss.* I shouldn't like the feel of his lips on mine, shouldn't feel anything at such a quick, nothing of a kiss.

"Is everything okay?" His hands have found their way to my back, fingers pressed into my body. He looks down at me, letting his gaze glide over my skin and end back at my lips.

His mouth moves as he says something else and waits for me to respond. Unable to take my eyes off his lips, I nod. I have no idea what he's said. Voices and Christmas music have morphed into vague, white noise, buzzing in my mind. When the corners of his lips turn up in a grin, longing tingles over my skin.

This time, when Sexy Santa pulls me closer, I go willingly.

It's just a kiss. A mistletoe kiss.

Our lips meet again, and my thoughts meld into the press and pull of his mouth. Heat dances through my body, and it's nothing for my hands to find their way up his chest to the back of his neck. Pressing my fingers into his skin and hair, I push his Santa hat askew with one hand and grip his velvet sleeve with the other. His hands answer me, sliding across the back of my waist and up my spine. Intoxicated by the gentle force of his lips, I let him lead me deeper into his embrace until the connection breaks.

The kiss is over.

There's no need to pull back.

Green eyes rove my face. We're separated by nothing but panting clouds of peppermint white breath. He strokes a thumb down my cheek, leaving a line of fire.

Desire rushes through me, sucked into my hollow chest like opening the window on a burning building.

That was not just a kiss.

I've never kissed a stranger.

I'm not like that.

Apparently, I'm boring.

Take that, Erik. I don't even know his name, and I kissed him. *Not so boring now!* Heat spreads across my neck and shoulders as the memory of Santa's kiss rolls through me.

I just broke up with Erik. How could I kiss another guy so soon? Even if it wins the title of sexiest kiss of all time. . .

No, I tell myself. *That was not sexy. It was bad.* I was lured onto the naughty list by Santa Claus himself.

Kissing that man is dangerous. Erik is safe. Slow burn versus wildfire. Compared to that kiss, kissing Erik was like kissing a brother. Not that I'd know, but . . . *Wow. I should have gotten Santa's number.* No, it's good that I walked away. I couldn't handle being around him any longer.

Rule number two of my dating list: *I will not date a man based on attraction alone.*

My suitcase bumps off the slushy sidewalk, tipping and jerking me to the side as it falls.

"You've got to be kidding me." My anxiety ratchets up as I step into the snow-crusted street to retrieve my suitcase. "Where am I?" I can still see the town square in the distance behind me. But somehow, I've made it to a residential area.

Yup. Way too much attraction to be clearheaded.

I'm supposed to be looking for a place to stay. But pretty houses, woodsy-smelling smoke, and holiday decor are not good indicators of hotels in the vicinity.

Jerking my suitcase up onto the sidewalk, I pick up my pace. A sign hangs in a yard up ahead. I take a few steps forward. *Please, let it be somewhere to stay and not a lawyer's office or funeral home.* When I'm close enough to read the scrolling letters carved into the rough wooden surface, tears prick my eyes. *The Sugar Creek Inn.*

My bag has somehow gotten heavier, and I pause on the front walkway to compose myself. I'm breathing heavy, and I'm ready to collapse in the snowy front yard. Even so, if they've got open rooms, I just might kiss another stranger smack on the mouth.

It's a beautiful Victorian home. A Christmas tree glows in the window. a sea of white paper stars dangling from the roof of the wrap around porch. The most beautiful thing of all is a little sign hanging near the front door that reads *Vacancy.*

It's going to be all right.

That simple thought seems to bring the day crashing down on me. Everything that's gone wrong is suddenly too much, from the breakup to losing my phone, and then getting stranded without anyone to care. Tears catch in my throat, but there's still no one to notice them. Pushing the door open, I stuff my emotions down and call out, "Hello?"

Golden plank floors and warmth welcome me inside. The check-in desk stands to the left with a bell on its dark wooden counter. It matches the rest of the trim boards, decorated with greenery swags and woven, paper hearts. A woodstove burns in the corner and my heart does a double step. The smell of smoke is light and delicious. It's like I'm in a gingerbread house, or a woodland cottage from a hundred years ago. Or I might be in heaven. Except that it's empty.

"Hello?" I feel a little like Goldilocks, ready to investigate the beds of the three bears. Scents of cinnamon and ginger mingle with something savory, pulling me past the entry hall.

A bustling sound comes from around the corner and an elderly man with his arm in a sling appears.

"*Ja? Hallo?*" speaking in a heavy Scandinavian accent. His wrinkled frown turns up when he sees me. "Ah, welcome to the Sugar Creek Inn. Do you need a room?"

Chapter 4

Torin

"And I want a soccer ball, and professional hockey sticks, and . . ." The little boy on my lap hasn't stopped for air since he started his list of Christmas wishes.

I discreetly glance at my watch while smiling at the little boy on my lap. Five minutes and thirty seconds until four o'clock. That's well into the Christmas-gimme monologue, and only thirty seconds since I last checked the time.

". . . I want a light-up frisbee for my puppy, with light-up shoes for me, and a skateboard, a BIG can of whipped cream, and a new game system—"

Pause.

"That's a big list, Zeke," I interrupt, grateful for the opening. "How did you remember all that?"

"Zack." The little boy on my lap looks up in horror. "I'm Zack. You're not going to give my stuff to someone else, are you?"

"I meant Zack." *How could I forget his name?* That's got to be a big no-no in the Santa handbook. "I would never give your things to someone else."

The little boy nods, picking up his monologue with more requests, and my jaw drops. Trying to give him the attention of a real Santa, my strained smile belies the truth. I don't want to be here.

Four minutes and thirty seconds until close.

Zack says something about a race car, or playing cards, and I glance to the end of the block. I could tell myself I'm not looking for the woman in the pink sweater . . . but it's not true. Her face is seared into my memory, complete with blonde hair, blue eyes, and soft lips.

Blaire clears her throat beside Zeke-Zack's parents. She's standing with camera in hand, waiting for my go ahead. I adjust the little boy so he's turned toward the camera and interrupt his Christmas wish list. "Let's take a picture for your parents."

Blaire lines up the photo as the boy protests. "But I'm not finished."

"It's all right. You've given me some good options." I smile and Blaire clicks the picture just before I lift him off my lap and set him on the ground. "Have a merry Christmas!"

Blaire ushers him back to his parents, rewarding his grabby attitude with a candy cane.

My eyes track to the end of the square again, replaying the kiss in my mind. I try to shut the memory down as soon as it pops up, but I can still feel her, as if I could reach out and pull her back. I'd been ready to ask for her number or a date or kiss her again when she'd cleared up any misconception I'd had about how great the kiss had been with a few words.

"That was a mistake."

Her regret added an extra bit of sting to the rejection that buzzed through me before she walked away. I shake my head, trying to free it of her memory. She just felt so right in my arms—against my lips.

It doesn't matter. She's gone and I don't have space for a woman like that in my life. A woman who's willing to kiss me and ditch me.

I'm not in the right headspace to play Santa.

Gearing up for the last few kids in line, I take a deep breath.

Blaire approaches the remaining crowd. "Thank you everyone for coming. Santa will be back tomorrow if you want to come see him!"

I start to remind her of the time, but when she raises eyebrow, I close my mouth and wave to the kids.

"You looked ready to go," Blaire whispers as the kids and families disperse.

"You have no idea," I mutter. The image of a gorgeous girl and the feel of her skin under my hands materializes again.

"Do you want to go get a drink? You could relax, and we could visit." Blaire smiles and the hair on my neck rises.

"Uh, —" That is one hundred percent not what I want. "I should get home. There's a leak in the kitchen waiting for me."

"Okay. That's fine. Are you caught up on repairs yet? I'm still having some issues with my fireplace. I don't know how—"

Not again.

"Oh, hey." I point toward the candy cane rope, where one little girl still pulls against her mother's arm, trying to keep them there. "There's one visitor left —"

"Don't you worry about a thing," Blaire says. "I'll take care of it." She bends down in front of the anxious pair. "Hey, I'm so sorry. Santa has to get back to Mrs. Claus. Can you come back tomorrow?"

The girl's lip trembles, and she looks up to her mother who shakes her head. "We can't come back, Joy. Your Dad will need us tomorrow."

"Ho, ho, ho! Did you say Joy? I've been waiting here, just for you!" My Santa laugh is very enthusiastic, considering how ready I was to leave only seconds ago. I turn to Blaire as we get settled. "I have enough time for one last visit. You can get going."

"Okay," Blaire glances between me and the little girl. "Are you sure?"

My answering grin is big enough to make Blaire flinch, and guilt tugs at my chest.

"Santa," Joy says, pulling on my sleeve. "I wrote you a letter." She has an envelope pinched in her fingers.

"Thank you." Taking the letter, I give myself permission to focus on Joy as Blaire goes inside the workshop. "Can you tell me what it says?"

Joy nods and glances back to her mother, lowering her voice. "I need some Christmas magic for my mom. The doctor told me it might help."

The doctor. Thoughts of Corrine's final days rush through my mind, full of sterile hospital rooms and hard truths. For the first time today, I can feel the snowy temperatures through my thick suit.

The letter slips from my hand, drifting to the snow at our feet. Scrambling to catch it, my heart pounds in my ears. What kind of doctor says that to a kid, gives them hope like that? Joy's mother looks overwhelmed and exhausted . . . but she's here.

Maybe it's not as bad as it was for my wife. I cross my fingers and give her what she came for—false hope.

"Christmas magic can do lots of things, Joy." I feel like a con artist. "I'll see what I can do."

"Thank you, Santa!" Joy beams up at me. "Can I have a candy cane for my Aunt Sarah too?"

"Absolutely." I pull two candy canes out of my bag and hand them to the happy little girl. "Merry Christmas."

As they walk away, I slip a gloved finger under the lip of the envelope.

Dear Santa,

For Christmas, I want a miracle for Mommy.
She's sick and the doctor said
she might not get to come home.

Help mommy get better, please.
Thank you, Santa!

Love, Joy

With a quick look up I make the real connection. Joy didn't come with her mother. She came with her Aunt Sarah. Her mother is in the hospital.

The memory of Corrine stirs painfully in my chest. How do you tell a little girl that wishes and magic, even the Christmas variety, aren't the same as miracles?

"Ma!" I call as Alice runs into the house. I sling my coat over the stair railing and set the Santa gear on the small table in the hall. I'm still wearing the Santa pants, but I can only take the itchy fur and beard for so long. "I'm sorry I'm late. Alice ended up at Colleen's, so it took a little longer to get her—" My breath catches as I push through the kitchen door. Dad's backside sticks out from under the sink. "What are you doing? Dad, I told you not to worry about the plumbing."

"I didn't do anything," My father says, adjusting his belt with his one good hand. "I was just looking."

Laughter bubbles behind me. Alice sits on the counter, as my mother feeds her ginger *pepparkakor* cookies. "Come, come, Torin. Your father isn't hurting anything," she says, holding out a thin, ginger wafer. "Have a cookie."

I scowl at her and point to Dad. "This isn't funny. He could hurt himself again. I thought you were on my side."

"I am." My mother frowns, taking the cookie back.

Before she can put it away, I snatch it out of her hand. "Fine. But I'm gonna need more of these."

"Wally?" A feminine voice comes from the hall, both familiar and completely out of place. "Here's that screwdriver. I tried what you said, but the faucet still isn't working—excuse me." She bumps my shoulder, stopping when she sees me. "What are you doing here?"

The woman who labeled me a mistake, before walking away, is in my kitchen. Her tousled blonde hair reaches well past her shoulders, perfect lips hanging open. In no more than a second, horror washes her smile out, showcasing a second helping of the stinging rejection she served up earlier.

After catching me completely off-guard, I look around at my parents and daughter. "I live here."

"Oh, Lucy. This is our son, Torin." Ma touches my shoulder as she interprets the recognition passing between us. "Lucy's going to be staying with us for the month. Have you two met?"

"No!" Lucy announces at the exact same time I contradict her with a "Yes."

The conflicting answers prod raised eyebrows around the room.

"Well, I guess we met briefly," she stutters. "I met Santa. But I didn't realize he was your son—not that I knew you guys at the time. And I, uh, I didn't recognize him—you know—without the beard." Her laugh doesn't sound normal, and her pleading eyes are the only thing keeping me from throwing out a round of sarcastic responses.

"I'm surprised you remember me at all. We barely spoke." Okay, maybe I can manage a little sarcasm.

She flinches, and her fake smile dims to a real grimace. "You're hard to forget. Yours is the only Santa beard I fixed today."

Ma looks at my chin, as if I might have magically grown bushy lumberjack whiskers in the past few seconds. "You fixed Santa's beard?" she asks. "What happened to my Santa beard?"

Instead of waiting for an answer, Ma pushes through the door into the hall, and I groan.

Lucy shoots me a wide-eyed glance.

"It's an heirloom," I hiss as I push through the door after Ma.

Lucy's eyes close, releasing her breath in a slow stream behind me. "Sorry," she says softly and follows.

"It's fine, Ma. The elastic came undone, but it was loose anyway. Now it's fixed."

Holding the costume in her careful hands, Ma doesn't respond for several seconds. When she turns, her gaze bypasses me and stops on Lucy.

"You are a miracle." She grabs Lucy up in a hug and pats her cheeks. "I've been meaning to repair that for ages. You did a beautiful job. Please, join us for dinner. Let me thank you."

"Umm." She glances up at me, with my mother's hands still holding her cheeks. "I guess so."

I stifle a laugh, and Ma releases her hold. "Good."

"Did you need some help with that faucet, Miss Lucy?" Dad leans around the doorway, coming to stand by Ma. "A lovely girl like you shouldn't have to work so hard for her bath."

Lucy's blush is mild compared to what it was earlier . . . in the cold . . . before I kissed her. Seeing it now, I want to pull her close and kiss her again.

"I'd like that," she says. It takes me a second to realize she's responding to my dad, not to my inner dialogue. "It's not the bath though, just the sink. I couldn't get the bathroom faucet to come on. I was going to wash up a little."

"Of course, I can help—" My mother grabs Dad by his good arm, cutting him off.

"Aren't you going to help me get dinner ready, *min älskling*?" she says and turns to me. "Torin would be happy to help you."

"Ma?" I start to object, not willing to embarrass myself again, but I quickly fall in line when she glares. "I'd be happy to."

I turn to the stairs, leaving Lucy's blushes and pretty face behind me.

Tucking the allen wrench back into the medicine cabinet, I turn to Lucy politely. "And that's what you do when the faucet decides it doesn't want to come on or shuts off on you."

Her lips purse and she shoots a wary glance at the faucet. "Does it do that? After it's running?"

"Yeah. It happens sometimes. At least it's not the shower." My eyes wander to the vintage tub and I'm suddenly picturing her in it. I clear my throat, patting the cupboard door, anxious to change the subject. "But we keep the tools right here. So, you can fix it. By yourself. In privacy."

She giggles and I look up, grateful she finds me funny instead of offensive.

"Well, that's the Sugar Creek Inn, where we treat you like royalty." I wink at her, opening the door.

I lead her down the hall, showing her the extra linens and communal areas. At the end of the hallway, we stop in the sitting room. Windows peek between bookshelves in a circle around the turret room. In the distance, Lake Champlain grazes the horizon in a streak of hazy blue-gray.

She takes in the view quietly until I clear my throat. "So, what brings you to Sugar Creek?"

"I came to meet my boyfriend."

She says it with complete nonchalance and a pile of rocks drops into my stomach. *Boyfriend*? "Oh, so that kiss—"

"Was a mistake." She smiles an apology to the window and turns to me as she explains. "We just broke up and I really shouldn't have done that."

A ray of hope.

I glance at her with relief. "You broke up?"

Her cheeks heat again, coloring her pale skin Poinsettia red. "I wasn't in a good emotional place."

She touches the divot of her clavicle like she's searching for something that's not there. My eyes follow the movement, and she pulls her hand away.

"So, you're single." I try not to smile too big. She's probably not as happy about her relationship status as I am.

"Technically." She takes a deep breath before finishing her thought. "I'm hoping not for long."

Cool fingers of icy heat trickle through my body. She's blushing again. Maybe I'm not such a mistake. "I could help you with that, too. You're here for a month, so I could take you out, or—"

"What? No! I didn't mean that. I meant, I'm trying to get back together with my boyfriend. He's staying up at the lodge."

The rocks in my stomach turn into an avalanche, crashing through my gut. "Right, that makes more sense." *Does it?* "Sorry. So—how are you liking things?"

"Torin, I didn't mean—the thing back there—it wasn't—"

"It's fine, really. I've kissed lots of girls."

Why would I say that?

"Uh-huh . . ." She sounds a little weirded out. "I'm sure that's very *exciting* for you."

"That's not what I meant." I shake my head. "I mean, what's a kiss, anyway? Just lips. And we were under the mistletoe."

She shrugs, agreeing. "Right, we had to."

"A mistletoe kiss." I fold my arms over my chest, and she nods. "Good."

Now it's just a matter of burying these feelings while she lives with us for the next month.

"And that concludes our tour." I gesture back down the hall, and she leads the way to her room.

Lucy's eyes drift from one thing to the next, taking in the lights and garlands over every door. It's the first time I've been glad Ma insisted on turning the inn into a holiday wonderland.

"How do you like it?"

"The kiss?" Lucy's eyes are wide, panicked. "It was good, I don't—"

I laugh, and she stops talking. Her brows pinch together in confusion, and I take a second to control my mirth. "I meant the house, the decorations—but thanks." I wink at her. "I guess that's better than a mistake."

"Oh, it was absolutely a mistake." Her smile turns up at the edge of an open mouth, like keeping her lips stretched wide will hide her amusement. "Doesn't mean I didn't enjoy it."

A crash sounds from downstairs.

"I better go check on that," I say backing away. "Where there's trouble, Alice usually follows. She's too curious for her own good."

"Who's Alice?"

For a second, I consider keeping my little girl a secret. Discovering my Daddy status is a make-or-break moment for most women. But I'm unapologetically proud of Alice and being her daddy.

"Alice is my daughter. You probably saw her downstairs, in the kitchen."

"She's yours?" There's no smile or frown. Her mouth hangs open in an "O," which is quickly becoming one of my favorite expressions. That combined with her blush might do me in for good.

"Well, no wonder," she says.

"No wonder what?" It's almost impossible to look away from her and the light reflecting in her blue eyes.

"No wonder you were so good with those kids today. Not everyone can pull off such a convincing Santa."

She's got her sights on another guy, I remind myself. "You really want to get back together with your ex?"

Her fingers dance across the base of her neck again, and the light in her eyes fades. "Yeah. I'm really sorry, Torin."

"It's okay. I understand. He's your guy." It's trite, but it feels like the only reason that she wouldn't want to even try being together after that kiss.

"Maybe if things had been different—" She stops, catching her bottom lip in her teeth, as if she already regrets the words.

If things had been different.

If she wasn't dating him? Then she wouldn't have come. And I never would have met her.

Maybe she'll change her mind and she'll be available after all. Except I don't want her to get hurt.

Maybe—but there's no guarantee in maybe.

As she releases her lower lip, I look away, trying not to remember how they felt pressed to mine.

"Maybe."

Chapter 5

Lucy

I have to stop thinking about Torin and that kiss.

But he's everywhere.

If I leave my room, he's in the hall. If I stay in my room, he's outside the balcony doors. He's walking around, being helpful and beautiful and . . . all I wanted was a place to stay. A place to strategize how to get Erik back.

And I will get him back. I love him.

Love is more important than attraction. Stability and security are better than passion and mind-melting kisses.

Be smart, Lucy.

Even still, it's probably best if Erik never finds out about that kiss.

Torin is a passing attraction, not the one I want.

Erik is my true love.

Not that I need to remind myself. It's just, the universe is testing me. To see how committed I am to having just one man in my life.

It's not like I'm not attracted to Erik. He's blond-haired and blue-eyed and gorgeously tall. He's got a great smile, just like Torin. His lean build is striking, though Torin's muscular accents have their own appeal . . . And I've never seen anything like Torin's eyes—crystallized pale green. Erik's are icy blue.

I love blue eyes.

I fall onto the bed, the coverlet fluffing around me. Tiny leaves that match Torin's eyes trail over a white background. I wonder if he's ever lain on this bed. The green stripes and climbing plants on the walls match the leaves on the bedspread. Does anyone know how Torin could disappear in here? Go invisible among the wallpapered vines. He could be anywhere in this room.

Across the room, a pair of French doors lead to the balcony where I saw Torin just moments ago. He's probably gone now.

I roll off the bed to check, crossing to the glass doors.

The view is amazing. Winter-clad rooflines and trees stretch across the distance, all the way to a stretch of Lake Champlain. It's almost as clear a view as in the turret library, where Torin took me earlier. I sigh, admiring the artfully discarded sleds in the yards below. Torin is still there.

The poster boy for relaxation wades through the snow in socks and house slippers, hauling something from the car.

Torin's mussed hair is nothing like Erik's smoothed and styled businessman look. It's almost as much a contrast as the long-sleeved t-shirt and jeans, to Erik's slacks and dress shirts. Erik would never be seen like that. He'd wear a button-up shirt in the shower if he thought it made him look more professional.

I like that about him — don't I? The formality makes me try harder. Though, it might be nice *not* to plan my yoga pants around the times Erik is gone.

I shake my head, watching Torin move across the iced path. Dating him would be so different.

Wrong. It would be wrong. So what if Torin has qualities Erik doesn't? Everyone has their own preferences, right? And I know mine.

The hair on the back of my neck stands up at the idea of just dismissing five years of my life because Erik got bored. I won't be that person. I'm loyal, and I know the difference between infatuation and real love.

My mother taught me that.

Dropping my head against the glass with a loud thump, Torin's head snaps up, looking for the sound.

I straighten quickly and wave, pushing the French doors open as if it was my intention all along to walk out on the balcony. If I hadn't been drooling over Torin a moment ago, I might even believe my own lie.

"It's cold out here," I call down to him, goose bumps rising on my arms. It's the only thing that comes to mind that is safe to call down to the helpful, casual, gorgeous man.

Torin smirks. "You know it's snowing, right? Welcome to winter, Florida Girl."

My cheeks heat despite the winter air.

"I know it's snowing." I do now, anyway.

I was so caught up watching him, I didn't notice the flakes drifting lightly through the air.

"Daddy!" Alice runs out, jumping into his arms. "I need kisses!"

Instead of pulling her close, he throws her up into the air, her hands extended wide. They turn circles, and Torin tosses the giggling little girl again, pulling her into a hug as he catches her.

I don't realize I'm staring until cold seeps through my jeans. The snow on the railing melts against my hip where I'm leaning against it, breathless. Still, I can't take my eyes off the blissful father-daughter moment unfolding before me.

A car pulls into the driveway, breaking the spell of the tender scene. I back up, shutting the French doors. That's not my world, or my family. I shake myself out of my imaginings just as a car door slams. Curiosity stops me, and I turn back. I don't know if I want a glimpse of the new guest or Torin and his precious little girl when my world stops turning.

Erik stands alone in the driveway.

My heart clenches, my breathing turns to gasps. I can't tell if it's nerves or hyperventilation.

He's here. He came for me.

It's my wish. Fishing my necklace out of my purse, I dash out of the room and down the stairs. It's going to be all right. The savory smells of dinner lift me out the front door. If this place has mistletoe anywhere, I'm going to find it and drag Erik underneath, so I can make a real mistletoe memory.

"Erik!" The front door closes behind me.

He doesn't respond. He's looking at Torin. The two of them are in some kind of staring contest. Erik hasn't even made it inside. Does he know? Did someone see us?

"Erik!" Trying again to get Erik's attention, I step to the edge of the porch. I left my shoes inside. "How did you find me?"

Erik's shocked gaze turns to my voice, and he does a double take. "What are you doing here?"

My smile doesn't quite make it out of its state of confusion, and I grip my snowflake necklace tightly. "I'm staying here."

Erik's mouth opens slightly and his jaw drops. "I thought you'd be back in Orlando, nursing one of your green smoothies on the beach."

Torin's eyes narrow at Erik. I'm not sure if I'm supposed to feel that as sharply as I do, but I'm not nearly as excited to talk to Erik as I was.

"I can't afford a new ticket." I laugh awkwardly. "And I just wanted to stay close, in case things change."

Torin steps between us, looking from Erik to me. "You two know each other?"

Possessiveness stiffens Erik's jaw. I've only seen him like this a few times, but a touch of relief winds through my anxiety. He still feels something for me.

"Do *you two* know each other?" Erik asks.

"Sort of." Torin swallows and glances over his shoulder. "We met on the square—"

"And I helped him fix his costume." I cut Torin off, praying he won't say more than that. Both men look back at me, and I catch my breath.

Something about the way they're standing is odd. Or maybe it's in their faces? "He was just giving me a tour of the inn . . . am I missing something?"

"Probably," Erik mutters. It stings, but I'm not sure Erik can see that through glaring at Torin. "Why are you here, Torin? I thought you moved away."

When did Erik learn Torin's name? I only have a second to wonder.

"I did. I came back after my wife died." Torin clenches his fist and takes a threatening step forward. Tension thickens the air.

His wife. He had a wife, and she . . . died. When? How? I grip the column next to the stairs. Wired garland bites my skin, but the pain of his words feels more real, twisting my heart.

With clenched teeth, Erik shakes his head, as if trying to make room for Torin's words. "Right. I forgot."

There's a beat of heavy silence before Torin responds. "Wow, I guess you forgot two years ago when it happened, too. You missed a big party. We all wore black. Shoulda been there."

His dark humor hits its target. Erik falters, running a hand over the back of his neck the way he always does when he's anxious. I feel it, too. Pain, deep in my chest. My heart breaks for this little family and what they must be going through.

When Erik responds, his tone is tempered. "I should have. I'm sorry."

"But you weren't." Torin's monotone response seems to shake Erik, but it's Torin who glances at me, remembering I'm there.

"I'm sorry." Erik steps forward, but Torin backs up, his whole-body tensing. He's coiled on a hair trigger. "I hadn't figured myself out yet. I needed space—"

"You know, most people go on a walk when they say that. They don't move across the country and disappear for years on end."

My breathing turns shallow. I'm trying hard to keep the pieces of this puzzle in the order I like.

"You know why I had to go." Erik's nostrils flare, battling to keep his calm.

Torin laughs, until his fist comes up, like he's gonna punch Erik.

"No!" I jump off the porch, throwing myself between them to block the threat. "Don't hit him!"

Erik rolls his eyes. "Lucy, chill out. We're not gonna fight each other."

"Are you sure?" I start tiptoe dancing in the remains of the snow-cleared path as my socks soak up the ice.

"I'm sure." Torin's fist transitions from floating near his shoulder to gripping the muscles at the back of his neck.

"So, you're not here for me—and you two have some serious bad blood going on." Bad blood. *No.* I look between them, and I can't breathe. "Why aren't you fighting?"

Torin snorts a laugh. "That's a good question. Because the last time we did, my *brother* gave me a black eye for something I didn't do."

I waver on the sidewalk like a drunken sorority student. One of them steadies me with a hand at my back. It's not Erik. Looking from Torin back to Erik, I point to Erik unsteadily. I have more than a few questions in my head, but only one comes out my mouth.

"Did he say brother?"

On a scale of one to entirely uncomfortable, making small talk at dinner with my almost-parents-in-law, their one son who just broke up with me, and another son that I recently kissed rates near jellyfish-as-a-shower-scrub levels of discomfort.

A chill hovers at the dinner table as soon as we sit. Torin and Alice on one side face Erik and I on the other. The entire family dances around the conversation, elephants in a tulip field. If I could just leave, maybe they'd actually be able to have a conversation.

I serve myself what looks like tiny green cabbages in caramel sauce on my plate and clear my throat. "Wow, Mrs. Nyström. I've never seen greens served like this."

"They're brussels sprouts, dear." She chuckles as Torin takes the bowl of vegetables from me.

A wave of embarrassment forces a breathy laugh through my throat. "Of course. That's what I meant. I, um, I'd love to get the recipe."

"I didn't know you cooked." Erik's monotone adds to the growing chill. I've never eaten a brussels sprout in my life, much less considered making one. I spear a green ball simply so I won't have to answer, but it smells sweet, and my stomach turns at the idea of sugar-coated vegetables.

"I like brussels sprouts," Alice announces. Erik and Torin's father, Wally, clanks a spoon on the side of the serving dish, helping her get some food.

A spoon clatters against glass and Torin makes a frustrated sound. Slapping a hand on the table, he leans forward. "Why are you here Erik?"

"I'm here for the reunion. Why do you think?" Erik pops a piece of ham in his mouth, and the two of them lock eyes in another staring contest.

Torin's jaw shifts as he breathes through his nose, analyzing his brother. Erik grins while he chews. "You want Lucy's number, little bro? You could steal another of my girlfriends."

"The way I understand it, she's your ex," Torin says.

I thought the same thing. I watch Erik swallow in silence, trying hard not to let hope bloom too quickly.

Finally, he shrugs. "Sloppy seconds are good enough for some people. That's your M.O., isn't it?"

"Erik," Ingrid says, and both boys look at her. "You apologize. To Torin and Lucy. We've all missed you, but I won't have people come to my table to be insulted."

It's quiet for a moment before Ingrid reaffirms her request. "Now, Erik."

"Fine. I'm sorry, Tor, and I'm sorry, Lucy." Erik's eyes are hooded and dark when he turns to me. "She's right. I really am sorry, Luce. I shouldn't have used you as bait. I'm sorry for a lot of things."

I wish he didn't have to be told, but I'm grateful anyway. The backdrop of Christmas carols softens me, and the hint of a smile tugs at my lips. "I know. Me too."

"What do you have to be sorry for?" Torin interrupts my sugar-coated thoughts and drags Erik's eye back to his side of the table. "Did you do something that caused his bad behavior?"

"Of course not. I'm not a pushover. But any long-term relationship has things both people can apologize for."

Erik's half grin is a gift, and I move to take his hand, but he pulls back. He's not ready yet. That's okay.

"So—long-term?" Ingrid leans forward. "How long have you two known each other?"

I glance at Erik, my body prickles with pins and needles of hope and anxiety. "About five years. We met his first day at college and we've been together since."

"Until now. We broke up before I came here. Lucy was supposed to stay in Florida." Erik says point blank.

"You told me that in a text." I force a smile and try not to notice everyone watching us. "And it's not like you canceled my flight."

"It was nonrefundable." Erik raises an eyebrow.

"So, I figured I should use it, and we could talk about what happened."

"You don't think that's a little pushy?" Erik drops his silverware and takes a deep breath. "I just needed some space."

Torin coughs and all heads swing to him. "You know, there's space in places not all the way across the country. But I guess it's your M.O., isn't it."

Erik shoves his chair back and stands up, turning back to me. "If you want to hang out with my brother, go right ahead. He knows everything I've done wrong in my life. I'm sure he'll fill you in. Dad. Mom. Thanks for dinner, but I've got to go."

"Erik," Ingrid calls after him. "Erik, please stay. It's been so long since I've had you both home."

"It's not worth it, Ma." Torin's voice is soft and strained and I almost don't recognize it.

"Family is always worth it," she says and pushes her chair away from the table. "Erik, we've wished you were back so many times. Don't go."

With a look around the table, Erik flinches and drops back into his seat. "Fine. For you, Mom."

"Thank you, Erik." Wally nods to his son and leans over, taking Ingrid's hand. "Your mother works very hard to keep us all taken care of, and I know she's glad to have you home."

Wally winks at her and Ingrid waves a hand at him. "Stop it. You're embarrassing me."

"Oh," Wally says, kissing her knuckles, "don't ask me not to appreciate you."

Erik groans beside me.

"I'll never get tired of you, Wally," Ingrid says. "You're just the sweetest."

"What was that? Swedish? Of course I am, lovey. We're all Swedish." He nods to the table. It's a terrible joke, but I smile anyway. I learned a long time ago to go along with whatever stops the arguing.

Alice bounces in her seat. "It's fun to be Swedish. I can show you how."

Torin's grin catches my eye. He's watching his daughter with a focus I've never known.

"Do I have to do anything different?" I ask, keeping my focus on the little girl instead of her daddy. Her blonde curls bob merrily.

"Yeah. When you're Swedish, you say things different. Like, '*talk so milk it*'. That means thank you lots and lots. And you call gramma '*far more*' and grampa '*far far*', 'cause he's really old."

A guffaw bursts from Wally and laughter fills the room. Even Erik grins at his fork.

"Oh, well, *talk so milk it* for the lesson." I glance around the table, hoping for a correction.

"Very good." Ingrid claps for me. "It's '*tack så mycket*', but my granddaughter did very well, *en söt*." She blows a kiss across the table, and I swear the whole room is brighter.

Her spoon moves something on her plate, but she isn't eating. I can't blame her. She looks purposefully at Erik. "What time should we head up to the Vanderberg's for sledding tomorrow?"

"Sledding?" Erik asks.

"Of course, it's tradition. You're coming, aren't you?" Her kind, motherly tone is cloaked with a coercive force. It's kind of impressive. "You could stay the night here and then go with us, if you'd like. We've got your room made up for you."

My eyes zip to Erik to catch the nuance of his response. If he stays, I could get a lot more time with him. That could be good and bad.

Erik puts on his I'm-a-professional face. It's the one he wears for big client meetings when he needs to close a deal. "No, Mom. I'm staying at the lodge. Let's not pretend that's a bad thing. The rest of the family is staying up there for the reunion. I'll be fine, at least until they go."

"But, honey—" Ingrid starts, and Erik shoves his chair away from the table. His expression isn't calm anymore.

"I'm not staying here with my ex and Torin!"

"Erik, *sötnos*, sit down. I didn't mean to upset you." Ingrid's pleading has no pull on her son.

"You didn't upset me," Erik says, stepping away from the table. "I stayed away because of him. Being gone, it was easy to let the time pass. I thought I would feel differently when I came back, but I'm not ready for this. Good luck, you two."

"Wait, no." I stand and reach for him, but he pulls away. "It's not like that."

He ignores me, walking toward the entry. "I'll try and come back in a day or so."

"Wait," Ingrid calls out, jumping from her seat to follow him. "What about sledding at the Vanderberg's?"

He pauses, looking back, and his eyes land on me. Tensing his jaw, he puts on a smile and raises his eyebrows. "I'm here for the reunion. If that's where the events are, I'll be there." Erik slams the door shut, leaving quiet behind him.

The soft melody of Christmas carols overpower the sudden quiet. With a small remote, Ingrid turns the music down till it's almost off.

Guilt builds in my heart, rising through my throat. This is my fault, but there's an easy fix. I push back tears and set my napkin on the table.

"I'm sorry, I should go. Thank you for everything you've done for me, but I'm causing a lot of problems for your family. I'll find another place to stay."

In my periphery, I catch what I think is disappointment on Torin's face before Wally sets his glass firmly on the table. We all look. "Don't be ridiculous. My son has the pride of a Viking. It will take time for him to learn someone else can be right. I prefer letting *min älskling* kiss me goodnight than to sleep in the stink of the fish."

I furrow my brow. "What does that mean?"

Torin rumbles a laugh and points to his father. His hand comes down on the table near mine, his little finger grazing my skin. Warmth trembles over my tight nerves. I feel the call to look, but outside of a quick glance, I stay focused on his face. "It's a folk tale about a stubborn sailor who refused to admit to his lover that he didn't know where her cabin was. Instead of agreeing to meet her, he said he had to clean fish . . . all night."

Wally chuckles, leaning toward Ingrid. "It's an old tale. We just tell it to keep our pride in check and a kiss on our lips."

"On the cheek," Ingrid insists, giving her husband a peck before settling back in her seat. Watching the two of them, I'm less curious where Torin's bold romantic moves came from. I do wonder where Erik's went, though.

My heart tugs. It's the kind of relationship I've dreamed about. I send a passing glance to Torin and look quickly back to Ingrid and Wally. "How long have you two been married?"

"Going on thirty-nine years, next spring." Ingrid smiles when Wally takes her hand.

"Oh, that is so beautiful. My parents didn't make it anything close to that. It's amazing to see a couple so in love."

"Oh, I'm sure they'll make it," Wally says, and I smile politely. "It's easy when you've got the right partner."

"Easy?" Ingrid says and scoffs. "Easy for him."

Wally looks slightly offended and kisses her hand. "I'll help you clean up, *min älskling*." And just like that, the tension is gone.

Ingrid and Wally gather plates and leave as Alice yawns.

A tiny laugh bubbles out of me as Torin helps Alice down from her seat. "What?" he asks.

"Nothing." I can't tell him that's the only family argument I've ever seen start and end in less than twenty-four hours, much less twenty-four minutes.

"Whatever you say. Are you ready for bed, Aly girl?"

Alice shakes her head and leans toward me. "I want to show Lucy the big playroom so we can play superhero princess."

"You'd rather have Lucy? You don't think I make a good princess?" Torin asks and Alice giggles.

"Lucy gets to be the princess, and you can be the bad guy who's getting eaten by the monster."

I bite down on a laugh. I might be falling more in love with Alice than Erik.

"Maybe I'll be the monster." Torin roars in jest, twirling her over his shoulders.

He starts to the stairs while Alice laughs through his volatile affection. When he finally puts her down, she wobbles unsteadily and looks at me. "Can you play?"

"Aw!" Torin throws his hands in the air in mock frustration, and Alice dissolves into more giggles.

"Anything you want," I say, winking at Alice, and Torin's laugh catches. He looks at me for several seconds of near silence, the hint of White Christmas drifting around us.

I have no idea how I'm connected to this family anymore, but my only hope is that I will be.

I can see two stories side by side as I imagine myself showing up to the Nyström's family dinner. Once beside Erik, apologizing for his attitude all night. Meeting Ingrid and Wally, Torin and Alice. Watching them through the screen of Erik's bitterness . . . and the other with Torin. I'm having dinner beside him, laughing with his daughter, and kissing him good night.

I follow Torin and Alice up the stairs. I have to do something, or I'll be explaining to the Nyströms why I'm kissing the wrong son.

Chapter 6

Torin

Lucy and my brother.

Of course they'd be together.

I made a promise to myself a long time ago that I would fix things with Erik if I could. I just didn't expect a complication like Lucy.

Leaning against her doorway, I wipe my sweaty palms against my jeans. I need to clear the air.

It's been five minutes since I decided to come talk to her, and I'm still dredging up my courage just to knock. My heart hasn't raced like this since my wife died. I don't know what that means, but, in a bubble of determination, I land my fist on the door, second-guessing every thump.

It's only a few seconds before Lucy opens it. Tension and relief flood my chest in unison when I see her face.

"Why did you kiss me?" I whisper. It's the question that's been burning in my mind since I saw my brother's eyes light with recognition when she appeared on the porch. She is—or was—important to him.

Lucy scans the hallway I already checked for vacancy and bites her lip. "I don't know." Long lashes graze her cheeks as she closes her eyes and when she looks back, they are filled with worry. "It was a mistletoe kiss, right? It meant nothing."

"Maybe if we were talking about the first one. But we both know that's not all it was. And then, I find out you were dating my brother." My voice spirals from crazy to hurt and back again.

"Exactly. *Were*. I were—I *was*—dating your brother." Lucy steps closer, surrounding me with the scent of citrus and flowers. I hold my breath as she jabs a finger into my chest. "But not anymore. And not when it happened."

"Does that matter?" I let go of my control and inhale deeply, raking my fingers through my hair against the growing tension in the base of my skull. In what world will my brother forgive me for kissing Lucy after everything else?

"It should matter." Her lips curl down in a pout, and I lean into the doorframe.

"But it doesn't. Not if you knew you still wanted him." I swallow hard, waiting for her to comment, but she won't even look at me. "Do you . . . want him?"

It's an unwinnable test.

Her breathing becomes the only sound in the house I can hear. The slow, rhythmic sound thrums a baseline to my ever-increasing heartbeat.

When she doesn't answer, I tap the doorframe. "That was a heck of a kiss for a woman that doesn't know who she wants to be with." Somehow in her loyalty, or insecurity, she's stringing us all along, the whole family included. "Maybe I don't need to know the answer to that, but you do, and eventually, Erik will need to know too."

"You can't tell him about the kiss." She reaches out and pulls back in quick succession.

"Why not?" I wasn't planning on it but now I'm curious about what she'll say.

Lucy shakes her head in frustration. "Because I don't intend to hurt him."

For a second, I think she's going to say, *like you*, but Lucy wouldn't know about that. If she did, Erik would have had to mention me, and he didn't. "Really? Tell me again, then . . . why did you kiss me?"

"You're the one who suggested it." Intensity permeates her hushed tone, and I lean in, matching her vibe.

"Well, you didn't seem to mind."

We're only inches apart when someone down the hall bumps their door and we both glance toward the sound.

Grabbing my shirt collar, she pulls me inside, shutting the door behind us. Dusky light fills the room, making it difficult to step away when she lets go.

With her arms wrapped around her waist, she watches me. "I wasn't the only one out there. Why did you kiss me, a random stranger, while you're out there being a role model to a crowd of merry little children?"

"You don't get to not answer and then turn it around on me. You just got out of a relationship." And then, because it's sitting on the end of my tongue like a hot coal, I spit out the real problem. "A relationship with my brother."

"I didn't know he was your brother!"

"That doesn't make it better."

"I know!" Lucy admits and walks toward the French doors. Moonlight reflects on the snowy world outside, bouncing off every surface like the questions in my head. Why is she here? Why is she with him? Why does she want to be?

And why does it matter to me?

I follow her to the doors, standing behind her. In the dim light, I can barely make out her reflection on the glass. Her lips open and she turns to face me. "I'm sorry, Torin. I know there was something between us, but I don't think—"

"I kissed you because I wanted to." I cut her off, not wanting to hear, or feel, the rejection again. "You asked why I kissed you. That's the truth."

"Oh." It's all she says, and her lips settle into that familiar "O" of surprise.

I have to tear my gaze away from her mouth to go on. "I figured I would let you know. Before we start dancing around polite ways to tell each other we're not interested, even though we are." Tension pulsates through my body as her jaw drops and I hear what I just said. "I'm not asking you to choose me, but I won't lie. And I'm not gonna say I'm sorry I kissed you, because I'm not. It was a great kiss. But that's why I did it. Because I wanted to." I can feel the real truth hanging on my tongue, and after a breath, I let it out, too. "And because I like you." I'm very aware that we're alone together in her bedroom as the cute little circle of her lips pinches slowly, gathering concern and doubt.

"And now you want to get back together with my brother," I say. Erik. Exactly the mood-killer I need.

"Yeah." Lucy steps back, and the air cools without her next to me. "I guess I do." She looks at the ground as if she's ashamed of this fact.

I nod. I knew it was coming, and still, I'm disappointed.

"We've been together for five years. There are still a lot of feelings there, and I won't give up on us after one rough patch. Not without trying to fix things first."

"I get it," and it only makes me like her more. "I'm gonna go." If I even want a chance at fixing things with Erik, I can't be alone with Lucy.

"Torin, I have to try," she whispers as I back away.

"Good. I'm glad you are." I pull the door open and breathe air that doesn't smell like fruit and flowers and Lucy. "I'm just glad to know we're on the same page. Good night, Lucy."

"Wait!" she calls, and my body responds with instant obedience. I don't look back, but I can hear her worry. "I need help."

I hover over the threshold, offering quick, Innkeeper-who's-not-interested-in-you answers. "Extra pillows are down the hall, toilet paper's under the bathroom sink. Let us know if you need anything else."

"I need help getting back together with Erik."

There's more of a sigh in my response than I'd like, and I turn to face her. "I am not the right person to help you get back together with my brother."

"You're the only person who can help me." She rests her hand at her collarbone, the barest movement, like the motion comforts her.

"Why me?" I ask at the same time I give a tiny shake of my head.

She reaches a hand to my lips, stopping just shy of touching me. I pull back a little, looking from her fingers to her face. "He's here for your family reunion. I'm not family."

"Well, Lucy." I put on an expression of severe penance. "Marrying you for my brother would be quite a sacrifice, but I'd do it for Erik's sake."

"Be serious." She punches my arm and I laugh. She has no idea. When she's satisfied that I'm done laughing, Lucy drops to the bed. "I took a risk coming here. And so far, it's not paying off. If I don't fix things with Erik here, I'll only ever be his creepy stalker ex." She gives an uncomfortable chuckle.

"That's probably true."

She glares. "Not helpful. You heard him tonight, he's here for the reunion and other than skiing, I think that's all he's planning to do."

She doesn't seem concerned by the obvious downfall of her plan. "But he's also pretty bothered by us being together. I don't think it's going to help if you come with me."

"I don't have another option. You're the only other Nyströms I know."

"It's an Olsson reunion. Ma's side," I say, and Lucy raises an eyebrow. The thought of spending a week with Lucy going to all my family events and explaining why she's *just a friend* doesn't sound appealing. "So, go skiing with him."

"I'm not big on skiing, and I'd still need a ride. We might as well go for the reunion?"

I shake my head, and she jumps up.

"Please, I'll help with Alice or anything you need. If you just get me in to the events—I won't bother you, I swear. I need time with Erik to help him see that what we have is worth fighting for. And . . . what do you need? I'll do it."

"You don't need to do anything." I hold my breath to keep the wounds from bleeding out. I've only known her a day. A few hours, really. This is how it was supposed to go. Maybe I can finally make amends for the relationship I helped destroy before Erik leaves for good.

I glance at her downturned lips in the dim light. All I want is to make her happy again. "Fine."

I close my eyes and nod reluctantly. When I open them, it's worked. Her cheeks are lifted, eyes smiling. A bitter victory.

"You'll help me?" she asks, confirming my downfall.

"Yeah." It's time to go, but I have one more question. "Lucy?"

"Yeah?"

"Why did you guys come back this year?" I trace the edge of her silhouette with my eyes, not sure I can bear to see her reaction. "We have the reunion every year. He never comes. Why this year?"

She's quiet for several breaths. "He talks a lot about missing the skiing out here, and I needed to meet his—your parents. When the reunion invite came this year, I made a plan. It took some convincing, but here we are. Sort of."

"You're here to meet my parents? You weren't engaged, were you?"

"No! Nothing like that. It's just one of my rules. I don't date a guy without knowing his family and what they think of him. It helps me judge character."

"Rules?"

She hesitates before responding. "My rules to keep from getting my heart broken."

A sliver of her commitment to Erik becomes clearer. "You don't make rules like that unless it's already happened."

"I've never actually had my heart broken. Thanks to my rules." She smiles robotically.

I don't believe that for a second.

"I guess you're the lucky one." I open the door again. "I'm gonna go. But skiing is a good idea. Erik loves skiing and I'm guessing he'll spend most of his time on the slopes."

"Skiing?"

I nod and escape the room, closing her door behind me.

Exhaustion rakes my body. With a heavy breath, I cross the hall, catching something on my toe. It flies at my bedroom door, hitting it with a clunk. I suck in a nervous breath and lean close, to hear if my little girl has woken.

A pink teapot lies on the ground with several other discarded tea toys. I kick it to the side, where the little pot twirls and tips near the stair railing.

"I feel you, teapot," I mutter to the fallen toy. I don't know how I'm going to survive being with Lucy every day. How long can I battle the need to touch her, simply because we walked into the same room?

"Torin?" Lucy taps my shoulder.

"Lucy?" I turn quickly at the sound of her voice and run smack into her. "Oh! Jeezum crow." I back up and hit the wall. *Alice*, I think in a panic, *please, don't wake up*.

"Sorry." She bounces nervously, looking at everything but me. "I don't know how to ski."

She blurts it out, louder by the second.

"Shush," I whisper. Grabbing her, I pull her close and rest a finger on her lips, listening for sounds of a child waking. We stand there together, neither of us moving until I'm sure the house is quiet. I let out a breath.

"Is it safe?" Lucy asks. Tucked in the crook of my arm, she's holding perfectly still, gripping the fabric of my shirt. The color has drained from her cheeks as she holds tightly to my chest.

She probably thinks we're being robbed.

I let her go and rub a hand over my jaw and into my hair. My whole body is alive with the vibration of Lucy. I swear, a team of giant moth-sized butterflies have woken in my chest, beating my insides black and blue in an effort to reach her. "Sorry. Alice is a light sleeper. What did you need?"

"You said I should go skiing with Erik. Well — Florida girl, remember? I don't know how to ski."

I muffle a laugh that sets her eyes sparkling. "Don't worry, I'll teach you."

She pauses, looking up at me like I just saved her. "You'd do that?"

"I can get you started, at least."

She laughs, and the world turns gold. The glow of the Christmas garland above glistens on her lips and turns her blonde hair to caramel, as if she's made of light.

I shake my head.

She's just like any other woman. Everything turns gold in dark hallways lit by Christmas lights.

"Yeah. I've got the Santa Claus thing most afternoons, but we can start practicing here. It'll be a good way for you to spend time together." I let out a breath and settle into the friend zone, where I should have been all along. "Erik's lucky to have you. I think you'll be good for him."

She smiles a genuine, sweet smile, and I know what I have to do.

I will let Lucy go.

"Thank you. I hope I get to return the favor sometime." She turns to go and slips, a plastic tea party plate zipping away down the hall.

I reflexively reach for Lucy, catching her halfway to the ground. The moth-sized butterflies inside me redouble their efforts to escape my body and worship her.

"Oh." She straightens, looking around as my heart pounds in my ears. "Thank you. Again. I think that's the second time? Or is it the third time you've kept me from falling today?"

"I must be getting pretty good at this game." I laugh, tamping down the rebellious butterflies.

A strand of hair hangs at her cheek. Sliding my fingers the short distance from her cheek bone to her ear, I tuck it back. Her blue eyes hold mine as her cheeks warm under a holly berry blush.

This is never going to work.

My heart races my spinning thoughts, challenging the idea that I could ever not be with Lucy.

Even for my brother.

Crap, Torin. You suck at this.

Blankets and pillows fly haphazardly across my mattress the next morning, as I search the layers of bedding for a lost sock. Normally, I wouldn't care so much, but it's one of a pair I got from Corrine our last Christmas together.

Guilt niggles in my heart as if this sock were something precious. "It's just a sock," I mutter. Almost instantly, I can hear Corrine's voice.

"Swedish colors," Corrine said as I unwrapped the yellow and blue striped gift. "And they're fleece lined—" She coughed, then recovered, as if nothing happened. "For when we go back home."

"Be careful, If you want to come home, you have to get—" Better. I couldn't tell her to do the impossible. "—some rest."

After helping her sip some water, I climbed into the bed beside her and held her.

"Don't be afraid of hope, Torin. I know it's not a guarantee. It's not a monster. It's just possibilities. It can't hurt anyone."

I stuck my nose in her hair and took a breath of lilac shampoo. It was the only part of her that didn't smell like hospital. "That's not true. I'm pretty sure it's killed me several times over."

"Don't say that." She laughs, and I scoot closer to feel her body shake.

I run my hands over her sides, trying not to use too much pressure, to avoid the IV drip line and the wrapping around her chest. My hands settle beside her shoulders. I'm sure she can feel me crying, but I pretend it's fine. "Thank you, Corrine. I love the socks. I'll have to get you a matching pair . . . when we go home."

"There you are." A bright blue fabric toe peeks out from under my pillow, and I snatch the wayward sock up, tossing it in the hamper with its brother. "Don't scare me like that," I mutter to the dirty clothes.

Alice is still asleep in her bed, just a few feet away, and I'd like to keep it that way long enough to shower.

I grab my pants and a towel and move into the hall. Lucy's door is cracked open, and a gentle moan stalls me before I make it very far. I can't tell if she's still sleeping or not, and I stand in front of her door for a second too long.

My mother comes down from her room, catching me there. Already showered and dressed, she grins and pats my cheek on her way to the kitchen. "How'd you sleep, my boy?"

I hurry past Lucy's door, following Ma toward the stairs. "Great. Do you need me for anything this morning? I was thinking I'd teach Lucy some ski techniques in the backyard."

She pauses at the top of the stairs and turns to look at me. "I don't have a problem with that." She looks me over and pumps an eyebrow. "Are you interested in Lucy?"

"Ma—" I glance over my shoulder and pull Lucy's door closed as quietly as I can. Turning to my mother, I throw my hands up and cross to the stairs. "Why would you ask that? She's right there."

"What? She's not dating Erik, anymore, is she?" Ma's worried frown doesn't help the hope eating me alive this morning.

"She wants to be. That's why I'm teaching her to ski. So she can go hang out with Erik."

"Oh." She nods and pats my jaw again. "Well, I just noticed at dinner that you two did a lot of visiting. I didn't know Erik was still—are you sure? He seemed very clear last night. They broke up."

"I know. It's not Erik, it's Lucy. She's trying to be faithful to him and show him she still cares." My throat swells like I'm having an allergic reaction as I talk about them. I take a deep breath and try to relax. "Lucy and I are just friends."

"That's good," Ma says. "Lucy's a sweet girl. I hardly slept last night, thinking about Erik breaking up with her. I'm glad they're getting back together. Maybe she'll help him be happy again."

"You don't need to worry about Lucy. Apparently, her heart doesn't get broken."

She smiles like she thinks I told a joke, before she shakes her head. "Everyone gets their heart broken."

I turn back to the shower. "I know, Ma."

"Torin?"

I look over my shoulder. "Yeah?"

"You're going to find someone nice like Lucy, too. Corrine would want you to find someone you can be happy with."

Ma's sentiment isn't the comfort she thinks it is. Setting Corrine and Lucy against each other pulls my loyalty in separate directions until my chest aches. "Thanks, Ma. I'll be on the lookout."

As I turn toward the shower again, her voice calls me back. "Torin?"

"Yeah, Ma?" I turn toward her more slowly this time.

"Maybe watch out for Lucy. I don't want anyone getting hurt, and if Erik doesn't realize his mistake, that could be hard on her." Her hand flutters out like she wants to take mine. "Do you think she'd like to come sledding with us and maybe some of the other reunion events?"

I bite down on my laugh so Ma doesn't misunderstand. I muddle out a nod. "Yeah, Ma. I think she'd really like that."

"Good." She nods happily, like all is right with the world again. "Now, go put a shirt on. This is a respectable place."

Half an hour later, I'm showered, dressed, and mostly dry as I step into the hall. Alice is up, peeking in Lucy's door. "Oh, don't go in there," I whisper as I scoop Alice up. "There's a princess sleeping, and we don't want to wake her."

Alice blinks up at me, her lashes brushing her cheeks. "It's not a princess. It's Lucy."

"It's a Lucy princess." I kiss Alice and bound down the stairs with her.

"You baby her too much," Ma says about Alice when we reach the floor. She holds her hands out and Alice slides into Ma's arms. "Oh, you're getting so big."

"Don't say that." I follow Ma and Alice into the kitchen. "She's my baby."

"A big baby," Ma says in a deep voice, bouncing Alice over to where breakfast is cooking.

Something clinks by the sink, and I realize there are tools on the counter. "Dad?" I say, circling the island counter. "I really hope you're not—"

I stop on the other side of the counter, because the legs sticking out from under the sink are not my father's.

"I don't know what you have against helping." Lucy's muffled voice is teasing, and I can feel the grin sliding up one side of my mouth. "But it may have to do with whoever was working on this before." She leans out and wipes a sheen of sweat off her nose. "They were awful."

"Hey, you don't know who you're talking about."

Lucy grabs a coat hanger off the counter. "Oh, I think I do."

She wiggles her way under the sink again and the hem of her shirt catches, lifting over her midriff on one side. My instinct is to reach out and fix it, though I'm not sure if that's my good Samaritan nature or the devilish side of me. How bad would it be to slide my hand along Lucy's waist? In the name of modesty and helping, that is.

Thankfully, she reaches down and tugs her shirt back into place, and the visions of sweaty summer rendezvous vanish.

Mostly.

I manage to help Lucy after all, handing her tools and at one point cutting up a bike tire innertube. When she emerges, I even help her stand.

"Thank you." She smiles and turns the faucet on.

I nod and look under the sink. "You're amazing." I stand to thank her, pulling back when she's closer than I realized. "You saved me a plumber visit. Thank you."

"Hmm," she says looking me over. "I saved your Santa costume and now, I've saved you here. I'm ticking off my debts, slowly but surely. What are you at? Three catches?"

I shake my head. "If this is how you repay me, I'm gonna keep you indebted to me for a while."

Lucy rolls her eyes and checks under the sink. "It's not a permanent fix, but at least you won't need a bucket for a while."

She walks past, and I stick my foot out, intentionally tripping and catching her.

I lift her up as she starts to protest. "That's one more for me."

"Seriously?" She folds her arms and shakes her head at me.

Her hair is long and loose around her shoulders, and she's wearing yoga pants and an oversized sweater. Her cheeks are warm with an involuntary blush after my trick, and she looks . . .

She looks just like a sister. I'm fine.

Chapter 7

Lucy

"Swear to me this isn't a isn't a joke. Because I thought you were teaching me to ski." I scan the flat ground and test a foot into the thick white snow. It sinks in past my ankle.

"I am. And you're stalling. If you want to be able to ski, you have to be able to fall." Torin stands impatiently in the snowy backyard. "You can do this. Falling is easy."

"It's not the falling I'm scared of, it's the landing," I complain. "How deep is this snow? What if I hit a rock or something?"

"Lucy." Torin folds his arms, staring me down. "You're supposed to trust me."

"I know but I've known you all of twenty-four hours." I look over my shoulder. "Everyone knows it takes at least twenty-five."

"We can come back in an hour if that's better for you."

"No." I roll my eyes. "I can do it." *I'll be fine.* I nod, giving myself a mini, silent pep talk. Torin says I'll be fine. So . . . I'll be fine. Right? Maybe?

"Come on, Florida girl," Torin grumbles. "Haven't you ever made a snow angel?"

"No." I shoot him a look of disbelief and shake my head. "I grew up in the South." I suck in a fortifying breath and stand backward to the landing area. "This is terrible. It's a trust fall with no one to catch me."

"Mother Nature will catch you. I promise." He grins lightly, and warm bubbles of pleasure dance in my chest.

I pop them quickly.

"I hope we get to the good stuff soon, because I really don't want to look like an idiot in front of Erik." I shoot a glance at Torin when he gives a sound of disbelief.

"Get on with it, Florida."

I make a point of not looking at him and take a deep breath. "One, two, aaagh..."

Adrenaline and frosty air take over for the few seconds before I hit the ground with a light crunch of crystallized snow. Torin's laughter fills the air and I fight the smile it draws from me.

"You pushed me." I struggle into a sitting position, and he laughs harder.

"Look, we made it to the good stuff." From his towering position at my feet, Torin holds out his hand to help me up.

I glare and fold my arms until his laughter calms.

"Come on," he says, a genuine smile on his face. "You did a good job, Florida."

I hesitate a moment longer before accepting his help. And only then, because I don't want to flounder through the snow like a beached walrus.

"Next time, lean more to the side. Try to hit the flat part of your hip, right here." He smacks my hip and I jump back.

"Hey," I protest, not sure if his hands on my hips in any form is normal interaction or not.

"Relax, if I wanted to fondle you, it wouldn't be over so quickly. And you wouldn't be complaining." He backs up, some of my dignity tucked in his back pocket. "Try it again. This time without my help."

I turn away from him and cross my arms over my chest. "I'm doing this for Erik," I mutter. And push back.

Gravity takes over and I land in thick snow. My hair flies in my face and laughter bursts out of me. I fling my arms out to the sides and move my arms and legs in wide arcs.

"What are you doing?"

"Making a snow angel," I announce, waving my arms in the snow. "Now you can't say I've never done it."

He chuckles and drops into the snow beside me, his arms pushing snow away in the same sweeping pattern. A second snow angel.

This time when he helps me out of the snow, I'm grinning. My angel has shallow wings compared to Torin's, but I think she's beautiful.

"Well, all right then." He looks down at our masterpieces while he brushes the snow off his clothes. "Not bad for your first."

"Thanks." I smile up at him, pleasure feeding the warmth in my chest.

"And next time will be even better."

"What are you saying?" I make a show of shock as I examine my artwork. "You think I could do better? She's perfect."

"Eh," Torin pinches his lips together, squinting down at the angel, and I grab a handful of snow, tossing it at him. "Hey!"

He lunges for me, and I dash away into the yard. His long legs swallow up the tiny advantage I had. As I scoop another handful of snow, he grabs me around the waist, dropping me in a snowdrift hear the house.

Snow wasn't meant to get in your ears. It's freezing. I gasp, but my shock is torn between the cold and what just happened. Torin is hunched over, laughing.

"You just threw me!" I exclaim, tightening my lips over the emerging smile and glare at him. "What if there was a rock in here? You could have hurt me."

"Not likely. I know this place better than you think. Here, let me help you up." He reaches out, and I grab his hand, pulling harder than necessary.

Torin jerks forward in surprise and tumbles face first into the snowbank beside me. He rolls over, sitting up with snow crystals stuck in his hair and eyebrows.

I can't help myself. The fizzy energy of the last few minutes explodes in my chest and sends excitement and giggles through me. He pushes the wall of snow between us onto my lap.

I gasp, more for fear of the cold than the actual result of the attack. "You never stop." The loose snow flies easily, now, and I send a wave back to his side of the snowbank. We're en route to an epic snow battle when his phone rings.

"Dang it." He holds a hand up, moving quickly away.

I'm still laughing as he takes his call and I help myself out of the snow. This is fine. Laughing is fine. We're just hanging out. I'm here to get Erik back, and nobody says I have to be miserable while I do it.

Torin is turned toward the mountain, the phone to his ear. Even wrapped in a snow jacket and gloves, he's easy on the eyes. He turns back and my eyes go straight to his lips. Oh, geez. I can't even look without my hormones taking over.

I'm still brushing snow off my clothes when he returns, but we've both sobered considerably. Torin claps his phone between his hands repeatedly, flipping it over and glancing from it to the house.

"Who was that?" I ask, trying to step out of the thickest snow, only to find even more snow.

"Oh, nobody. Just business. Stuff about the inn." He shrugs, pocketing his phone. His lips have turned down and he lets out a heavy breath before he notices me struggling. "Here." He takes my hand and helps me out of the drift. "There you go."

"Thanks." We lock eyes and I pull my hand away, dropping my gaze . . . all the way down his body, till I finally hit snow.

Why is there so much of this man to look at?

"Umm, why don't we—" I point to the house, and Torin follows my gesture.

"Right." He starts toward the house.

I tromp after him, hiking my knees to climb slowly through the thick snow. "Did this get deeper?" I ask, stumbling along.

Torin turns and gives a humorless laugh. "No. We're just not chasing each other. Adrenaline and speed help a lot."

"And you carried me over it before, to fling me in that snowbank."

"Oh, yeah," his smile curls the corner of his lips. "That too."

The fizzy warmth returns, shooting a wave of energy over my skin. Dang hormones. Trying to hide my reaction to his smile, I look to the house and search for a distraction. "So, is everything all right? With the inn?" I ask, only sending brief glances at him. "You seem concerned. Did you have a cancellation?"

He looks over and his expression darkens. "I wish that was it. I'm trying to figure some things out with the inn. This may be her last season."

I frown. "Why? Is it struggling?"

He smiles vaguely and looks back at the house. "The inn is great. We should be doing fine, but I just can't get people to come stay."

"Oh, I'm sorry."

His step stutters. "Um, not that you wanted to know."

"I do, actually." I take several big steps to catch up, now that the snow isn't as deep. "I'm really surprised it's not doing better."

"I know. Like I said, the inn isn't the problem. I'm the one failing it—and everyone else."

"Is it really your responsibility?" I ask. His tone is spiraling as he talks about it. I miss the jovial man laughing and throwing me into snow drifts.

"It's in trouble because of me. So yeah, it kind of is my responsibility." We walk quietly, me wishing I could do something. The inn seems like such a treasure to this family, and it's becoming one to me, too.

When Torin stops several yards from the porch to look up at his home, I follow suit. "You know my wife died a couple years ago. I was working in Seattle at a startup company, and they had very little insurance. My parents re-mortgaged the inn on a business loan to help pay for some experimental treatments. Before, they owned it free and clear."

"Oh, Torin. I'm so sorry." I second guess my ability to help with this but I want to say something anyway. As a friend. "No one needs that kind of burden associated with the loss of someone they loved. Maybe I could help."

"What would you do? We can't seem to make this place bring in any more than it used to. It's like, no matter what we do, the inn has a certain level of income it likes to make, and that's all it ever does." He scrubs a hand over his jaw and back to the muscles in his neck. "We should get inside. You look cold."

I reach out, grabbing his hand, and he looks back. "Maybe I can help."

"That's sweet, Lucy, but we've really only got through Christmas to decide what we're doing. I'm meeting with a realtor next week. That's what the call was, setting up the appointment. There's not much else to do now. They trusted me. I can't fix it. It's pretty helpless."

"There are things in life that we can't control, but that doesn't make us helpless." My worry for his family and the inn aches within me.

"Excuse me?" He looks at me with confusion.

"Don't give up. You love this place, I can see it in your eyes."

"But what am I going to do? What did you say? There are things in life we can't control."

"Yeah, but that doesn't make us helpless. You find another way."

Torin looks at me warily as we reach the porch. "Okay. what are you saying?"

"I'm saying, I'm in marketing and this place is amazing." I look back over the property.

"I wouldn't ask you to come in here and set up a marketing plan at the eleventh hour."

"I wouldn't give you a choice." I pull my phone out and snap a picture of the yard with the mountain climbing through the sky in the background. "They really should be jam-packed in here. I can't believe your parents would even consider selling."

Torin pulls the door open, and I follow him inside. "Yeah, well, they don't exactly know."

It's quiet inside as we pull coats and gloves off, hanging them in the mudroom to dry.

"Want some hot chocolate?" Torin asks, grabbing a mug.

I nod and lean against the counter. "Can I ask you a personal question?"

Torin nods slowly, grabbing a teapot of steaming water from the stove. "Sure." Then he points to the island. "Will you get the spoons?"

I grab two as he fills the mugs with steaming water and cocoa packets.

"How is it that I didn't know Erik had a brother?" I don't admit it, but I could have sworn Erik said he didn't have one at all.

"Isn't that a question for him?" Torin offers me a mug and I accept it.

"He's not exactly talking to me right now." I stir my cocoa and breathe the chocolatey steam, letting it warm my hands before I drink.

Torin turns and leans against the counter beside me. "Honestly, it doesn't surprise me," he says softly. "We've had some misunderstandings. The last one sent him to Florida." He takes a drink, looking across the kitchen at nothing. He swallows. "I didn't think I'd ever see him again."

"I know the feeling," I mutter.

"I think he wanted to forget I existed. And unfortunately, I let him."

I don't know what drove them apart, but it had to be big for Erik to want to leave this place.

"I'm sure you weren't the only one to blame. Erik ran away from me, too."

"I know! It's not my fault his brother is gorgeous." I hiss the words into the phone and look around my room as if someone might be listening.

"It's not your fault, but dang, girl, it might be your blessing." My best friend's voice rings over the line. "Who's the better kisser? Erik or the brother?"

"Oh, my gosh, Shaunda! That is not the kind of help I need." I crack the door open as Shaunda shrieks in my ear.

"Holy Hannah! It's the brother, isn't it?"

The hall is empty, and I pull the door closed on my nuclear-level phone call. "Calm down. It was just a kiss."

"Apparently a good one. What's his name?"

I probably shouldn't tell her that. "I just need to know what to do. I'm trying to get Erik's attention—"

"Well, that'll do it."

"Not like that." I roll my eyes and drop on the bed. "I'm trying to show him what he's missing. I want to get him back."

"Oh, damn. It wasn't just a good kiss, it was great, wasn't it."

I sit up straight, leaning into the bed. "Shaunda!"

"I'm just sayin'. You don't worry what your ex is gonna do about a kiss if it meant nothing. But you're freaking out over—" She gasps, and I pull back, looking at the phone as if I can see what's wrong. "Lucy Sweet. You like him."

I blink, trying to follow her thoughts. "What? How can you tell?"

"Girl, you've got to figure out what you're doing."

"That's why I called you." I drop back into the covers and bury my head in a pillow with the phone still to my ear.

"Is he willing to move to Florida?"

"Well, since Erik already lives there—let's say yes." Obviously, this doesn't matter. I throw the pillow off and stare at the green vines of the wallpaper, imagining Torin standing there. "I just— I've got to stop thinking about Torin. How do I get someone out of my head when my own stupid vulnerability let him in?"

"Oh, Torin? I like it. He sounds like one of those Norse Gods. Maybe he's related to Thor."

I close my eyes, annoyed that I couldn't keep a secret from her even for the length of a phone call. "What would you do?"

"I think you know what I'd do. I'd go find that gorgeous, godlike man and drag him off to have intergalactic relations."

I gasp a laugh at her ridiculous suggestion. "He's a single dad. Leave the man alone."

"Oh, so he's got a cute little godling to play with."

"Stop," I laugh. "She's precious, but there is nothing going on. He's helping me get back together with Erik."

"No. Tell me you didn't rope him into this. Wait . . . you've been there two days—"

"A day and a half."

"Whatever. Has this cousin of Thor kissed you again?"

I hesitate. He almost did. I almost let him. Last night after I tripped. With the dim lights, and his fingers on my neck, and his lips so close —

"Oh, thank goodness," Shaunda breathes.

"Wait, I didn't say anything."

"Girl, you didn't have to. I can hear your sexy thoughts."

"Well, you're wrong. We didn't kiss."

"Well then, he must have tried. And that is good enough for me. I was just worried when you said he was helping you with Erik that maybe he wasn't feeling the same way as you, if you know what I'm saying."

"No, Shaunda, I'm not feeling any way. I'm not interested in him. Right now, I'm trying to see if rekindling things with Erik will work."

"Fine. Get back together with the guy who dumped you twice. I don't have to date him. But when you come to your senses and want to talk about this brother, let me know. You said you think Erik is scared of being with you? Well, I think you're scared, too. But not of Erik. Of real emotions. Of what they might feel like."

"Wow, and this is the advice of my best friend. I feel better." Sarcasm drips in my voice.

"You should. I'm not saying Torin's the one, but it seems like you like him, and he likes you. Right now, that's a massive change of pace from you chasing after a guy who hasn't been invested for a while."

"What are you talking about? Erik and I were great all the way up until a few days ago."

"It's never perfect until—"

"No relationship is perfect." I interrupt her.

"Maybe just give this guy a chance. A little one, for me."

"It's not like that. It can't be."

"All right. When it is, you let me know, okay?"

"You'll be waiting for a while."

"I'm patient."

I shake my head and say goodbye to my friend.

The French doors frame the view of Sugar Creek's snowy vista, and I stare out into the cold, beautiful world. There are so many differences between Erik and Torin, but when I see their faces in my mind, they have the same spicy, pine tree scent and a smile that lights up my world.

Erik hasn't smiled at me like that in ages.

I do a quick check of my hair before stepping into the hall. 'Voices drift up from the main floor, and I turn toward them.

Ingrid and Wally are talking quietly in the dining room as I approach, but it's Alice who spots me first.

"Lucy! Come see my picture."

"Sure," I say, leaning over her shoulder.

Ingrid looks up in surprise. "Lucy, I hope the ski lesson went well."

Wally prods her, and she waves a hand, stopping him under my curious glance. She smiles innocently, watching me with interest.

"It did. Thank you." My reply is a little slow, but Ingrid doesn't seem to notice.

She smiles up at me. "Would you have time to help me with something today?"

I glance from her to Wally with curiosity. "Of course, what do you need?"

Ingrid's eyes light up. "Oh, thank you! I guess it's really Torin that needs help. Our neighbor who normally volunteers as the elf in Santa's Workshop just called and said she can't make it today. I would really appreciate it if you'd step in."

"Oh." Remembering Torin's attempt yesterday to handle things by himself, I nod. "I can do that. Santa really shouldn't be left alone."

Ingrid's relief comes out in a breath. "I have an extra outfit in the hall closet. Thank you so much."

"When do I need to be ready?" I ask as I wait for her to retrieve the costume.

"Torin should be leaving in the next five minutes or so." She hands me the costume. "Thank you, again, dear. I didn't know what we were going to do."

"Five minutes?" I squeak. It's a good thing I already showered. "Oh, goodness." I take the stairs two at a time as I fly onto the landing by my room and right into Torin, dropping half my costume.

He's only half dressed, towel drying his hair in a pair of suspenders and red Santa pants. Not looking at him is not an option.

"Oof, hello to you too." He picks up the pointy elf ears and hands them to me. "You've been recruited, huh?"

I nod, trying not to notice the muscles he's left on full display. A wave of heat licks up the walls inside me like someone lit a yule log in my chest.

I dowse the flames as best I can and scoot around him. "I'm going to change. I'll be fast."

"Well, be careful, too. We've already lost one elf today."

Chapter 8

Torin

The sounds of tiny bells dance over the chattering chaos of children. My ears perk up, anticipating Lucy's appearance in the jingle bell-clad skirt of her elf outfit.

"I'm so sorry I'm late." Blaire's voice precedes her as she appears from around the corner of Santa's Workshop, wearing a familiar elf costume. She slides behind my Santa seat and through the door of the workshop as Lucy exits. "Oh!"

"Hi, you must be Blaire. I'm, Lucy, your replacement for the day." She circles away. She holds out a candy cane to the little girl who just climbed down from my lap. "Here you go. Have a merry Christmas!"

Both women reach for the bag of candy canes as the little girl and her mother leave.

"I'll take care of this part," Blaire says, gripping the bag. "You can help with the line, way over there."

Lucy's shoots me a questioning glance, but I can't help. The next little boy in line is already running to greet me. "Ho, ho, ho. You've gotten very big this year." I turn a quick look to the quarreling women and try to disguise my impatience. "This is a happy place. Why don't you try working together?"

Blaire prances off with several pointed looks at Lucy. This workshop may not be big enough for both of them.

Two hours later, Lucy flips the *Santa's In* sign to *Santa's Gone Packing Presents*.

In the doorway of the workshop, Blaire stops me, with a pile of candy cane rope in her arms. "How are your parents, Torin? It's been too long since I've stopped by to say hello."

"They're doing fine. Can I, uh, get past? I need to help Lucy." Blaire looks over her shoulder where Lucy is trying to manage a large wooden gift box.

"The new girl?" Blaire asks. Lucy's gift box has fallen in the snow several times now, and I'm halfway past Blaire when she clears her throat. "I thought I was your only elf this season," she laughs awkwardly. It's impossible to miss her frown at Lucy. "We don't really need two elves here."

"I know. It was a little crowded today. Since you told my mother you couldn't make it, she asked Lucy to come in your place." I don't know why I need to explain, but I am. "She's just filling in."

"And yet—she said . . . replacement." Blaire squeaks a tiny sound of surprise. "Oops. I really was just going to be gone this one time. My cousin came to town and surprised me. So, you won't have to worry about me being late anymore. She asked me to help her out with—some work things. She just got a house out here to rent. But I'll still be able to help here too—I swear!"

Blaire starting a job could solve a lot of problems.

"If things are too busy, I'm sure Lucy could keep filling in," I say. "It would make sense. She's staying with us, so she'll just ride with—"

"No! I wouldn't do that to you, I've committed to help you. And after everything you've been through, and now you're alone in that big inn—"

I open my mouth and Blaire starts talking faster.

"Besides, it's a great experience for me, um, I get to spend time with you, the owner of a local inn—" She scoots closer and straightens my collar. "I've always been so interested in what you do. It's a perfect situation for me. And Santa's Workshop is sponsored by the inn, right? So, I really should stay."

"This place, the holiday activities, don't really have anything to do with the inn."

"But you do. And with all the challenges you've been through personally, and then all the struggles at the inn, I just want to help, and I thought you could use a . . . friend."

I step back nervously, "How do you know about everything I've been through?"

"Oh, I listen. I was thinking maybe we could go out some time, or back to your place."

Challenges? My throat contracts, like I'm sucking a lime. "My late wife was a bit more than a *challenge*."

"Oh, um, I didn't mean—" She stutters over simple words like her tongue has gotten in the way of her voice.

I take a long breath. "Look, Blaire. I'm not sure what you heard, but I'm afraid you've gotten the wrong impression here."

Her smile stays pasted in place, staring up at me. "I don't know what you mean?"

I try again. "I'm not going to be able to have you keep working here. Like you said, we don't need two elves, and Lucy's dating—she came with my brother. So, she's practically family, and the inn is family-run, so—" I pinch an unapologetic smile on my face. "Santa's Workshop should be family too."

She shakes her head at me, speechless and staring. It's as rude as I've ever been to anyone, but Corrine's memory is not going to be bait to this woman's mid-life crisis.

"Don't say that. We don't have to make a decision now, I have big plans. Everything is finally coming together."

"I'm not sure I'm ready for those kinds of plans. I'm sorry, but you're fired."

"I'm a volunteer!" She shouts and throws her elf hat on the ground. "You can't fire me."

"Then, until you get word to come back, there's no need for you to show up anymore."

Lucy peeks out the door of the workshop, her eyes the size of quarters. Blaire has her hands out, taking deep breaths and looking at the shops and trees behind me.

"Fine," she says. "If you don't want to be in this together, neither do I. Goodbye." Jingle bells serenade her exit, taking it from dramatic to theatrical.

"I thought she was supposed to be nice," Lucy whispers, crunching her way over the salted path.

"Lucy?" I ask, without looking away from Blaire, fighting with her jingling shoe covers. "Do you think you can be my elf while you're here?"

"She's really not coming back?" Lucy's voice radiates surprise, and concern.

Across the square, Blaire finally rips the shoe covers from her feet. Aiming them in our direction, she yells something I can't understand and throws them on the ground.

I pick up Blaire's discarded elf hat and shake my head. "Nope. Definitely not. I'll give you a discount on your room."

"Are you sure?" Lucy's eyebrows raise. "I mean—that's really nice, but is that a good idea?"

I don't know if she means us spending time together or what I told her about the inn's finances, but I don't have time to fish around. I can't take another minute of Blaire.

"We'll get by." I ignore the twinge in my heart. "Will you do it?"

Lucy laughs. "Well, since you're helping me fix things with Erik, it's only fair if I help you here. As long as you say please."

I laugh. "Please. I'm not above begging."

"Perfect. Looks like I'm finally winning the Who Saved Who contest," Lucy says innocently. "I've never had anyone indebted to me before. This should be fun."

After finishing day two at Santa's Workshop with Lucy, the sound of jingle bells has become a trigger. Her musical movements hold my gaze as she takes the stairs in her short skirt and candy cane tights.

No one should look that good in an elf costume.

Focus, I think. Then I promptly trip over a bench that's been in the entry since I was sixteen and knock over a nearby table stacked with Christmas books.

Lucy spins around and my mother appears in the doorway.

"Who's ready to go sledding?" I ask, standing with the books in my hand, like I went down just to pick them up instead of the other way around.

Lucy laughs, continuing down the hall. She wasn't supposed to see that.

I push through the kitchen door after my mother to find Alice standing on a chair by the wide island. Around her the counter is spread with thin layers of brown dough, ambiguous shapes cut and laid out on trays.

"We're making a village!" Alice says, pointing to the big squares of cookie.

I slip a heart-shaped gingerbread cookie off a plate and bite the corner before kissing Alice. "I can't wait to see it."

She frowns. "You're supposed to wait till we decorate them."

"If you didn't make them so delicious, maybe I could wait."

"Your daddy's never been very patient." Ma lifts Alice over to a different stool. "Can you cut some more gingerbread shapes?"

Alice carefully sets out her cookie cutter, pressing it into the dough, as my mother pulls me aside and asks, "Are you ready for sledding tonight? We have to beat Nils to the hill. He's always the first one there."

"I didn't think the competitions started until Monday."

"It's not a competition," Ma scoffs. "It's a matter of pride. We're hosting everyone, and he's always there before me." She picks up a gingerbread cookie and bites the head off the little person. "I know my brother. If there's a way to win at something, Nils will try."

"Is there something I can do to help?" Lucy walks in as Ma shakes the decapitated cookie at me. "Oh, woah." She gives the waving cookie a wide berth. "Is Torin in trouble?"

"Ha!" Ma takes a vicious bite of the cookie's arm. "Not yet. But just wait. This man can make trouble out of thin air."

"Hey!" I hold up my hands and turn to Lucy. "Woah."

She's changed from her elf costume into a pair of very tight black pants and a red turtleneck, just tight enough that I don't have to wonder what she's hiding.

"That's, um, —" I tug at my collar. "You look—" My tongue seems to have lodged in the back of my throat. I look her over, from head to very long legs. No words come to mind that I can say in front of my mother and daughter.

"Yes?" Lucy tips her head in question, crossing her arms over her chest. She knows exactly what she's doing as she watches me struggle with a smug smirk on her pretty face.

I swallow and shut my mouth. There's no way for me to say the right thing.

"Out of thin air," Lucy turns to my mother. "Very impressive."

"Uh-oh!" Alice exclaims as something clatters to the floor. My dad reflexes have developed a serious lag as I pull my eyes off of Lucy.

"Oh, *sötnos*, let me help you." Ma lifts a dripping Alice down from her chair. A glass of juice pools over the counter, around the cookies, and down Alice's clothes.

"Shoot. Let me help." I grab a towel and start mopping up juice.

"Thank you," Ma says. "If you'll get that, I'll take care of Alice."

"Sure," I say at the same time as Lucy. She's got a towel on the floor, mopping up the opposite side of the counter.

"Thanks, Ma," I mutter, but she's already gone and I'm alone with the housewife version of Nightclub Barbie.

I swallow as Lucy stands up, rinsing out her soaked towel. She gives me a funny look, and I start wiping off the counter in slow motion.

"Where are the extra towels?" She's pulling drawers out, looking on the wrong side of the kitchen. It takes me too long to respond. "Is there a problem, Torin?"

I shake my head. "Nope."

After kissing her breathless, spending mornings together before she gets ready for the day, and dressing up in costume together, I thought I was prepared for every version of Lucy. No such luck.

I go to the mudroom and grab a short stack of extra towels. When I return, I'm more prepared. I hand her a towel and hold it, keeping her there for a moment. "You look amazing, Lucy."

"Thank you." She grins and I release the towel. "I hope Erik likes it as much as you do."

Erik. I have a mental fist fight with my brother, prepping myself for bad news. *I knew this wasn't a sledding outfit.*

"Oh, he'll like it. Are you two going out tonight? Because—" I make the mistake of looking down her long legs again and have to take a moment to clear my throat. "I thought you were coming sledding with us."

"I am going sledding." She looks down at her outfit as I finish wiping down the counter. "These are sledding clothes. Long pants, turtleneck . . . sledding."

Red lips, blue eyes . . . therapy session.

"Right, I can see your logic. But we're going to be out there for several hours. You really need something more . . . water resistant. Or you're going to freeze." *And I'm going to crash on every run.*

"I'm not wearing a trash bag."

"No. Did you bring snow pants? For skiing? You might want to try them out today for sledding."

"I don't have any snow clothes," she complains, "but these are long pants. How much warmer can I get?"

As a general rule, I try not to laugh at Lucy. But sometimes, I can't help it. "Let's go find my mother. She'll find something that won't turn you into an ice cube by the end of the night."

An hour later, and thirty minutes before anyone from the reunion is going to be here, we're pulling into the Vanderberg's Christmas tree lot. Lucy's still wearing the black pants, which isn't such a bad thing. She looks amazing in them. And my mother got her to put some thermal leggings on underneath, so she won't freeze.

Around the side of the barn, the lower area of the sledding hill is filled with crowds of people in thick flannels, scarves, and heavy jackets. Sleds and smiles don most every guest. It doesn't take long for my mother to claim triumph over Uncle Nils, setting her post by the check-in station to welcome her siblings as they arrive.

My dad wastes no time claiming Alice wants hot chocolate, and heads off to find marshmallows. Lucy puts a hand on my elbow, natural, like it doesn't make her proximity sensors go off and her skin light up with heat where she touches me. *Yeah, no biggie.*

"Do you want to go up with me?" She points to a fat wheeled vehicle hauling people and sleds to the top of the sloping hill. "I've never been sledding on anything this big."

"Absolutely. I was going to take Alice up soon, but we can go first."

"Would Alice come with us?" She grins. "That'd be fun. We should go soon, though. I don't want to be gone when Erik shows up."

"Erik, yeah. I didn't think about that. Good idea." We're not going alone, and we're going now, so she can see Erik later. I'm the backup dude. "I'll go get Alice."

The sled rental line weaves, snakelike, past the red barn, ending with a blond guy in a thick brown jacket. He turns as I approach, and my footsteps stutter. I do a quick look to see if there's another line or a shoe that needs tying—anything I might be able to take care of until there's someone between us.

His blonde hair is plastered up in a wave, and he smirks when he recognizes me. "Hey, Torin. How's it going?"

"Sanford . . ." A groan rises inside me as I push out the expected pleasantries. "How are you?"

"Your parents haven't given up on that inn yet, have they?" Sanford chuckles, and I cringe. "It's got to be rough taking out a mortgage on a place they owned free and clear."

"How would you know that?" It's a fight to keep my smile in place.

"I recommended my mortgage banker for them, a couple years ago." *A couple years ago,* around the time Corrine got sick. He carries on the conversation without my help. "I offered to buy the place when they said you needed the money, but they weren't interested." He slugs me in the shoulder, laughing. "Rough that they picked the house, over paying off your debt, isn't it? Let me know if they're ever interested in offloading it."

"It's still not for sale." My upper lip hitches into something closer to a sneer than a smile.

Even if it is, it won't be for sale to him.

"That's too bad." Sanford's grin sours. "I'm always ready to help."

He turns around in line and I bite my tongue. I need to confirm with Max that Sanford doesn't come anywhere near the Sugar Creek Inn.

"Merry Christmas, Torin! What can I do for ya?" Mr. Vanderberg greets me in his bright red bib overalls and Santa hat after Sanford walks away with his rented sled.

"I'd like a three-man sled." I don't see any of the tall sleds against the wall.

Mr. Vanderberg frowns and points to Sanford walking away with a bright green sled under his arm. "Just rented the last one. There should be more coming back soon, if you want to wait."

"No, it's fine." I grumble and look back at the stacks of colorful plastic. "Two-man?"

"Only singles, sorry about that."

I dig into my wallet and pull out the cash. "It's fine. I'll take two."

I leave with the sleds stacked under my arm, and find Alice with my dad and a half-full bag of marshmallows. When I pry her away from the sugary treats, she bounces ahead of me. "I like s'mores," she calls loudly. "Marshmallows are so—" she holds out the O until she can't breathe— "yummy!" she finishes, and my eyebrows lift.

Thanks, Dad.

This will be an epic sugar rush and crash.

I don't even get to respond before Alice hurtles across the snowy ground, colliding with the back of Lucy's legs. Lucy stumbles forward and laughs.

"Aly girl!" I call after her. "Since when do you like her more than me?"

I adjust my grip on the sleds, jogging over to rescue Lucy. At the appearance of hands on her waist, something rears up inside me.

Erik.

Of course he'll be helping her, I reason with the beast in my head. She's been waiting to see him for days.

Only, that's not Erik.

My protective monster wakes again and I finish my jog to the girls. "Sanford! I see you've met Lucy."

When Sanford retreats, my hand settles on Lucy's back. It's possessive, but someone has to stake my brother's claim, and he's not here to do it himself yet. Lucy gives me a look and steps slightly to the side, till my hand drops from her back.

Sanford's gaze bounces from Lucy to me. "Do you know him? I thought you were visiting."

"I am," Lucy says, her smile dimming when she looks at me.

I must not be hiding my irritation well. I push a tight grimace onto my face and glare at her new friend.

Shaking her head, she turns to Sanford. "I'm staying at the Nyström's inn."

"Nice, it's a good place." His eyes are locked on Lucy. "You know, it could be mine one day. I'm trying to buy it."

I shake my head at Lucy's shocked glance. "You ready to go sledding? Lucy." I put my hand at her back again, and this time she doesn't leave. "Alice wants hot chocolate when we're done."

"Why don't I come with you guys?" Sanford says. "I've got a three-man sled. We can ride together." He winks at Lucy.

I step forward, fighting the skepticism in my voice. "Are you serious?"

Sanford gives me a wicked grin.

Shifting tactics, I transition my tone to one of gratitude and mock shock. "That is so nice." As innocently as possible, I set a hand on his shoulder and look at Lucy. "We wanted to ride together, and they were out of the triples after yours." I hand Sanford my two sleds and trade him for the three-man.

"Thanks, Sandy," I say, leading Lucy and Alice quickly to the sledding hill.

"Thanks, Sandy!" Lucy echoes, and I choke on a laugh, coughing while Sanford glowers after us.

String lights blaze over the fire pit, reflecting warmth across the snow. A smattering of stars greets the remaining guests of the annual Vanderberg Tree Farm sledding event. They gather to the flames, s'mores, and conversation under the lights.

"Are any of your cousins still here? That girl who tripped you was so funny."

"You *would* latch on to Emma," I tease as Lucy finds an open spot on the bench closest to the fire.

"Emma! That's right." Holding her hands out to the heat, Lucy removes her gloves and looks up. Her nose is tinged pink by the cold, and I set my wrist against it, trying to warm her without holding, kissing, or caressing her.

"What are you doing?" she laughs, dodging my odd gesture and patting the bench beside her. "Are you going to sit?"

"After I get some hot chocolate. Want some? You look cold."

She nods and I press into the crowd, her eyes sparkling as she watches me go. When I look back, she drops her gaze. There's a touch of satisfaction just knowing she's aware of me.

The cocoa station isn't far, but it takes a few minutes to find it with all the people milling around. My phone dings as I get in line.

"Finally," I mutter, opening Erik's text.

— *Hot tubbing all night. Couldn't make it out.*

The text is accompanied by a group shot of several bikini clad women smiling at the screen. Scowling, I shut the screen off. It's a good thing Lucy didn't have to see that.

It's only a few more minutes to get two cups filled with hot cocoa and make my way back to where Lucy sits. Holding her cup out to her, she takes it and presses her pink nose to the side.

"Thank you," she says behind the steaming wall.

I chuckle, holding mine to my lips. "Normally, people *drink* their hot chocolate." I twist the cup in my hand as my phone buzzes a reminder about Erik's text.

"Are you gonna check that?" she asks, taking her first sip of the hot drink. "Maybe it's Erik. Would he come just for cocoa?"

"Good question," I lie. My stomach bubbles with deceit and the rich, chocolatey drink. Setting my cup down, I pull out my phone before I raise my eyebrows and make a disappointed groan. "Oh, that's too bad." Lucy glances at my phone screen and I click it off quickly. "It's Erik. I guess he hurt himself on the slopes and the lodge medic gave him some serious meds that just knocked him out. He's really sorry about missing the night with us, though."

"It must be pretty bad. He doesn't usually do much pain medication." She shakes her head. "Either that, or he lied just to ditch me." She smiles a sad smile and slumps closer to the fire.

"No." I suck in a breath and try to adjust the story so she won't think it's her fault. "It sounds like it was a pretty big crash." She looks up, worried, and

I adjust again. "But not, like, dangerous big, 'cause he, umm, hit his head, and they were worried about a concussion. But he's fine . . . so they just gave him some big ol' horse pill things." Her eyes only get bigger as I go and I taper the story again, trying my best to end the lie. "Over-the-counter ones, you know. But big ones. Really big . . . Tylenol, or something." I try to keep my face normal as I second-guess myself and nod.

"Tylenol? Are you sure?" she asks, her face twisted in confusion. "Oh, no."

"Yeah," I say, regretting the contorted lie. I'm already not sure of what I told her. "I think he's going to be all right in a day or two. He's just a little banged up, you know."

"He's banged up? No other – problems?"

"Mmhmm." I pinch my lips together and nod. Sometimes no words are better words.

"So, the medicine's helping, then?"

"I guess so," I mumble to my cocoa cup. "Erik said he's waking up, but still tired."

"Well, that's just terrible." She starts to laugh, and my worry switches from her being sad to her being crazy.

"You're not you upset?"

Lucy's grin grows wide enough she can't hide it.

"Oh, I am—I'm really upset." She furrows her brow over an exaggerated frown. "I bet Erik is having a really rough day."

"Yeah. Poor guy. He'll be all right, though."

"Most likely, after the blisters go away." She shakes her head and I do a double take. "I bet they're just killing him."

"Blis—what?"

"The blisters. From the Tylenol. Cause he's allergic to acetaminophen." My jaw drops. "No, he's not."

"Sorry." Lucy shrugs. "He is. It started last year."

"Crap." I take a long drink of my hot chocolate and exhale through my nose. "That's what I get for not staying in touch with my brother."

"Yeah, well, it's not like you missed his wife's funeral." She only glances at me when she says it, but the dark humor feels justified.

"Truth," I mutter.

"So, why do you think he actually ditched us?"

I look away, losing myself in the crackling fire for a moment. Some answers aren't easy, and I'm not sure if I can or should tell her what Erik's really doing tonight. "He's probably just tired."

Lucy throws a stick in the fire and sparks fly in the air. "Or maybe I just need to admit he doesn't want me."

Chapter 9

Lucy

Hot chocolate scalds a river down my throat. I should have let it cool. I keep drinking until I see the bottom of the paper cup.

"Erik's not the only guy out there." Torin's tone is defensive, but it's like he's defending me, not himself or his brother. It's as if he wants to wrap me up and keep me safe.

"I'm very aware." I give him a tight smile and twirl my empty cup on the bench. "I just, I had a plan."

"Plans can change. What do you want now?"

"I want Erik to stop being an idiot." I look away.

People are still milling about, and the fire glows in the middle of it all. I reach for my necklace on instinct. As I dig through my thick scarf, I remember that my snowflake isn't there.

It's fine. I know better than to let my hopes get so high they can break you.

"Well, I can't help you with that." Torin sits back, shaking his head.

I laugh softly as my phone lights up with blonde hair and a hot pink smile, beneath the name Deronda Sweet.

My mother is calling.

I hover my finger over the call slider. "I should take this," I say to Torin. "Would you mind getting me more hot chocolate?"

He nods and I slide my finger over the screen, answering the call. "Hey, Mom!"

"Lucy!" She sounds too excited, and I rush to get her talking before Torin comes back.

"How're things with An-dy-Drew—Andrew—Brian!" I applaud myself for coming up with the name that feels right. Torin steps over the bench, and his phone falls out of his pocket. "Oh!"

"I imagine he's fine. Thanks for asking, sweetie. But I'm not dating him right now."

"Torin." I jump to grab the phone and hold my phone to my chest while I call after him. He doesn't hear me.

When I put the phone back to my ear, she's not talking. "Mom?"

"Who's Torin?" She sounds a little too enthusiastic.

"No one. Erik's brother," I say, taking my seat. He'll be back. I'll give it to him then. "What were you saying? You dumped Brian?"

"Weeks ago. Oh, honey, you've got to keep up." While she gives me a timeline of her last month of boyfriends, I flip Torin's phone over and slide my finger over the screen.

I gasp nervously when it turns on. Who doesn't have a passcode on their phone? Looking around, I check the crowd to see if anyone's watching me. The text screen is open to the thread with Erik. It's short, but the last message stands out. A picture of a hot tub full of girls.

The real reason he couldn't come tonight.

A wave of nausea sweeps over me. Residual hurt for not being chosen. He picked hot tubbing with them over coming to see me. I drop the phone to the bench and look up. My goal was to prove Erik still loved me, and I haven't even had the chance to attempt it yet.

"So, tell me about what you and Mr. Perfect did tonight. You know that's why I called."

The text flashes in my mind and the air sticks in my throat. "He isn't Mr. Perfect."

"Fine. Don't tell me." My mother replies to my non-answer. "He's probably being disgustingly perfect, anyway."

"You could say that." *He's disgusting all right.*

Across from the firepit, Torin walks toward me with two hot chocolates and a big smile.

I pick up Torin's phone as he approaches, holding it out to him. I don't bother closing the screen with Erik's text.

"You dropped this," I whisper, holding the phone away from my mouth.

He sets my cocoa on the bench as he takes the phone and sees what I saw. "I'm sorry."

I shake my head and try to focus on my mother as he straddles the bench in front of me.

"Can I talk to him?"

"No!" I blurt, and Torin looks up at me curiously. "Uh, no. Sorry, Mom. He's not here right now." Guilt wraps me in its silken grip as Torin, not Erik, sends me questioning looks from the bench beside me.

"Then where is he? Is everything all right?"

"Yeah, he—uh—got hurt on the slopes." My nostrils flare, and Torin tenses, watching me. "I'm learning a lot about him, though. I went sledding with his whole family tonight." Keeping my eyes on Torin, I feel my body heat rising.

"You didn't stay with him? He's hurt, honey. All women know how much of a baby men are. They need us to take care of them. Maybe I should come help you out, I could use a break."

"You don't need to do that." I laugh weakly. "We're coming for New Year's. So it's really not necessary."

"Oh, I knew that. I guess I'll see you soon."

I say goodbye and Torin scoots closer, worry pinching his brow. "How's your mom doing?"

I'm surprised he wants to know. I give an uncomfortable smile. "She's fine. Just wanted to know about my trip."

He nods, splaying his hands against the bench and waits. Eventually he shakes his head and reaches a hand toward mine. "And . . . you told her you've been hanging out with a great guy and his family?"

"Are we talking about you or Erik?"

"You tell me." He looks down at his phone and the picture of Erik's hot tub full of women shines in my mind.

He's not technically doing anything wrong. We're not dating. But it still hurts. Can I even blame him? The day we broke up, I walked through his hometown and kissed the first guy I saw. I kissed his brother. My breathing picks up, and I open my mouth. Erik has been a part of my plan so long, I don't know what it looks like without him.

"Tonight, I cannot honestly say it's Erik. But he's not like that. He's a good guy, and we've been together a long time. I hope we'll be together a lot longer."

"Wait, are you saying . . . you still want to be with him? After treating you like this?" His jaw tenses and one eyebrow drops low. "Lucy, my brother can be a good guy when he wants to be. I've always looked up to him. But are you sure this is what you want?" His hand twitches toward his phone, and I silently beg him not to pull the picture up again. There's so much hot chocolate in my stomach, I might barf at the sight of those swimsuits.

"Relationships are hard work. I'm not ready to give up on it yet. We've been together five years. If you're not committed, you break up after a few months, a year. When you hit five years, it's gold bands and wedding receptions. There are expectations and unspoken promises."

"I can't tell, are you committed to Erik or the relationship? You keep talking about how long you've been together and working hard for this. But he's out flirting and dating."

I shrug and look down at my hands. "We're not together right now. And him being like that doesn't mean I didn't make those promises. I can't just walk away because it's suddenly inconvenient to my hormones."

Torin looks up when I mention hormones. I close my eyes.

"So, you want to be with Erik because you've been together a long time. That's it? Do you even like him?"

"Of course I like him."

"Okay, do you love him?"

I blink at him, opening my eyes in surprise. "Isn't that what we've been talking about?"

"Not really. You've talked about commitment and expectations, but don't you both deserve to be with someone you love?"

"What is love? Being 'crazy' over someone?

"No, but hopefully that's part of it."

Torin stares into my soul, his green eyes challenging the entire reason I'm here.

"Why does love have to be crazy? Why can't it be happy or calm?"

"It can, but that's not all it is. Don't you want that feeling? To be so in love with someone you *can't not* be with them? If you find someone that you're *that* in love with, wouldn't you try to be with them? Choose to feel that every day? To love and be loved?"

"Crazy isn't usually a good thing," I point out. "People get that way because they let attraction and desire rule their choice. What if I don't want to feel crazy? I've seen what relationships are like that way. Giddy feelings don't last, and jumping in headfirst only gives you a headache."

Torin nods to the fire. "I'm sorry Lucy, but that's crap."

I look at him sharply, tears pressing my eyelids. "Excuse me? Why is it crap to want a partner that really fits me? I'm not looking to get my heart broken." He's quiet, and I'm furious. "Love shouldn't rip your heart out. It should heal it, support it, make it stronger. That's the love I'm willing to fight for. Not the one that makes me lose control of my fingers and toes until kissing someone I just met feels like the only logical answer."

Torin pulls back. I didn't mean to reference our kiss, but I don't take it back. The way Torin makes me feel is not safe.

"I don't think you can have one without the other. This safe, kitten love you're talking about . . . it doesn't exist. Love isn't a tame emotion. 'Like' is. You like Erik. But do you love him? I have yet to hear you say that. Don't you want to feel your heartrate pick up when your person walks in the room? To know what they're thinking when they smile at you? To want their touch so badly your body tingles at the brush of their skin?" He's leaning in and his breath warms my skin, sending those very tingles over my cheeks and down my spine. He pulls back, drawing my energy away with him. "Do you love Erik?"

I feel dizzy. His question is unfair, forcing me into a confrontation I don't want to have. The threshold between discussing and arguing has always been made of eggshells for me, and Torin is tap-dancing across it with bravado.

"I've been with him for five years. I'm committed to being with him forever. Isn't that love?"

"Maybe. It's one way to put it, anyway." Torin's finger brushes mine as he shifts on the bench. "Love is commitment. But it's also fun, and laughter, and excitement, and desire. It's giving up your wants for theirs because your biggest want is for them to be happy. Lucy—you deserve to be happy."

"I want to be happy. But how do you know if you have some epic love or if it's just wash, rinse, and repeat?" I'm terrified of what he's going to say, but I ask anyway.

"Epic love?" Fire dances in Torin's eyes and he takes my hands, sliding closer. "You don't need to worry about that. Every love story is epic. And tragic. No matter how long they last. They go hand in hand. Love is epic."

As his words hit my heart, I want more of them. I want his kind of love to be real. I just don't know if I can trust it. It's never been like that for me . . . until him.

I tip my head forward and our foreheads touch. Every breath tastes like Torin, till I'm drunk on wanting him. "And if you want it forever?"

His eyes dim and his grip tightens. "That's not a choice you get to make on your own. You can't force your partner to stay, whether they want to or not."

The transition from Erik to Corrine is so smooth I don't even notice until I can hear her unspoken name between us. I sit up, letting the air take up space between us. "Corrine's illness made the choice for you."

He drops his eyes. My heart aches for him and what I wish he was offering me. She is the one who taught him about epic love. She is the one shaping his heart. Without her, it would be easy to tamp down the little voice in my head chanting that my rules are the only thing keeping me safe.

But if I'm choosing between brothers, it doesn't really matter who I love. Torin's heart is already taken.

And neither might be my only option.

"I may not be able to make that choice for Erik," I sigh, "but I'm not ready to be the one that sends it away."

Alice giggles at the edge of my bed, a blond head of bobbing laughter. Almost in slow motion, I roll over. Then, making a quick jump, I pounce on the sheets in front of her.

A squeal of giggles erupts, and she runs a wide circle away from the bed and back.

Voices drift through the now-open door, calling my attention. "Everyone's awake, huh?"

Alice's head bobbles. "*Farmor* says it's time for breakfast."

"*Farmor*?" It takes me a minute to remember. "Oh, your grandma?" I give myself a mental pat on the back when Alice nods, and the two of us make our way down the stairs.

Torin does a double take when I reach the bottom of the steps. "Where'd you find my sweater?"

His sweater?

The blood drains from my face as I drop my gaze to the oversized top. The unidentifiable logo has hockey sticks under it and weird slasher letters that spell out *Go Carvers*.

I should have known it would be his.

I didn't even look in the mirror before coming down here. Then Torin sees me, or I see him, and I'm suddenly self-conscious in my choice of sleepwear.

Crossing my arms over my chest, I lean away from him in the corner of the dining room, where the family has gathered for breakfast. "Your mom said I could borrow it."

"I'm surprised we still have it." In his confusion, he quickly scans me and looks away.

"It was in the mudroom closet. I didn't realize it was yours," I whisper, regretting the found clothes. My tank top nightdress was freezing, but at least it was mine. "I'm sorry. I'll put it back if you want me to."

Alice climbs up the chair beside me and into my arms.

Torin can barely look at me. "No, it's fine."

"It's not fine." I can feel his anxiety, and I shift Alice toward him. "I'll change. I'm sorry."

"Lucy," he says with more force, his gaze dropping to the sweater again. "It's fine. It's an old sweater, and it looks better on you than it ever did on me."

My cheeks heat as he holds his hands to Alice, who bails from me to him.

Our gazes lock, and my breath grows heavy. The kitchen door swings open, breaking the spell, and I look away, brushing my hair back. *I'm primping again.* Dropping my hands, I inhale sharply. This is not who I am.

"Why can't they stay here?" Ingrid sails into the dining room, with two bowls of fruit in her hands. "Why do they need skiing and a hot tub? It's only thirty minutes to the lodge, and now we won't even get to see them." She plunks the fruit onto the long buffet cabinet at the side of the room. "Who knows when they'll clear the mountain pass?"

"Is it so bad?" Torin asks. "We only have a handful of rooms, and it'd be nice to get paying guests in them, so we can make our payment."

"We always make our payment. We're not the Laurents, but we're fine, and now we won't get to see the family at all." Ingrid pushes her way back into the kitchen and the door slams closed behind her.

Torin sighs, turning back to me and leaning against the archway between the hall and dining room.

I go up on tiptoe to whisper, "Who are the Laurents?"

"Rich people. They've lived in Sugar Creek forever." He glances down at my sweater again. "I played hockey from sophomore year and on. I haven't seen that sweater in ages."

I chuckle, grateful he no longer seems upset over it. Though his frequent glances could make me uncomfortable for another reason.

Ingrid bursts back into the room. "Well, Nils just confirmed it." Upset wouldn't even begin to cover the way she looks right now. She is a hurricane of her own making, sweeping arcs of chaos from one side of the room to the other. Ingrid picks things up in one spot replacing them indiscriminately on tables or shelves. "They've moved all the reunion activities to the lodge, which means we're the only ones that can't go."

"Why can't we go?" I ask.

Torin points to the window. "It hasn't stopped snowing since last night. The rest of the family is staying at the resort, and it's drifting on the mountain, so they closed the roads."

"But it's fine," Ingrid says, her face puckering with frustration. "Erik is there, so they said we have representation."

"*Älskling.*" Wally stands, holding his arm out to his wife.

She redirects his hand with a push, waving a serving spoon at him. "Don't you 'darling' me. Being unhappy is perfectly reasonable, considering we've been ousted from our own reunion."

"It's a week-long reunion. Why be upset? It's one or two less days to risk Linnea's cooking."

"But she won't even see the stars I put up."

"I put up—" Torin clears his throat and Ingrid glares at him.

"*We* put up. It took Torin two days of climbing ladders and hanging lights to create the beautiful decorations *she* insisted on. Even Alice helped."

"Your sister will see the decorations. They'll all see them. Aren't we hosting the snowman contest on Santa Lucia day?"

"Yes." She calms slightly, and Wally kisses her.

"They'll clear the snow, and when the roads open, they'll all be back." He doesn't look overly excited.

Ingrid puffs her chest and pokes her husband with her wooden spoon. "They'll clear it when it stops coming down. Look at that!"

I follow her gesture to the window, expecting snow piled up to the windowsills. It's a little disappointing to find the view clear, though a blanket of white has obscured the features of the lawn and sidewalk beneath a heavy dust of falling snow.

"Perhaps it will stop sooner than later." Wally laughs and settles back in his chair. She pokes him again for good measure, and he waves her off, chuckling. "Go poke the road men with your spoons. Then you'll get your work done, and I won't get bruises."

Ingrid harrumphs. "Just watch. It'll keep snowing and we'll be alone the whole time."

The breakfast meal Ingrid has set up, is filled with an array of fruit and a bowl piled high with fluffy white cream. Torin hands me a plate.

"Are we getting snowed in?" I whisper.

"Not likely," Torin says. "We're only expecting six to eight inches. They'll have the roads cleared pretty quick."

"Six to eight inches . . . of snow?" I stare at him. "I've never been snowed in before."

"You still won't be." Torin looks back at me, bemused. "You don't need to worry."

"Worry? It's amazing. I mean, it's not past my knees or anything, but that's so much snow!"

"I'm glad someone's happy about it." He sets a thin washed-out pancake on my plate. "How do you feel about Swedish Pancakes?"

I look at the unfamiliar food with wary eyes. They seem closer to crepes than the pancakes I'm familiar with. "Never had 'em."

After teaching me to build the perfect Swedish pancake, Torin watches as I add a muddle of berries over cream and wrap it carefully. Wally comes up behind me and drops a couple folded pancakes on his plate, dollops whipped cream on top, and heaps piles of juicy fruit over that.

I look from his plate to mine and its carefully filled and folded fruit and cream combinations.

Torin shakes his head. "Don't follow his example. He's a heathen."

Wally looks up from his plate long enough to shake his head and dig in, holding up his fork once it's loaded with food. "The important thing is that you enjoy it. And that you add piles of lingonberries."

His accent is thicker this morning. I want him to keep talking.

"Sit by me, Lucy," Alice begs.

I oblige, watching the Nyström family enjoy their morning.

A single other guest joins us briefly before Ingrid helps them check out, and I can't help it anymore. I have to say something. "I can't believe this place isn't jam-packed with people. It's such an incredible home."

Torin nods. "It should be. It's been here for years and has all the right ingredients. People just don't find us."

Across the table, Wally's newspaper covers his face. I lean toward Torin and lower my voice. "What kind of marketing do you do?"

I have a list of things I hope he's going to say, but nothing prepares me for his answer.

"Not much. We have a website, but I'm afraid it's as hard to find as the inn."

"You're joking, right?" My brain clicks into problem-solving mode and I start throwing out ideas. "I've seen the reunion itinerary. I know the kinds of things they do around here. You really don't market with any local venues? Cross-promote?"

Torin's eyes dash to his mother, and he pushes away from the table. "We haven't had time."

"It's a great marketing tool. Community outreach is important." I frown as he circles the table.

Leaning over my shoulder, he takes my empty plate and whispers, "This isn't the best time."

I glance over to see Wally tip the corner of his paper down. "Okay," I nod. "But we do need to talk."

"Of course," he says and turns to Alice. "Want to help me clean up?"

"Yeah!" Alice jumps down from the table to run after Torin.

"Did you get enough to eat?" Ingrid asks before I can make my exit. "My son didn't take it all, I hope."

"No, it was wonderful. I'm sorry you're missing the reunion, though." I'm sorry for me, too, but that feels selfish to say.

Ingrid flashes me a friendly grin. "That's very kind of you. And as much as I hate to admit it, Wally's right. The roads will be cleared soon enough. And next year we'll do it all again."

"That sounds exhausting," I laugh as Ingrid gives a happy sigh.

"It is . . . a bit. It would be better if Torin would hang around, or Erik. I'd be more than happy to turn this place over to one of them. But for the first time in a hundred years, the Nyströms don't have a descendant that wants to carry on the legacy."

"Have you talked with them about that?"

"Not really." Ingrid looks at Wally and purses her lips. "We were trying to wait and see what happens with their families, but Erik left, and then Torin's wife passed. I just don't know when they're going to settle down. Or if they'll want to stay in Sugar Creek. We may have to turn the inn over to a non-Nyström."

Chapter 10

Torin

"**D**addy? Is Gramma sad that it's snowing?"

"No," I say, taking Alice's clean dish and setting it to dry on the counter. "Gramma just really loves her family. She's sad she won't see them because of the snow."

Alice nods, like she understands, then frowns, leaning toward the window. "But the snow isn't hard to see through yet."

"You are so right." Happiness seeps through me, soaking Alice's innocence up like I'm a paper towel. "Maybe we can help Grandma be happy. What should we do?"

"Gramma likes cookies. We could make chocolate chip."

"Aren't those *your* favorite?" I tickle her lightly, and she squirms away. "We should do something for Grandma, though."

From the time I woke up, Ma has been complaining about the family reunion at the lodge. But it wasn't that surprising. They'd been holding the reunion on the mountain since I was a kid. The risk of getting snowed in is ignored in favor of the convenience of skiing out their back door.

"Does Gramma need angel kisses? So she could get a second chance?"

"Does Gramma need a second chance?"

"Mmhmm. So she doesn't have to be sad about the snow."

"Oh, I see." I nuzzle my daughter and sit back in the brightly lit kitchen. "That's a great idea." Ma finished cooking breakfast a while ago, but the smells of baking linger. Nostalgia clings to the room. Images of friends, family, and food play in my head as I snuggle my daughter. "You could go give Gramma angel kisses right now, cause you're my angel."

"No, Daddy," she laughs. "Not those kinds of kisses. *Snowflake* angel kisses."

Carrying her toward the mudroom, I pause by the large fireplace. "Well then, if we find your coat, maybe you could go get some snowflake angel kisses, and share them with Gramma."

"Can I?" Alice shouts. "I want to share some with Lucy, too!"

"Of course you do." The thought of Alice sharing kisses with Lucy buzzes inside me. Happy and excited, but also potentially dangerous.

"Yay! Then we'll both have another chance, and maybe then, Lucy can be my mommy!"

Her comment takes a moment to process. When it does, I almost drop her. "You already have a mommy. Lucy's just our friend."

"I know." Alice's joy droops with a tiny frown. It's contagious. "But mommy's gone."

"But she's still in our hearts." Fighting my worry, I place my forehead to Alice's. "I know it's hard to remember, but she loved you very much. And I love you very much."

Alice puts her hands on my cheeks. "And I love you very much, too. 'Cause you're funny, and you help me fly like a angel."

"That's because you are an angel." I kiss her nose.

"I'm not a real angel. Mommy's a angel. I'm Alice. Alice C'rinne Nyström, like Mommy." She points a finger at her chest as she says her full name . . . minus the 'o' in Corrine. I hold her close while she squirms.

"That's right. Alice C'rinne. Like Mommy."

"When Lucy's my mommy, will I be Alice Lucy Nyström?"

My heart tugs again. "Alice. Lucy's a really nice person, but she's not your mommy."

"But my mommy's gone, so I need a new one."

I kneel to face her, tucking her into the corner by the fireplace. "I'm really glad you like Lucy, but you don't need a new mommy. Grandma helps us with good things to eat and taking care of you. And Grandma, Grandpa, and I will always love you so much. And when you get angel kisses, that's mommy sending you her love, too."

"Wow." Alice's eyes grow wide. "That's a lot of kisses! It snows every day."

"Just about." I laugh at her obvious excitement. "You don't need a new mommy. But I do want Lucy to be our friend. Do you understand?"

"Okay. Lucy? Will you be my friend?"

Oh no. My heart sinks to the floor, followed closely by my stomach. I turn around and see Lucy watching us from the kitchen door, lips twisted in a confused smile.

"Cause Daddy says you can't be my mommy, but that's okay. Cause I still love you."

"Of course, Alice. I would love to be your friend."

Alice hugs her around the knees, and I force a smile.

"Do you want to come get angel kisses with me? I'm gonna share some with Gramma, but if you get your own, then I can keep some, too."

"Of course. Where do we get these angel kisses?" Lucy asks.

"Outside, silly."

"Well then, you better go get your coat."

Pattering feet answer Lucy's request as Alice runs off to find her coat.

Lucy turns to me. "Is this alright? I don't want to intrude, and I don't want her to think I'm trying to be her mother. I'm so sorry."

"No, not her mother. Maybe her aunt." I laugh awkwardly, following with a quick, "It's not your fault. She just gets attached quickly."

"Her *aunt*?" Lucy looks even more confused before she connects the dots. "Oh, gosh. I wasn't thinking about that." She shoots a look back to where Alice left the room. "It seems like a long shot right now. . ." She looks up at me like she wants to cry. "But who knows what will happen."

Her eyes are so soft, so full of hope. My heart races to believe the impossible. "Right." I want to reach over and run my thumb over her pinched brow. "I'm just trying to make sure Alice doesn't get her heart caught up in something that isn't—"

"Got it. Loud and clear."

My tripping over icy, careful words is cut off by Lucy's cleaver of a response, ending the conversation as Alice runs in.

"I'm ready for kisses!"

Lucy instinctively reaches for her, until she pulls back. This is not what I was trying to achieve. I spin my little girl and send her to Lucy. "Will you show Lucy what to do?"

Lucy grins with a flash of gratitude, as Alice takes her hand. "Let's go!"

"Throw me, Daddy!"

I catch Alice up off the ground and throw her high in the air, a peal of laughter shattering the quiet of the snowy yard. When I catch her, Alice leans back, turning her face to the sky with her arms stretched out wide, and we spin.

I don't stop until her giggles taper off, holding Alice close until the dizziness is gone.

Lucy watches from several feet away, and I give myself license to watch her back. Lucy claps for Alice, who is now spinning on her own. The falling snow paints the sky around them with a hazy fog.

"That looks so fun, but I catch snowflakes from the ground," Lucy laughs. The blurry, distant mountain looms behind Lucy as she holds her hands out, doing her own spin. I set Alice down.

"They're not just snowflakes." Alice lifts her head up with white specks clinging to her eyelashes. "They're angel kisses."

"Are they?" Lucy asks. "I thought they had to get on your eyelashes first. Isn't that what you said?"

Alice nods and Lucy taps her chin. "Snowflakes must be pretty magic, because when you catch them on your skin, like right here on your cheeks, they do something different." She glances at me like she's asking permission. I don't know what she's getting at, but I'm curious, so I shrug my vague approval. She turns back to Alice and bends low, getting at her level. "If you catch it and make a wish before it melts, it might make your wishes come true." Alice nods, watching Lucy intently.

Can Lucy be my mommy?

My whole body is torn up trying to sort through how I feel about that conversation. I hate that Alice doesn't remember her mother well enough to know what she's giving up, but I do. And still, Lucy has been dancing in and out of my head since the first day I met her. If there was to be another woman in my life, it would have to be one like Lucy.

Watching her enthrall Alice with stories and laughter, I won't let myself admit that she has the same effect on me. *Aunt Lucy,* I think. *How will I ever handle seeing you with someone else? How will I ever make it when you're really with my brother? Till death do you part.*

Can Lucy be my mommy?

The real answer to Alice's question is—I wish I was allowed to find out.

"You have to get a really good one," Lucy says, holding Alice's gloves and catching snowflakes in her bare hands. "Very nice! Did you wish? I bet that one had a lot of magic inside."

"I missed it," Alice complains happily, waving her hands to try and catch more. "I only ever caught kisses. I didn't know they had wishes, too."

"They don't have wishes, they have magic. The wishes come from you."

"Wishes and kisses," Alice calls prancing through the snow. "Daddy, can I make a angel for my angel mommy?"

"Of course, sweetie."

Alice runs back toward the house and drops into the falling snow. Lucy stands to watch Alice with me. On instinct, I reach over and squeeze her hand. She smiles at me and gives my hand a quick squeeze back.

It feels right, having her hand in mine. I could quite possibly stand like this forever. I let go and quickly shove my hand in my pocket.

"I love these traditions you have with her," Lucy says.

"Most of our traditions are my mother's fault. She has always been good about keeping our family heritage alive. But these ones came from Corrine. Snow angels and angel kisses." The similarity strikes me, and I let out a breath. "Maybe she was always destined to be an angel."

"Lucy?" Alice calls from the porch. Finished making her snow angel, Alice is dusted in white and running toward us. My mother waves to us from the porch. "Lucy? Will you be here for Santa Lucy Day? Gramma wants to know! And you can be the princess. Cause you're Lucy!"

"What's Santa Lucy day?" Lucy whispers on our way across the yard. "A Christmas celebration of Lucys?"

"No," I laugh, and she grins, kicking snow at me. "Oh, you've got good aim," I say, jumping back.

"Well, you're not being very helpful." She elbows me.

"All right, then." I give her a quick rundown before Alice gets there. "It's a Swedish tradition, called Santa Lucia Day, or Sankta Lucia, if you want to sound authentic. Not Santa Lucy, sorry."

"Oh." Lucy sighs heavily as we reach the porch. "So, I don't have a day?"

"You should be celebrated every day, dear," my mother says, holding the door open for us. I couldn't agree more. "Sankta Lucia is in December around the shortest day of the year. The oldest daughter wakes everyone in the household with candles and treats dressed as Saint Lucia. It represents overcoming darkness and welcoming the season of light."

"You can be the Santa Lucy princess with me." Alice exclaims with bouncing and giggles as she takes Lucy's hands.

"Sadly, there's not actually a Santa Lucia princess," I say. "But I do think Alice gets to dress up as Santa Lucia this year." I gather Alice, before she can pull Lucy over, and I put a hand at Lucy's back, trying not to enjoy the feel of her too much.

"This is Alice's first year to be Santa Lucia." My mother glows looking at the little girl as she traipses into the house trailing ice crystals.

"Ma's been waiting a long time to have a little girl to dress up," I explain. "My mother was cursed with two sons, so she was the only Santa Lucia in our household."

The fire is still going in the kitchen, and it feels amazing. Shedding our snowy gear in the mudroom, Ma follows us.

"No Lucias, but we had star boys, and they were adorable," she says, "Shall I pull out the pictures?"

Shock rolls through me. "You wouldn't."

"Show off how proud I am of my sweet sons? Of course I would."

"Ma." I shake my head and glance at Lucy. "We dressed in white robes with wizard hats that had giant stars on them. I still don't know why it's a thing."

"Gramma says I get a crown." Alice turns bright eyes on Ma who winks and bends close to her.

It feels like I'm watching the coronation of a princess. "That's right. A Christmas crown, with candles, and a red bow."

"Oh," Lucy says, widening her eyes dramatically. "So, there is a Santa Lucia princess!"

"I guess so." I kiss Alice. "But her outfit is a lot cuter than the one I had to wear. We'll just keep those pictures buried deep in an album somewhere."

"Daddy?" Compassion and worry flow from Alice's eyes. "Do you want a crown too?"

I chuckle. Lucy leans over, whispering, "I bet your dad would look great in a crown." Her eyes sparkle with mischief and maybe a bit more.

Alice giggles with Lucy and Ma. My heart jolts.

Alice's words from earlier jump back into my mind. *"My mommy's gone, I need a new one."*

"Are you allowed to cancel Santa's Workshop for snow when it's less than six feet?" Lucy sits on the edge of the back porch, bent over Ma's old ski boots, buckling the straps like I showed her. "I would have thought elves are used to this kind of weather."

"Not usually," I say as she finishes the first boot and holds it up. Giving her work a once over, I nod my approval. "I hear he's recruiting elves out of Florida. Besides, it's the perk of being in charge."

"Santa," Lucy scoffs, "thinks he can do whatever he wants. I can tell you from personal experience, he works the elves pretty hard. No wonder he has to recruit so far away. The elves can't take it anymore."

I snort and look doubtfully at Lucy. "Right, handing out candy canes is exhausting."

"I know!" She flips her hair back to look up and shakes her head. "Not to mention the cookie-making and present-wrapping. There's so much more than toys and candy canes." With a shrug, she turns back to her second boot. "That's probably why he's struggling to find good help. The elves are being worked to death. All work and no play means no baby elflings to grow the labor pool."

My guffaw is not attractive, but Lucy doesn't seem to mind. It's fun laughing with someone that isn't two and a half feet tall. "We should write a letter." I add, "The Elvish Worker's Union needs to hear about this. Elves need romance, too."

"We could form a protest."

"Or a petition."

"Nice. Hold on, I got this. . ." Lucy wrinkles her nose and looks off in the distance. I love watching the wheels turning in her head. When she turns on me her hair flip sends a wave of fruity floral scents my direction. My breath sticks in my throat as she points at me. "The Modern Elf—no, Mobilizing Elves for the Rediscovery and Regularization of Intimacy petition. It's MERRI, with an I. I'd sign that petition." She jerks a satisfied nod at me and tries to stand, almost falling off the porch.

I'm laughing and I don't know if it's her sense of humor or her lack of grace that's got me so entertained. Helping her up, I hold her hands as she finds her balance. "Just move around a little, then I'll show you how to clip in to the skis."

"I feel like Frankenstein." She holds her hands out and wobbles a few steps away from the porch and back.

"You're in a good mood," I comment, enjoying her smile and banter.

"I am. I figured something out today."

"What's that?"

"Your marketing campaign."

It's a good thing I wasn't holding her, because I would have dropped her. "I forgot you were working on that."

"I've been working on some logos and slogans. I really think we need to focus on the family and tradition that you guys have here. The history of the Sugar Creek Inn is amazing."

"Uh, yeah." I rack my brain over our current marketing efforts. "Isn't that what we've been doing?"

"No," she laughs. "You're living it, but we need to sell it to people who don't know you already. I made some notes after finding your website. I'm afraid all people will see online is an out-of-date website that looks like it will steal their identity. That's not the kind of impression you want to make."

She holds her foot over her ski. I quickly help her clip in, and she starts testing the stiff angles of her boots and body.

"Here. Bend your knees like this, and I'm going to pull you over here."

I can't believe she's really helping with the inn. We haven't even made any moves, but her putting a hand out to help hold this burden is making me feel lighter than air.

We work on posture and clipping in and out of skis long enough to get Lucy familiar with the boots and angles. After dinner, she shows me her marketing notes and we work until the smell of ginger and molasses call me to the kitchen.

Pepparkakor.

"You have to come try these," I say, dragging Lucy with me. "They are your reward for giving me the first seed of hope I've had in two years."

"That smells amazing." Lucy follows me into the kitchen. I wrap my arms around my mother.

"I wasn't expecting you to make these again so soon. You're my favorite mother ever."

"Well, thank you." She glances at Lucy, as if my good mood needs an explanation, but Lucy is just as pleased.

I grab a stack of my favorite cookies, passing a thin, golden wafer to her. "Here, have one."

She takes the cookie delicately, and I shove one whole in my mouth. "Where's Alice?" Lucy asks. "I haven't seen her for a while."

"She's sleeping over with a friend tonight. And it's a good thing, or she'd totally try to talk you out of yours."

Lucy bites her lip and looks up embarrassed. "I don't like raisins."

Ma laughs and I shake my head. "It's one raisin. You have to try them."

I grab several more and Lucy looks at the stack of ginger cookies like they might eat her.

"So do we have any plans for the evening?" she asks still pinching her thin cookie between two fingers.

Right then, something catches my eye through the window. The sky is just barely starting to change colors, the snow turning an ethereal, dusky blue. A spark lights in my brain. Maybe it's because Alice is gone for the night, or maybe it's just working with Lucy on anything, but I feel *alive* right now. More than I have in ages.

"Follow me. I want to show you something." I grab her hand in the dimming light and pull her to the stairs.

"Why are we in such a rush?" She almost trips in her rushing to keep up and I slow.

"Sorry, it's my favorite view, but it's a little time sensitive. And we need to grab sweaters, because it will be cold."

"We'll be fine," she says, her face slightly pink at the edges. "The cold's not so bad with you around to keep me warm."

A smile glows in her eyes, and my chest swells with heat. I swallow the words and grab a blanket as we fly around the corner.

Chapter 11

Lucy

My face flames with heat as I realize that it sounded a lot more like an invitation than I meant.

"If you keep running me up and down stairs and feeding me cookies, anyway." I can't meet his eye, but as I mention the cookies he reaches over and snatches one off my stack.

"The cookies won't do anything unless you eat them. They taste like Christmas. I think you'll be surprised." He eats the stolen cookie in one bite, and I hold the others away from him protectively. Not because I want to eat them, I just don't want him to take them.

"You can't steal my cookies," I protest, and hold one up to eat it.

The wafer-thin cookies still smell great but they're each topped with a single black raisin. I stare at the tiny dead grape in a standoff.

"It doesn't look like you're going to eat them." He reaches around me and takes another cookie.

"Hey," I pull back and look at my dwindling stack. "I was gonna eat that."

"Eat what?" He flings open, empty hands to the side, looking around like he has no idea what I'm talking about, then swallows and reaches for another.

"Hey!" I jump away and shove one of the little cookies in my mouth, raisin and all. "Mmm, I should have known," I moan. "These are amazing."

Torin stands like a superhero with hands on hips, triumphantly watching me shove the last two cookies in my mouth. "I knew you'd like 'em."

"And yet, you still tried to take them from me." Fighting over cookies is almost as much fun as eating them.

"I may have pushed my luck a bit. Now, come check this out. Not many guests get to see it." He opens the door across from mine—the one leading into his bedroom. "After you."

I raise an eyebrow and step past him. "Your favorite view is in your bedroom?" Our shoulders brush, and I look up at him. "It's a good thing I trust you."

All day, I've been saying things without thinking twice about them. But those words jar me more than anything else.

In the fireside talks and snow angels. A wave of emotion rolls over me.

I trust him.

A toddler bed is tucked in the corner next to a large queen size, both with rumpled covers. A dresser is scattered with trinkets, aftershave, and Alice's hair bows. He doesn't seem bothered as he crosses the room to the French doors on the outside wall. It's set up similarly to my room, but on the dresser near the balcony, I spot a picture on his nightstand.

A family. His family.

I only recognize Torin, with his arms wrapped around a smiling woman and a newborn Alice.

"Lucy?" Torin follows my gaze. "Come on, you can dig through my things later. It's almost time for the sunset."

I step out onto the balcony, and Torin hands me a blanket, wrapping it around my shoulders. A breeze chills my skin and I take it gratefully.

Torin's room is on the backside of the house, facing the mountain. Even though I've already seen Mt. Ambrose, watching it dominate the sky from this vantage point takes my breath away.

"It's beautiful," I say. "And massive. But won't the sun set on the other side of the house?"

"It's not even the good part yet," he laughs softly, his warm breath sending shivers across my skin.

The depth of the shadows has turned the snow a grey-blue nighttime shade, rather than white. Trees paint speckled trails over undisturbed snow, condensing until the texture unifies at the mountain top, stony peaks tearing free of the icy insulation to reach rocky fingers to the sky.

The cold air touches my skin, and I adjust the blanket around my body, trying to become one with it so I don't have to go back inside. In one smooth step, Torin moves behind me, wrapping his arms around me and pulling me up against his warm chest.

"Is this okay?" he asks, and I tense momentarily. His body against mine sends tendrils of heat coursing through me. "You looked cold."

Of course, that's all it is. He's just being thoughtful.

I nod, chastising myself for letting my brain make the gesture anything more than a nice guy noticing I was cold. I am cold. I lean into his warmth and duck my nose below the edge of the blanket, grateful that I'm allowed to be okay with this. It's like a group hug with only two people.

A spray of snow blows off the railing, dusting us both, and Torin leans into my neck with his lips near my ear. "Do you mind if we share?"

He slides his hand along the edge of the blanket, and I let him have it. He wraps it around us both and I can tell the difference immediately as the blanket and coat cocoon our bodies, pooling our combined heat.

I lean against him. "What are we watching for?" I ask. "The mountain isn't gonna do tricks, or magic, or anything, is it?"

His laugh rumbles through me and I let myself lean into him. "That depends on what you think of as magic."

A flash of golden light hits the top of the mountain and I gasp. "Is that it?" I snuggle into the warmth of his arms, training my eyes higher up the snowy peaks.

"Do you like it?" He pulls me close, his chin tucked into my shoulder.

"Mmhmm." I mumble my approval, not taking my eyes off the sunset as it reflects color and light over the icy surface. Everything about this feels safe and comfortable. Not conditions I usually associate with Torin.

He points to the top of the mountain where the reflection is brightest. "Just like the sunset changes color and intensity each night, the mountain does the same. See how the gold pours out over the mountain like that? It's pretty vibrant tonight. Some days, you can just barely see it."

He's right. It's gorgeous. In the warmth of his arms, a halo of rightness perfects the scene. Rocking side to side in the dregs of the sunlight, golden streaks fight their way through the trees to land on the mountain, until the very crest of St. Ambrose Peak tinges pink and goes dark.

"God, that was beautiful." His voice is rough against my ear, and I look up.

"Complementing God on a job well done?" It's hard to gauge in the dark, but he feels close. If he turned his face down toward mine, our lips would touch.

"Maybe I am." He chuckles softly.

I hold position, watching his silhouette as if I'm testing him, daring him to turn my way. A kiss in the dimming light would be so easy. So natural. I finally look away, back to the darkened mountain, and I feel him turn. He waited until my lips were out of reach, but I was right about the kiss. His lips brush my hair, and I close my eyes, feeling him against me.

By the time I can let go of the moment, it's fully night and we're bleeding heat from one body to the other inside Torin's quilt. No snowflakes have fallen but I can feel the magic of the moment.

"I've never seen anything like that."

"Best view in the house."

I nod. It feels like I've been granted an unspoken wish. "Thank you," I whisper, pressing my cheek into his chest. "It was magical."

Over the next couple days, Torin and I manage to find time for a couple more backyard ski lessons, progressing from equipment use and basic stopping to beginning ski positions. I even manage to make it down the small hill in the yard with Torin's help.

When they finally open the road, we head up the mountain to join the rest of the family at the reunion.

"Are you're ready to go skiing on an actual slope?" Torin asks when we pull into the parking lot of the ski lodge.

"*Ready* is a very strong word," I mutter as trees and cars pass. I reach a hand to my collarbone, grateful to have my snowflake back around my neck where it belongs.

It's the first day they've cleared the road for tourists, and my heart is beating a million times a minute. *I'm here to get Erik back.* I look at Torin and my heart tugs. *I'm here to get —*

No. I can't even think it. Erik hasn't even tried to contact me since I got here. So why am I here? *I'm here to learn to ski.* There. That I can do.

Maybe I'll just stay with Torin.

Torin circles the car, while I bemoan my choices, and he opens the door for me. "No one ever feels ready their first time." His smiles and waggles his eyebrows in a suggestive way, and I can't help but laugh. "It's going to be different skiing up there on Rosie."

"Rosie?"

"The mountain. It's short for, Mt. Ambrose."

"Oh. Are you sure we shouldn't go back? I like the little hill in your yard."

He laughs and takes my hand helping me out of the car. "The only way to be more ready than you are, is to get out there and try. You'll be fine. Promise."

I smile weakly and follow him in. He sets me up with beginner rental equipment and we make our way to the outdoor back of the lodge.

Finding a spot on one of the benches, I begin adjusting my buckles and clipping into my skis. "So, Erik knows we're coming?"

Torin shrugs. "How are you coming with your boots?" He latches into his skis.

I frown, anxiety stiffening the boots more than expected. I swear these ones have twice as many straps. "One of my straps is twisted . . . I think."

"Let me see." He slides over and squats in front of me, fixing my strap. It takes him no time to straighten me out and help me onto my feet. He doesn't let go of my hand for several seconds after I'm up. He's right in front of me, blocking out the chaos of the tourists and skiers and lifts.

"Thank you," I say. "Putting on boots shouldn't be so difficult. They're Velcro, for goodness sake." I'm only half making fun, and before I can set the helmet on my head, Torin takes it from my hand.

"Hang on." Removing his glove, Torin takes my sunglasses off the top of my head and hands them to me. "You won't want to lose those. And—"

He twists back a stray piece of hair, stroking his fingertips down my jawline to my chin. He holds my gaze, and the chaos of the lodge drowns into the background. "Lucy, I'm really glad you're here. I—"

"Hey. guys!" Erik's voice sends us scooting apart. A pair of bright red skis swoops in beside us, still shiny with new-in-the-box polish. Erik pushes his goggles up on his helmet. "You look good, Luce. Are you here taking lessons?"

"Hey," I manage. Erik's attention is overwhelming at best. "You could say that. Torin's been giving me lessons."

"Yeah," Erik says, sending a glare at Torin. "I can see he's taking care of you."

I shrink back, and Torin shifts closer. "We're heading up one of the smaller runs, if you want to join us."

He glances down at me. I wish we'd talked about this before. "Unless you don't want to," I say to Erik. "I'm sure it'll be nothing compared to what you usually do."

"I'd love to. And actually, if you want to go do a run on your own, I'll take Lucy."

Erik's assertive tone catches me off-guard. I started lessons for this very reason. But now—Torin takes my arm and looks down at me. "Do you want to? I know it was the plan but—" Sad green eyes travel from me to Erik. I'm learning to ski so I can be with the right brother. "You are pretty new to this though, so, if you want to stay with me, I'm here for you."

Erik side-shuffles to get in front of me and leans in on his poles. "Of course she wants to come with me. We haven't talked in days. Let's do it. You can show me what you've learned, and honestly, I'm a much better teacher than Torin."

Torin glares at Erik.

"I guess it wouldn't hurt." Erik takes my hand, pulling me away.

"Have fun, Tor." Erik jabs Torin with the end of his ski pole. "You ready, Luce?"

"Umm," I send a glance over to Torin, but he's already gone. Erik clears his throat. "Ready. Yup. That's me."

I shuffle after him and spot Torin already in line at the lift. He looks back and we lock eyes as Erik takes my hand.

"Where are your poles?"

"The handle things? Torin said I wouldn't need them yet."

"That's because Tor doesn't trust you." Erik moves away, talking to a random skier and returns with a pair of borrowed ski poles.

"Did you just steal poles for me?" I go for a joke.

"Nah, I know him."

They're long and gangly, but when he lets me push off with them it does feel like they'll help with balance—or trip me in the middle of a run.

Either or.

"Hurry," he says. "We won't have much time before they shut us down to light the lanterns. We can still do the Hot Wings Trail if we go now. It'll be more fun than the bunny hill."

A sign showing the various trails and ski runs is posted near the lift. Hot Wings is fairly high on the list, but it's not black. A little blue box is next to it.

"Do you think I can handle it? This is my first time on an actual hill. I'm new still." Only a few shades from brand new.

"Yeah, it only sounds scary. It's rated a medium, so really, it's a great one to learn on."

"Oh." Even I can tell I don't sound convinced.

He winks at me. "Skiing isn't hard. You just gotta let yourself go, balance a bit, and be brave."

Soon we're on a chair lift and riding up the hill. With minimal problems and barely-voiced panic, I successfully use the third lift exit.

"I did it!" I'm ridiculously proud of having not caused a pileup in the lift area.

"Good work. You're going to love this run. Let's ski."

The idea of pushing myself over the hill with other laughing ski-lemmings terrifies me. Erik doesn't give me a choice. He drops down onto the hill without hesitation, forcing me to follow.

"Keep your skis parallel, angle them across the mountain to turn or slow down, and if you want to stop, just dig in. Or fall back, that's the fastest way to stop."

"And bend my knees, right?" His directions aren't the same as Torin's. Facing the long white slope on a pair of slippery boards, I can't remember what Torin told me to do. anyway.

"Sure, some. Do what feels good." He pushes off with the poles and slides several feet down the hill, stopping to watch me.

It can't be that hard. I have Torin's lessons. I have all the gear. I have Erik. He knows what he's doing. It may not be graceful, but I can make it down . . . one way or another.

I push off and stutter down the hill.

Trying to turn and stop myself, the edge of my ski sinks in the snow, almost landing me on my face instead of my backside. I only catch myself by shoving my flailing handle into the ground in front of me.

Erik's jaw drops as he watches me. "Oh, God. You really don't know how to do this."

"No, no. I'm fine. See—" The balance of my pole lets me push off, and miraculously, I swivel several slow feet down the hill and recreate Erik's stop, digging the sides of my skis into the snow. I look up and grin.

Erik has a faux smile on his face. "That looks good, Lucy. Come on, let's see what else you've got."

After several repeats where I only fall about half the time, I turn to see how far I've come. The lift exit is still right there.

Not as far as I thought.

The twenty feet I've moved feels like a thousand.

I push off again, determined to get away from that blasted landmark. One of my skis dips into the snow, and in seconds, I'm face-first in icy powder. A spray of snow hits my face as a line of laughing teens skids around me. I've become an obstacle for other skiers.

Erik tromps his way back up the hill and holds his hand out to help me stand. I can hardly look at him. All I see is frustration on his face. I just might die under this landslide of embarrassment.

"I guess that's gonna happen a lot," I say, and Erik answers with a tight smile.

Over the next twenty minutes, Erik's patience runs out. His mood turns from thinly veiled annoyance to out-and-out ignoring.

"Hey, I've seen you before!" Erik laughs as a group of skiers pass, apparently lapping us. I can tell he would rather be with them instead of babysitting me down this stupid slope.

"You can go with them if you want," I offer hesitantly, silently begging him to stay with me.

He looks back at me with hopeful eyes. "Are you sure?"

I push the corners of my smile up. "Yeah, I'll be fine. We're probably close, right? I mean, we've been working our way down for a while now. You go have fun."

Don't go. Please, don't leave me here.

"Okay," Erik says. "But I'll come back around and meet you after a few runs."

I nod, no verbal responses left in me. My lips tremble, tears so close I'm afraid to breathe. *Please let him leave before I cry.* Erik winks at me and disappears over a rise in the hill, and just like that, I'm alone on the side of a mountain. My only way down involves a lot of bruises.

Skiers zip by, giving me a wide berth as I perch in the cold. I'm alone enough to be scared, but not so alone I can sit in the snow and cry. I want to.

I force my body to get into position and try to ski again. It goes about as well as it did before, until I reach the next rise. There, the hill drops. I'm nearly hyperventilating at the looming slope. There's no end in sight.

My tears pool into swells of liquid shame. I'll never make it down before the hill closes. They're going to have to send someone up to rescue me, and then I really will die of embarrassment.

I force a slow breath. Then my skis slip out from under me, and I'm on my backside again.

"Lucy?" A voice calls my name, but it's not Erik. A snowsuit and ski gear slides to a stop beside me.

"Torin?"

"Of course it's me." He balances in front of me, reaching out to help me up.

"Thank you." The small act of kindness wells inside me, and I find myself trying not to cry again.

"Where's Erik?" Confusion and worry meld through his tone. "Did he leave you here?"

"Well, yes. But I told him to go on without me. He was getting frustrated, I didn't want to ruin his day." I wave like it's no big deal. "But he did say he's coming back around. So . . ." Even as I say it, I know it's not going to happen.

Torin looks down the hill and turns back. "Well, until he does, I'm going to ski with you. Is that okay?"

"You don't have to do that. I'll—I'll be fine." My voice catches as a hot tear slides down my cheek. I force a watery smile and get my body set up to go again.

Torin nearly jumps at me. "Oh, no you don't. I'm not leaving you by yourself. You're stuck with me. Got it."

More tears slide free as I nod and swallow down my panic.

"Okay, first, let's get rid of these." He grabs my ski poles.

"But I need those." It's like he's stolen my security blanket.

"No, you don't. Where did you even get them?" He sets both of our sets of poles against a tree at the side of the trail before he moves back in front of me.

"Erik borrowed them for me. We can't just leave them here. They help when I fall."

"Well then, let's not fall, okay?"

I laugh. And he frowns.

"Okay?" he asks again.

This time I nod.

"Good. I'll come back for those later. Beginner V. Just like I taught you. Are you ready?"

"Yeah, but is position really important? I'm not worried about learning how to ski anymore. I just want to get down the hill and never come back up."

"Unless you want to roll all the way to the bottom, yeah, your form is important."

The pain of rolling might not be as bad as it sounds, since I've already started a collection of bruises across my body. But Torin is waiting, so I give in.

With a sigh, I move my skies into a pizza shape and get set to try again. Torin makes small adjustment to get me in the correct position with my ski tips pointed toward each other, and then he moves out in front of me.

"Looks good. Now, focus on your heels, push them down. Don't let your ski tips cross. At the bottom of this hill is a cozy fire and hot chocolate. You want that, right?"

His enticement is entirely unnecessary, but I nod anyway. "Just get me down this hill."

He laughs and sets his skis a few feet down from where I am. "I'm gonna be in front of you in a reverse wedge. And you're going to ski toward me."

I shake my head. "You don't want me to do that. I'll fall on you."

"That's okay. I'll catch you." He looks so confident, I almost believe him.

"I'm going to fall," I say, leaning forward.

"You will if you move like that. I can't believe Erik let you ski this way. Keep your shoulders back, and your body upright. You aren't going to need help going forward, gravity and your skies will take care of that. Keep your weight above your feet." His hands hover in front of my waist, and I straighten up.

"This feels weird."

"Good. 'Cause you don't want to keep doing what you've been doing." He's holding my gaze like a leash. "Okay, push off when you're ready. I'm right here."

I swallow. Directly ahead of me, Torin is waiting. I push off, and for the first time, I don't immediately feel like I'm going to fall. Maybe I can do this.

"Good, now we're going to turn."

My eyes dart to the terrain. We're coming to the edge of the trail. My heart rate spikes and my body reels forward, tumbling into Torin, but we don't fall.

His hands find my waist and, as promised, he catches me.

I almost hit him with my flailing arms, but we're both still upright.

"Sorry," I wheeze. "I guess it's a good thing I'm not wielding poles."

His deep laugh actually slows my heartbeat. "One of the many reasons beginners don't need them." He helps me get in position again and nods at me. "Keep those hips and shoulders back. Here we go again."

Moving down the hill, his hands hover in front of me. He catches me every time I get within arm's reach, guiding me forward, pushing me back.

For a moment, I can feel the wind against my face and the rush of gliding over the snow. "This isn't so bad."

"Eventually, it might even be fun." He catches me and his eyes sparkle with reflected light. "Watch your ski tips." His warning draws my eye down and I witness my skis cross and catch, jerking me forward, right into him.

"Are you alright?" he asks, softly.

His voice is so tender, it feels like I'm the only one there. Our faces are only inches apart as he holds me, and I can't tell if it's Torin or the momentum of my fall that has me pressed against him. I don't care.

"If I say yes, are you going to let me go? Because I'm not sure that's safe."

"It's pretty safe, considering we're almost to the bottom." His laughter warms me against the cold air, and I miss his closeness when he sets me back on my feet.

"Why can't I see the lodge?"

"It's just over there." He gestures with his chin, not taking his eyes off me. "We'll cross-country ski over this flat ground toward the trees over there, and then we'll catch a ride down in the gondola." The slope has tapered significantly. Skiers below us push off toward the trees.

"We made it?" I look to the trees, relief gripping my heart with fizzy fingers, and I throw my arms around Torin. "We made it!"

He laughs, slipping under my momentum now that we're on flat ground. "Hang on," he laughs, steadying himself and wrapping his arms around me. "You did really well."

He presses his cheek to mine, and I close my eyes, reveling in the warmth of his skin.

"Your nose is cold." His whisper holds the hint of laughter, and I pull back, turning my face up.

Brushing the tip of my nose against his, I whisper, "So is yours."

He glances down at my lips.

"You promised me hot chocolate." My words produce clouds between us, and he leans forward, as if pulled by an invisible thread.

"Hot chocolate and a fire," he says.

My smile grows as his eyes flash hotter than any fire at the lodge. I try to move closer, my skis catching against each other. Still in the pizza position, I can barely maneuver, but all I want is to be closer to Torin. Thanks to our padded snow clothes, I can't seem to get close enough. The distance of the snowsuits and my awkward ski position feel like major deterrents to my goal.

I notice the crinkling corners of Torin's eyes.

I don't care if I thought I came here for Erik, who my mother expects me to be with, or my ideal of true love. Right now, Torin has his fingers around my heart. And I like it.

"Are you playing with me?" I smack his shoulder while gripping his arms tight. He's still holding my body, and I lean as close as I can. "If you'd help me out here, we'd be kissing already."

He lets out a laugh and finally—finally—he leans in, closing the distance between us. His lips meet mine in sweet victory. The heat of his mouth is better than I remembered. The chill of our skin warms quickly, and I lean against the thrilling pressure of his lips.

With a gentle tug, he shifts closer, gripping my hips and waist. But I want more. I shift to the side, pressing my leg to his thigh.

Crossed somewhere between the snow and skis below us, my feet are caught. It's an easy problem to ignore, since I'm not going anywhere until his lips release me. Shifting a foot, my ski suddenly comes free of its tether and my knee jerks forward—directly into Torin's thigh.

He groans, releasing me.

"Oh!" I gasp as he hunches over. I hold my hands out, trying to assess the damage. "I'm so sorry! Are you okay?"

Please let it have been his thigh.

Trying to give him room, I trip over my skis, falling backward into the snow. My ski tips flip up behind Torin's legs, catching the backs of his knees. I knock him forward and he cries out, unable to stop his collapse. Flailing for support, he lands on top of me. We'd be perfectly nose to nose if it weren't for our helmets cracking against each other.

With a groan, he rolls off, lying back in the snow. Our feet and skis are tangled together, the top half of my ski hooked painfully behind his knee and the other half pinned over his opposite leg.

"Hey, you two. Back to the lodge," someone calls. "We're prepping the lanterns. You can come back out in thirty minutes." The employee shoves past us and mumbles, "Or get a room."

"Did that just happen?" I start to laugh, lifting myself off the ground. "I'm so sorry. I didn't hurt you, did I?"

I set a hand on his chest, and he flinches. "Careful," he says bringing a hand to cover mine. His eyes are closed, and he barely peeks one open to look at me before his own laughter starts to eke out, mingling with a breathy moan of pain. "You really know how to make an impression on a guy."

I laugh harder and lean forward, trying to unhook our skis. As he relaxes, he lifts his upper body off the snow, propping himself up on his elbows.

I shake my head at him. "I'm so sorry."

Slowly, I lean forward, keeping my eyes on his. I carefully close the distance between our lips. His nose is still cold, but I press gently against his mouth, seducing his lips open to deepen the kiss. With tongues and lips, we explore the desire that's been building since our first meeting. When I finally pull back, I look around as if waiting for something to happen.

"There," I say with a sigh. "That was better. I kissed you, and nothing broke. No one fell."

"What about me?" he asks, pulling me back to him. I rest my head on his chest, his heartbeat tapping a quick rhythm behind the layers of his snowsuit. He lifts my chin and I turn, looking into his eyes. "Feels like I've fallen pretty hard."

Chapter 12

Torin

Lucy's fingers fit with mine like they've been waiting for her. Our gloves are stuffed safely in my pockets so I can indulge in the feel of her skin on mine.

Being near her has added a glow to the world. The lodge glitters against the snowy landscape, tourists smile bright, and lanterns illuminate the darkening sky. A horse-drawn sleigh pulls around the back of the building as a light snow drifts in the dusky evening.

I can't tell if it's fresh snowfall or just the wind blowing snow dust off the roof and treetops. Either way, it's the most magical scene I've experienced since the day Alice was born.

Shuffling her skis alongside mine, Lucy swings our joined hands. The pair of Texans we sat next to on the lift pass us with easy movements and heavy glares. Lucy's blush warms her cheeks. I can't take my eyes off her.

"I'm sorry!" she calls after them.

I squeeze her hand. "You don't have to apologize. Everyone trips getting off the ski lift at some point."

"But they got stuck in the chair on the way back up."

"Not completely in the chair." I stifle my laugh for Lucy's sake, but she groans, remembering the image of the man hanging half-out of the stalled chairlift. "Really, Lucy. They'll be fine." There's no denying the laughter underlying my words now. Lucy's blush hurdles from sugar plum pink, straight to Rudolph's nose. I try to catch her eye while soothing her embarrassment. "It only took a couple minutes to get them down. We all helped. It turned out fine."

"You couldn't save the chair of people I took out before them."

I chuckle at the priceless image of skiers trying to avoid Lucy as I tried to help her up, only to get knocked over time and again. "That was a pretty epic pile up."

"Skiing and I don't get along." Lucy's hands come up, shielding her face as people stream around us. "I think we're breaking up tonight."

"Lucy." I pull her hands away from her face, waiting until she opens her eyes and looks up at me. "Let's not be rash. Some partners are just harder to get to know than others."

She shakes her head, but she's smiling, and I start to pull her on her skis. She cries out, gripping my hands as I increase our speed. She stiffens like she'll crash and burn if I let go.

"See, you're better at this than you seem."

"This is not skiing."

"Hey, Harold!" I call.

The man in the driver's seat of the sleigh waves at us, lifting his top hat at Lucy. "Evenin'. Can I offer you a ride?"

"You have real, horse-drawn sleighs here?" Lucy's eyes are wide.

"Yeah, but the only one has a driver with a faux Cockney accent." I let go of her as we get close and lean up to whisper to Harold. "Could I get you to take a long detour off the loop if I tip you well?"

Harold looks at Lucy and smirks. "Anything for one of Wally's boys . . . I'll take care of ya."

"Harold, you're the best." I pat the side of the sleigh.

"How long until you're ready?"

"Probably twenty minutes to get changed and return our gear." I fish out several bills, and he nods.

"Done. I'll meet you in the front, but make sure you're there. I've got to keep Charlotte movin'," he says, patting the horse's neck. Harold snaps the reigns and tips his hat to Lucy.

"We—umm, aren't we . . . we aren't?" She watches him go with dismay, before giving me a suspicious look. "He seemed nice."

"He is." I grin, secret intact. I leave it at, "He's a good friend of my dad's."

Lucy raises an eyebrow as we make our way to the back entrance of the lodge. Removing our gear, Lucy stops only steps inside the building.

"That's him." She's staring across couples and families sharing dinner in the restaurant. Erik leans over a table as a brunette laughs and chatters with him. "What's he doing here?"

I quickly steer her away from Erik's betrayal. I don't want it to matter, but even I want to slug him. "Maybe he was just taking a break."

"He's wearing jeans and a sweater." Lucy looks over her shoulder, and I dodge the swinging ends of her skis. She shakes her head. "He wasn't ever going to come back for me."

I exhale slowly as we get in line to return Lucy's gear. Piling our things together, though only hers are being returned, we slide forward slowly. The line snakes around the room.

"We hit the wrong time to check out," I whisper and Lucy laughs. A burst of laughter from down the hall stops us – Erik's laughter. Lucy quiets, and we slide our things forward.

Wrapping my arms around her, I hold her against me. "He's probably leaving." Eventually, she drops her head back, leaning against my chest. I reactively flex, only to quickly relax. Hoping it feels like a breath. Lucy doesn't care about my ego and all I want is for her to feel safe. Well, that and to slug Erik for leaving Lucy, a brand-new skier, on an advanced ski slope . . . alone. I curse my brother silently when she wipes her eyes trying to hide it with a yawn. "He should never have left you."

I don't know if she'll interpret that as on the slopes, or at all, but both of them are true. "I know. I had really convinced myself that he cared about me. It doesn't even matter but it still hurts. I'm okay, it's just—I'm trying to be okay . . . with not caring. But..." she fades off and my contentment goes with her.

Holding her in my arms, I want to stay there to buffer her in my protection. But she's hurt. I kiss the top of her head and release her. "Wait here for me. I've got to go take care of something."

Leaving her with the skis, I follow the laughter toward the entrance and find Erik and the brunette in the lobby. *He better not get her a room key.* I storm over, without really thinking, to interrupt whatever is happening. "Erik. We need to talk."

Plain, simple, to the point. That's a good start.

Erik barely looks at me, turning back around to say something to the clerk.

"Now, Erik."

"I'll be right back," he says to both the counter clerk and the girl he's been flirting with. "Does Lucy need another lesson?"

I stare at him through narrowed eyes. "What the heck were you thinking, leaving her up on that mountain? I told you she was new. We've had a few lessons in the backyard. Surely you figured out she needed help."

"I wasn't looking to spend hours with a noob that shouldn't be on the mountain."

"*You're* the one that put her there."

"So? It's not like she couldn't get down." He angles back to the brunette. "Lucy had skis. It was a waste of my time to be there. I wasn't doing anything but waiting."

"You were supposed to be teaching her." I turn around to leave, but swivel back just as quickly. "Why did you even offer? Why toy with her like that?"

Erik smirks, his eyes narrowing. "Please. You already know."

The moments before Erik showed up come to my mind. "Right. Well, I'm sorry if you don't want me showing interest in Lucy, but this time, you made the deciding choice. You hurt her. You walked away. Just keep walking, okay?"

"As if I'd want anything to do with her." He grins at me, like the idea is ridiculous to him.

My nostrils flare in a snarl, and I take a deep breath. Lucy wouldn't enjoy finding me and Erik in a fist fight. "You don't know what you're missing."

"Right, so now you're gonna tell me about my ex? You've known her for a little more than a week. This should be interesting."

"Seems like I know her better than you do." I love and hate that he's uncomfortable when I talk about Lucy.

"Hmm, single mom, trailer-park girl with daddy issues. Nope I think I got it."

"I guess you like to see what you like to see, don't you? You probably have no idea, she's setting up a marketing plan for the inn. Our parents' inn. Something their son should've been doing, but he hasn't been home. She's been here a week and cares more about what's going on than you do."

"Shut up," Erik sneers. He looks back to the counter and turns back with a sharp whisper. "Since when does the inn need a marketer?"

I swear under my breath. He really knows nothing. "Since our parents mortgaged it."

"Holy crap. You let them mortgage it?"

"I didn't *let* them do anything. It's their place. I'm trying to take care of it, and Lucy is the only one helping. How did you manage five years with such a hardworking, compassionate woman?"

"She's hot." He says it like it's the obvious answer.

"That's all you see?" You paid as much attention then, as you did today."

"I didn't have to pay attention. She was high-functioning arm candy. She even impressed my boss."

I cock my fist back, and Erik flinches.

"Torin?" Lucy speaks up from the hallway entrance to the lobby.

"Lucy is so much more than arm candy." I turn toward Lucy, ready to be done with this conversation.

Erik grabs my shoulder and pulls me back. "So it's true? You always want what's not yours."

"You don't know what you're talking about."

"I'm talking about Hillary, and now Lucy. Is that clear enough?"

"Who's Hillary?" Lucy asks, coming up behind me.

Our eyes lock. Erik's smile lifts at the corner of his mouth.

Then, Lucy takes my hand.

Erik looks from our joined hands to my face, and the world slogs into slow motion, like I'm watching a movie. With a single step, Erik pulls his fist back, swings his arm in a low arc, and lands a punch at the side of my gut.

Movies don't usually hurt this much.

"Erik!" Lucy shoves him away, and her hands land on me. "Are you all right, Torin?"

I clench my jaw as Erik shakes his fist out against the pain of contact.

"It's been five years," I hiss. "I didn't touch Hillary. I've tried to tell you that."

"I don't believe you. I never have. And now—" He glares at Lucy. "I never will."

"Go away, Erik. Nobody wants you here." Lucy arm is wrapped tightly around me, her elbow dangerously close to the injured section of my core.

I'm gonna have a bruise from that one.

"You're wrong, Lucy." He takes the brunette's hand and smiles. "I'm pretty sure she wants me. At least she did last night, several times in fact."

The brunette looks ticked-off, but that's not who I'm watching. Lucy's shock is evident in her dropped jaw and wide eyes. I feel her pain deeper than Erik's punch.

With a sharp glare at Erik, I turn to Lucy and lift her chin. Not waiting for permission, I drop my mouth to hers pressing fluidly over her lips. It only takes a single pull to convince her of my plan and she responds to my forceful seduction with an audible moan.

She's the drug to my desire and I clutch her body to mine. My blatant display of affection deepening as Lucy presses back, burning through my urges. Unhindered intensity rises inside me. Her fingers thread their way into my hair and over my back as she drags us closer, my heart beating wildly.

It doesn't last long, and we pull back, locking eyes before finding each other again in short echoes of the kiss. Until being apart doesn't feel as jarring.

She stares up at me, a faint smile slowly building, as I let my hands drift down her body.

Footsteps pass us as Erik's voice reminds us we're not alone. "At least we had the decency to get a room."

"Thank you for not slapping me." I slide across the velvet bench of the sleigh, putting my bruises on the opposite side of Lucy, who climbs in after me. "After he targeted you like that, I just couldn't let him win."

"Well, I'm happy to award you the gold medal." I almost kiss her again. But, a little restraint is good, probably. "I would have loved to see the look at Erik's face."

Lucy snuggles into my side, as Harold leans back greeting us with his terrible Cockney accent. "Good evenin', loves. 'Appy 'olidays. There's blankets on the bench, and I'll be serenadin' you as we go. I 'ope you enjoy the ride."

Lucy bites her lip and looks at me, holding back her laughter as Harold clicks the reigns. The horse pulls forward with a jolt and a jingle of bells. Cockney Christmas carols start on the driver's bench.

"Ouch." Lucy flinches. "So, I was wondering about Hillary."

The horse hits a bump and Lucy pulls her feet up on the bench, adjusting her position.

"Oh, that." I'm not looking forward to this conversation. "If I promise to tell you everything, can we wait until after the sleigh ride?"

"Mmhmm," she nods affirmatively and takes my hand. "Of course. Now pass me that blanket, and let me lean on your shoulder. Harold's singing my favorite Christmas song."

"We Wish You a Merry Christmas is your favorite?"

"No. We Wish You a Merry Christmas in cockney. It just became my favorite." She spreads the blanket out and leans against me.

Snow covered trees and mountains dance by as we travel the lantern-lit, cross-country ski path. The sun sets as we circle out to the mountain road. Lucy's hand is soft in my own as I run my thumb over her knuckles. I try not to think about how sore my ribs are as we jostle our way along the extended sleigh loop.

We hit a particularly large bump, and Lucy lifts herself up off the seat for a minute before settling back and looking up with a pained smile.

"Are you all right?" I run my hand over her shoulder, forgetting for a second that I've got a growing, cantaloupe-sized bruise on my side.

"Everything is so beautiful," she says skillfully, not answering my question.

Harold's sleigh jogs into a rut on the road.

"Ow!" It just slips out, and Lucy looks up, tears forming over quiet laughter.

"Sorry about that, mates," Harold says over his shoulder. "This road's a mite bumpy."

"Torin," Lucy whispers. "This hurts so bad."

I look her over and flinch as we jolt again. It's as if her confession gives my body license to feel it, too.

"Are you okay?" I ask.

"I'm so bruised, I can barely sit." She looks up at Harold to see if he heard her.

"Harold!" I'm laughing and cringing with every move now. "Harold, can we pause at the Big Sugar? I want to show Lucy the falls, and then we're going to cut the ride short after that."

"Oh, feeling romantic, are ya?"

Lucy laughs, and I smile up at Harold. "You'd be doing me a big favor."

Harold grins widely and tips his hat, pulling off the road as the entrance to Big Sugar Falls Park appears.

I help Lucy out of the sleigh, and she limps for the first few steps.

"I'm so sorry." I laugh, limping alongside her until my body loosens up. "I really thought it was going to be a good idea."

"It was. It really was. I've just been trying to hover in that sleigh for the last five minutes. I swear, I must be a canvas of purple bruises under all this." She takes my hand, walking close beside me as we head down the trail toward the falls.

Her thick coat doesn't stop me from pulling her close, but as she wraps her arm around me, I gently slide it up over my bruise. "Right," she giggles. "I'll watch that."

"Thank you." I lean into her hair, kissing the side of her head. She smells like sunshine and flowers. Like summer, pulled from that season and brought here for me. "This wasn't in the plan, but I'm glad we got to stop. Big Sugar Falls is one of my favorite places in Sugar Creek."

"Really? Better than the covered bridges and Mt. Rosie?"

"I have a few favorites," I admit. "This one is not the most popular this time of year, but I've always loved it. I like going when the crowds are low, so I can listen to the water. The Little Sugar falls are closer to the lodge, but this falls right into Crystal Gorge."

When we reach the bridge that spans the gorge, I can already hear the waterfall.

"The falls?" she asks.

"Yup. This is Crystal Gorge." As we walk out over the open crevice, her gasp is validating. "It's over a hundred-foot drop, and the falls are right over there." A wired fence stands between us and the view, but the falls put on a good show despite the barrier.

"Oh, wow," she says, leaning out over the railing.

Water plummets from high on the wall of Mt Rosie all the way down into the floor of Crystal Gorge. Barren maple trees decorate the cliff edges of the gorge with silver branches, a skeleton of the seasonal view when the deep walls are covered in gold and red leaves.

The creek isn't as full as it is in the spring and fall, but it's full enough, showing the Big Sugar Falls that pour through fat white icicles into the frozen edges of the Grand River.

I stand behind her, wrapping my arms around her waist. "If you sit here for very long, these falls can make the world disappear."

"I could use a little time away," she says. "I love the ice fixtures on the waterfall. It's a living sculpture."

"I've never looked at it as art."

"How can you not?" Lucy's elbows rest on the railing as she stares out over Crystal Gorge. "See how the sheets of ice hang over the water as it pours through them? It's like threads of life, stretching from mountain all the way down to the gorge. Even the icy mist down there is stunning."

I hadn't even noticed the fog billowing below. It's so far down that it's nowhere near touching us, but it floats there at the bottom of the gorge like crystalline magic. She's right. "You just made this place even more beautiful." I slide my arms further around her, rubbing my hands over hers to keep the chill away. "You make everything more beautiful."

Lucy sighs, watching the icicles of the Big Sugar Falls protect their still-moving fountain. "Is it time to talk about Hillary?"

A twinge passes through my chest, releasing in a heavy breath. "If that's what you want to talk about."

She turns in my arms to face me. "I don't need everything. I just want to know what's going on. I'm sorry Erik hit you. He shouldn't have."

"You don't have to apologize for him."

She shifts closer, and I wrap her back into me, pressing a kiss to her forehead. We lean against each other.

"I'm sorry for fighting. That's not how I like to handle things."

"Oh, I experienced how you like to finish an argument." She grins up at me and then drops her eyes. Her hand hovers over my coat along my side, but she doesn't do more. "You're the one who came home with the battle wound."

With one finger, she traces the line of my lips. I feel her touch deep inside my chest. Then, slowly, she leans forward. "Torin," she whispers as her lips touch the corner of my mouth. Her finger continues to outline my face, down my jaw. Her soft touch trickles the full length of my neck.

Her lips slide across my cheek and down the trail of her fingertips. I'm afraid to breathe, to break the spell of Lucy's touch.

I'm breathless, in another world, until she pulls back and bites her lip. "We should talk. Just tell me the quick version."

Pain spears my heart, and I nod. "Did Erik ever tell you he was engaged?"

Her brow pinches, and she shakes her head.

"About five and a half years ago." Images run through my mind that I wish I could forget. I take a deep breath, focusing on Lucy's face and breathing the citrus and floral scents of her hair. "Her name was Hillary. I think she genuinely liked Erik, but on the day of the wedding, we were getting ready at the hotel. And when I came into the room, Hillary was there. In my bed. Completely undressed." The visual of that moment never seems to fade, but I close my eyes anyway, trying to shake it. "I left immediately, but Erik was already in the doorway, and he just never believed that nothing happened . . . I didn't even like Hillary. Brunettes are not my type." I curl a lock of hair around my finger and let it go with a sigh. "Erik walked away from the family that night."

"I'm so sorry." Her thumb runs across my jaw, and I close my eyes.

"Me too. Before that, we were friends. I was his best man. He was going to be mine."

"Were you and Corrine together when that happened?"

I nod. "We were both engaged." A painful laugh jerks from my chest. "It seemed like a perfect situation at the time."

"I'm so sorry. He should have believed you." She shivers in my arms, and I hold her tight before letting go.

I look down into her eyes and the world stops turning for half a second as my heart jumpstarts into a new rhythm to match hers. Erik was right about one thing—I've only known Lucy for a week. And yet, I'd do just about anything for her.

"We should go." I hold her hands to my lips, warming them with my breath. "We need to get you back to the car."

"Let's go home," she whispers.

Home? The word sounds lovely on her lips. I nod, and we hold hands as we walk back to the parking lot. Harold and the sleigh are waiting. As I help Lucy into the back, my phone buzzes with a text from Max.

> — *Big news buddy. I've got a buyer for the Inn. They're anonymous, which isn't great, but I think you'll be happy with the offer.*

An offer. Relief and confusion pick at the pieces of my brain holding my little world together. We didn't even put it on the market, but selling could ease a massive stress. I just don't know if we can do it.

"What's that?" Lucy asks, glancing at my phone.

I click the screen off and breathe. "Nothing important. I'd much rather talk about kissing you."

Chapter 13

Lucy

"*N*atten går tunga fjät. Runt gård och stuva.*"

Coupled with quiet voices, foreign lyrics drift through my room, muffled by walls, sleep, and lack of understanding. Moonlight spills over the snowy balcony as the lyrical melody rouses me to a state of semi-consciousness. It's still dark. People are clearly awake, but that doesn't explain why they're singing at this hour. I roll over, barely able to think.

"*Sankta Lucia, Sankta Lucia.*" Ingrid's soft voice seeps through the bedroom door as the handle turns and the latch clicks.

Music and light fill my doorway, and Alice steps through wearing a white dress tied with a red bow around her waist. Her hair has been braided in two, tiny blonde braids under a crown of evergreens and electric candles. Between Alice's crown and the real candle glimmering in Ingrid's hands, the tiny Lucia is lit with a magical glow. Flickering light illuminates their sweet faces, grandmother and granddaughter together.

I breathe it in, sitting up to see them better. If I could stay at this inn forever, with family, friends, and the smell of sweet rolls wafting through the air before dawn, I would.

"Happy Santa Lucia Day!" Alice whispers with rosy cheeks as the song ends. Her giggle melts my heart.

I want to hold her and kiss her and keep her forever. "You are the most precious Santa Lucia I've ever seen."

"I agree." Torin's deep voice is such a contrast to Alice, I can't help but look up.

He's leaning in the doorway behind the women, holding a small, lit candle. His plain t-shirt sets off bright red, cotton drawstring pants with cartoon Christmas trees that dance up and down the fabric. I slow blink, taking in his drowsy grin and tousled hair.

He's perfect.

"Please," Ingrid says, offering her hand to help me out of bed. I do a quick check of my pajamas and climb out to join them. "For the record, I'm the only one of you who's actually seen another Santa Lucia. So, when I say you're the most perfect Santa Lucia I've ever seen—" she leans down, tapping Alice's nose, "—I actually mean it. You are perfect, *min älskling.*"

"*Jag älskar dig, Farmor.*"

Ingrid's hand hovers over her chest at Alice's words, as if her heart is moments from bursting. "Did you teach her that?" Tears sparkle in Ingrid's eyes reflected by the candlelight.

Torin slips an arm around his mother. "Happy Santa Lucia Day, Ma."

She kisses him and moves into the hallway, where she hands me a candle. "I'm so glad you're here." Turning to include Alice and Torin, she holds her hands out. "*Glad Lucia, mina älsklingar.*"

The music and light act as a pied piper, leading me after the little Santa Lucia. I'm enthralled with this walk in the candlelight.

Torin falls back, as his mother leads Alice with her tray of rolls. Moving carefully up the stairs, she coaches Alice on another verse of *Sankta Lucia* as they prepare to wake up Wally.

"What did you teach her to say?" I ask Torin, joining him at the tail end of the group.

"*Jag älskar dig.*" His deep voice caresses the words. "It means, I love you."

My step stutters, and I can feel his eyes on me. The candlelight dims as Alice and Ingrid ascend, leaving us in the hall with our two small candles. I look up into Torin's eyes.

"That's so sweet."

"I knew it would mean a lot for her to hear Alice say it in Swedish." He smiles down on me, his unshaven jaw lit by the barest candlelight.

His face is so familiar now. Looking up at him feels almost like the day I met him, when he was Sexy Santa, and I was only kissing a stranger under the mistletoe.

Now it's different. He's different. He's not some gorgeous, pin-up Santa Claus to dream about, though I wouldn't mind if I did. He's a dad, a son, a brother. Experience assures me, he's not perfect. He misunderstands, rushes into things. But he's kind. He's compassionate. He watches out for people.

He watches out for me.

My breath catches, as my rules come to mind, like they always do when I start thinking like this.

Rule one: *I will not add to the parade of men in my life.* I reach up, brushing my fingertips down his cheek bones. Torin doesn't feel like part of a parade. Someone only around for the fun, ready to leave when they've filled their belly and their bed.

Rule two: *I will not date someone based on attraction alone.* There's no denying the attraction between us.

He studies my face with his intense eyes, and my skin heats like he's physically touching me. But there's also so much more.

Slipping his hand around my waist, Torin strokes a thumb down my cheek. My heart clenches and I don't want him to stop.

If I didn't know his four-year-old was awake and walking around, I'd probably have my legs wrapped around his waist right now. Still, the heat between us isn't the only thing here. Attraction doesn't comfort me when I'm nervous or defend my value. His actions simply make me want him more.

And then there's rule number three. I've never changed my rules for a man, but I'm considering it after this week. I set my free hand against his chest, hovering there not sure if I want to reach up to his neck or lean into him and let him hold me.

Rule number three: *I will not date someone who doesn't see me or my potential.*

Erik saw potential in me, but it was always more about what I could be for him. Like the job at the marketing firm and helping him get promoted. It was only about him. Torin sees my potential, but he's not trying to shape it for me. He sees me as more than what he wants me to be. He sees me as I am.

"Lucy." His fingers slip behind my ear and trail down my jaw to my neck. My snowflake necklace rests there. I put the necklace back on after spending time with this family . . . with Torin. They make me want to believe that I'm here for a reason. Maybe true love isn't what I thought, but it could be real. And just maybe, I was too hasty to rid myself of this snowflake's magic.

Picking the tiny pendant up, Torin's fingers brush the curve of bone below my throat. "I have a wish to make."

He sets our candles on the hall table and pulls me close until we're breathing the same air. His lips press gently to mine several times, passing short gasps between each other. I lean into his form, my body screaming for more. Not from Sexy Santa, but Torin.

"Happy Santa Lucia!" Wally's voice booms from the third floor and I jump backward.

For a second, Torin still looks like he's holding me, his face full of the longing I feel. Footsteps bound down the stairs as his dad bursts into the hall and wraps Torin in a hug. It's followed with the smack of a kiss on his cheek.

Turning to me with wide arms, he bellows a similar greeting. "Happy Saint Lucy's Day, Lucy!"

He chuckles at his joke and gives me a bear hug as well. Torin watches me, and I miss being in his arms. This embrace, though welcome, is entirely different.

Tears prick my eyes as I soak up Wally's generous spirit. I can't remember ever being held like this, by someone who loves me as a daughter. He kisses my cheek, and laughter swallows my tears. I pray that one day, this story I tell myself will be real. One day, it will be mine.

In the dining room, bottle brush trees of all sizes fill the center of the table, interspersed with candles and shiny metal reindeer.

"The Season of Light has begun!" Wally announces and sits where Ingrid has set cups of hot chocolate and plates full of saffron buns.

Laughter fills the air as everyone compliments Ingrid's cooking. The buns are sweet and soft like cinnamon rolls, complimented by the unique flavor of what must be saffron. I could eat hundreds.

"Do you like my crown, Lucy?" Alice has a bun in one hand and a cup of cocoa in the other. The wreath on her head tips haphazardly to one side. "Do you want to wear it?"

My eyebrows lift in surprise, and the other adults laugh. "Can I?"

"Uh-huh." Alice leans her head toward me. "The green stuff itches."

I remove the wreath from her head ceremoniously, electric candles flickering, and place it on my own. "How do I look?"

"Like a Santa Lucy Princess!"

"That is so lucky," I say, "I've always wanted to be a Santa Princess."

Alice giggles and stuffs her mouth with a bun, holding everything she can in her cheeks.

Lucky.

Being here . . . with this family . . . finding this place . . . this is lucky.

Joy builds inside me. The space between that letter K and me is the shortest it's ever been. In fact, my breakup with Erik may be the luckiest thing that's ever happened to me.

"Should I be more worried about this? Is the Nyström Family snowman contest pretty high stakes?" I adjust my box of snowman hats as we head to the backyard.

Torin's got one arm wrapped around my waist, with his other arm holding a box of buttons, pipes, and holiday accessories. "Definitely high stakes. The winner gets bragging rights, at least until sundown." Torin's hand slips up my back. I pretend not to notice the thrill it sends all the way to my fingertips as he points to where we'll set up the snowman gear. "Also, it's my mom's side. So they're Olssons, mostly, not Nyströms. Probably should know that before you go off insulting anyone."

"Well, thanks for the warning. You know me. I love to insult important people."

He laughs, and a familiar face appears on the porch.

"What's her name again?" I whisper, from the corner of my mouth.

"Emma, the one who tripped me. She's Linnea and Henry's—" His lips brush my ear and my box tumbles to the ground.

"Just her name is enough." I lean, straightening the box. "How about here?"

Torin waves to her as he laughs at me. "Perfect."

He drops his box next to mine.

Together, we cross the snow to greet Emma before going back inside, where the crowds have arrived in an overwhelming chaos of smiling faces and laughter. I smile anxiously as I greet people I've met but don't remember. Ingrid has set out a full array of snacks, sweets, and breads.

Erik comes through the door, and I squeeze Torin's hand. It was only yesterday that two fought, leaving Torin's body as bruised as Erik's ego.

"It's okay," Torin says, and goes back to talking with his cousin.

I nod, trying to process the differences in a family so unlike mine. The cousins and people and forgiveness that Erik somehow missed out on. Maybe that's why I was always so comfortable around him. And why, even though I love the way I feel with Torin, his ease in all of this is a little disconcerting.

The thought that I may be more fit for Erik than Torin makes me sick. Torin turns me around as an older woman claps her hands and starts giving out instructions – I don't have time to worry.

"Aunt Linnea," Torin mutters softly. "Ma's oldest sister."

My lips quirk up on one corner. I had been just about to give up the mental search for her name. "Thanks."

"Let's play by the rules, and make sure everyone participates!" Linnea calls, and the crowd erupts with movement as teams gather and boxes of supplies are decimated.

I hurry to the scarves behind Emma to find a selection of single gloves and an empty box. "Oh, my gosh. Is there anything left?"

"You'll be fine." Emma nods back to Torin. "He always sneaks first pick. We mixed up family teams one year, and I worked with him." She breathes on her knuckles and shines them against her shirt. "We won."

True to Emma's reassurances, Torin has a full bag of snowman gear for the Nyström family and is already forming a large snowball.

"Here, Lucy, help me get this snowman going." Torin asks for my help and advice, laughing and talking with me the whole time we build. Only a few minutes in, Erik is apparently exhausted after a late night.

"I'm gonna go lie down, if that's all right?" He kisses his mother and leaves without waiting for anyone's approval.

"It's all right," Ingrid says, obviously disappointed that her oldest son has disappeared. "He technically helped. So, as long as we finish his snowman, it still counts."

Things go basically back to normal. Torin teasing Alice and I, and all of us building the worlds quirkiest snow people. Emma's has sunglasses and a waist. Ours dons a tweed hat, giant slippers, and as many pinecones as Alice could find for hair.

Alice helps our team prep both snow people, adding buttons and hugging them, because, "Love makes them real."

Patting Erik's snowman, she compliments our work. "He's so fat, Daddy. I like him."

Ingrid's voice interrupts the festivities. She's speaking to Nils, but aiming her comment at Torin.

"Oh, things are great. The inn's doing better than ever. Right, Torin?" she asks. "Torin's been helping manage it over the last couple years. He's doing a great job."

I'm not sure Torin agrees with her assessment, but he smiles anyway as Ingrid's brother dismisses her.

"Interesting, I heard someone mention it might be for sale when I went into the real estate offices last week."

Torin turns quickly toward his uncle. "Who told you that?"

Nils shrugs, and I lean over, whispering, "What was he doing in the real estate office?"

Torin glances at me, distracted. "Nils has always wanted to get out here. All of them would if they could. But Nils goes house hunting during every reunion. He's too cheap to find anything."

Ingrid scoffs at Nils. "You need to go back to your snowman building. The inn isn't for sale."

"Good, because you should be giving family the first option."

"Because you'd give us such a good price?" Torin snarks.

"Because we'd keep it in the family."

"Wrong side of the family." Torin rolls his eyes and looks to Wally, who's carving impressive swirls in the bottom of his and Ingrid's snowman, like an embossed dress.

When Nils leaves, Ingrid bustles over. "Why didn't you seem surprised by that?"

Torin's gaze darts to me his eyes wide with worry.

"Something is going on here, Torin Nyström. And I want you to tell me what it is."

I nod, trying to encourage him. I know how scary hard truths can be, especially when you have to tell them alone. I take his hand. "It's time," I whisper, and his shoulders sag.

He calls his dad over and with everyone there Torin turns to Wally and Ingrid. "We need to talk to about the inn."

The family contest continues while Torin takes his parents and I inside, leaving Alice with Emma.

"What's going on?" Ingrid asks. "Why did Nils think the inn was for sale?"

"I've been talking with Max. He was supposed to keep it quiet. I wanted to find out what it would look like if we sold it."

"But *why*?" She emphasizes her question, and I can see Torin tense.

"Because we're not making enough money." He drops his gaze, tracing invisible patterns on the stone planter he's leaning against. "We haven't been since I got home."

"We have savings," Wally says.

Ingrid grips Wally's hand. "But that's our retirement."

Torin nods. "And I don't want to burn through your retirement money trying to keep a dream alive, if it can't do it on its own." He glances at me, and I squeeze his hand. "And that's what keeping the inn alive is, right now. A dream."

Ingrid sucks in a breath. "Wally?" She looks to her husband.

A deep frown creases his face, and my heart jumps up into my throat. Anxiety for all of them ties knots through my chest.

"Unless we can figure out how to turn things around," I add. "I have a few ideas."

Wally looks at me hopefully. "What are you saying?"

"They're just ideas . . . But I've noticed your marketing could be a lot better. Torin and I have been talking about the website, and promotions, and local companies we can work with to promote your business. You've got business neighbors all around here. I'm sure they'd all be happy to help."

"You want to ask our neighbors for help?" Wally bristles, and my eyes widen at his pride and misunderstanding.

I glance at Torin, and he steps in. "It's not charity, Dad. She's not asking them to pay our rent. She wants to work with them."

"How would we do that? Do you know other inn owners?"

"They don't have to be inn owners," I try to clarify. But his tone has brought on an air of tension. "I want to find people who would be willing to promote you and you'd do the same for them."

"Wally," Ingrid sets a hand on her husband's. "Selling the inn has always been a possibility. We've known for a while that it may come to this."

"But not because it was failing."

Torin's expression sets to ice. That must have hurt him pretty badly. I slide a hand over Torin's, but he only slightly thaws. After a bit more discussion, frustration, and understanding, Wally and Ingrid rejoin the family outside.

A sound comes at the top of the stairs, and Torin starts searching the visible landing, but no one's there. He gestures to the front door, and we step onto the porch, claiming the rockers at the side.

With the family engaged in the contest, no one is on this side of the house. Torin drops his head into his hands.

"Torin!" A man in a thick leather jacket and deep green scarf stops on the sidewalk. "Am I interrupting?"

He looks between us, adjusting a pair of wire-rimmed glasses. A dark yellow beanie hugs low around his face, light brown hair curling from under its edge. Deep dimples set off a bright smile.

"Max!" Standing to greet him, Torin takes long strides across the snowy yard, barreling into his friend. "Dude, I'm so glad you're here."

My pace is less enthusiastic, but when Torin looks back, his expression is lighter, and I follow suit.

Torin's got his arm slung over Max's shoulders when I reach them, and Max swings his arm from around Torin to extend to me. Torin flinches, but only when Max hits his bruised side. "You must be Lucy."

"I am," I say, trying to keep my attention on Max. "And I guess you're Max? How do you know me?"

He grins. "Torin mentions you every time I, oof—" Torin elbows him in the side— "I mean, he's mentioned you a couple times. Maybe once or twice . . . an hour . . . since you got here. What's your name again? I can't remember."

"Dude!" Torin smacks him, and he laughs.

"It's good to meet you." I'm laughing, too, as we all go back up to the porch.

"Max is my realtor friend." Torin playfully shoves him into a rocker and pulls a stool over to round out our group.

"Oh, nice." I shoot him a smile. "Torin mentioned he'd met with you."

"You talked about me?" He winks at Torin like they're flirting. "Of course he did. I'm Max Crew! Your real esta—"

"Not now," Torin says, kicking the arm of the rocker and sending Max reeling backward.

"Hey!" He shoves Torin back. "I didn't even get to finish my tag line."

"Sorry. Not feeling the cheesy cheerleader vibe today."

"Geez, that turned fast. What happened?" Max asks, scooting his rocker closer to the wall.

Torin shakes his head. "Sorry, but I know why you're here, and I barely talked to my parents about the inn."

"Oh?" Max raises an eyebrow. "How'd it go?"

Torin shoots me a look and presses back anxiously on his stool. "Could have been better."

"Could have been worse," I counter. My phone dings and when I look, I realize I have several missed calls and texts from Shaunda. There's also multiple from Cormac Walters, the first of the Walter & Walter's marketing firm brothers.

I excuse myself while Torin and Max discuss the benefits and disadvantages of selling. I glance back, and Torin looks more relaxed than earlier, but the stress still weighs on him. He catches me watching him and his smile droops.

I must be showing my concern.

My phone buzzes again, and I slip into the house.

Shaunda sent me three messages, and typing bubbles are still cycling at the bottom of the screen.

They don't make a lot of sense.

> — *Why does it look like they're moving your desk? Did you get a promotion and not tell me?*

> — *Looks like they finally realized who's been doing all Erik's work.*

> — *So, this isn't right. Call me. I don't understand.*

Torin strides up beside me. "Is everything all right?"

"Unless I got a promotion no one told me about." I shake my head. "I don't know."

I start typing out a reply as her last text comes through.

> — *They FIRED you?!?!?!*

My fingers freeze on the phone screen.

They *what?*

I start typing a question, then delete it. I can't get anything out. I try again, only to delete a second question. I rub my frozen fingers over my forehead.

"Lucy?" It's Torin's voice, but when I look up, Erik's face is there, watching me.

"What?" I shake my head, and Torin steps around his brother.

"You need to leave her alone," Torin says, wrapping his arms around me.

Erik ignores him. "Is everything all right?"

I shake my head, looking up at Torin. With a trembling finger over the name Cormac Walters on the voicemail list, I tap the screen.

Mr. Walter's voice comes on the recorded line. "Ms. Sweet. I'm appalled at your behavior. Skirting company policy and putting our clients at risk is bad enough, but you signed a non-compete disclosure when you came on here, and considering it's been going on for some time now—I'm shocked. Effective immediately, you have been fired from Walter & Walters marketing firm. Your desk has been cleared. All personal belongings will be sent to your home address. I am sorry to do this over the phone, but considering the situation, I didn't feel I should wait for you to return. Please call with any information on unfinished projects you need to pass on to someone else her at the firm."

Silence.

Short breaths suck into my lungs, stuttering bursts of air as I replay the voicemail in my mind. *Clearing my desk . . . considering the situation . . .* What did I do? Somewhere in there Torin's hand slips around me, holding me upright.

"What is it?" He pulls me into a hug, my stiff body conforming to his.

"They fired me." I look up into deep green, worried eyes as reality rocks through me. "I don't even know what I did. I just lost my job."

Chapter 14

Torin

Bitter elves aren't great for business.

Today's whispered complaints are slightly less hostile than yesterday's. But considering that yesterday, Lucy told several kids that she had access to Santa's email and could put them on the naughty list, today has been a huge step up.

Lucy grimaces at the line of kids while eating a candy cane she had offered to a little boy and then took back after he got too energetic.

"Ho, ho, ho!" I say, welcoming the next little girl in my jolliest voice.

"Parents stay behind the ropes, please." Lucy counteracts my festive persona with the opposite side of the spectrum. She steps into the aisle, blocking the way as the curl of her elf hat bobbles, its bell glinting in the sunlight.

It's not really a rule. The dad's only a few feet away, but it feels like she's trying to pick a fight. The man opposite her stumbles when confronted with the barrier of the angry elf, and I can hardly blame him.

It's getting harder to focus on why I'm here. The kids. I'm doing this for the kids. I lift the next youngster in line onto my lap, praying Lucy will relax.

"Merry Christmas," I say, without looking down.

"Santa? Thanks for letting me come again." *Again*?

I look down, and my chest tightens as I recognize the little girl from the beginning of December. The one who asked for a Christmas miracle for her mom. Joy? Yeah, Joy. Under her wide-eyed stare, the image of Corrine, pale, exhausted, and dying, returns. Joy's miracle is a request I won't soon forget.

"How's your mother?"

"Not better." Her lip trembles. "Did you forget to send your magic?"

"No, Joy. I'm so sorry. If your mom's really sick, Christmas magic may not be what she needs."

"But it is. Daddy said we need a miracle. That's Christmas magic. I brought you the address." She holds a little card out to me.

I take it and try to explain. "Joy —"

"I really want her to get better by Christmas. I've never had Christmas without my mom."

Lucy turns, and the shock on her face swims, mixing with the man's anxious restraint. Focus. Everything I try to say sticks in my throat, until I'm choking on my good intentions.

I nod and, like a scale tipping, she lights up. A pit forms in my stomach.

"Thank you, Santa!" she says, and hugs me around the neck. She jumps down and runs back to the haggard man.

Even with her curly-topped elf hat, Lucy's not as tall as Joy's dad, but she's blocking his path, showing off the stubborn streak that I've only seen during our ski lessons. "Next," Lucy calls sharply.

"You might put on a smile," the man says.

Lucy speaks through gritted teeth. "I'm smiling on the inside. Next. Please."

Oh, *crap*. "Lucy?" I try to keep my voice pleasant, like Santa Claus should be. "Let's help the other kids."

"I'm trying," she says. She doesn't turn to me. "Are you complaining about how I do my job?"

"We're just here to see Santa." The man shuffles away, taking Joy with him. "It shouldn't be this difficult."

"Everyone's here to see Santa." Lucy waves a hand to them as they leave. "Santa's got the best job in the world. Right kids?"

The remaining kids cheer, but her tone has me worried. I put my hand on her back and whisper against her ear. "Lucy, this is probably not the best time."

She pulls away. "Well, it's true. All Santa has to do is hand out presents once a year!" She turns to the crowd. "Who thinks they could do Santa's job?" Some kids bounce and raise their hands. Others look nervous, sensing the trap. "I bet you could! Work one day a year, and everyone sings his praises. I could totally do that! But do they let me be Santa? No. You can't be Santa, kids. They won't even let me market Santa, much less anything else. How could I screw that up? Everyone *loves* Santa."

"Okay!" I jump in front of her, I don't know if that was really what her job entailed or not but taking Lucy by the arm, I stand between her and the crowd. "Merry Christmas everyone! Santa has to leave early today. Be back here tomorrow at noon with your Christmas wishes!"

Lucy looks up and opens her mouth to say something, then shuts it, pressing her lips into a flat line and her blush rising in mottled red blotches.

Pulling Lucy with me into the workshop. I yank my beard off, I can't talk to her dressed as the jolly old elf. "Lucy, you have got to stop. They're just kids."

"That was not a kid," she spits. "He was a full-grown man."

"Who doesn't care that you lost your job, or if you want to be Santa Claus. I, on the other hand, would be happy to relinquish that position, if it will keep you from sending kids home crying."

She huffs and leans back against the wall. "I don't actually want to be Santa Claus."

"Lucy, this isn't like you. I thought you liked kids. I thought you liked being here."

"I do." She looks up, meeting my gaze.

The trust in her eyes makes my heartrate rise. She's letting me lead this, and I don't want to screw it up. "Then don't let that idiot you used to call your boss ruin this for you, too."

I set a hand against the wall by her head, creating a bubble of imagined privacy.

"I know I'm wallowing," she squeaks. "I just don't understand. None of his accusations are founded. I work hard. I help people. I don't ask for much. Just to be valued." On saying that, her breathing immediately spikes. "Oh gosh, I'm just like my mother. That's exactly what she says right before she breaks up with a guy. Torin, what am I going to do? I'm jobless and single, and I don't want to turn into my mother—"

"I'm certain you are not your mother." With my arm by her head, I take her hand and lower my voice. "You're smart. You're beautiful."

"I have a degree in marketing."

"You've got a degree in marketing." I laugh, but let the words sink in as she nods, and I keep going. "You're independent, creative, determined." The image of her staring down a man twice her size flashes in my mind, emphasizing her instinctual qualities. I take a deep breath hoping I never have to see that again. "There are a lot of marketing firms in Florida, and they'd be crazy not to want you."

I want you. Emotion stirs like angel kisses in my chest, snowflakes dancing inside my once-cold heart. She could be my second chance, but can I do that to her? And what about Alice? When Lucy finally looks up, her eyes shake me like a snow globe, sending my heart swirling.

"Lucy, you're incredible. I know I'm not the only one that sees that."

She sniffs a laugh and tries to look away. "You have to say that."

I weave to stay in her line of sight. "Why? Why do I *have* to say that?"

"Because you're a nice guy." She turns her head to the door, looking away.

She looks back at me. So close, I can feel the heat of her skin through the cold air. I sigh and lean my forehead against hers. "If you could hear my thoughts right now, you'd see I'm not that nice of a guy."

Feeling her skin against mine, I don't care about anyone who might see us, or anywhere else I'm supposed to be. Her lips part and I stroke my thumb along her jaw. Several blonde curls tumble loose along her cheeks. Brushing them back, I lean in to kiss her, and something crashes outside our bubble.

"I knew this was too good to be true," I mutter. "Hang on."

She doesn't follow me out. I find several children running away from a nutcracker, lying face-down in the snow.

"Lucy?" I lean back in the workshop. "I could use a hand."

She's leaning against the wall with her eyes closed until I appear. "Oh." She's a little breathless. "Um, yeah. What do you need?"

I take a step around the corner and lift her into a kiss, taking her lips in hungry anticipation of her soft mouth and body. But she responds with strength, and I feel the pressure of her body, her lips pulling a reaction from every part of me before we let go.

Now we're both breathless.

It takes a few minutes to get the nutcracker to stand upright, but after, I take Lucy's hand. "Come on, I have an idea." Leading her to the other side of the square, we stop in front of a wide, awning draped in evergreen swags and bows. "Have you ever tried a Mistletoe Hot Chocolate?"

Thick webs of Christmas lights crisscross the windows below the name, My Sister's Soda Shop.

She shakes her head. Her expression shifts quickly from confusion to surprise. This shop is a lot to take in the first time—dark and light checkerboard wood floors, drink machines, and stacks of vintage mugs along a pale pink back wall. Customers chatter, scattered about the place, as Christmas music plays above it all.

"This place is so cute." She sounds less grumpy than she did twenty minutes ago.

163

I try to pull Lucy's stool out before remembering the ones at the counter are affixed to the ground. She takes the seat anyway, and I settle next to her, slapping my hand down on the polished wood counter. Lucy jumps as I call to the nicer of the two proprietors working the milkshake blender at the other end of the counter. "Hey, Lydie! I've got a Mistletoe virgin here!"

"Well, kiss her already," Lydie calls over her shoulder. "We've got the stuff all over the place."

Lucy's blush rises as the rest of the patrons laugh, warming her cheeks to match the red Christmas bows on the salt shakers.

"Oh my gosh," Lucy mutters, and I follow her gaze to the garland hung along the perimeter of the room. Every few feet it swags up to the ceiling, accented with a bundle of mistletoe. "It's a never-ending loop of kisses. I'd have come here earlier if I knew you meant real mistletoe," she teases. "I'm sure I could've found someone to bring me."

"Lucy, that hurts," I tease. "Unless, of course, you meant me." I give her a peck on the cheek and her smile lifts where I kissed her.

She turns a full circle on her spinning stool as Lydie slides over.

"Unless you've got some new holiday magic worked up, we'll both take a Mistletoe Hot Chocolate."

"Well," she says, squinting, "I've been perfecting a few things. How do you feel about Chai and caramel?"

Lucy raises her hand without hesitation. "I feel good about it."

"Great. One Mistletoe Cocoa and one Sticky Gingerbread Boy, comin' up." Lydie scratches her pen over a notepad and bustles to the stack of oversized mugs.

"Perfect. Now we can share," I say.

Lucy nods her agreement. "My Sister's Soda Shop, huh?" she says, turning another slow circle.

"Just a soda shop, run by a couple of sisters who can't stand each other." Sherry, Lydie's older sister and partner, comes out from the back office, accenting my statement.

"I thought we weren't allowing men at the bar," she snaps at Lydie.

More than half the counter customers are male, and though I know nothing will come of it, I shrink a little when Sherry's gaze lands on me.

"You decided that, Sher. Not me. If someone likes my drinks, they're welcome here."

"I'm just trying to simplify things," Sherry says coolly, and turns, as if trying to hide her words. "Men are bound to cause problems."

"Yet another place we don't see eye to eye," Lydie says, wiping a tiny pitcher clean and carrying it and two mugs to the counter. "Customers are never a problem."

Lydie starts to pour our drinks, and Sherry huffs and glares at the entire counter of people. "Fine. They can stay if they've got someone to vouch for them."

Slight panic agitates over several men before Sherry disappears into the back room.

"I thought she was going to make me fight for you," Lucy whispers, squeezing my forearm.

I snicker and lean an elbow on the counter. "Would you have done it?"

"No way. Did you see her? She's scary. Not worth it."

"Oh, but you haven't tried the drinks yet."

Lucy's lips press together in an amused grin. "Oh no, I wasn't going to give up the drinks. I was going to let her send you off. Then I could drink both." Her wide-eyed shrug is adorable.

Lydie approaches us, laughing. "I like you," Lydie says, keeping an eye on the drinks she's just crafted. "Don't worry about Sher. Half the time, she conveniently forgets that we run on happy customers. And the other half, I tell myself she's just being extra cranky as a novelty to our guests."

Lydie flashes a smile and slides two bowl-sized mugs across the counter. One is filled with golden brown liquid decorated in a cream gingerbread man, and the other is pale green with a perfectly swirled sprig of foamy mistletoe on top.

"These are gorgeous!" Lucy says, turning her mug gently. "I didn't know you could make shapes like this out of frothy cream."

Lydie puffs a laugh and wipes her hands. "They're not that great."

"Uh, yeah, they are." Lucy hovers a finger over the surface like she wants to touch it but knows better.

"Well, thank you. Stay as long as you like. You can even keep him around, if he's nice." She smirks at us and pulls out two canisters. "Now that you've seen my masterpieces, who wants whipped cream?"

"Me," I almost shout, but Lydie knows me well and is already adding a mountain of thick cream to my hot chocolate, with a sprinkle of miniature green beads.

Lucy's hands cover her gingerbread man protectively. "This Sticky Boy is perfect as he is."

"Sticky *Gingerbread* Boy," Lydie laughs, and I pull my drink closer as she moves on to the next customer.

Lucy's mug is already to her lips, eyes closed in obvious enjoyment. I take my first drink as well, savoring the perfect blend of mint and white chocolate.

When Lucy releases her cup with a sigh, I slide my mug into her hands and trade for the caramel brown colored drink. "Switch."

"I don't think I need to switch." Lucy's eyes follow her mug to where I place it in front of me.

"Trust me. You're going to like that one."

She takes a slow sip, followed by a moan and a much longer sip.

"That's what I thought." I turn to her drink, sampling Lydie's new creation. The Sticky Gingerbread Boy is reminiscent of an extra spicy gingerbread cake with caramel frosting, sprinkled with more cinnamon. It's good.

I set the cup down, only to lift it for another drink. It's really good.

"Okay, buddy." Lucy's voice calls me back to the counter, her hand already on the mug I'm holding. "We're sharing, remember."

"Oh, but Lucy—" I don't finish my thought, unsure if I'm pleading or stalling. We lock eyes, and I keep hold of the large cup. "Have a little compassion. Thanks to you, I just found my new favorite holiday drink."

"Unfortunately for you, I ordered it." She scrunches her cute little nose to match her mocking tone. "But you can always order another one. I'll keep both of these."

"Hey," I say, reclaiming the cup of whipped cream. She seems to have the same trouble letting go of my cup as I had with hers. "I'm sorry, but you picked." I earn a groan of disappointment.

"How do you choose?" she finally asks.

I set my drink back on the counter. "You don't," I say honestly. "You just come back . . . a lot."

"Lydie?" Lucy calls to the chef like she's a local.

I look over her impressed. "You really want more hot chocolate, don't you?"

Lucy chuckles. "Yes, but this is more important." She takes another drink, waiting for the smiling barista to return. "Lydie, would you be willing to keep a stack of business cards and fliers here for the Sugar Creek Inn? And recommend them to guests who may still be looking for a place to stay? The Nyströms are expanding their marketing and I know they'd be happy to include your place in their welcome gift bags. They go out to every guest."

"We don't have a welcome gift bag," I whisper.

"Shh," she hisses, "you do now."

Lydie tips her head, looking at me curiously. "Are you guys still running the inn? I haven't heard anything about it for years."

"Of course we are." The question takes me completely by surprise, and I have to work to cover the dumbfounded tone that slaughters what should be a pleasant response.

"That's great," Lydie nods, "we'd love to. I thought maybe your folks had transitioned the place to personal use. Get me some fliers. We get tons of tourists through here, and we always want more." She glances toward the backroom and chuckles. "Well, *I* always want more."

By the time we finish our drinks, Lucy has committed Lydie and Sherry to not only keeping a stack of fliers but providing coupons for the Sugar Creek Inn guests.

Outside the soda shop, I grip her hand, keeping her from trekking into the snow. "You're amazing. I don't know if I'll be able to turn things around at the inn, but what you're doing gives me more hope than I've ever had on my own.

"That?" She looks over her shoulder toward the soda shop. "That was nothing. Honestly, that's the easy part. You shouldn't have any trouble networking here. People like you and your family—you guys are friendly. You've just got to learn to ask for help."

"Ha!" My laugh is layered in fear and insecurity. "That's the hard part."

She chuckles, and her smile is so genuine and irresistible, I lean forward, pressing her up against the brick building to cover her smile with a kiss. As our lips come together, I taste chai and caramel. The air around us is frozen, but her mouth is warm, and as I pull against their softness, heat rises till our connection breaks. I stay there, resting my nose next to hers. A breeze dances around us, tossing her blonde curls against my cheek.

"What prompted that?" Her whisper is breathy and sweet, and I steal one more pull of her lips.

"You." *How can she not know what she does to me?* "And everything you're doing. I don't know how anyone could let you go. You have amazing instinct and no fear. I can't think of anyone I'd rather have with me than you. Uh, you know . . . helping . . . me with . . . all of this . . . mess." I stumble over the words as I realize I've gotten way more personal than I intended.

It's the kissing.

I let go and step back, trying to smile like a normal human.

Kissing screws up my brain.

She's still looking at me, but her smile has turned a little sad. "Thanks. You're very sweet, but I'm sure there's something I could have or should have done. People aren't let go for nothing."

I wasn't talking about her job, but that's where her head is and I step back from my worries to try and help her. "Have you talked to anyone from the company? Gotten an explanation at all?" I want to fix her scarf or brush her hair back, but obviously, touching her turns me into an idiot, so I don't.

Lucy's head shakes gently as her gaze drops to the ground. "No one will talk to me but Shaunda. And she only knows gossip. Besides, what good will it do?"

"Maybe none, but it might give you the answers you need, or at least a little closure. This was so out of the blue. You deserve to be given a reason. And, if they don't want to give you real answers, they deserve a lawsuit."

She laughs softly, and when she looks up at me, her smile has brightened with only a touch of the sadness from before. Her hand slips into mine, and she pushes up on her toes to peck a kiss at the corner of my lips. A ripple of pleasure travels over my body from that single point.

"Thank you, Torin." She wraps her arms around my waist and lays her cheek against my chest. "I'm sure it doesn't feel like much, but thank you for believing in me and pushing me to do what needs to be done."

I no longer feel cold. Holding Lucy both turns the world upside down *and* sets it right again. Heading home after all this will end the night too quickly. I'm not ready for it. But we hold hands as we walk in the entry hall of the inn, and we're greeted by Alice, my mother, and a loss of privacy I suddenly miss desperately.

"Hi, Ma." I give her a hug, but her smile is all for Lucy.

"I hope you're coming tonight." Ma brightens as she speaks, excitement leaking into her words. "The play won't start until seven, but we'll want to get there at least an hour earlier to get good seats."

"The play?" Lucy looks at me like I have the answer.

I shrug, and Ma brushes me aside, walking with Lucy toward the living room. "*Ja*, everyone is going to see White Christmas, the town's Christmas play. It's our big goodbye event for the reunion, so we need to be there, and we're trying to coordinate colors to wear with the whole family. So, if you have anything in red, that would be perfect."

Just outside the living room, I put a hand up against the wall to stabilize myself while I watch the two of them talk. From the inclusion of Lucy as family to the word goodbye, I'm in an emotional grinder.

Lucy squeezes my mother's shoulders as they talk on the couch. Every cell in my body pulls me toward Lucy. Having her here, as a part of us, is right. Goodbye isn't part of the plan anymore. At least, I hope goodbye isn't part of the plan.

I have to say something. I have to keep her here. "What are the guys going to wear?"

Both women look at me like I've just said I'm starring in a fashion show, and I give myself a mental kick. That isn't what I was supposed to say, but they're the only words I can make come out. As much as I want to, it doesn't feel like the right moment to ask her to stay. What if she doesn't want to stay? What if I was just a distraction from her breakup? She told me she had rules, and I don't fit them.

I swallow and run a hand over the back of my head, smiling weakly at their confusion. "I, uh, don't know if I have anything in red."

"Sure, you do." My mother sends me a look that clearly asks, *"Are you drunk?",* then she stands, clasping Lucy's hand with a smile before she turns back to me. "But I'm not worried so much about the boys matching. Just wear something nice, like we usually do for going to the theater. I can't even get Erik to respond."

"Wait, seriously? You're just going to trust me with a major fashion choice? That seems risky. You could at least give me a few parameters?"

My mother shrugs. "Why don't you ask Lucy?"

"Me?" Lucy coughs and gives my mother a terrified look. Ma seems happy to have pawned the job off. Lucy clears her throat and looks back at me. "I don't know. You're a big boy. Pick your own clothes."

"Well, what's your favorite color then?" I ask.

Lucy's grin doesn't come with a blush this time. I miss it until she stops beside me and touches my arm. I forget to be disappointed.

"Lately . . ." She hesitates, looking directly into my eyes like she can see inside of me. "I've really been liking green."

Ma chuckles, and Lucy's blush appears, splashing red on her cheeks.

"Green and red together are very appropriate for the holiday." Ma giggles on her way back to the kitchen.

I furrow my brow. "What's so funny? I can do green."

"Nothing. Dinner is in an hour. We're leaving by six. I want good seats." The kitchen door shuts behind her.

"Is something wrong with green? Am I gonna match the seats or something?"

"You don't—" She smiles up at me, a touch of confusion in her eyes but it fades with her blush. "You don't know why green is suddenly my favorite color?"

I shake my head. We're alone in the room. I don't know where Alice is, my father isn't in his usual place at the table, and my mother has conveniently excused herself. And Lucy's smile is effectively holding me in place.

I want to come closer, but I can't seem to bring myself to move. My mind entwines with hers in a consensual grip. She could scrape out my heart, examine it, and replace it any way she wanted to. I wouldn't even notice a change as long as she stayed beside me.

"I better go change." Lucy laughs, lightly pressing a kiss to my lips and walks away, releasing her hold on me.

I inhale sharply, not sure if I stopped breathing, or if I just need to clear my head.

It's a few seconds before I'm able to follow, still confused as to what is so funny about green being her favorite color. I go up to my room and pull my shirt off to shower. Grabbing a towel, I pass the mirror and pause.

Green eyes stare back at me.

I've really been liking green lately.

A soft laugh escapes me.

She's been liking green.

My heart understands the implication of her statement before my head does, and I'm at the bedroom door with my hand on the doorknob before I realize I'm shirtless and need to shower.

Happiness settles around me as I head back to my bathroom. I'm positive Lucy will go into green overload tonight, since my eyes will likely never leave her face.

Chapter 15

Lucy

"I never said he was hot." A scrap of emerald catches my eye. Pulling the green skirt from the hanger, I hold it against my red lace top.

Shaunda gives an audible eye roll on the other end of the line. "But he is."

"Shut up." I try not to laugh, but it's there, and Shaunda knows it. I pinch my snowflake necklace like a security blanket. The red and green of my skirt and top go nicely together, and it's the color of Torin's eyes when they get intense. *I like it.* "I really like Torin. But they're brothers, and he lives in Vermont! I'm not supposed to fall for him."

"Ha! I knew it! Turn on the fire, my girl is maple tapping in Vermont."

"Stop it! I am not." She's ridiculous. She always has been, and it's part of why I love her. "That doesn't even mean anything." *I hope.*

"Can you just tell me I'm gonna see you in a week? Because you are coming home, aren't you?"

"Of course I am. I'm not uprooting my life for a guy." *Except—it's Torin.*

"Maybe you should. I'd miss you like crazy, of course, but don't you like it there? I mean, outside of the hot Scandinavian guys, which we know you like."

I scoff and try to remove the image of my favorite Scandinavian kissing me outside the soda shop on our way home, and at Santa's Workshop, and . . . as my brain tracks further back, I have to shut it down. That is not what she asked me.

"Thanks for that. I'm sweating and I still have to do my makeup." Shaunda laughs and I look over to the balcony. "As for Sugar Creek . . ." I tug the French doors open and let the icy air hit my skin, cooling the heat created by the memory of Torin's kisses. "I actually love it here."

One day, I could be standing here with Torin behind me and Alice playing in the yard. My gaze falls on the spot where I first saw Erik after arriving here.

Erik would always be here, too.

"This is never going to work, is it?" Guilt crashes through me as I realize what I've done. I've wound my way into Torin's life and sewn our hearts together. There's no way out without hurting someone. "They're brothers. I came here for Erik. That was the plan. I had rules. I'm not supposed to go falling for his brother."

I lay the green skirt on the bed, letting go of the brightly colored outfit. I can't choose it.

"Lucy, you know I say this with the best of intentions and all the love I can send you." She pauses for effect, letting the phone gather silence like empty wishes. "Screw the rules."

"I can't do that! They're brothers!" I bury my head under a pillow, only coming out to explain the vision of chaos running through my mind. "How could I do that to this family? Family dinners would be awful. It would never work."

"How do you know? At least give it a chance." Shaunda's voice gets soft and serious. "This is a love story, for goodness' sake. It's still playing out.

174

Don't decide what the ending is before you've made it there. Just move it along."

When I don't respond Shaunda sighs, "Tell me what you want."

"Umm." It's not a what, it's a who. "I want . . ." A bubble of fear holds his name down in my throat and my mouth hangs open without sound for several seconds.

"Oh my gosh! Do I need to help you? You want Torin. Say it all ready. Why not give this a chance? People fall in love in all kinds of ways—"

"I never said love." Brick by brick, I struggle to put my walls back up. "I just met the guy. I said, 'falling for'. I did not say love."

"You didn't have to." Shaunda's disbelieving tone shimmers with excitement I can't feel right now.

"That is so scary." I roll over, playing with the hem of the green skirt.

"It is scary. But it's also amazing. And fun. And exciting," Shaunda sighs into the phone.

"And what if I'm wrong? What if I'm too boring for him, too? Or one day, he wakes up and realizes I'm not the woman he wants in his or Alice's life?" I'm drowning as reality wells up around me and I can't breathe. "He knows what love is. What if I can't live up to it?"

"You're missing the point of your own rules. There is no list in the world that can keep you from getting your heart broken. All you can do is try your best to find someone that wants to help you protect it."

I already know Torin wants to protect my heart. And if I ever had to do the same for him, I would. I pick up my green skirt. "Why are you always right?"

"Because I'm your best friend and will always try and protect your heart. Everyone makes mistakes, and everyone makes choices. Don't regret yours."

Maybe it's because Shaunda's my best friend, but she's said exactly what I needed to hear. I slip my feet into the green skirt, zip it, and look in the mirror. It looks good. Really good.

I can't wait for Torin to see me in it.

"You deserve to be happy, Lucy. Remember that. Now, go make some sweet, Sugar Creek, maple syrup, romance, okay?"

"You're an incredibly bad influence. You know that, right?"

"And you're lucky to have me. Have fun tonight. Call me with the juicy details later."

I laugh. "Talk to you later."

It takes me a minute to regulate my breathing and fix my makeup after we hang up.

Getting it wrong sounds so scary. Shaunda's right, though. I get to choose. And hopefully, if it's right, he'll choose me too.

Somehow, I can only imagine Torin's green eyes looking back at me.

This was so not the plan.

Christmas lights glow in the dusky evening light as we pass the town square and head toward the community center. The wide steps and cream stone of the beautiful, old building set the stage like we're going to a grand party.

The community theater is performing White Christmas. We're later than we planned but still early enough to catch hints of melody spilling out the wide double doors. A clash of conflicting notes greeting us as the orchestra warms up and we climb the icy steps.

Holding Torin's arm, I climb the wide stairs with the whole Nyström family, minus Erik. While Torin's assistance is more for stability than grace, I've never felt more elegant.

"Careful, *sötnos*," Wally says, following Alice with his hands out on either side of her. Glittering snowflakes decorate the sheer layers of her red skirt. She seems to be doing her best to make them dance below her thick jacket.

"I'm a pretty snow globe." Alice does a twirl to make her skirt and its printed snowflakes float around her. Alice makes it up to the top without incident, though Wally's breathing heavily and has to stop and rest.

"Walfrid," Ingrid says, taking Alice's hand, "you're sweating. She's just a little thing."

The three of them go in ahead of us. Torin stays with me.

"You look beautiful," Torin says softly, walking beside me.

"Because you can tell under my giant coat?" I tease.

"You are always beautiful. Even in the coat." His reply feels entirely serious. "But I am looking forward to when you take it off." And now he's teasing.

I can feel my blush rise anyway, heating my skin. "Thank you, I think. It's not what I had planned, but the green skirt felt right. I think it's even better than my plan." The duplicity of my words is intentional. He holds the door, and my heart swells with gratitude that I get to choose him.

As we step inside, the sounds of the orchestra grow. Greenery and mistletoe hang everywhere, as if the decorator anticipated a lot of couples needing that holiday nudge.

A familiar voice squeals, and the click of high heeled shoes rushes toward me. The sound pulls my gaze, filling my head with anxious panic. All I have to do is follow the sound until—

It can't be. She wouldn't. I just talked to her about this.

"Baby girl!" Her blonde hair is sprayed in thick loops of honey gold curls, dancing around her head as she hurries across the brightly-lit lobby. My brain fights to reason away the appearance of my mother in Sugar Creek.

"No," I gasp. "What is she doing here?"

"Are you okay?" Torin's whisper cuts into my awareness. "Ma told us to keep it a secret. I hope it's all right."

"You should have told me," I whisper back, just before my mother crashes into my arms.

"Oh, baby, I've missed you so much!"

Ingrid did this? How? I want to ask, but I can't.

Ingrid and Wally are standing at the theater doors, watching us, hands clasped in restrained joy.

"Mrs. Sweet. It's nice to finally meet you." Torin squeezes my shoulder, prompting me into a breathy, fake laugh.

It's the only sound I can manage that is nicer than screaming and running back to the car.

My mother releases me and wraps Torin in a hug. "This must be Erik. I've waited so long to meet the man that makes my Lucy so happy." She scrunches her nose at me, and I jump away from Torin. The realization of what she's seeing slams into me.

"Oh no, Mom. This is Torin. I mentioned him to you the other day."

"Oh," she steps back looking at him. "Torin? You're very good looking."

Torin clears his throat and raises an eyebrow at me. I smile uncomfortably. "Torin is, uh, Erik's brother." I pause, searching for more description. "We're just friends."

The words are out, and Torin pulls back. Hurt lances through his eyes before his expression smooths of any emotion.

"Oh, look, Alice is climbing on that priceless statue." He points past us and walks off. "I should go, *friend*." He doesn't look at me. His emphasis of the word friend slipping its fingers in an iron grip around my heart.

"Torin, wait." I reach for his hand without catching him as he passes my mother.

I regret everything.

My mother doesn't even notice. "Well, where's Mr. Perfect? I want to talk to him."

"He'll be here soon. Why don't we get our seats? Did anyone . . . come with you?" I remove my coat. On my way out of the lobby, I spot Erik near the concessions.

Mr. Perfect doesn't even realize I've arrived.

"No! I'm just here to see you, baby," my mother croons. "I'm just so thrilled you're with this nice young man. You seem so happy. And you know that's all I ever wanted."

"That's all you ever wanted?" The sarcasm stays in my head. I don't fight with my mother. "Right." I make her happy until I can escape. That's how things work. "Well, Erik and I, um—he's not—"

I try to tell her.

I really do, but saying we broke up would make her so smug. She'd be all over my poor, broken heart, setting me up with anything that walked, and Torin—Torin would become fodder for her insanity.

I can't do it.

"He's not here yet. Let me introduce you to Erik's parents, Ingrid and Wally."

"Oh, I met them just a minute ago," she says as I put my hand at her back and usher her into the theater.

"Come on, Mom." I drag her down the aisle to where Wally and Ingrid are visiting with local friends. "Ingrid, it was so nice of you to invite my mother out."

"Oh, sweetie, it wasn't my idea, though I wish it were."

"Sure it was!" my mom says. "She called me and masterminded it."

"But Erik suggested it." Ingrid makes a face like she thinks it was so sweet. Has she not seen everything between Torin and I? Doesn't she know? "He didn't want you to miss Christmas with your mother."

"Erik suggested she come?"

"Oh." My mother presses her hand against her heart and sinks back with a slight bend of her knees. "That is just so precious! He really is Mr. Perfect. Where is he?"

My smile is full of clenched teeth and frustration as I turn to find him. I love my mother, but Erik knows how much she affects me. And to bring her here without warning. . . he knew exactly what this would do to me.

Every piece of my plan is falling apart.

"Why don't you find us a seat, Mom. Wally, Alice—" I smile down at the little girl. "I'll be right back. I have to go find Mr. Per—Erik."

"Oh, but honey—"

I don't wait to hear what my mother wants to tell me. Turning on my heel, I stride up the aisle, passing Torin on my way to the lobby. Erik is still there, on his phone.

Come on, Lucy. He's doing this on purpose. And he's not going to stop, unless you make him.

My mini pep talk fills me with crackling energy, and I march across the room and corner him.

"Erik." I stand there in the outfit chosen specifically for Torin, my hair curled and pinned, with silver heels, red lips, and fire burning in my veins. Instead of sitting with Torin and finally getting to choose what and who I want, I'm standing here, waiting for Erik to give me the time of day.

"Erik!" I hiss, with as much hushed urgency as I can muster.

I've waited for this man for five years. How did I not see it? Was I so used to being ignored that I didn't even notice he was already gone?

"What?" He finally looks up, casually stretching his neck like he could care less that I'm standing there.

This is so Erik.

"I need you to pretend to be my boyfriend tonight." My smile is tight, but I keep my tone pleasant, folding my arms across my chest.

Flexing his shoulders, Erik leans forward, glaring at me. "There's not a chance in hell I'm gonna stand next to you and pretend things are the same as they were. Not after you followed me out here. You weaseled your way into my family's house. You begged me to take you back. You made me watch while you and my brother went front-and-center romance."

This is not my fault. But it's also not the debate I need to have right now.

"Remember the last project you signed for Walter & Walters? The international Glow Pen campaign."

Erik doesn't respond. We both know he does. It's the campaign that got him promoted.

"I'm prepared to forward Cormac Walters a particularly interesting email you sent me several months ago, where you begged me to help you get them back after they dropped you. And the subsequent emails, documenting my design ideas and how I saved the client." I say it all with a plastic smile on my face.

Erik narrows his eyes and slides his phone in his pocket. "You little witch."

"I have others, too." I glance over my shoulder as the lobby begins to fill.

"That's not possible." Erik grabs my arm and I jerk away "It only happened the one time."

"The baby food? There was the ground beef. Oh! And last summer, you lost—straight up lost—the contracts for Health-Bee." One of Walter & Walters' biggest clients. My bright smile doesn't fit, but it's exactly the expression I need. "I still don't know how you managed that. So, you are going to put on your perfect little smile, the one you've been wearing for five years to placate me, and you're going to walk in there and play nice for my mother."

I turn around and stop.

Torin stands in the doorway to the theater, watching us as people stream around him.

"Fine," Erik says, grabbing my arm and jerking me to stand next to him. "Come on, *darling*."

We walk together to the theater doors, and I pull my arm free as we reach Torin. "I'll be right there."

Erik looks from his brother to me. "Be careful. You wouldn't want mommy to see what's really going on here."

His bitter tone comes through a perfect smile with only a single hitch of an eyebrow before he walks away. Torin steps to the side with me.

"I'm sorry. I asked Erik to pretend we're still in a relationship for tonight. At least, until I can figure out how to tell my mother."

"You're not serious . . . are you?"

I nod, and the pain in his eyes nearly guts me. "Torin—"

"I'll go along with it because it's what you want, but don't try and pretend it's okay. You should tell her. What we have means something to me. I thought it meant something to you, too."

"It does, and I'm not pretending it's okay. I will tell her. I just need to do it in a safer space. I don't want you, or Alice, or your parents to get caught in the crossfire."

"You think she'll be mad if it's me? Is Erik so much better?"

"No. It's not that at all. She'll probably be excited. Is it weird to say it's not you, or her, it's me? I just . . . my mother requires a special hand. I'll fix it. I promise." I step close and rest my palm along his jaw. "Just, please, trust me. I can't tell her now."

I push up to kiss him gently, but he presses into the simple movement. Cupping my jaw in his hands, he moves his lips over me. Pressure and passion flutter wildly through me as my sense of awareness vanishes in the heady scent of him. His hand sliding behind my neck he deepens the kiss, only letting me go at the sound of my unbidden moan.

"Okay." He strokes the line of my jaw. "I don't want you to have any questions about how I feel."

The feel of his lips clings to my skin.

I jostle my head slightly to confirm I have no questions.

Torin presses his lips to my forehead and leans down, his lips by my ear. "You'll probably want to go check your lipstick then. I might have smeared it."

He straightens and moves past me, as if he didn't just tangle my hormones into a mess of overheating Christmas lights before walking away.

I don't have time to feel any of it. The lights dim giving a five minute warning, and I rush to the bathroom to clean up the edges of my red lips.

When I make it to our seats, my mother has Erik seated next to her at the end of the row, and she's questioning him like she has flashcards tucked away somewhere. Surprisingly, he plays along.

Alice and Torin are on the other side of my mother, next to Wally and Ingrid, near the middle of the row. "Oh, Luce, this is your seat," Erik says, scooting one over so he's on the end. "I thought you'd want to sit by your mom."

Good, that puts at least three seats between him and Torin.

"It's no wonder you never introduced me to your mother before. She's like a forty-year-old teenager."

"She's fifty."

Erik coughs and my short breath punctuates my tight smile. "Thanks for saving me a seat," I say to my mother. "I'm still just so surprised you're here."

The overture begins and my forced calm relaxes as the story of White Christmas plays out on stage. Onstage, the two main characters sing and dance in military uniforms and Santa coats. I glance past my mother at Torin, but he doesn't look back. Alice has climbed up on his lap, and he's whispering to her. Then, suddenly, he turns toward me and my heart clenches.

I look away and Erik grabs my hand. With my eyes between Erik, Torin, and my mother, I miss most of the first scenes. Vague glimpses of men onstage meeting two women is all I can process. Miraculously, these men know exactly who they're interested in, and don't change their minds.

About halfway through the first act, Erik drapes a hand over the armrest and runs a finger over my thumb. I used to love Erik's discreet touches. I pull my hand away and his finger drops to my thigh.

My skin crawls at the feel of him.

He's just playing the part of a boyfriend. A real couple would be fine with this. I shrink in my seat. Trying not to feel Erik's touch, I can't make myself small enough to disappear.

"Excuse me—sorry. Just a moment." Torin's voice pulls me out of my head as he slides past my mother and myself, to Erik and the aisle. With a shove he manages to push Erik's shoulder back, flat against the seat as he passes. It removes Erik's hand from my thigh. Erik chuckles softly.

Erik's smile softens to a smirk, and he leans over as Torin disappears up the aisle. "That was fun."

"You don't have to touch me," I mutter as softly as I can. I shoot a glance at my mother. I don't think she's listening, but only one seat away, how can she not?

Torin returns with a drink and snacks, managing to knock Erik's knees and even bump Erik's head with the side of his elbow on his way past, he leaves the rest of us unscathed.

Erik's enjoyment of Torin's annoyance is disturbing.

The first half of the show is full of trickery and manipulation. It feels surprisingly true to life at the moment. It doesn't take long before Erik throws a hand over my shoulders and begins stroking my knee.

"Cut it out," I whisper, discreetly shoving his hand away.

Erik leans against my ear. "But it's so much fun to irritate him."

"Sorry, I need to—just a second."

I glance at Torin. He's already up and heading back the way he just came, still holding his drink.

As he passes Erik, he tips the drink right in Erik's lap. Both men are up and in the aisle in seconds. Whispers flow away from us in a ripple across the crowd. With an excuse to my mother, I join them both, taking the two angry men by the elbow.

"Let's go, boys." I intentionally downgrade their maturity.

In the lobby, Erik jerks away and smacks Torin's shoulder. "I was just doing what she asked." He brushes a hand down his soaked pants and storms off to the bathroom.

Torin turns on me. "Did you ask him to do that?"

"No!" I pace past him. "He was trying to bother you."

Torin glares in the direction Erik left. "Well, it worked. I just spent an hour watching him be close to you and your mother, knowing I can't tell her how amazing I think her daughter is. Because you're too embarrassed, or scared, to tell her you care about someone new."

The lobby is mostly empty, but a few personnel hover at the edges by the concession stand and ticket counter. I step close to Torin, dropping my voice low. "I'm just trying to get through the night, Torin." I exhale sharply, nostrils flaring. "I'm sorry if I'm handling this wrong, but I'm doing the best I can."

"No. The best would be honesty. You need to tell your mother the truth. She's a grown woman, she can handle it. And so are you." He's standing close without touching me. He seems to be actively holding back.

"It's not that easy." I turn away, pacing to the door and back. "She's my mother. She's supposed to take care of me, but I've spent my entire life making sure she's okay. She's the only constant in my life, and all she does is fall apart. I can't be the one responsible for breaking her. I need her to be okay. I need her to see there's a way out of this cycle she's created. If that means sucking up to Erik for one night, so be it."

Erik appears at the end of the hall, and the pressure of having to perform settles on my chest, pushing the air from my lungs.

Torin's voice pulls me back. "I understand what you're saying, but it doesn't hurt less. I hope that soon you can be proud to be with someone like me."

I don't want someone like him. I want him.

"I need some air." I push through the front doors without a response. I don't know if I want Torin to follow me or not. Wrapping my arms around my waist, I walk in aimless circles over the landing, rubbing my hands over my arms and pinching my snowflake pendant.

I wish things would just go right. I wish I knew what to do.

The doors push open behind me, and I glance back.

"Here, I thought you might need this."

Torin's there with my coat. He brings it over, wrapping my shoulders in the thick fabric.

"Thank you." I let out a breath.

"Are you coming back inside?" He asks.

"In just a minute." I twist the metal snowflake at my neck. "I have some things to think about." With a tiny snap, the snowflake necklace pops free of the chain and my fingers slip. "No!" I try to catch the charm as it hits the steps, and bounces away. "It's from my mother!"

My foot hits an icy step and pain spiders through my world before the world goes black.

Chapter 16

Torin

Bright lights reflect off hospital-white walls, forcing my eyes to the floor, the slate blue vinyl chairs, the random paintings on the wall—anything but the reflective, white emptiness.

Nothing sticks.

I can't focus. I can't see a thing, except for Lucy tumbling down the steps of the community center.

Automatic doors at the front of the room slide open, and my dad comes inside, sitting beside me on the plastic chair. "How are you doing?"

I grip the muscles at the back of my neck in a useless massage. He always seems to know when things get hardest for me. "I think Lucy's fine. Deronda went home. Lucy woke up on the way here, and sent her off." I shake my head, "I don't know what happened. And I'm not family, so they won't let me back."

My dad nods, probably hearing more than I've said. "That's good to know. But it's not what I asked."

I know what he means, but I've been avoiding reality very well up until now.

"I hate hospitals."

Saying it out loud doesn't help. The hum of anxious voices and staccato footsteps in echo-chamber hallways is the soundtrack of death.

Dad shifts back in his chair. "Not everyone comes here to die." *How exactly did he learn to read minds?* "Most come to be saved."

"Not in my experience." The ominous bird painting watches me. I stand, anxious to be moving, and walk over to the desk. "Lucy Sweet? Do you know her status?"

The nurse is familiar with my question by now and does a quick tap to check her information. "I'm sorry. It's a busy night, Mr. Nyström. She's still waiting."

My dad comes up beside me, hands in his pockets. "Lucy's a special girl, isn't she?"

I don't know what I can say without him figuring out everything I'm *not* saying. Based on my behavior tonight, I can't risk it. So I keep quiet and nod.

He reads me anyway and turns to the nurse. "Excuse me, Miss? My son's fiancé has been here for a while. Can you tell me when he'll be able to see her?"

The woman at the counter looks at me with wide eyes. "I'm so sorry. I didn't realize. You said there was no relation, and I didn't even think to ask. I can let you go back with her now, if you'd like."

I might have the worst brother in the world, but I have the best dad. He wraps an arm around me in a hug. "Call me when she's all fixed up."

"Thanks, Dad."

He pats my shoulder and turns back to the door.

"If you'll follow me," the nurse says. "Ms. Sweet is around the corner." Her staccato footsteps lead me down the hall, our feet tapping out the intro to a familiar hospital death march.

I hum to block the hospital's unique funeral dirge out of my mind. What starts as random melodies morphs into Christmas carols.

"Torin?" Lucy's voice comes from inside a curtained cubicle. A smear of red stains the paper bedding behind her, and my stomach contracts. Strands of worry thread sharply through my body when I think of her pain.

The pins that held the little twists of hair back over her ears are gone, leaving haphazard strands of tangled blonde ringlets. Sitting on the edge of the bed, I push the stray hairs back, touching the sides of her face lightly. There's something so reassuring about having my hands on her skin, knowing she's there, real, safe, alive.

She looks up at me curiously. A polarizing charge buzzes in the air between us. Being this close sets my body on high alert.

"Hey, beautiful." I kiss her forehead to sell the fiancé story, hoping she doesn't try to run away again.

When the nurse leaves, I cross to the door and pull open Lucy's chart. I've gotten pretty good at reading these.

"What are you doing here?" she asks from her place on the exam bed.

I glance up and back at her chart. Her injury is minor in the scheme of things. A scrape and a single stitch in her hairline. But she was out there because of me. I put the chart down and run a hand over my jaw.

This is my fault.

"Torin? Where were you? Is anyone else here?"

"No, I'm by myself. But if you want someone else with you, I can go."

Her nose scrunches lightly, and she quickly reaches out, putting her hand on my arm. "No."

I don't know if I've ever been stopped so quickly by one word. "You don't want me to go?"

She shakes her head. "And I don't want anyone else."

I've stopped breathing. *Does that mean what I want it to mean?*

She doesn't elaborate. Taking her hand into my own, I sit beside her, running my fingertips over her skin, playing with her hand and wrist until she relaxes. "I'm so sorry for all of this. For not warning you about your mother coming, for not understanding enough what your feelings are. For not catching you the one time you really needed me."

"Torin, I—"

Regret is heavy in her tone, and I know immediately I can't handle it if I hurt her. I can't do it. "I wanted tonight to go very differently. I could have done better—"

"Hello there, Ms. Sweet." A doctor comes through the curtained barrier in a wave of oblivion. "How are you feeling?"

I swallow my plea as Lucy waits and turns to the doctor. "I think I'm fine. I feel better now than I did before the fall. I'm just tired and –" She looks at me as if she wants to say more, then turns back to the doctor. "And sore."

The doctor probes along the side of Lucy's head until she winces. "Can you turn this way for me?" He shines a flashlight in her eyes, checks her head again. "Well, since you've got someone with you, I can sign off on dismissal." The doctor turns toward me. "It's a good idea to keep her awake for the next few hours. Walking, talking, playing games, anything she's comfortable with, as long as she's alert." He signs a piece of paper and tucks her folder under his arm before he leaves.

"Wait, are we done?" Lucy asks as the curtain swings shut behind the doctor.

I lift my eyebrows and quirk a half smile. Do I continue my begging, or does she want to move on? "That's it, I guess. You ready to get out of here? Everyone's at home waiting for you."

Helping Lucy up, she latches onto my arm. "Everyone who? Is my mother there?"

"I think so. Do you want me to call her?"

"No!" Her fingers clench around my arm. "I mean, that's all right. I think she and I do better with a little space."

I stifle my laugh, and Lucy sighs. "Laugh all you want. I have mommy issues." She points to her coat on the chair in the corner. "Would you get my things?"

"Sure." I'm so grateful we're laughing again. I shoot my parents a quick text and pick up her coat, revealing her metallic shoes from earlier. The image of her long legs in these spiked heels hits me with physical memory. I hold them out to her. "Do you want these? Or should I throw them out? I'm not sure I can condone the possession of dangerous weapons."

"Don't you dare. I bought those my first year at college."

"And they haven't killed you yet?"

"Tonight was their first attempt." She takes the shoes, slipping them on before I help her stand.

"Let's get you home. We don't need shoes there. You'll be safe."

Stopping us at the curtain, she grips my arm tighter. "Actually, can we walk the halls for a minute? I know I said I was fine . . . but I just want to make sure before I leave."

I don't feel any weakness in her stride, and I understand. "Your mother?"

She looks up at me in surprise, then nods. "I need a little time to adjust to the idea of her being around."

I look down the long, white hallway. "Then we'll walk the halls. I'll take you home when you're ready."

The emergency room is attached to a larger hospital. We walk slowly, following the signs toward the main lobby. I hum absently as we go, until Lucy's giggle interrupts me.

"Chestnuts roasting on an open fire, huh?" Laughter sparkles in her eyes.

"Was I humming that?" I really didn't know. "I guess the Christmas Song is on my mind. Sorry, I can stop. . . probably."

"No, you don't need to. You're pretty good. Just unexpected." Her amusement is contagious. "Why are you singing?"

"I don't love hospitals." I try to explain without getting too depressing. "Music drowns out the sounds."

"So you sing Christmas carols?"

"It's Christmastime. That's what's in my head right now." Without the music, my mind drifts to other days of walking the halls. Breathing machines. Squeaky IV pole wheels. Oxygen tanks. Precious, stolen moments. It's quiet again. Footsteps and thoughts echo through the hallway.

"It's beginning to look a lot like Christmas . . ." Lucy's jaunty carol rings beautifully through the hall.

The melody jolts my mind from the padded cell it was crashing around in. She's several lines in before I begin to hum a coordinating harmony, squeezing her hand when she gets to the end. "I'm impressed you know all the words."

Her body shakes and my vision snaps to her silent laughter. "I don't," she says. "I make them up as needed."

We're holding hands, now, instead of her hanging on my arm.

"What's your favorite?"

I hesitate, then chuckle, "I don't remember the words."

Her smile spreads from cheek to cheek. "Perfect. Then you won't know when I mess them up."

Humming a line from a carol my mother used to sing, Lucy squeezes my hand. Starting over, with the words this time, she sings, "City sidewalks, busy sidewalks, dressed in holiday flare. In the air . . ."

"That's it." I close my eyes as she builds to the chorus: "Silver bells, silver bells." I sing softly along with her, not wanting to disturb the silent corridors. Lucy's clear voice is angelic. I never want her to stop singing.

Someone claps as we finish and Lucy blushes. Her fingers move to lace through mine, stepping closer as if she can hide from the praise. Stopping under a large, chandelier-style art display, she tucks herself into my side.

I watch her embarrassment in wonder. "You know, applause means you did a good job."

"It just means I was noticed. People are nice."

"Okay, let me tell you then. You sound like an angel."

She bumps my shoulder, looking up into the suspended glass and plastic shapes. I bump her back.

"Thank you."

"What for?"

"For singing." I let out a breath, hoping she'll understand. "I have too many memories in places like this that hurt. This is going to be the first good hospital memory in a long time. It's a nice change."

Footsteps alert us to a young girl's approach. I recognize her.

"You sing really well," the girl says.

"Joy?" Her name pops out without a second thought.

She looks up at me curiously. "How do you know my name?"

"I, umm, is that your name?" I glance at Lucy but her single furrowed brow is of no help. "You just looked like a Joy. It came to me, like magic."

It's work to keep my voice from going into Santa mode, and Lucy's quiet chuckle tells me she notices.

Joy's face lights up, her eyes wide. "*Christmas* magic?"

Oops. I glance over to where her dad stands against the wall, but before I can reply, Lucy kneels to Joy's height. "Do you like to sing, Joy?"

Joy nods emphatically. "My mommy likes it, too."

"That's great," I blurt. "I hope you get to sing lots of songs this Christmas."

Lucy tilts her head at me, a silent question marking her features. She doesn't know about Joy's mom, or the letters, or her wishes for a Christmas miracle. She doesn't remember her at all.

"Will you sing a song for my mommy?"

Lucy looks at Joy and gives her a smile. "Sure." The lobby is empty except for us and her dad. "Is she here?"

"She's upstairs. She's sick. I really want her to get better."

"Oh." Lucy locks eyes with me. "I don't know if we're allowed to do that."

"It's okay. Mommy's heart is sick but she's not contagionous. Umm, I mean, she won't give her sick to anyone else. My daddy's over there. He said it was okay." When Joy points, the man smiles and comes forward.

As soon as Lucy sees him, she blanches.

"Hi, I'm Charles—" He looks between us again and shakes his head. "I know you, don't I? Oh, I—oh." Charles nods and sucks in a deep breath as he recognizes not me, but Lucy. "You're that elf?"

I get the feeling there aren't very many people she's stared in the face and tried to intimidate. This man is undeniably one of them.

It's okay. I'm right here with you. Lucy's whispered reassurances repeat in my mind as she squeezes my hand and the elevator dings.

The doors open on the fourth floor and a rush of memories hits me as we step into the sterile hallway. *It's not the same*, I remind myself. Corrine had an autoimmune disease and died after a massive battle that started as the common cold. *It's not the same.*

The sterile scent of the Cardiac unit carries a touch of plastic. The sound of nurses and patients making quiet life-or-death decisions in lobby corners is familiar. But it's also fading, and I can't tell which fact bothers me more.

After checking in at the nurse's station with Joy and her dad, Charles leads the way down the hall to room 414. Inside, his wife is propped up on the bed. The whir of heart monitors and machines spins my brain and skyrockets my heartrate.

Lucy starts singing.

I check back into reality, joining her.

I add harmony to the chorus of Silent Night, and both Joy and her mother, Dora, light up. We sing through two more carols, and by the time we finish, Joy is the only one not crying.

And then it's over.

We wish Dora a merry Christmas before Charles walks us out. He leans against the wall once the door is shut.

"Some days, I can't breathe in there," he says. "Some days, I can't breathe unless I'm in there."

I laugh softly, brittle understanding rattles my heart.

"I'm so sorry about the other day," Lucy jumps in. "You've got so much going on in your life, and I was just having a really bad day—week. A really bad week." I run my thumb up and down over her spine, hoping she'll relax. "I lost my job, but I wasn't dealing with anything like—"

"It's not a competition." Charles's soft voice doesn't hold any judgment. "If I lost my job, I don't know what I'd do."

"The insurance. I remember feeling the pressure to keep my job, for the insurance." It pops out as I recall harboring the same worries.

Calling my office daily to catch missed due dates and worrying about what would happen if they decided to get someone without so much baggage. . .

"Yeah. My wife is dying, and I'm worried about missing emails and getting into the office."

I can feel the weight of his burden, and I let out a breath, heavy with understanding. "I've told myself a lot of things since my wife passed, but the worst is how I should have spent those last days with her."

"But—" He stands straighter, looking between me and Lucy. "I thought—"

I shake my head. "My wife passed away about two years ago. She used to say, 'Hope isn't a monster. It's just hope. It shows us possibilities.' I never believed her until I met your daughter."

"Joy? She's got too much hope."

"I would have said the same thing. And —I know how you feel right now. What it's like to want your wife back, and know it's never gonna happen. Hope feels like a monster, taunting you. You start wishing for moments or hours of frozen time. One more day, and one more beyond that, and one more."

Charles nods but doesn't respond. He just stares at the ground, like his ragged breaths are the only thing holding his life or his mind together.

We wish him one more merry Christmas, and then leave. Lucy follows me until we round the corner to the elevator. She hits a button, and the doors open, letting us in.

Waiting until the doors close, she sets her hand on my arm and looks up into my face. "I didn't mean to put you through that."

My body trembles under the pressure of the memories. I thought that conversation was for him, but as I try to get it together, I can feel Corrine here, holding me. I wrap my arms around Lucy and fight to stay whole.

"Losing Corrine changed everything," I say weakly. "It's all going to change for him too."

"They'll make it," she says.

"You don't know that."

It's several seconds of quiet before I realize she might not mean Charles and Dora. She means Charles and Joy.

They'll make it.

I take a deep breath. They will.

"There are things in life that we can't control, but that doesn't make us helpless," I whisper.

Lucy tilts to look up at me. I can't tell if she recognizes her own words, but I've been carrying them since she first got here. She nods and leans her head against my shoulder.

"There are always choices. It's his turn to make them."

A late-night snow glows through the twinkling Christmas lights as we pull up in front of the Sugar Creek Inn. I follow Lucy onto the front walkway, and she turns a slow circle on the powder-dusted ground, her face to the sky. If she was younger, it would remind me of Alice.

"Be careful," I say. My emotional state has numbed since the hospital. I can still feel Lucy in my arms, comforting me, and I don't want her to get hurt again. My hands hover alongside her like an overprotective lover.

Maybe I am one.

She laughs and spins faster.

"Lucy," I groan.

Her eyes are closed, and she bumps into my arms. With a slight sway, her spin ends facing me. The giddy rush has added a glow to her cheeks, and the moonlight brightens her smile.

"Be careful," I repeat gently. "I don't want to have to lie to more hospital attendants so I can follow you into the emergency room again."

"That's right, you were my fiancé tonight." She winks at me and leans back, looking up into the snowfall. I hold her waist, and she leans further.

"What are you doing?" Amusement colors my voice, and Lucy stands up, her hands planted side by side against my chest.

"Enjoying the snow. I'm catching angel kisses."

"Not likely," I say, but I'm smiling. "According to Corrine, you have to be flying to be kissed by an angel."

She chuckles softly. "Well, I'm trying."

"Here." I take her hand, in a formal dance position and sway. She's not flying yet, but soon. "Let me help you with that. Just like a traditional kiss, angel kisses require two people." Spinning her in close, our faces are inches apart when we stop. Nearly lip to lip, she's so close her breath warms my skin. I start the sway again and my nose brushes her cheek. "But, unlike a traditional kiss, your lips never touch."

"That's too bad," Lucy teases.

"I know." I let my lips brush her ear as I speak.

Lucy shivers, and I spin her on the slick sidewalk, keeping her upright by willpower alone. She stumbles back into my arms and grins.

"But if our lips never touch, how do I know if I've been kissed?"

"If you can't tell you've been kissed, then I'm not doing it right."

She smacks my arm playfully. "I meant angel kisses."

I shrug and make myself let her go. "They're just snowflakes on your eyelashes. A silly little tradition."

"I've never heard of them before you and Alice. Where did they come from?" she asks. "Is this another of your mother's traditions?"

I hesitate, not sure I want to explain. Watching Lucy's smile, part of me would rather just stay in this moment with her. When I don't answer, her smile dims, and she pulls back.

Denying her escape, I slide my arms around her waist. "Angel kisses are Corrine's tradition."

She looks up when I speak, meeting my eye. "That doesn't sound silly."

I sway with her in the pale light, memories of Corrine overwhelming me, shutting me down again. I don't know how to handle holding Lucy while remembering tender moments with my wife.

"You don't have to talk about it," Lucy says, stepping away.

I loosen my grip, letting her go, but as she slips away, it's like she's pulling threads of my heart with her. I don't want her to leave. Before she's out of my hands, I start dumping words.

"Corrine always loved winter, and Alice was barely two when she passed away. Angel kisses are how Corrine told me she'd send her love. In the snowflakes." I hesitate, not sure if I should keep going or if I can, but memories have begun to spill like syrup, sticky and messy, into the space between us. "That's another piece of why I came home. In the winter, it snows here almost every day. Alice will always know how much her mother loves her."

"And you." Lucy bites her lip. "You will always have that reminder, too. That Corrine loves you."

I nod, not sure how to soften it, because it's true.

Having Lucy here seems to color the memories with happy nostalgia and it's not so hard to keep talking anymore. "I was having a rough day after Corrine died. It was snowing, and honestly, I could have stood out there for hours, but Alice was cold. And, well, you try explaining to a two-year-old why Daddy wants to stay out in the snow after they're done playing. So, I told her that Mommy was sending angel kisses, and that angel kisses could make sad things go away, and we'd get to try again. But we had to catch them first."

Lucy smiles a sad smile and reaches up, smoothing my jacket collar. "That's really sweet. You've done a wonderful job giving Alice ways to remember and love her mother."

She pulls back, as if that's her sign to go.

"Don't leave."

"Torin," she sighs.

I pull her close, she leans in, and our lips meet. The snow falls gently around us. It's been a long time since I've longed for someone besides Corrine in my arms, and as she presses her body against me, our lips eagerly seeking each other, I long for this woman.

I pull her closer to deepen the kiss, and whisper her name, "Corrine."

Chapter 17

Lucy

The door across the hall shuts and my smile dissolves.

Corrine.

Is this what choosing Torin means? Becoming his wife's replacement?

My heart has rocketed from purpose, to hell, to bliss, to painful acceptance. The story of angel kisses with Alice and Corrine was precious. A vulnerable moment that meant something. . . until he needed her more than me.

"That was some kiss out there."

My mother sits on my bed. The shock of her appearance throws me into a new loop of emotion and confusion.

I turn away, as if not looking will make her disappear.

"But that wasn't Erik. Do I need a name for the new Mr. Perfect?"

The doorway holds me suspended between worlds, staring at Torin's closed door. As painful as my worries are, I'd still rather be on the other side of the hall, wrapped in a place where I know what I want.

Exhaustion has eaten my soul. I just want Mom to disappear, so I can fall into the comfort of my mattress and sleep until the world is right again.

Ignoring her doesn't work. She's still here, facing the French doors with what would have been a perfect view of our kiss.

"Don't you have a room somewhere?" I close the door.

"I came to be with you." Her questioning eyes carry both guilt and sympathy. "And you've been with someone else all night."

I can't tell if she's serious. "I was in the hospital."

"And I wanted to be there too. I was worried about you. I've been here, waiting for you to get back." She slides off the edge of the bed and walks toward me. I skirt her trajectory, heading for the closet.

"Don't be like that, Baby. I just want to spend time with you."

I strip the green skirt from my body like it's a cocoon, only instead of revealing a glorious butterfly, I'm a more bedraggled insect. My red blouse is torn after my fall, and with my limited sewing skills, it may never return to its former glory. I repair elastic costumed beards, not lace.

Everything I do highlights the inadequacies of the person I will never be.

Corrine.

I pull Torin's sweater and my yoga pants from my suitcase and slide into them, imagining I can smell Torin's fresh pine scent on the sweater he hasn't worn since high school. I drape my disheveled, exhausted insect body over the bed. Maybe by morning, I'll be a butterfly.

"So, do you want to tell me about Torin?"

"No." Silence drips like melting slush, while my mother perches on the bed. She's an insect in her own right, a praying mantis.

"Then tell me about these rules."

"What rules?" Play dumb. Don't get hurt. It's a simple plan, but it's served me well over the years. "I don't know what you're talking about."

I know exactly what she's talking about. I just don't think she does.

Mom holds up a piece of paper. "*Lucy's Don't Get Your Heart Broken Rules.*"

I pick myself up off the bed to look at her.

"Where did you get that?" I stare at her through her heavy makeup.

She waves the list in front of her, glancing at the words I know so well. "It was in a book."

She gestures to the nightstand, and I pick up the pale leather book. "My journal?" I barely remember writing them there. "What were you doing with my journal?"

"I didn't realize that's what it was. I was just looking at what you'd brought with you. And you always tell me you don't have anything to hide."

"I don't, but—"

"Kind of like you don't have anyone but Erik?"

"Mom." My heart aches just thinking about Torin. "Not now."

"Why not? You were limiting yourself with just one man. Now, as soon as you realize there's no reason to be with just one man, you suddenly have no time for me? We could have so much fun! This list is ridiculous."

I snatch the list from her hand, and she shoots me a glare.

"Fine." She pulls out her phone. "I took a picture of it."

My heart drops. "Don't pick this apart. This list has kept me from a lot of bad situations. Guys who weren't really interested in me, who would have treated me like a toy or made me into something I'm not."

"Wait—would have? Are these actual relationships or hypothetical?"

I slide back against the head of the bed. My answers feel more like empty holes in reality than solutions. "It's not a bad thing to spare myself pain when I know who a guy is or isn't. I don't have time to invest in people who won't put me first. Who need me to be weak so they can be strong."

"So, hypothetical," she says and I grip the pillows beside me. "Or are you talking about me?"

"Mom—"

"No. It's all right." She stands and holds her position by the bed. "Just so you know, you can't know what will happen if you never try."

"I can. I've seen it. I know what it's like to be talked over and used because I've seen y—" I stop myself, and my mother looks up.

"Oh, still me . . . Do I treat you like that?"

"No. Men treat you like that." My heart clenches so tight it's tearing. Tiny rips across the protective barrier that keeps me safe. I've never said this to my mother.

It was selfish. She was hurt by so many of the men she brought into our lives but if I didn't say anything I didn't have to be the one to hurt her. I swallow hard, stepping across the fears that have kept me trapped in my childhood.

"I've seen you in relationships that I never want to be in. The guys you date are just here for fun. I want you to have someone who will treat you well and loves you. I can't take care of you, and I don't want you with some fly-by-night guy who's gonna break your heart." I hold the list out and my mother laughs.

"You don't need to worry about me. Nobody can live up to that list."

"Torin can," I mutter, until I remember the very last rule.

Rule number ten: *I will NEVER be his second choice.*

I can still feel his lips as he whispered her name. I know he values me. I know he wants me, but does he want her more? Will I ever be able to live up to the perfect memory of a woman who is gone forever?

It's a terrible, cruel thing to think. The weight of my unanswered questions curls me onto the bed.

My mother leans over me, brushing my hair back like she used to do. "Okay, so you've finally given up on Erik. Is the brother your new 'true love'?" She gives it air quotes.

Tears push against the backs of my eyes, and I reach for my snowflake necklace.

It's not there. I splay my fingers around my neck.

My mother doesn't miss the movement and it doesn't take her long to realize what I'm looking for. "Snowflake wishes used to fix everything." My mother sighs. "Maybe you're getting a little old for it, anyway."

My lip trembles, and I bury my head in the pillows before she starts talking again.

"You should be more careful. I may go through a lot of guys, but I know what's important. I'd never want to lose you."

I look up from my pillow. "Am I supposed to feel flattered? Or loved? Is it some miracle that you hold me higher than your revolving door of boyfriends?"

She laughs and brushes my hair back.

I push her hand away.

"Baby, you're having a rough night. I don't understand why, after what I saw happening out there on the lawn with that tall, dreamy guy. God, if he was a little older or I was—no, actually, that doesn't matter."

I suck in a breath, holding down bile as she laughs. Paper crunches under my palm, and I smash the paper list into a ball.

"Do you know why I had this list, Mom?" Words I never intended to say are bubbling just below the surface, and I can't stop them. In this moment, I don't want to. "It's because of you. You only ever saw me as a mini you. But I don't want to be you. I don't want to have so many men in my bed that I can't remember their names or where I met them. I don't want to be so flippant with relationships that I use people up without considering their feelings or needs. I don't want to be so broken that my children aren't enough to fill the gaping empty holes in my life. I don't want to need so much validation that the only fix is another new man, and another new man, and another new man. I don't want to be like you."

I throw the list across the room as my mother stares at me.

"I think you need to get some rest."

"I tried for so many years to be enough for you, but I never am." Tears gush over my face. "And now, I just want you to leave me alone."

She doesn't say anything for several long moments.

She leans forward to brush my hair back again, or touch me, or something but I recoil and she stops.

"Okay." She pulls back, hesitating. "I'm sorry," she whispers as she leaves.

Over the next several days, Torin and I work together prepping marketing displays and gathering sponsors for the last big event the Sugar Creek Inn sponsors over the holidays. The Great Candy Cane Hunt. The event has come together nicely, but we've had to do it all while moving to a new dance. The I-called-you-by-my-ex-wife's-name dance, paired with the coordinating I-know-you're-sorry-but-I-never-want-to-feel-like-that-again dance.

It sucks. Emotionally, I've been run over by a herd of reindeer and head-butted by the one with the flashing nose.

For the moment Torin is nowhere to be seen. It's somehow better this way.

Wrapped in scarves, gloves, and hats Alice and I wait, huddled with other cozy bunches of people, in the middle of town square. Santa Claus will arrive soon and begin the hunt and I'll officially accept that we're not going to be at this event together.

He's here somewhere, of course, in full Santa gear . . . rosy cheeks, and all. If Wally had been a little more confident in his wrist, Torin would be a breath away, standing with Alice and I.

"Lucy?" Alice holds my hand tightly, just as I asked.

"What is it?" Leaning down to hear her better, her eyes shine, and she lifts up on tiptoe to whisper to me.

"I really want to win."

I point all around us where candy canes wait in not-so-hidden hiding places. "There's a lot of candy canes out there," I whisper back. "I'm sure you'll do great."

"But I want the big candy cane." Her fists clench in contained excitement as Torin appears in front of Santa's Workshop.

"Well, he's really let himself go," Erik says at my shoulder.

Standing next to Erik seems to be my lot in life. I keep my eyes trained on

Torin as he waves gloved hands to the crowd. Ingrid is dressed as Mrs. Claus. She steps forward, as jolly as her son. "Alright, everyone! The Sugar Creek Inn and Santa Claus welcome everyone to the Great Candy Cane Hunt!"

Just like they practiced. I grin, watching Ingrid applaud with the crowd. "Remember, the kids who collect the most candy canes will win a ride on the North Pole Express. And the lucky one to find the special candy cane gets to ride in Santa's train car, with treats, a couple's stay at the inn for their parents, and—" she takes a deep breath, "—a hundred dollars to spend at My Sister's Soda Shop!"

"Honestly, that place is too expensive." Erik watches his mother and brother, shaking his head.

"Quiet. They're doing a great job."

Erik scoffs. "The poor kid who wins will think they have a year of drinks. It'll last 'em a week." His breath hits my ear and I cringe. "Also, I know where the candy cane is."

Alice, thankfully, doesn't acknowledge him. I don't think she heard, but I shoot Erik a dirty look. "How would you know that?" I hiss. "And why does it matter? It's for fun. Do you really feel like you have to win at everything?"

"My mother told me where she hid it." Eric wags his eyebrows, as Mrs. Clause opens the hunt.

Alice dashes to the first candy cane she sees, dragging me along.

Erik follows leisurely. "I'm not saying anything, but there's some really nice candy canes over by the knit shop tonight. You should really go look . . . at the red and white decorations."

I glare harder and spin Alice in the opposite direction.

Erik shrugs and follows us. "Suit yourself."

Candy canes get slim fast. Kids run back and forth, parents following close behind with cameras and phones, capturing precious memories. I don't turn toward the knit shop until Alice moves that direction on her own. Loud cheers erupt ahead of us, and someone is standing up high, waving a giant candy cane wrapped in a red bow and holly.

He wasn't lying, at least.

Alice doesn't even seem to notice as she continues to spot candy canes tucked in unusual places.

After the winners are crowned, and the last of the candy canes are found, happy children and families wander around the square, eating peppermints, playing games, and making crafts sponsored by local clubs and businesses. It's a marketing dream. And with the Sugar Creek Inn banners up near Santa's Workshop, they're creating a buzz about the inn as well.

Alice seems content with her basket of treats as she finds a group of other kids to play with.

"Ugh, isn't there someone else who can watch her?" Erik waves a half-eaten candy cane at Alice.

The rudeness of his undesired attention has worn my last nerve to pieces, and I turn on him. "You've been following me all night. Is there something you need? Because I'd really like you to go bother someone else."

The noise is somehow louder, the people more pressing as the revelry of the community grows.

"Sheesh, I was just trying to talk to you."

"Go talk to your hot tub girls. Or ski bunnies. Or anyone else that doesn't already know what a selfish jerk you are." I spit the words, only remembering to keep my voice down after several faces turn raised eyebrows at me. "Go find them," I hiss, glancing back to Alice. Her red sweater and blonde curls are crammed among the busy crowd of active children.

"Fine." He doesn't even fight me on it. "I will. Maybe then, you'll realize what it's like to miss me." As he turns on his heel, I want to throw something at him or swear or throw a tantrum.

I settle for deep breaths. My stress is not currently his fault. He's just a thorn in my already-irritated side.

"Lucy?" I turn to my name. Max, the dimpled real estate agent, is waving at me. "Lucy! Have you seen Torin?"

My eyes dart to Alice. She's not moving, but I'm anxiously headed her way. "Not really, he's kinda busy doing the Santa thing right now."

"Shoot, I need to see him. The buyer I told you guys about is getting anxious."

"I can let him know you're looking for him. Is it a big deal? Marketing's going pretty well," I say, gesturing around us. "I wasn't sure he was still planning on listing."

"Last I heard, he was, and on my side they're getting antsy to finish the sale. If he doesn't want to lose the buyer, we need to let them know tonight."

"Tonight?" Holy cow. "Okay, I'll let him know, I guess."

"Yeah . . . I'd hoped the Nyströms would be making some decisions, since he said he needed to get it listed by Christmas." Max pushes at the bridge of his nose. Shoving at invisible glasses, he catches himself in the habitual motion and turns it into a quick scratch of his nose. "I'll keep looking for him." He waves. "Later, Lucy."

I return a quick goodbye and work my way into the group of kids, pushing after the little girl with the blonde curls. "Alice," I call and take her hand. "We need to go home. Let's go find Grandpa."

The little girl screams, and I turn with a start. "Alice? What's—oh, no." I drop the miniature hand that I'm holding. Tears pool in the child's eyes. "You're not Alice."

I don't have to tell her twice. She knows she's not who I'm looking for. But Alice isn't next to her, either.

At the edge of the crowd, Erik watches me with more amusement than he deserves. I'll give him a piece of my mind later.

I scan the crowd of little people, and my brief panic drains, as another blond head bobs in a red sweater. I work against the sea of children and adults, all playing and making ornaments.

"Alice!" I call. My frustration compounds with worry. She doesn't turn to her name, and when I finally reach her, I spin the girl around.

She's not Alice, either.

Ice settles in my chest.

Everywhere becomes a hiding spot. I search, and ask, and search again. Nobody has seen her.

A red velvet suit walks nearby, and I race for Torin, slamming into him.

"I'm so sorry. She's gone. I looked and she's not um—" My brain trips over the information, moving faster than I can process, and it takes a minute to get the words out. "She's missing. Alice is missing."

I don't know if I've ever seen fear like the kind taking over Torin's eyes. He steps back, pushing me away from him. His eyes have been stripped clean of his usual humor and joy. I've ruined him, ripped him apart.

"We have to find her," is all he can gasp out.

I nod wildly as he turns away, yelling her name. "Alice!"

I can't keep my emotions in check any longer, and tears spill over, pouring down my cheeks.

Ingrid turns the entire crowd into a search and rescue team, sweeping the square. The evening fades to darkness. Streetlights blink on. The police go further, to parks and creeks.

My panic matches Torin's. I want to hold his hand, feel his touch, but they keep us busy searching. Brief glimpses are all I've gotten of him since I told him I lost his daughter.

My heart pumps on overdrive, hiding the pain of branches and rocks as I dig and crawl through low bushes, and search around parked cars. Reality stalls as I crash into Torin outside Santa's Workshop. He's racing around the back while I race to the front. I wrap my arms around him as sobs rack my body. He pulls me close and holds me briefly before letting me go and shaking his head at me.

"No," he whispers, backing up like I burned him. "No. I have to go."

He wants nothing to do with me.

I hold it together for seconds after he leaves. Splatters of snow and ice speckle the wall of Santa's Workshop. I slump through it, all the way to the ground, heaving sobs into the night until I can't breathe.

How do I fix this? Even if he never forgives me, I have to try.

Moments of Alice flash in my mind as I try to remember the things she liked, places she'd go if she could. Her precious smile and blonde curls. Her daddy holding her. Holding me. I imagine Ingrid's voice, Wally's bass . . .

Alice's giggle . . .

Wait.

"Hello?" I say.

That wasn't my imagination—the giggle comes again. Alice's giggle. Her larger-than-life giggle.

"Alice?"

Another giggle.

"Alice."

The giggle is soft, yet clearly hers. Inching around the tiny building, I follow the sound. It leads me around to the front of the Santa's Workshop. At the door, I grab hold of the knob, pushing.

The giggle gets louder.

I shake the door again. It's stuck.

"Torin!" I turn my face and yell in the direction he went. "Torin, I can hear her. She's over here."

Seconds later, Torin appears, running toward me as I continue to rattle the doorknob.

"It's locked," he says. "She couldn't be in there."

I shake my head. "No, she's in there. I heard her." I twist and struggle with the doorknob again.

Torin takes the doorknob, forcing long, slow breaths. With a jerk and a lift, the door swings open.

"Alice?" I call, then bite my tongue and step back. I let Torin in first. He should be the one to find her.

He pushes his way inside.

My whole body shakes as he emerges with Alice, holding her close.

"Did I hide long enough?" Alice asks. "Uncle Erik said I'd get a big candy cane."

I crumble to the ground, aching, with tears in my eyes.

"I'm so sorry, I'm so sorry, I'm so sorry." The phrase just keeps coming, trembling through my body.

Wally is the one who, after kissing his granddaughter, sits on the floor next to me. His arm drapes over my shoulder. "Oh, Lucy."

Wally pats my back. His aged hand rubs support and strength into my shoulder. I wait for his wisdom and storied guidance, but it doesn't come. He simply says, "It's a good thing you heard her, Lucy. You did good."

I feel raw, empty. With a final pat, he stands and returns to his wife and family. My lip trembles as I watch them.

I will never be part of this family.

How could I, now?

I lost Alice.

She was in danger because of me.

How can they ever forgive someone who put their daughter and granddaughter in danger?

It's dark before the crowd thins and my breathing is normal enough that I can stand. When I do, Torin sees me.

For the first time since Alice has been found, he lets go of her. Ingrid and Wally each take a small hand. "I'll meet you at home," Torin says, and his parents lead Alice away. Soon, she'll be safely home.

Through the crowd, I continue to hear his voice. Thanking people. Offering rides home. His thrum of depth and patience is astounding.

When I realize he's walking towards me, my breath and tears catch again and again, like hiccups without a cure.

My instinct is to run, to turn and hide. I don't want to know how much I've hurt him. I don't want to see the disappointment in his eyes. I back up into the workshop. It's dark. I can hide in here. Just like Alice did. I settle into the farthest corner behind a thick beam.

If I'm lucky, Torin won't follow me.

Chapter 18

Torin

Santa's Workshop has become an ominous traitor in the darkening night. It hid my daughter from me for over an hour, and it's the last place I saw Lucy.

I should have come to her sooner. I don't know if I mean tonight or over this last week since I called her by my wife's name, but after nearly losing Alice, I can't lose her, too.

I can't let Lucy go.

My chest tightens as I surrender to my need to see her and step through the doorway. The darkness is nearly complete, but she's here. I can hear her muffled tears.

"Lucy?" With only a small window on either side of the unlit workshop, streetlights filter in thin streams, only hitting her corner of the building with ambient glow. She's barely visible, but now more than ever, I need her.

"I'm sorry." Lucy stutters a breath from the opposite side of the tiny room. "So, so sorry." She begs for forgiveness, as if she's guilty of something, when she's the one that saved Alice.

She pulls back when I move closer, and I slow my movements, but I can't stop myself from crossing the darkness to hold her. "Lucy?"

The dim light hits her face when she finally looks up, and I wrap my arms around her. She's limp in my arms. I kiss her anyway, emotion pressing against my heart and my tear ducts. "Thank you for finding her. In all the chaos, you heard Alice. You found her. Thank you. For listening. For saving her."

My heart is pounding, as if she rescued me.

I slide my arms around her waist, up her back, tangling my hands into her hair. She flinches at my touch, but I need to tell her how much I want her.

"I don't know how it happened," she says, shaking her head against my shoulder. "I was watching her, I promise. Erik was following me around—I got upset with him—and then she was gone. It's my fault. I just feel so terrible—"

"Lucy." I lift her face to mine. Even in the dim lighting, I can see the reflection of tear-stains. "It's not your fault."

"I lost her." Anxiety weights the air, and her body droops limply against me.

"You found her. Erik did this." My fists clench, arms coiled tight. It's probably good that he disappeared like he did, because I'm not sure I could keep myself from striking back after this. "He distracted you on purpose. Alice said she was playing a game, that he promised her candy if she hid in here for a long time. It's not your fault."

It was a terrible thing to do, but after what Alice said, and everything that's happened between Lucy, Erik, and I . . . I can guess at my brother's reasoning.

Lucy only shakes her head.

"That can't be right. Why would he do that?" She's too trusting.

A gust of wind blows the workshop door open, and it smacks against the wall. She turns, but I ignore it, pressing my lips to her forehead. "I can only guess it has to do with this, how I feel about you. Maybe. . . it went further than he meant it to."

She whimpers, sinking deeper against me.

"Lucy." I can't let her keep thinking this is her fault. "I don't know what I would have done without you tonight."

"You wouldn't have lost Alice." Her voice is so soft, I almost miss the words.

She steps back, and I follow. I need to keep her close. "No. I wouldn't have *found* Alice." Setting my finger to her chin, I wait until she lets me guide her eyes upward to meet mine. "Lucy."

For a second, I think I can hear her heartbeat, but it might be my own pounding in my ears. I spent the evening thinking I'd lost Alice. Now that I'm with Lucy, all I can think is, what would happen if I lost her too?

I can't lose her too. It's been more than a week since I called Lucy by my wife's name, and I've been avoiding the conversation. I don't know if I want to know what it will mean. But if it keeps Lucy here, I'll say it.

"No one has ever been more important to me than Alice or Corrine. . . *until now*. It hurts to think about shifting my heart, but Lucy, I want you in my life."

"And I want to be there. But, Torin—" She doesn't know, she doesn't understand that I would do anything for her. "I will never put you into a situation where you have to settle for your second choice."

My heart thumps hard and deep in my chest.

"You have the memory of Corrine, and you have Alice, the sweetest little girl on earth." She reaches for me and instead wraps her arms around her waist, closing me off. Though she doesn't pull away, she's stiff and unresponsive to my touch. "That seems like it's been enough for you. I'm sorry. I just don't see any room for me."

She steps back again, and this time, I let her go. It feels like she's cutting the tethers that hold us together. Without them, I might collapse. "I'll make room. Lucy, I want—"

"No, it's not that simple. I don't want this. There's only one way to avoid getting my heart broken like this. I'm sorry. We already knew we couldn't work. My past with Erik, yours with Corrine . . . It would only hurt us. If we try—" She shakes her head. "I'm not going to be your second choice. And, what if I'm not capable of being a mother? The first night I'm in charge, and we end up searching for Alice for an hour. Just look at me."

"I see you, Lucy. I know we can figure this out."

"Some people really aren't meant to be in permanent relationships. It's too scary—it's not just about Alice. Knowing how I hurt you . . . knowing I caused you panic and pain, I don't want to be responsible for you feeling like that ever again, I can't be with you. There's too much at stake."

Her words take my breath away. The thought of not holding her, not laughing with her, not having her to share my joy and pain tears the life from my limbs. "That just means that you care. All of those things are exactly why I need you. That's what love is."

"Love shouldn't break your heart."

"It broke mine." I almost tell her it broke me tonight, but I can't seem to get any more words out.

Pressing her fingers against my chest, she looks at me with anxious eyes. "I don't want your daughter to end up with someone like my mother, someone like me. The world already has enough broken people. And she's too precious."

I take her hands, kissing her fingers and she lets me, pain etching her forehead, sadness dripping through each breath.

"We can figure that out. We're all broken. I'm breaking right now. If you love us, there's no wrong way to do it. Stay with me."

She shakes her head and steps back, letting her hand slip down my chest. I catch it before she can pull away.

"Please, can't we try? I'm falling in love with you."

She sucks in a breath. In that half a second, I feel her considering. She has to know I'm right. Please, God, let me have convinced her.

She removes her hand from mine in a careful cold motion. "Sometimes, love isn't enough."

Her fingers find her collarbone, where her lost snowflake used to sit. After opening and closing her lips a few times, Lucy pushes past me, straight for the door. I didn't hear it close, but when Lucy reaches the far side of the building, she tugs at the door handle.

"You've got to be kidding."

She pushes against the door, but it doesn't open. With pleading eyes, she turns toward me. I'll never be able to tell her no. Not really.

I walk up behind her, slipping my hand around her waist. My fingers tingle as I wrap them around her body. Holding the handle, I carefully lift, and jerk the door back.

It opens and I take her hand as Lucy walks out. Her eyes find me, and I stare, pleading silently for her to stay as I search for the right words. "You know I'd do anything for you."

"Me or Corrine?"

The question lays bare the hurt I caused and her pain crashes over me.

"Please don't ask that. It's you, *of course* it's you. You have to know, when I said Corrine's name, I didn't mean—"

"Torin, you don't have to explain. You just have to let me go."

I bring her fingers to my lips without kissing them, feeling her skin against me as she turns away, eyes closed. "Lucy, I need you to understand, I will never not have Corrine as part of my life. But I know she's gone, and I'm not looking to bring her back—"

"Torin," she says, and I bite my tongue. "I don't blame you for loving her. You should love her." Her breathing is shallow. She puts a hand up, balancing against the workshop wall. "But don't ask me to live in her shadow. I can't do that. Not even for you."

Quiet infects the air around us, infiltrated with pain that eats through my skin, to my heart and bones. Every layer of my body aches. My mind, heart, soul—everything hurts.

Lucy bolts into the empty square. It makes no difference. We're going home together.

Thankfully, it's a short drive. Just over the threshold of the inn, Lucy stops, looking toward the living room.

"What are you doing here?" She glances at me, and I turn to see Erik sprawled out on the couch, like he's settled in for the night.

"Just here to show my support. I heard it was an exciting night." Erik grins lightly, watching Lucy.

"Get out." I point to the door. I'm serious, and I'm done.

"I'm going to bed," Lucy says.

I don't watch her go—I can't take my eyes off my brother—but I hear her footsteps on the stairs.

"Don't stay up too late, boys." My dad is at the top of the stairs. "Erik, I didn't know you were here. Your mother put Alice to bed. Erik, your room's made up."

"I don't need it. I'm staying at the lodge," he calls after Dad, fidgeting now that we're alone. When Dad doesn't respond, he turns back to me. "I don't need it."

"Then leave." I stare at him, not sure if I'm waiting for him to explain or just cataloguing the string of cuss words I want to call him.

"What's wrong with her?" Erik gestures to Lucy.

"None of your business." It doesn't matter that Lucy has chosen not to be with me. Maybe she won't be with me, but she sure as hell isn't going to be with him. I take several steps into the living room, standing over him. "What were you thinking? You promised my daughter candy to hide from us?"

"I didn't expect her to do such a good job," he snickers. "She's, what— like, two?"

"She's four, almost five. She's determined, and smart—She's my whole world."

"Come on, you found her. No harm done."

"Maybe if you'd told anyone where she was, or that she hadn't been taken. Lucy blames herself."

"She should have been paying closer attention." Erik shrugs. "Maybe she should blame herself."

"For something you did? Alice is my kid, Erik. She's off-limits." Any kid is off limits, for that matter.

He leans forward. "Yeah? Well, my girlfriends should be off-limits to you, but you have a habit of stealing them anyway."

"She's not your girlfriend." My phone rings. It's Max. I groan and hang up on him.

"Maybe not, but you and her—that's not going to happen."

"You're right. It's not. Thanks to you." I'm almost yelling, and I have to forcibly keep my voice down.

"Please, I've seen you kiss her. I knew this was gonna happen. It's not even the first time."

There it is. The real reason Erik is freaking out about Lucy. No. I head toward the stairs. I take two steps, and pause. This is a conversation that never goes well. I should let it go.

I turn back to face him. I have to defend myself. After all these years, he needs to understand.

"I'm sorry your fiancé wasn't exactly faithful. I'm sorry she hurt you. It doesn't make me a liar." I want to smack the scrunched-up grimace off his face. "You and I used to be friends. Remember that? Thanks for trusting her word over mine."

"You don't think there's a reason for that?" He shakes his head, lips curling in disgust. "You want me to believe women are just drawn to you? That you flirt with them and then nothing happens? Well, I don't. I don't believe you, Torin."

"Nothing happened!"

Erik's eyes are daggers, and I'm their target. "So my fiancé just happened to show up, in your hotel room, in your bed, on my wedding day?"

"You're forgetting to mention the part where I left the room as soon as I realized she was there. I'm the one who asked you to come to my room. I didn't know she was there!" It's the same defense I hurled at him five years ago. We haven't really talked about this since he left, no more than accusations and assumptions. "You knew that's who she was. It's why you didn't believe her stories. Your relationship imploding on your wedding day was not my fault."

217

"It's never your fault, is it? Must be nice to be the golden boy."

"Me? You're the one who has shrine upstairs even though you chose to leave. You never helped, never stuck around. And still, Ma keeps your room all made up in case Erik comes home to grace us with his presence. Somehow, you're still allowed to get close enough you can *put my daughter in danger.*"

"Oh, I'm such a terrible person. I gave my niece a candy cane." He sprawls back on the couch and sneers up at me.

I swear again and pull him up by his collar. He laughs, and I shove him against the wall.

"I don't understand what you're still doing here. You're not welcome."

"Just, stay away from Lucy."

"Why do you even care? She's not your girlfriend. *You* broke up with *her.* You don't even want to be with Lucy. Look at how terribly you've treated her since she's been here. Why do you have to keep hurting her? Why can't she have a chance to be happy? Don't you think she deserves that?" I run my hands through my hair, looking to the stairway, and realize I still haven't heard Lucy's door shut. With a growl, I turn back to my brother. "It doesn't matter anyway. She doesn't want to be with either one of us."

Erik laughs out loud until it turns into a snarl. "You finally found a girl that doesn't just fall at your feet? I guess she's smarter than I thought. Maybe I shouldn't have told the firm to fire her after all."

"Wait. You did that?"

His glare intensifies. "I wouldn't say I'm the only one responsible. You're the one that told me she was consulting for the inn. I just informed the boss of her breach of contract."

I'm speechless, stunned that my brother could have been so cruel. This whole night, and honestly, his whole trip, he's done nothing but mess with people's heads, showing his true character in the worst light. "You are —" I stop myself, and Erik takes a step forward.

"I'm what, exactly?"

Not worth it. "It doesn't matter. You won't listen to me, and it won't change anything." I turn headed for the stairs. "I'm going to bed. There's a scared little girl upstairs needs me."

"Alice, or Lucy?"

I freeze in my tracks.

"Come on, what were you going to say? I want to hear it. What is it that Mr. Golden-Boy-Perfect-Son thinks of me?"

I shake my head. "You know what's really sad? I used to look up to you. We used to be close. Now, you're just a waste of my time." I start up the stairs.

"Lucy was mine long before she was yours," Erik calls up after me. "I had her first, in *every* sense of the word. You can just think about that as you fawn all over each other."

A door slams upstairs, and I hope it isn't Lucy's. I hope she didn't hear what Erik just said. My mother appears in the hallway before I can give in to my urge to head downstairs.

"*Sötnos*, can we talk?"

"Do we have to Ma? I've had kind of a rough night." I grab the door handle to my room, and she stops me with a touch.

"You should probably give Alice a little more time. She didn't get to sleep right away."

Waking Alice is never a good idea.

"Okay."

Ma holds her hand out. I sigh and follow her down the hall to the library. "Sit, Torin."

I can't quite bring myself to obey. "I don't think we have anything to talk about."

"Why is Lucy crying?"

"I didn't—is she?" I glance over my shoulder toward Lucy's door. Lucy must have heard everything Erik said. Everything I said. My heart breaks for her. When I look back, the intensity of Ma's one raised eyebrow pushes me back a half-step.

She points at the seat next to hers.

I sit.

"Ma, there's nothing I can do—"

"Of course there is. She's crying. You boys were yelling. What happened?"

"I told her how I feel. That's all." I can't take a steady breath.

My mother purses her lips. "So, you've talked to her?"

I shrug.

Ma huffs and folds her arms, glaring. "Then why isn't she in here with you?"

"I don't know."

"You don't know." She stares at me.

I run a hand through my hair.

"What exactly did you say to her?"

A simple question, with a simple answer. "That I was falling in love with her."

Hope languishes in her expression as I stand. She reaches out taking my arm. "Are you?" Her question takes me by surprise, and I nod slowly. "It's been a while since you cared about someone like you did Corrine, and I just want to make sure—"

"Ma. I don't want to talk about it." I stand up and walk away, useless thoughts running through my head. I know what it means to love someone, and tell them how I feel.

I also know what it means when they don't say it back.

I hesitate by the bedroom door.

Alice is sleeping, and I need space. Backtracking down the hall, I close myself inside the bathroom.

Water sputters from the faucet, pouring hot into the tub. I flip the knob to the shower, letting steam fill the room as I remove my clothes. The scorching water soaks through me, softening the shell I've built up to protect myself. Regret and sadness tingle through my chest, pooling behind my burning eyes.

I don't deserve to feel bad about this. I couldn't separate Lucy and Corrine. I was supposed to be *helping* Lucy and Erik. Even when Lucy told me not to, what happened? I fell in love with her anyway.

A bottle of soap slips from my hands, hitting the floor with a clatter. Frustration and unshed tears overwhelm me as I hit my palm against the wall. Smacking the hard surface, I lean my face against the smooth tile. Cool stone beneath the hot rain of the shower tries to level my emotions, until the first round of tears begins.

I fell in love.

I knew I couldn't have her. I knew from the beginning she wasn't mine.

My body contracts against the piercing wound in my chest as I sink to the floor of the tub. Hot tears spill over my cheeks in rivulets of pain that join the steaming waterfall washing down my face.

I knew she couldn't love me back. So, why does it hurt so bad?

Chapter 19

Lucy

"*T*his is not your fault." Wally's words to me in the upstairs hallway echo in my heart. They'd been overlaid with Torin and Erik, throwing words at each other like poison darts.

As quietly as I can, I move my suitcase to the front porch and close the door behind me.

"*I have two very good sons, but one is blind, and one is holding the poker. My fear is that I don't know which is which.*" His attempt to comfort me, left me alone in the hallway, the walls closing in around me.

What if it's not his sons holding the poker at all?

Sweat coats my hands in a clammy sheen before I wipe them on my coat and heft the suitcase down the steps to the walkway. I've taken two good men, and set them battling till they are both blind.

I don't belong here.

If things go smoothly, in about twenty minutes, I won't be here anymore. It's after midnight as I hit the button on my phone to call the QuickLyft driver. I head toward the town square to meet him.

"Erik, she's my whole world." Torin's voice slides into my mind, another piece of the arguments circling my head all night. My throat constricts against the emotion inside me. Alice is his world. Between Erik and I, we lost her.

Slush and dirt scrape beneath the wheels of my suitcase as it bumps along the sidewalk. I thought I'd cried all my tears between losing Alice and Torin, but as the lights of the inn fade behind me, my chest heaves, threatening more tears. I don't want to go, but I can't stay.

My suitcase hits a crack in the sidewalk and jerks to the side, tipping over the curb and taking me with it.

"No," I moan into the night and grip the errant suitcase, pulling it back onto the sidewalk. *I just have to make it to the square.*

It's only a block or two more, but I'm so distracted I can't even walk straight. Alice's tears while her dad and uncle fought on the floor below. Erik's voice as he confessed to getting me fired, all to drive a wedge between Torin and I.

Two brothers hate each other because of me. An entire family is at stake. Sweet Alice doesn't deserve to have her world torn apart because of my lack of willpower. She has an amazing dad who works hard to put her first.

I may not be able to fix my life, but I can fix this.

I am strong enough to stop the yelling for her.

"You don't understand, I have to get on a flight." I complain to the man at the airline counter. "I've been here all night, and I will ruin lives if I stay any longer. I have to leave."

"I can get you on standby, but it's a long list. I can't guarantee you a flight for two days."

"Fine, book me on that one."

"Okay. Flying out, December twenty-third, a single one-way ticket." I push my credit card to him. "That's eight hundred forty-four dollars."

I pull my card back. "Are you serious? My original flight is only a few days later."

"Oh, how nice. You could stay and spend Christmas?"

"I don't have anyone to spend it with here."

He gives me a strange look. "So, standby?"

"Forget it. A hotel will be cheaper."

"Oh, yeah. It definitely will."

I glare at his smile and shove my card back in my wallet. Trekking back across the airport, I debate living in the lobby for the next four days. Security may not like that.

My next QuickLyft driver is only a few minutes away. I call him anyway and begin the hotel search. Even closer to Christmas than before, I'm facing the exact problem I had when I first arrived. There is nothing available in my budget.

When my driver pulls up, I'm still homeless, but I climb in anyway.

"How long you stayin' in Sugar Creek?" he asks.

"Hopefully not long."

He gives me a funny look and I sigh. "I was trying to get an earlier flight than I'd planned, but they were going to be on standby for two days." I scroll through another page of sold-out hotels in the wrong places.

"Hey! I recognize that phone. You're the one who lost that earlier this month."

My jaw hangs open as I flip my phone over. "Yeah, I guess." Have I become known among the QuicklyLyft driver circuit as the girl who lost her phone? Surely, I'm not the only one.

"It's me, Gary." His smile in the rear-view mirror is far too wide. "I brought you into town after your boyfriend dumped ya!"

Him and his giant smile wait for my answer as I come to terms with it all. I'm not just the girl who lost her phone, but the girl who sobbed, confessed all her feelings about a breakup, scared her driver, and lost her phone in his car.

Maybe it's an omen. A bad one.

"Oh, right. Nice to see you again . . . Gary." I give a weak smile. Will I see him after every breakup?

"Where are you staying? You can't really want to get dropped at the square. It's barely five in the morning."

"I don't know. Anywhere that's not the Sugar Creek Inn."

"Oh, yeah, I've seen some fliers about that place. I'd forgotten about it." He nods and looks up with wide eyes. "Wait, are you saying you don't have a place? Everywhere's gonna be booked up, it's only a few days 'til Christmas." He snaps his fingers and looks up after making a sharp corner. "What about the cabins by the bay?"

"They're too much for a single night." I clear my throat and look out the window. "And, I lost my job recently."

No. Stop confessing. My tears are heavy against the back of my eyelids.

"Well, I might know someone, if you'd take a referral from an old codger like me."

"Someone? Like, not a hotel, just someone?"

He nods, watching me through the mirror while my mind muddles through the mixture of hope and turmoil inside me. I can't just stay with a random person my QuickLyft driver recommended.

Unless I do.

"She's an older lady, a good friend of mine. And she doesn't normally rent out rooms, but I've seen her take in a stray or two."

"Great, I'm a stray." I do feel a little lost. "Maybe you could take me by and let me see it first? I don't want to just disappear in some random lady's house."

"I can do that. Her name's Colleen, on Sugar Tree Circle," the QuickLyft driver says. "In case you want to message it to someone."

"Oh." I pull up Shaunda's contact screen. "Good idea." I feel a little silly taking safety measures from the old guy driving me to a random address. But, his pleasant smile is feeling more and more like a grandpa's, and I relax as he drives past the square.

I look at my phone and remember how early it is. "Will she be up at this time of day?"

"Yeah, I already messaged her. Just tell her Gary sent ya."

Colleen's home is a little yellow, split-level house on a circle drive. The front door is unlocked. And a blonde woman opens the door with a smile.

Thank goodness for small towns and good friends. I would never chance this in Florida.

Gary takes his hat off. "Mornin', Colleen. This young lady is in a spot. She's been visiting for a while and had a rough go of things. Can you put her up for a bit? I'd consider it a personal favor."

She winks at him and reaches out a hand to greet me. "Of course. What was your name?"

Gary checks his phone as I take her hand and introduce myself. "I'm Lucy Sweet."

"Lucy—oh," she says. "I've got breakfast right through here, if you want to join me. Then we can get you all settled into the guest room. Thanks, Gary. This'll work out just fine I think."

Curiosity wakes in my mind as Gary leaves, and Colleen gives me an appraising look. "This way," she says, ushering me through the hall.

The sounds of pots and pans and the smell of bacon and potatoes greets me as I enter. The entire house is done in a formal, floral style until you reach the kitchen. It's all yellow and bright colored dishes, with fabulous smelling food. There's not as much variety as Ingrid's table would hold, but I recognize every dish. Only a couple bites into my plate full of bacon and eggs, Colleen sits in front of me.

"So, Lucy." She clasps her fingers together and rests them on the table between us. "You're the one who's been spending so much time with Ingrid's boys."

The bacon slips out of my hand, and I spit orange juice into my cup.

Colleen raises her eyebrows as I scramble to replace my food. "Umm, yes. I, uh, I dated Erik and–uh," I realize the rest of that explanation will probably end up more confusing than helpful, so I stick with the old version of the story. "How did you know about that?"

Colleen takes a long drink of her juice and sets it down between us. She narrows her eyes, one hand coming up to straighten her earring. "Never mind about that. It's interesting that Erik is the one you mention, but you've been spending all your time with the younger son, haven't you? It's been quite the talk of the town. Torin, opening his heart up again. He's a good man."

I can no longer swallow.

"I know." I croak the words out. My food has expanded in my esophagus like those grow-a-dinosaur sponges you get from drugstore toy dispensers. What kind of explanation can I give this stranger? "He was helping me learn to ski."

"Really? That's interesting. When Ingrid spoke to me before, she seemed to think there could be more between the two of you than that." She smiles, adjusting a piece of hair back into place.

I shake my head and chug as much water as I can, praying that it will clear the growing blockage of food in my throat before I choke. "No. Torin and I are—not a thing. We're just friends."

"Friends? So, you'll meet up with them for skiing tonight."

I set my water down and push back from the table. I may not be able to eat after all. "No. I have three days before my flight leaves. My only job until then is to avoid that entire family—especially Torin."

Colleen smirks and picks up my plate. "I thought you were just friends."

I open my mouth and close it, dropping my eyes. When I look up again, Colleen is watching me in silent laughter, like she's discovered a secret she wants to share with me.

"Can you show me that room now? And, thank you. I don't know what I would have done if you hadn't been willing to take me in. I couldn't bother the Nyströms again."

"But you'll bother me?"

I'm speechless. I just want to crawl inside my body and disappear.

Colleen starts to laugh, running the sink to rinse the dishes and offering me a bowl of fruit. "I'm just kidding. We Sugar Mamas have to check up on each other, and I haven't seen any young ladies around Ingrid's house since Torin's wife passed."

The Sugar Mamas . . . One of Ingrid's friends. I smile vaguely, tapping my foot while I process Colleen's intimidation. It makes a little more sense, but does that mean I should go?

When I don't respond, she gives me a funny look. "Anyway, I've got a full schedule of hair and nails for the Winter Ball tomorrow, so I won't be much help keeping you entertained until your flight. But you're welcome to stay. And, just so you know, you were never a bother to Ingrid."

She dries her hands on a towel after cleaning up breakfast and finally stops moving, putting her hands on her hips. "You know, if Ingrid approves a match, then the rest of us will fall in line."

". . . Thank you?" I can't tell if that's the appropriate response or not, but Colleen grins and walks around me.

"You sure you're not interested in Torin? I could do you up real nice for the ball. You two would make a beautiful couple."

"No." I stand and back my way out of the kitchen. My phone rings, and I apologize to Colleen hurrying back to the guest room as I answer. "Hello?"

"Baby?" It's my mother. "I'm so glad you answered. You haven't responded to my texts, and your young man told me you left. I didn't know if I was going to get to see you before I head home."

True to her word, my mother has left me alone since I asked her to the night of the play . . . a week ago. Regret plays in my heart and I close my eyes before I respond. "I'm so glad you caught me. My flight leaves the day after Christmas. When do you leave?"

"I've got a flight out this afternoon."

A pang of loneliness nips at my heart till it bleeds. Just a trickle. I shouldn't have asked her to stay away in the first place.

My mother clears her throat as if she's nervous, and the trickle of loneliness in my chest thickens, leaden with guilt.

"Do you want to go to lunch?" she asks. "It would be nice to see you one more time."

My mouth goes dry and my heart swells. "I'd love that."

The polished wood countertops of My Sister's Soda Shop reflect the Christmas lights and my melancholy. I sip my Sticky Gingerbread Boy latte as I wait for my mother. Sherry, the less cheerful of the two shop owners, leans across from me. While she doesn't sugarcoat her attitude, she is a great listener.

The tall, thin woman taps a finger on the counter and leans in, commiserating my dating life. "Men are just terrible, aren't they? I mean, after five years—"

I put my hand out on the counter to stop her. "I'm not worried about that." Over the last twenty minutes, I've somehow spilled my life story to this woman, and I'm just now realizing I've overshared, as usual. "Erik and I should have broken up a long time ago. But Torin—"

"Those Nyström boys." Sherry swoons a bit, fanning herself. "They're beautiful, all right. It's too bad I'm too old for them. And, too bad they're men. Dooms them right from the start. No men are good men. But if you have to pick someone to play around with—" She lets out a smiling breath, "—they're hot ones at least."

I glance at Lydie. She rolls her eyes, handing off a tall, thin, sugar-rimmed glass of pale blue slush to a smiling woman.

"But by all means, play, have fun." Sherry waves a hand nonchalantly. "Then, when he inevitably forgets which woman he's with, or cancels on your date for the third time, you don't even have to feel bad when you put ketchup under the door handles of their cars. Because it was all just for fun, and they were nice to look at for a while."

"I don't want to ketchup their cars."

"It's the best in the winter, cause it freezes—" Sherry shrugs. "Oh, well we'll, plastic wrap felt cliche, but you do you. And watch out for Torin. As a general rule, I advise not playing around with people who've got kids. Too messy."

She's not wrong. I can still see Alice curled up to Torin's strong shoulders or in my arms. I can see the look in his eyes the night I told him I couldn't be with him. That I couldn't be a mother. I reach for my snowflake necklace, wanting to wish away the ache in my chest. It's gone for good.

I close my eyes as the thoughts play on a reel in my mind. Whether the aching is for him or me, I don't know, but it consumes me. "I'd recommend not playing at all."

Sherry opens her mouth to respond as Lydie slides her an empty mug. "I need a fat Mrs. Claus." Sherry flinches and turns away grudgingly. Lydie watches her go before turning back to me. "I know you're new here, so I'm just gonna let you know, Sherry may not be the best to talk to about men. She's put up a few walls."

I sip my drink as Lydie wipes the counter. "She's nice to talk to, though. I just needed to get some things off my chest, I guess. You don't have to worry about me vandalizing any cars."

"Yeah? Good to know." Lydie stands back, watching her sister top a steaming gold drink with cream, orange curls, and a sugared cranberry ball before passing it back to her.

"Who's this for?" Sherry asks. "I didn't see anyone waiting."

"Me." Lydie winks at her sister and adds a cinnamon stick to the very full mug of creamy cider. "Thanks Sher."

Sherry scoffs, laughing softly as Lydie walks away with her drink and the bell over the entry door jingles.

"Brr," the newcomer announces to the whole room. "It's cold out there!"

There are a few chuckles from tourists, raised eyebrows from the locals, and a bittersweet sigh from me. My mother has arrived.

"Hey, Mom." I stand hugging her and taking my drink to a table.

Lydie sidles up to the table after us with pen and paper in hand. "What can I get you?"

"What are those blue sparkly things?" My mother looks back at the sugar-rimmed slush the woman at the counter is slowly working on.

"A Blueberry Snowflake." Lydie examines my shivering mother. "But we also make it hot, with coconut, as a steamer if that sounds more appealing."

"Yes, please. I love coconut." My mother makes an excited face, clenching her hands together.

"All right, one Blueberry Snowflake, melted. Coming up." Lydie makes a note and turns on her heel.

"I'm so glad I get to see you." My mother reaches across the table, squeezing my hand. "I didn't like how we left things before. I want you to know, I'm here for you. No matter who you end up with." She takes a deep breath. "And, I'm sorry if I haven't been who you needed."

"I'm sorry too. It's been a really emotional couple of weeks for me. I really—I don't want you to feel like you're not who I need for a mom. You've done a lot to be there for me. I just need you to see that I may be different than the woman you expected, and that can be a good thing."

My mother's lips pull into a tiny frown. "Is it you that's not who I expected, or me who's not what you thought?"

I shake my head. "Maybe we're both fighting who the other is. I'm just worried about you. I don't want you to be stuck with these terrible guys who cycle through your life. I love you too much for that. You deserve better—" My breath hangs in a heavy sigh. I know what I want to say, but it all feels judgmental. I can't bring myself to point out mistakes I've seen her dealing with or ones I've had to deal with for her. Those are my problems, not hers. Instead, I look up as she squeezes my hand again. "Are you happy, Mom?"

She flinched under a beaming smile. "Of course I'm happy. What makes you think otherwise?"

"I don't know." Her response has me on edge. I really don't want to hurt her. "You always seem to end up in temporary relationships. It's not good for you. You're going to get your heart broken one of these days."

"Honey, they can't break my heart if I don't give it to them." She pauses to consider something, then continues carefully, "You're the same way. You realize that, don't you?"

"I'm not like that. I don't let people trample my heart just for the sake of being with a man." I didn't mean to be so blunt, but my mother's sympathetic look is under my skin in point two seconds.

"Oh, baby. Nobody wants to get hurt." She pats my hand, and I pull back. "That's why we do what we do. I am happy—I've just never had the desire to put my heart at risk like that again."

I didn't want to hurt her, but she for sure isn't supposed to be pitying me.

Lydie sets a mug down full of steaming, light blue foam, with a tiny scoop of melting vanilla ice cream in it and a rim of sparkling sugar. It's beautiful. "Drinks like this can make me happier than any man." My mother croons over her cup.

Sherry hoots from the counter and my mother laughs with her.

"Wait." I have to interrupt their giggling to bring the conversation back to my mother's revelation. "Are you saying you choose to not fall in love?"

"Of course. I have my share of fun, and I have you. You are my long-term commitment." She smiles at me, glowing with happiness I only see in her when we're together . . . without her extra guys. "Don't let trauma make your life choices for you."

"I don't—"

Do I?

She takes a long drink from her cup, and her lips pull into a frown that doesn't touch the smile in her eyes. "I have to get going, baby, but go have fun. Don't get hurt." She takes a final drink from her cup and stands to leave. "I tease you so much about your 'Mr. Perfect', but you put your heart out as much as I do. It didn't matter how perfect he was. I couldn't see you giving your heart up before now."

"What do you mean?"

"I mean, watching you and the brother—"

"Torin, Mom, his name is Torin."

"Okay, Torin." She gets a little stern, like she hates being forced to acknowledge him as a person. "You're different with him. It makes me worry. I don't want you to get hurt."

I stand up wrapping my arms around her. "I love you too."

She walks out the door with all the energy in the room leaving only her words to taunt me. As great as her advice is . . .

It's already too late.

Chapter 20

Torin

I've walked past Lucy's door three times today.

Once to go downstairs when I couldn't sleep, once getting Alice dressed, and once to stand and pretend she's waiting on the other side.

Then my mother appeared in the hall, and I pulled my phone out pretending to be busy. That's when I realized I'd been ignoring Max.

The phone dials his number as I kiss Alice and send her to play.

"Torin?" Max says, answering the call. "Finally. Why haven't you called me?"

"Sorry. With everything that's been going on, I didn't even realize you had reached out."

"Yeah, well, didn't Lucy tell you what was going on?"

"No." I frown, thinking back trying to remember if she said anything about Max. "What's going on?"

"You lost the buyer."

"I what?" Panic sets in for a problem I didn't even know I had. "How can I lose the buyer? I didn't even know if we wanted to sell."

"Well, do you?"

I shove my hand into my hair, gripping a fistful of short strands in frustration. "I don't know. Nobody really wants to."

"Then why are we having this conversation?"

"Because I can't pay the bills." I slump to the wall, and a hand settles on my shoulder.

My mother is beside me.

"Torin?" she whispers. "We need to talk."

"Wow. This is almost twice what I thought we could get." *I wish I could show Lucy.* I try unsuccessfully to banish her smile from my mind's eye. The question of her opinion weighing heavily on my mind.

"I wouldn't have let you sell it for half, but—" Max leans toward me over the table, a self-satisfied grin lifting one side of his mouth. "It's more than what I was planning to suggest. So, if the buyer maintains interest, you could get a really good deal. And in the meantime, let's get it listed. Maybe we can get you some competitive offers and drive the price even higher."

"Higher?" Ma is trying to hide her sadness, and my fists clench under my crossed arms.

"Torin." My dad puts his hand on my shoulder. I jump a little when he aims his raised eyebrow at me. "Relax. It's not your fault."

It's not my fault. But it is.

"Sorry." The vacant word doesn't mean much when I'm glaring at everyone.

"I can't believe you're doing this," Erik whines from the doorway.

"Don't be a jerk, Erik. This isn't about you." I say it despite the tension it adds to my parents' demeanor.

"Like hell it isn't. You're calling me a jerk? You're the one off convincing our parents to sell our home without even talking to me. *That* is a jerk move."

"Calm down." Dad stands between us. I'm shaking with accusations and the weight of the failure burying me. "It wasn't Torin's choice."

Erik steps around him to continue his complaints. "He took your money and didn't pay it back."

"I'm working on it." I turn on my brother with a force I don't want to control. "What do you think I've been doing out here?"

"Stop right there." Dad's hand flies between us. "We were thinking about selling long before Corrine got sick—when both our boys chose paths far away from Sugar Creek."

Ma nods without speaking.

Erik's glare doesn't subside but he stays quiet as our parents finish the paperwork to list the house. Within the hour, it's done, and Ma gets her coat. "I'll be at Colleen's."

Dad pauses at the stairs. "I thought you'd come with me to Santa's Workshop for my first day back."

"We've got an emergency Sugar Mamas meeting. I can come by in a few hours."

"I'll be done in a few hours." He winks at her and starts up the stairs. "Don't worry about me, *min älskling*. I'll see you back here."

I hold the door for Ma. "What's the emergency? It's only a few days till Christmas. There're hardly any events left to handle."

"There's still the Winter Ball. But who said it was about an event? The Sugar Mamas deal with a lot of things you don't pay any attention too." She kisses my cheek and steps out the door as Erik strides up in her place.

"Well, that was exciting," Erik says. "I honestly thought we'd inherit this place one day."

"Why would you want that? So you could sell it? You can't tell me you want to run it."

"Oh, I don't, but I'll let you know next time I have the chance to take your inheritance and flush it." He doesn't confirm that he wanted to sell it, but his anxious tapping tells me enough.

"You cannot be that selfish," I say. "They should be allowed to retire. Paying back the inn won't let them do that. Losing it would be worse."

"I'm not that selfish. Their retirement was fine when I left." He might as well have me by the collar pushed up against the wall. I'd be able to breathe easier. All my defenses are futile. He backs away and his sneer practically leaves me bleeding. "I'm gonna go call the airline and see who I have to bribe to get out of here early."

"Let me know if you need me to contribute." Regret follows my final jab as the words leave my mouth. It's unnecessary.

"You're a saint." He pulls out his phone and walks out of the room.

Watching him go, I have to remind myself that he's my brother, and my parents would frown on his accidental disappearance.

"He's just as self-absorbed as he used to be," Max says from across the room. "I'll get the contracts written up. Don't beat yourself up over this, it's a smart move."

He smiles and nods encouragingly as he zips his bag closed over the worst decision I've ever had to make.

What would Lucy say if she knew we were selling? Would she even care? I drop to the couch. She doesn't want this life, so she probably wouldn't.

"Dude. Quit moping." Max sets his bag down on the coffee table and towers in front of me.

"I'm not moping," I mutter, still imagining a distant, cold, uncaring Lucy. It's harder than I thought.

"You're totally moping."

The acidic sting of bitterness eats away the locks on my emotions and I turn on him. "Fine, I'm moping. I just lost the only woman I've been able to care about since Corrine, and I burned my parents' dream to the ground. I'm failing at my entire life, but it's fine. I'll suck it up."

"Yeah," Max says, dropping onto the couch beside me. "You do kinda suck."

I punch him in the shoulder, and he laughs. Somehow, his levity is a salve to my pain. It's Max. He doesn't deserve to feel the brunt of my inadequacies.

Standing, I pace the floor. "I don't know how I misread her so badly. That's the hardest I've fallen for a girl since Corrine. I wasn't ready."

"Ready? What does that even mean? You forgot to add it to your weekly schedule? Fall in love, check." Max shakes his head. "No one is ever ready for love. I don't think it's something people plan on. It just happens."

"Well, I have too much to deal with in my life, okay? I wasn't expecting to feel this again. I've ruined everything I've touched. How can I expect her to love me? Of course she doesn't want me. I'm a complete screw up."

"Did Lucy say that?"

"No." I can't bring myself to tell him what she really said. That she doesn't want to be second choice. It still hurts too much. Because she's right. She should never be second. She deserves more than that. More than I can give her.

"Okay . . ." Max's brow pinches and he looks at me oddly. "You do know you're lying to yourself . . . don't you?"

"Am I? Maybe you haven't looked at my life recently, but aside from Alice, there isn't anything I haven't screwed up." The whole world seems to pulse around me through the film of failures, all leading back to this. "I even screwed up there. I lost her at the Candy Cane Hunt. I let my brother manipulate us, and I didn't even notice until Lucy told me."

"You haven't screwed anything up," Max sighs. "Life is just different now. Decisions are bigger. This isn't high school, and all these decisions we're making have permanent consequences."

I nod. "I've had to come to terms with that every day since Corrine got sick. Death and parenthood make you grow up pretty fast." I can feel the weight of my life more than ever as I remember what it was like before I became a single parent and widower. Before I carried someone else's world on my shoulders.

"I wouldn't wish what you went through with Corrine on anyone, but I would give anything to have even a portion of what you had. And you found it again with Lucy, ya lucky jerk. Things are going to work out."

"Will they?"

"Yeah." Max stands and grabs his bag. "You're not the only one that makes mistakes. I know how it feels to think your life is so messed up you'll never dig your way out."

I roll my eyes. "Well, you did light the science lab on fire freshman year."

"That doesn't even count!" Max belly laughs his smile lighting his face, burning off the insecurity and pain I put there earlier. "It was high school, and it was as much your fault as it was mine. I think you got me into all my teenage scrapes."

I sober, realizing he's right. "Point taken. I've been screwing people up since I was a teenager."

"Dude—" he says, sobering with me.

"No, no you're right. I don't know if you even make mistakes." I'm teasing, but it hurts. "You probably make rent payments a month in advance, scented in cologne."

"Don't judge," Max says. "The cologne keeps the landlady on my good side. Her favorite is Moonlit Mahogany, or Lumber Yard Rain." He laughs at his obviously fake man scents. "If I dowse the envelope, she basically gets drunk and won't know if I pay the full amount or not. I keep extra on hand for emergency get-out-of-anything situations. I can send you some."

His response pulls a grin from my sour expression.

"Seriously though, thanks," he says. "No matter what happens with the house. I'm glad you're here. Thanks, man."

I wrap him in a hug, and as he heads to the door he pauses, quiet for several seconds.

"We're all good at screwing things up. But, if you care about Lucy, you need to keep trying. She's good for you. You're happier with her than I've seen you in a long time. I think that's what most of us are looking for. Someone to be happy with."

"I am happy. I was happy. She doesn't want my life." The words are out before I have time to shut them down, and they burn, raw and red. My vision blurs, and I blink back the emotion Max doesn't need to see. "She said she can't be a mother, or my second choice."

"Ouch. She said that?"

"Yeah. She did."

He cringes. "That's rough, but to be fair, none of those things are 'I don't love you'."

"I know. That part isn't the problem."

"Well, what then? If you love her, and she loves you . . . go fight for her. Nothing she said makes this a deal breaker. Ball's in your court, buddy. What are you going to do?"

"I guess I have to figure that out," I say.

I have to let go of my past enough to make her first. Can I do that? I can't just track her down and kiss her breathless. No matter how much I want to do that part.

Max makes it all the way to his car before the phone rings. "Max Crew, your real estate guru. How can I help you?"

From the porch steps, I lean against the railing watching him go. I can't hear him well, but I know his introduction enough to follow along. Max nods and looks at me, holding up a finger for me to wait.

"Yeah? Okay . . . really? Sure." There's another pause, and Max hangs up, he shakes his head. "It's a good thing your dad hasn't left yet, because we need to talk. This is big."

Chapter 21

Lucy

"The dress isn't the problem," a woman on the far side of the garage spins a tape measure and laughs. Colleen's garage appears to hold an entire beauty salon. The chatter of women spills out into the driveway, and I instinctively turn toward them.

"I know! But the Ball is the perfect opportunity to fall in love." The comment comes from a thin, tallish woman with dark hair, standing beside a pink hairdresser's chair. "Some people can't see what's right under their noses."

For a moment, I'm afraid they're talking about me, but I'm not going to the Ball. I heard about the Winter Ball while Erik and I were making plans back in the fall, but I'd all but forgotten about it until Colleen mentioned it this morning. Besides, there's no way they're talking about me. I've already fallen in love . . . and walked away.

"Hello," I say, alerting them to my presence.

"Oh, Ingrid's girl is back." Colleen's whisper isn't very soft, and as she waves to me, Ingrid appears from the corner.

"Lucy!" Ingrid calls.

My anxiety coils tightly around the longing and nerves twisting inside of me. I have never wanted anything so badly as I want to be part of her family. "Hi, Ingrid. How's—" I almost say Torin and quickly swallow his name. The thought of him blocks my airway, like an avocado pit in my throat. I rework my question, trying to appear as natural as possible. "How's Alice? And Wally? How're you guys doing?"

"We miss you."

"I know I've only been gone a day and a half, but—" I stop, processing what she's said. "I, uh, miss you guys, too."

"Here Lucy, come have some food." Ingrid ushers me into the converted garage full of pink accessories and vintage hair salon supplies. "If you come to the meeting, you've got to eat the food. It's a Sugar Mama tradition. Isn't that right, Chief?"

A man with wide shoulders and a buzz cut is parked in front of a small television playing the opening musical montage of a reality show. He's surrounded by well-dressed, gray-haired women, and his huge frame makes him stand out like a palm tree on Mount Rosie.

My first thought is that he's either military or mafia. The idea of a Sugar Creek mafia makes me giggle. The big man shoots me a glance before he aims a chunk of glazed bread on a pink fork at Ingrid. "It's the only rule I enforce."

"Is not." Colleen tosses a jumbo pink hair roller at him that he easily swats away. "You enforce all your made-up rules. Just try and get away with watching the seasons of the Bachelor out of order."

"I like order."

"Thanks, Chief, you're lots of help," the tall woman laughs. "Make sure you wear your tiara at the next event if you want to keep your honorary Sugar Mama status."

So, these are the Sugar Mamas. Looking around at them, I do recognize a couple from various events. Admittedly, I spent a lot more time thinking about Torin than the community over my time here, but they're familiar.

Chief turns up the volume on the television. "Quiet, Rhiannon's telling Brett about Kelly's fight."

"What's going on?" I whisper as Colleen laughs, and Ingrid loads my plate with some kind of pudding and glazed cinnamon roll bread.

"Nothing," Ingrid says and gestures to her friends. "They like to stick their noses in everybody's business."

"They?" A short woman barely taller than Ingrid with a long white braid nudges her, prompting a groan from Ingrid with her simple question.

"Fine." Ingrid rolls her eyes. "*We* like to help things go smoothly around the community and make . . . connections with people who need it."

"See," the woman responds. "It sounds so much better now." She winks at me. "We're thinking of starting a matchmaker company. You could be our first client. I hear Ingrid's got a handsome son you get along with very well."

My stomach churns with anxiety and my chest lights with frantic butterflies. "No, really," I beg, as the women close in around me. "Please don't do that."

"It would be a great idea. Don't you like him?" A stylish woman with rosy cheeks grins at me like she's sharing a secret.

"We need a few more details if we're going to help at all," Colleen jumps in.

"We do!" That's the thin woman again.

I glance at Ingrid, who's standing innocently to the side. What has she told them about me? Then the questions start coming in rapid fire.

"How long have you known him?" One woman asks in a thick accent I can't place.

"How do you feel about kids?" The gray-haired woman says.

"What qualities does he have that you don't?"

I've stopped trying to track the questions and who's asking them. They keep coming. I close my eyes.

"I don't know." It's all so overwhelming. "Torin and I were just supposed to be friends. I was helping market the inn, and he was helping me get back together with Erik. Things got—messy, and I don't know how to be with him." I shoot a glance at Ingrid and regret washes over me. "I'm sorry Ingrid, but I don't want my heart broken again. He still loves Corrine. And I can't ask him to let her go."

"No. You shouldn't have to. I warned him about that." She wraps her arm around me. "Ladies," she says to the rest of the women. "And Chief. We're going inside for a minute. I'd like to talk to Lucy."

"Thank you," I whisper as she escorts me into the house.

Stopping in the living room, she puts both hands on my shoulders. "It's been a busy day, hasn't it? Were you able to get your flight figured out?"

I shake my head, and tears well up, for my lack of progress and for her thoughtfulness.

"I shouldn't be grateful, but I am. I'm going to miss you, *älskling.*"

When she calls me by the endearment I've only heard used in her family, the tears fall. I never really figured out what it meant, but it makes me feel like I belong. I feel a different kind of love from her than I do with my mother, and when she wraps her arms around me, I cry even harder.

"Don't go, Lucy. I know we can figure this out. He loves you. You know that, right?"

I pull away and nod, choking on the truth I'll never be able to embrace. "I do. But it won't work. He doesn't want to love me, and he shouldn't have to choose between me and the memory of his first wife. I have to go. It will be easier on everyone."

"Oh, I feel like I'm losing a daughter," she sighs and pulls back. "Losing a daughter and my home at the same time."

"Your home? Are you losing the inn?" All our plans to save their home flash through my mind. Torin must be in a panic. "I didn't know."

"Not losing it in a bad way. Sort of—" Ingrid opens her mouth and hesitates. Taking my hand she looks me in the eye, sorrow overwhelming her green eyes. I never realized how much like Torin's they are, just a little more muted. I don't know how I never noticed that. "We're going to sell it. It's for the best."

"Is it?" I pull back. "I thought you wanted to save it. That's what Torin said. You don't have to sell."

Ingrid's smile droops. "That's what I had hoped too, but we have to. Max and Wally are signing the papers now. We accepted a new offer just a few minutes ago."

"No." I jump back, shaking my head. "He can't do that. He can't take your life away. We were trying to save it."

They can't sell the inn. In all of three weeks, the Sugar Creek Inn has become the hallmark of this wonderful place for me. That's where I learned to ski. That's where I fell in love—with Torin, with Alice, with Ingrid and Wally. With peace. With myself.

Before I can think, I run outside and remember I don't have a car. I step back into the garage. "Colleen? Can I borrow your car? I need to go talk to Torin."

"Of course," she says. Her surprise holds the vague sense of being impressed. "Good work, Ingrid. I'm so glad you've come to your senses." She hands me the keys, and I take them hurrying away. I'm in too big of a rush to correct her.

I'm behind the wheel and driving before I can think about what I'm doing, or why it matters so much to me. As I pull up outside the Sugar Creek Inn, Max is shaking Wally's hand. By the time I stop the car and get out, he's hugging Torin.

"No!" I yell stumbling up the walk. "Don't sell it. You don't have to, there's so much we can do! Don't—"

Confronting the three men, I pause on the front pathway. Wally's in the Santa suit, and Torin gives me a look that reflects the confusion swirling around inside me.

Max straightens his glasses and speaks out of the corner of his mouth. "I'm not gonna tell her." He nods to me and turns back to the two Nyströms. "Thank you, gentlemen. I'll let you know when I hear back."

He strides through the silence, passing me in the snow to get to his car, which I, thankfully, have not blocked.

"Dad?" Torin says, as if asking him to explain, but Wally retreats.

"I'm sorry, son, but I think I hear Alice calling me. Yup, she needs some tea for her dolls."

And then, it's just Torin and me. Alone. Suddenly my mouth goes dry, and my words float away into my thoughts. I can't remember if I came over to discuss the inn or if I came to ask him to take me back. The sound of Max pulling away reminds me, I am very unclear on what I've missed.

"What are you supposed to tell me?" I climb the steps of the porch to face him.

"Nothing. You don't have to worry about us. We'll be fine."

"Your mother said you're selling the inn." I watch him closely and he nods looking away. "Why would you do that? We were making great progress."

"There's no *we* anymore, Lucy. Unless—" He shifts closer, and the space between us grows heavy. "—you've changed your mind. Is that what you're saying? Lucy?"

He asks like he's offering an olive branch, but I can't take it.

He's so deeply rooted he is in his life and the family he built with Corrine and Alice I don't know if he'll ever be able to really choose me first. And I won't ask him too. His deep roots are part of what I love about him, and I won't ask him to give that up.

As much as I want to give him the answer that would make us both happy right now, I shake my head.

"Then I don't owe you an explanation. We're doing what we think is best for our family." His words set me outside his family in a sentence. It cuts me deeper than I knew he could. He takes a step back. "You left, remember? It's pretty clear you don't care enough to be involved here."

"I do care," I whisper. I can hear my mother spouting words about not getting hurt and I package my heart up quietly. I can't have Torin but there's a need in my heart that this place will still be here even after I leave. "You don't have to do this. Don't sell. Give it another chance. You don't have to let go yet, just let go of how it hurt you. Please, there's new possibilities here. I saw it. I know you saw it. Don't sell the inn."

"I don't have a choice. I'm not a marketer. I can't keep doing what I don't understand. I needed you for that."

"You can choose to do this. I'll still help. You don't have to be perfect you just have to try. There's still time. I'm still here." I'm crying, begging. Every word twisted as I pray he can see the connection of choosing a new future with me. To choose us.

"Are we talking about the same thing?" Torin furrows his brow.

"The inn," I insist through stifled tears. The implications should be clear enough for him to see.

"Okay," Torin says slowly. "Then, I'm sorry, but I can't do that. It's already sold. We listed it this morning, and almost as soon as Max left, he came back with an even better offer from the same buyer. We had to accept it. Dad just signed the papers. I couldn't save it."

"What if it didn't need to be saved? What if it just needed to be loved? To be put first."

He steps back, taking a deep breath. I can almost see the pieces clicking together. "There's nothing else I can do. It's been first in my life for a long time."

I was wrong. He doesn't see it at all. My vision blurs as I feel every bit the analogy of myself as the inn. "Why did you let it go? We were supposed to fix it. We failed." The words pouring from me are a little bit hysterical.

"No. Your plan was working. *I failed.*"

His misinterpretation twists in my chest. "That's not what I said—"

"But it's what happened." He cuts me off, taking another step back. "I've failed at a lot of things lately. I think you should go."

"Torin—"

"Goodbye, Lucy." And with no further explanation, he disappears into the house and closes the door between us.

What have I done?

The Sugar Mamas are still in the garage as I pull into Colleen's driveway. I wish I could bypass them as I make my way inside, but I have to return Colleen's keys.

"Thanks for letting me borrow the car." I hand off the keys and immediately turn to leave.

"Not so fast." Colleen holds out a hairbrush like a railroad blockade, thwarting my escape. "How'd it go?"

Chief snickers on the other side of the room.

I glance at Ingrid, worry creasing every line of her face.

"Don't worry about Ingrid." The tallest of the women steps into my line of view. "She loves her boy, but she knows how this works. The heart is a delicate organ, and not every set of hearts will match." She holds out her hand. "I'm Deb. So, how did it go?"

Several pairs of eyes turn my way, and I'm ninety-nine percent sure every ear has tuned in for my answer.

I accept Deb's hand, blinking back threatening tears. "Not great." Their eyes are still on me and I know they expect more. "I don't know what I'm going to do. He doesn't want to keep trying."

"No." Ingrid's disturbance repels my gaze, though the chorus of pitying sounds from the other women aren't any better.

"Oh, honey," the woman with the short, styled hair laments—for me, and all of us, apparently.

My defenses rise, and I shake my head. I've never done well with pity. "It's fine. I'm fine. If he's not ready for a relationship, then I'm better off without him—sorry, Ingrid." I set my shoulders and close my lips. It's enough, but the moment one of them gives me that *poor baby* look, I crumble and start defending myself again. "I'll be fine. I've got options, sort of. Anyway, that's what the list says."

"What's *the list*?" Colleen asks.

I would deflect, but my walls are in shambles, and I'm spilling everything today. It's not like I'll ever see these women again. "I have a list of rules I follow to prevent heartbreak. And one of the rules is that I will never be helpless in a relationship. And I know that's not exactly what's going on, but I refuse to be desperate. If he doesn't want to be with me, I'm not going to beg him. Another rule says, I won't date someone who bases their happiness on me, and that's not really the same either . . . but if you take the reverse of that one . . . then, I can't base my happiness on him, either. So, I've got to let him go, if that's what he wants. You know? And then there's the rule that says—"

"Oh goodness, how many rules do you have?"

I sniffle. "Ten. But I'm thinking of adding another. 'Don't date him if he doesn't want to date you.' That seems logical and necessary right now."

"Why wouldn't he want to be with you?" Chief stands outside the group, every bit as interested and ten times more intimidating.

I shake my head. "It was all my fault. He poured his heart out the other night, and I said I couldn't be with him. I just kept hurting him. I caused so many problems, between him and his brother, his daughter, the memory of his wife. And today, I rushed over and stuck my nose where it didn't belong, which was the completely wrong thing to do. So, he asked me to leave."

"Leave, leave?" the woman asking this has her hand to her chest in shock.

Deb shakes her head at me, patting my hand as another woman squeezes my shoulders. "We all make mistakes. It's okay," Deb says. "This is totally fixable."

"We'll bring him around," another Sugar Mama says.

All I can do is smile at the well-meaning women. "Thanks, but I think I'd like to go inside and cry a little."

"Not on your life." The short woman with the braid puts her hands on her hips and stands as tall as she can manage.

I back up a step, and Colleen leans over my shoulder. "Lucy, how would you like a trim? I think your hair would look gorgeous with a few layers in it, maybe some gold highlights to brighten up that blonde. What do you think? It's on the house."

"Umm—I don't think a haircut is going to fix anything." I've never done much to my hair, but Colleen turns me to the mirror and starts fluffing my loose strands.

"We'll see about that. Sit." She turns me into the nearest salon chair and immediately starts brushing and examining my hair, while several other women take up the nearby seats.

"So, tell us how you feel about Torin. Is he worth all this? What do you think the holdup is?"

I shake my head. "I really don't think it's Torin at all."

"Lay back, dear." Colleen twirls the chair, and we slide over to a sink where she starts washing my hair.

"If it's not Torin, what are your concerns?"

I can't see who's talking anymore, but I think I heard Ingrid's accent.

"Uh, well." I'm talking to the ceiling, but attentive voices ebb and flow around me. "If you listen to my mother, I don't ever let myself fall in love. But— "

"It's possible," a voice says. "Do you know the difference between being in love and loving someone?"

"Of course." I frown and there's a smattering of laughter.

"When was the last time you gave your heart to someone?"

"Well, I dated Erik for five years."

"Okay," the same voice comes closer. "So did you ever *give* him your heart?"

"You can't actually give your heart to anyone. You'd die."

"Oh, honey. That is not exactly true," another disembodied voice says, as Colleen sends warm water through my clean hair. "Haven't you ever heard the saying two hearts are better than one? And when you love someone, you've got two hearts beating for you."

I take a deep breath. "How could Torin ever want me after what I said?"

"Don't you worry," Deb says. "We'll get things figured out."

"You really think you can help me?"

Colleen sits me up, and Ingrid is standing in front of me. "Do you want to be with my son?"

"I do. Torin sees me in a way no one else ever has. He makes me feel things I didn't know I could feel."

"Aww," Colleen warbles, "now you're gonna make me cry."

The Sugar Mamas all start in with their crooning. "That's so sweet." "See, we need to help them." The woman in the beaded glasses fans herself, and I think I hear her whisper, "Who needs a romance novel when we've got stories like these?"

"Well, I guess there's only one question left." Ingrid smiles. "Are you ready to give your heart to Torin?"

"But what if he won't take it? How can you trust someone that much?"

"A good man," Colleen says, pulling a comb through my hair, "will help you protect it."

"Torin's a good man," I say, and Ingrid smiles.

"Then you have to be vulnerable," the short, white-haired woman says. "Just remember, it's your heart, not your brain. Feelings rule the day, not thoughts."

The short haired woman laughs. "That's a very good distinction, Dory."

I glance at Dory and her long braid. "Noted," I say. "So how do I do that? How do I give him my heart, without worrying it will get trampled?"

Deb leans forward. "It's a delicate process, but at this point in the game, there's really only one option. What do you think ladies? Grand gesture?"

Several women smile and nod. Colleen leans over my shoulder and smiles at me in the mirror. "Oh yes. Grand gesture for sure!"

Chapter 22

Torin

Alice jumps into my mother's arms at the mention of cookies.
"No," I insist, crossing my arms over my chest. "I'm not going to the
Winter Ball."

"Well, I am going to be there, your father is going to be there. And
Colleen has already agreed to watch Alice, so you are going. I want to enjoy
one last Christmas event as a family before the end of the season."

"We're having the *smorgåsbord* tomorrow. That's our last
Christmas event."

"Not one that we'll get dressed up for. Go put on your nice suit." She
twirls Alice, and when I finally move to obey, she calls after me. "Wear the
green shirt."

The shirt I wore for Lucy at the play— "Not on your life," I call back.
"But I'll wear the suit."

I'm showered and changed in too short a time. Wishing I'd stalled
the process somehow, I load Alice into the car and we head toward
Colleen's.

"Every time we drive away from our home, I can feel my heart tear a little," Ma whispers softly to Dad.

I'm not meant to hear her, and I look backward at the house disappearing behind us as my heart buckles in my chest. Ever since we signed the papers, I've regretted it.

"There should be lots of ladies to dance with tonight," Ma says happily, as if she wasn't just whispering about her broken heart with my father.

"I think I'll be too busy checking my emails to dance. Sorry, Ma."

"You can dance with me," Alice says. I tweak her nose, and she giggles.

It's not long before we drop Alice off and make our way to the Community Center. The Christmas lights haven't changed on the building's facade, but garlands and musicians have appeared, with a quartet of singers stationed outside the doors. The whole town seems to be pouring through the doors, and even though it's early in the evening, Dad has to drive a little way off to find a parking spot.

"I'll be right in, okay?" Dad pulls his suit coat on and smiles at us. "Don't wait for me, I've got to go check something at the Workshop."

Ma narrows her eyes. "What's going on, Wally?"

"Nothing," he insists.

She gasps. "Where's your belt?"

"It's nothing. It was tight. So, I took it off at the workshop, and I forgot to bring it home. I just need to go get it. I'll change into my nice suit as soon as Santa's visit is over."

I laugh at the two of them and leave my parents to settle the matter of Ma's precious costume.

The last time I was here, Lucy was by my side. I can see her walking up the stairs, smiling, holding my arm . . . and then lifeless, her body against mine as I carried her away after she fell. A flash of green moves in the doorway, and for a second, I swear it's Lucy.

Get it together.

I'm never going to survive if I see Lucy everywhere I go.

253

Inside, a live band plays Christmas carols, and several of Ma's Sugar ladies are setting up a table with information and dance cards. There are various booths of local businesses, selling ornaments and souvenirs. If Lucy were here, she'd tell me the inn should have a table too.

But that doesn't matter anymore.

I bypass everything, going straight to the ballroom. A large refreshment table sits along the back wall. If I'm lucky, someone will have spiked the punch.

Halfway there, I spot Max in an intense conversation with a woman in a black dress. As much as I'd like to rope him into being my permanent sidekick for the evening, I don't want to interrupt.

I grab a drink and scan the room. Movement catches my eye, and I'm drawn to where Max and the woman in black are having a heated conversation. I'm about to give him a mental pat on the back for bringing a date when she turns my way, and I choke on my punch.

A flush covers Blaire Thomas's face, and Max slips his arm around her waist, pulling her into a corner. *Holy crap.* Our neighbor Blaire? The Christmas elf? He was the one teasing me about playing Santa with her, and here he is, getting cozy with her in dark corners.

I guess, if they really get together . . . I can gift them an elf costume.

My drink's gone in one gulp, and I set the tiny crystal cup on one of the bussing trays. The rising temperature in the room has me loosening my tie as I walk toward the exit. I came at Ma's request, but I have no intention of staying.

I give myself props for not having to deal with any drama during my very short evening out, and shove aside a décor snowflake as I pass through the doorway. In the lobby, my mother finds me and halts my great escape. She tightens my tie and generally straightens my appearance before I can pull away.

"Ma." I swipe her busy hands back, and the nearby Sugar ladies laugh. "What are you doing, Ma? I'm a grown man."

"I just want you to look nice," she says.

A sound of frustration bubbles at the back of my throat, and I fix my own hair after she's messed with it. Then, near the front doors, a green dress appears and vanishes into the crowd. A crystal bead of hope tugs from the center of my chest, and I take several steps in that direction. Her hair is different, but the rest of her looks the same.

What would I even say to her? I knew what she meant when she was talking about the inn. *It doesn't have to be over.*

"Torin, I need you to help set out some chairs." Ma has my elbow, and I glance at her.

"Can I do it later? I need to go see if Lucy —"

"Oh, look, there's Max."

I turn to see my friend striding out of the ballroom, minus one Blaire Thomas. When I look back, I have no idea where my woman in green went.

It doesn't matter, anyway. Lucy is no longer in my life.

I run a hand through my hair, and my whole body groans in frustration. The constant rise and fall of my hopes are crushing.

When I turn back, Max is talking to Ma. They both look my direction, and he calls out to me.

"Torin? I didn't think I'd see you here. After our last conversation, I thought you'd be home, eating your mother out of cookies and carbs for at least another week."

I put an arm around his shoulder and walk away from my mother's ears. Max steers us into the ballroom and I look back to see Ma watching us go. "Honestly, I thought the same thing, but Ma insisted I come, so here I am."

"Well, maybe that's a good thing," he says and slows our progress through the ballroom, "I have someone here that wants to talk to you."

"Really?"

He takes a deep breath and gestures to one of the side doors. "Yup. Out here. But I don't know if this is a good thing or not."

I walk outside, and Blaire is waiting there. Her black dress reaches to her toes under the thick coat wrapped around her shoulders. Her dark hair is pulled up off her neck and her face is more made up than usual.

She smiles and I turn, looking for Max. "Hi, Blaire, uh, Max is right here. I think this door is for you," I tease. "Did you want me to give you guys a minute?"

Max stands behind me, hands shoved in his pockets. "Torin, she wants to talk to you." Max nudges me out the door and follows. "Blaire, explain, please. Or this is gonna get weird."

"Sure. Yeah, of course." She fidgets with her hands and smiles at me. "I was expecting Wally. Sorry, it's a little strange to do this with you."

"What did you want with my dad?" I ask getting a minor creeped out feeling.

"Torin, I know you guys are selling your house."

"Okay. It's not exactly a secret." My curiosity is piqued. "But it's already sold."

"Yes, that's what I wanted to talk about." She looks to Max. "Shouldn't we have the owners here? Wally or Ingrid? I'm not sure I feel comfortable doing this with Torin."

My eyebrows lift in shock. She doesn't feel comfortable doing *what* with me?

"What's going on?" I ask.

Max sighs. "I talked to Ingrid first. Wally's busy, and she is too. She said Torin has the final decision on the house, so here he is. He'll talk to them, too. He's a good guy, and it's the best way, I think. Tell him what you're thinking."

"Okay, umm, since it's you, maybe I should explain. I know I've been a little weird this year. I don't know if you remember, but the last day I volunteered with you, I mentioned my cousin bought a house. Well, I've been hoping to buy a place too."

"That's great. But like I said earlier, our place sold already. It's a great offer, and we already signed the papers."

"I know. I know, that's not it." She pauses taking a deep breath. "I spent a lot of time trying to get close to you while we were working together at Santa's Workshop."

"Wait, is that what this is about? I thought I explained—I'm just not interested. Why are we doing this with Max?" I glance back, and Max is rolling his eyes so hard his head tips back.

"Would you just be quiet?" Max slaps the back of my head, and Blaire chuckles quietly. "She's got something important to say. Just listen. Sorry, Blaire, he's not usually so jumpy. He has a lot on his mind, these days."

She smiles at Max and turns back to me. "First, I never meant for you to think I was interested in you. I'm sorry. But I've got a boyfriend a bit more my age." She grins, and I'm already relaxing. "Second, the reason I wanted to build a relationship with you was so I could potentially buy your parent's place. Sanford—he's one of the other realtors—"

"Oh, I know who Sanford is." I shoot Max a glare, remembering the sledding night and him hitting on Lucy.

"Oh, good," she says, and I raise an eyebrow. "He mentioned your family was in a tight place, and I wanted to be ready. I thought Wally would be Santa but, when it was you, I figured I'd do my best."

All the conversations about home repairs, and getting to know my family, take on a new light. She looks a little sheepish, and I instantly feel like a jerk.

"Oh my gosh," I mutter as Max laughs silently, and I release my final dregs of tension. "I'm usually not so self-centered. I just couldn't think of any other reason you'd want to get my attention." I run my hand through my hair, wishing I could take back the last month for more than one reason. "I guess that's good news. So, what's this really about?"

"Well, I'm the one who put an offer in on your house. I'm your anonymous buyer." She holds her hands out, like she's saying *ta-da* at the end of a magic trick.

"Wait, what?" I look from her to Max, not sure if I trust what I'm hearing.

Max gives a tight smile. "Yup, that's what I was waiting for. Okay, Blaire, I'm gonna let you finish this. I'll be right inside if you need anything." I shift from one foot to another as he leaves.

Blaire gives an awkward laugh. "Well, I wanted to talk to you because I know I made a fair offer, but I'm not sure how you feel about everything. Or your parents."

"Oh, well, it's hard of course—we've owned the place forever, but it's a great offer, and honestly, knowing it's you makes me feel a little better. You wouldn't raze the place to the ground or anything . . . would you?"

"No. But that's not really what I meant. Being your neighbor, I've overheard a couple of, um, arguments recently."

I close my eyes and try not to replay all the family drama over the past week. "I'm sure you've heard some interesting things."

She chuckles softly. "Well, I just wanted to let you know, that if you don't want to go through with the sale, I'm okay if you back out. I don't want to hold you to anything you don't want to do."

"You really mean that? You would let us out of the contract?" My mind reels at the opportunity she's gifting us.

"I would. I love your place, and I think it's worth every penny I offered, but I don't want to hold you to it if you're having second thoughts. There are other places I can buy." She steps to the side and sets a hand on the door handle. "You can think about it. I just wanted to let you know."

As she pulls the door handle, I take her hand, stopping her. "Blaire, I need to apologize. A lot. I'm sorry for misjudging the situation. And I want to thank you for being willing to be flexible on the contract. I don't know what we'll do, but knowing we still have options is huge."

She shrugs and looks at the ground, embarrassed. "It's fine. We both made some misjudgments. Let me know as soon as you can about the house. My cousin and I are wanting to move forward, and finding the right house is important."

"Absolutely," I say.

She turns to leave, making halting steps toward the door before she stops, spins around, and pulls me into a hug.

"I hope that, whatever you decide, your family is one hundred percent happy with the decision."

"You're making that much easier to do. Thank you, Blaire."

She lets go and squeezes my hand before walking inside. For the first time in days, I feel really good about life.

Then, Blaire walks by the woman in the green dress.

She's watching me through the glass doors. Blonde hair curls softly around her face, falling to rest against her shoulders. Sparkles drape her body in delicate folds. Twists of deep forest green fabric wrap her waist, slinking all the way to the floor and leaving her sides exposed. My eyes trail her shimmering curves from to the tip of her silver shoe, all the way up to her red lips. They open slightly as our eyes meet, and I let myself see her face.

Somehow, impossibility has coalesced into reality, and Lucy stands in front of me.

Chapter 23

Lucy

My idea of love wasn't entirely wrong.

When you give your heart to someone else, you most definitely die.

I'm dying, as I watch Torin through the glass doors holding a beautiful woman in a black dress. He pulls her close and holds her tight, cutting me open, and I bleed freely.

Hearts are fragile and so easily broken. It's just a hug, but I can feel his arms around me, while she's the one in them.

Maybe it's karma. He handed me his heart, and I dropped it at his feet. Now, while I'm prepping to give mine away, I'm helpless, watching him discard me the same way.

Snippets of my useless rules flash bright in my mind. I'm going to be second place. Even if he can see past Corrine, this woman looms, threatening my forever — maybe it's not about being my mother. Somehow, I convinced myself that my heart was the only thing holding us back.

No wonder I've never truly given my heart to anyone.

Why would I allow my chest to be ripped open, heart torn free and left pumping on the floor.

For the first time in a long time, the answer comes to my mind, true and simple. Clarity is a gift.

Because I cared about him enough to try.

As I scoop up the pieces of my shattered heart, Torin releases the woman in black and she comes inside. Her dress hugs her every curve, and she has many to admire.

"Hi, Lucy." Her nonchalant greeting knocks me back a step.

I know her.

"Blaire," I barely get her name out, in a rush of breath, before she's past and gone.

Through the open door, Torin's eyes are on me. Deep green emeralds, cutting through my defenses. I want to scramble away before he can see how broken I really am.

Across the room, three Sugar Mamas—Deb, Annette, and Rose—watch me closely. I take a step back, and they make frantic gestures toward the door. I'm supposed to be going outside. That's the plan.

Succumbing to their wishes, I move myself forward. My confidence is shot. So much for my grand plan.

Maybe I can at least get closure.

The women in tiaras clap silently, their tiny fluttering motions trigger a wave of nausea. With a slow breath, I swallow, pushing moisture through my dry throat like wet sandpaper. I shouldn't have waited so long.

Torin doesn't move until I reach the door. Then he pulls it open for me, and the cold hits me all at once. I wrap my arms around my waist, falling into myself before I step outside.

This will be quick.

"Lucy?" He closes the door carefully behind me and brings me close in the dark courtyard. I pull back, until he lets go. I can't be held by him, not right now. "You're still here." It's not exactly a question or a statement. It's

261

like he's acknowledging the impossible. His wide eyes hold me in place sending my heart racing. "I thought you'd be on the first flight out."

"Turns out, there aren't as many flights from Sugar Creek as you'd think. But, don't worry." I offer him a soft smile. My exposed skin is already pimpling with goose bumps. I don't care. I need to say my piece and be done. "I saw you and Blaire. You guys look good together. I understand that you need to be with someone else, especially after what I said. I won't get in the way."

I take the door handle to go back inside, and with one hand on my arm, Torin stops me.

"You can't really believe I'd be interested in Blaire."

"You were hugging her." A clear visualization of the moment accompanies my point and I look away. "It's fine. She's beautiful, and good with kids, and –"

"Blaire is the buyer of the inn. She just told me we didn't have to sell, if we don't want to."

The door slips from my hand, clicking shut on the noise of the growing party. The sudden quiet creates a bubble of intimate privacy. "She's the—you don't have to sell?"

"We don't have to sell." He laughs lightly, and peppermint fills the chilly air between us. "But, if we're going to keep it, I could really use a partner. Someone to be there as I make a mess of the marketing, to keep me in line."

I flinch. He's holding his heart out. He's been holding it out all along, and now, it's supposed to be my turn.

Give him my heart. Be vulnerable.

I can do this.

"I, uh—was hoping—" *nothing.*

I can't do it.

Words fail me. I'm frozen in place.

Say it. I'm going to stay. I sold my apartment. I'm getting a job . . . here. Say any of it.

If he loves me, I can do this.

But Erik loved me.

My father loved me.

Even all the men my mother *loved . . .* I used to think one of them would try to love me too, be a new father, but they couldn't even love her.

Love doesn't last.

I can't do it, and I'm not going to wait around for the day Torin doesn't love me either. "I shouldn't have come. . ."

"Wait. Lucy?"

"I'm getting cold." I turn back to the door, shivering. I was never going to be able to give him my heart. I'm just like my mother. The door catches on solid commercial grade locks as I pull. "Torin? Do these doors auto-lock?"

He reaches around me and pulls. It doesn't open. "Hang on." He knocks on the glass. "Someone will let us in."

I rub a hand over my frozen arms. "I don't think so." On the other side of the door, the Sugar Mamas have their backs to us. One by one they turn, looking over their shoulders and waving. "They're trying to give us privacy."

"But they have to let us in. You're freezing." He knocks again and makes a gesture like he's wrapping a coat around himself and points to me.

They laugh and gesture back at his own coat. He groans and takes it off, handing it over.

"I'm sorry. You don't have to." I accept the coat any way and slip my arms inside. Fresh pine scent and warmth surround me as I breathe him in, filling my senses with the memory of Torin. It almost changes my mind about giving up on the Sugar Mamas' plan.

"I'm not upset about giving you my coat. I'm upset that they won't let us in. Everyone is right there, and we can't get in." He goes back to the door handle and shakes it. He really doesn't want to be out here with me.

All my plans dissipate into the night air with a frozen sigh. My grand gesture is a grand thud. It doesn't matter anymore. I box up the shattered pieces of my heart, shoving them deep inside while I look for an escape.

A low hedge surrounds our little courtyard. I hike up my skirt and shimmy between the hedge and the building.

"Where are you going?" Torin calls after me.

"Not here." Tiptoeing through snow and plants, I don't look back. There has to be a path somewhere. I just keep walking until I reach the treacherous front steps of the Community Center. My pulse jumps into my throat, as I look down them. Images of falling replay in my mind.

"Lucy!" Torin calls behind me. He isn't far off.

I have two choices. The doors to the Community Center would lead me to warmth, mistletoe, Sugar Mamas, and a host of questions. If I step through those doors, everyone knows what I've done.

Or I can take the steps.

It's sad when the treacherous steps, leading to the dark, cold night seem like the more desirable option.

"They're just stairs," I tell myself aloud. I put one heeled shoe on the top step and start down them as quickly as I can. I'm slow but I make it to the bottom in triumph. Only to hear Torin's voice above me.

"Lucy." He's at the top of the steps.

"Please, I can't—" My lungs pinch over my heart, vacuum sealing it from the air, but I'm still breathing. "I can't stay here. I need to go." I lift my skirt, hurrying across the street, as if I were a Christmastime Cinderella.

Colleen's car is on the other side of the square. If I can just make it there— Torin hits the ground behind me. His pursuit driven by the same need that sent me away . . . love and fear. Only he's afraid of losing love, I'm afraid of finding it.

This is crazy. I grab the handle of Santa's Workshop as I pass the little building and tug. It's stuck again and I don't know Torin's trick to open it. His footsteps close in behind me and I circle the side of the building. I just need a moment to breathe, to think without his eyes freezing time or his hands sending me on a roller coaster of trembling and heat.

I need to breathe.

Falling against the wall of Santa's Workshop, I try to calm down as Torin runs past.

Tiny specks of white drift from the sky, reflecting pale light in the darkness. Snowflakes. They could be wishes—kisses—anything. I have no idea what they are anymore but if they can save me, I'll take whatever they have to offer.

A tiny ice crystal lands on my cold skin and I gasp a sob. A perfect snowflake and I have nothing to wish for. I can't wish Torin away and I can't wish he were mine. Then it melts and the magic is gone.

I'm on my own again.

I should have wished for his happiness, for him to fall in love with the right woman. I should have wished Torin and Erik would make up. I should have tried to fix this, but I couldn't even do that.

"Lucy!" Torin's voice calls me back and I have to remind myself that I can't go to him.

I tiptoe to the corner of the building and he's on the other side.

"There you are." His relief inexplicably lightens my own burden, before I hurriedly back up.

He's poured his heart out to me already. I know how he feels. I don't want to hurt him, but I can't let him say he loves me again. I'm not strong enough for that.

I scuttle back another step and trip.

He lunges for me, catching me mid-fall. "We haven't played this game in a while," he whispers.

"I'm lucky you're so good at it." My mind goes blank the instant I look in his eyes. *Lucky*. Am I? He lifts me upright, as I keep my eyes trained on him. "Please, Torin. Please go."

"I'm exactly where I want to be." He pulls me close to his chest.

Christmas lights in the distance going blurry with tears. My body falls limply against him, fists curling against his suit as I cry. "All I do is hurt you."

"It hurts me to see you cry." He wipes a thumb over my tear-stained cheeks. "So, if you could not . . ."

"See?" I choke on a tearful laugh, but the humor doesn't last. I'm overwhelmed by what could have been. As the tempo of my heartbeat quickens, I look up into his kind face. "I can't be here."

"I don't want you to leave. What did I do?" His hands tighten around me, heat radiating from his grip, and for a moment I let myself live in his touch.

"Nothing." I can't think straight as I stumble out of his grip. "You didn't do anything wrong. I shouldn't have come."

"Then why did you? Why come and why run away?"

"I don't know. I'm trying to do the right thing!" Tears streak hot trails down my cold cheeks as Torin catches me bringing me back.

"This does not feel like the right thing."

My heart is racing my thoughts. Both flying against the walls of my mind and body at breakneck pace. Both try to lead me out of the mess I've created. Neither love or logic will win this battle. "It's not supposed to happen like this."

"What are you talking about?" Confusion pulses behind the tension in his jaw.

"Me! You! If loving you means, I'll lose you, I won't do it." My heart wages war on my body as I try to hold myself together, under his fierce attention. "You can't break my heart if I don't give it up." Only it's already done. My heart is gone. I never gave permission but I finally know what it feels like to give it away because I might die right here in this man's arms.

"Do you love me?"

Our eyes lock together. Torin's silent gaze holds off the night, slowing the gentle snowfall until my emotions settle on the only truth left in me. "I do."

I can hardly breathe. Even knowing he feels the same, I'm shaking as I nod, holding my raw heart in my hand.

"Then let me love you. I may have been in love before but you and I—we'll have something different, something more. I want you to be the woman in my life, the woman in my daughter's life. I want to share everything with you, good and bad, for the rest of my life."

"You can't promise that. You don't know—" Fear and insecurity ripple over the words like pebbles on a pond, shuddering the breath in my throat. "I love you but every—every man I've ever had in my life has walked out on me."

His smile dims as understanding wakes in his beautiful eyes. "Then they never deserved you."

"They are all I know."

Emotion rolls over his face in the pinch of his brows to the tightness in his jaw. He strokes a single line across my cheekbone, resting his palm against my neck. "That's not true."

His hurt startles me and I reconsider my statement as the last few weeks with Torin rock through me. His kindness, caring, and consideration of me and my needs. "You're right." I grip his arms as I can almost feel my world shaking beneath me. "But, Torin— I don't know. I'm sorry—"

I'm still collecting the words to apologize when his deep voice whispers between us. "Our pasts are not simple. Mine is a minefield. And I can't promise you forever, perfect love. I can't even promise you I won't break your heart." His forehead presses to mine as his words strike like arrows through my chest. "I can promise to love you as long as you will let me."

"Will it always be so hard?" I close my eyes, and Torin presses a kiss to the tears on my face, gently clearing my worries away with kiss after kiss as I breathe against his skin.

"Loving you is simple. Not loving you . . . that was the hardest thing I ever attempted. Trying to let you go nearly killed me. I can't do it anymore, Lucy. Don't stay away. Don't ask me not to love you. Please, let me be yours."

"I tried to walk away. I can't do it again." I shake my head against him, sliding my hands up to cradle his jaw. Pulling us together, until we're close enough I can feel the brush of his lips as I speak. "I love you. I want to be where you are."

His mouth closes the breath of space before I can get anything else out. Desperation presses from his body to mine, arching my back and pulling me into his need. Heat builds between us as his lips draw on passion and intensity I didn't know I had. The thrill of him spreads from the center of my body, until I'm holding him with my own desperation. Desperation to feel him, to believe he could possibly be right, and to never let him go.

When breathing becomes more necessary than the pressure of his lips, I pull back . . . slightly. Resting my brow against his cheek, I can still feel the heat of his mouth. Our lips hover a breath apart and I wait, breathing his air.

"You know, Florida is nice." His lips brush mine as he speaks.

"Florida?" my grins spawns organically curling beneath the burn of questions and tears. "I—uh— I hope you have fun."

"I will." Torin's eyes trace the lines of my face ending at my lips. "If that's where you are, that's where I want to be."

"Well, then you may want to stay put. I gave up my apartment back in Florida. And I'm not going to try to get my job back."

"You're not?"

"I've fallen in love with this cute little town up in Vermont, Sugar Creek. And there's this amazing guy . . . I'd like to see if there's anything there."

"You're not leaving?" he asks.

I shake my head.

"And you're staying here in Sugar Creek?"

I nod and rest my hands behind his neck. He wraps his arms inside my coat, finding the bare skin at my waist, exposed by the intricate twists of my dress. "That sounds perfect."

"I didn't think you could promise perfect."

"This time perfect is your fault." His hand slides to the nape of my neck, cradling my body. He brushes his lips across the side of my face, and down to my ear, trailing all the way along my jaw.

Opening my neck to his touch, I tip my head back and laugh. A fluffy bunch of white-berried mistletoe hangs above us.

"What?" he pulls back, eyes twinkling.

"Look where we are." I glance up and he follows my gesture, grinning at the mistletoe where we had our first kiss.

When he looks back, his eyes meet mine, and I lose my breath. He sees me. He wants me. In all my imperfections, he stares into my soul and wants to hold my heart.

"Should we?" he asks. And I look up at the perfectly placed decoration.

"It's just a kiss." I shrug, and he leans in, pulling a quick kiss from my lips.

"Not anymore. Now, it's tradition." He runs his fingers along the back of my neck, sending shivers through me, curling me against him. I push up slightly from my heels and return a quick peck to his lips.

"Like you needed any help," I tease.

"I'm not one to ignore tradition." His green eyes take on a mischievous sparkle. His fingers slide into my hair, the hand at my back hugging my body closer.

I slide my knee along his thigh. My hands travel the surface of his back, absorbing every curve of muscle until I'm wrapped around him, my hands over his shoulders and in his hair.

His lips secure our bodies together with the seductive crush of his mouth. His fingers burn hot trails over my cold skin, and I wrap my arms around his neck. Pressing my body closer, I deepen the kiss. His hands echo the curve of my ribcage, tracing heat across the bare skin at my back. His lips move in sync with mine until he breaks the connection with a light gasp.

Torin leans his forehead against mine. "You really love me?"

I close my mouth over his lower lip, pulling against him then fully press my mouth to his until steamy breath fills the space between us. My hands slide slowly down his chest. "Yes." I tip my chin up, kissing the corner of his mouth, feeling him smile as I press tiny kisses over his chin, lips, and nose. "I love you."

"Thank, God," he sighs. "Because I've been in love with you since you fell in my lap and ripped the beard off my face." An embarrassed laugh tumbles through my body and his strong fingers coax me closer. "Shh, there's more. I've been in love since you fixed our kitchen sink with an inner tube, and knocked me out with your skis."

My heart quakes, expanding in quick palpitations, changing shape and time as it beats to a new rhythm. Soaring higher and higher, it sings to the intensity of a drum beating inside my chest.

A memory plays in my mind. "When I got here, I wished to be with my true love." I hadn't planned to tell him this. But the thought makes me smile, so I keep talking. "That obviously didn't work out like I thought but wishes have a way of doing that. Coming true in ways you never expect." I reach up, touching his cheek with my cold fingers. "I gave up on wishes. But all this time it was bringing me to you."

Torin slides his lips to my fingers kissing warmth into them. "So, you believe in wishes again?"

"I believe in you."

Epilogue
One year later

Lucy

Snow falls outside the balcony doors as Alice's customary wake-up giggle rouses me from drowsiness.

"It's Christmas, Lucy!" She's a year older but her childlike voice still thrills me.

Dim morning light fills the room, glinting off the diamond on my left hand. I give a lethargic greeting as I stretch and roll to the edge of the bed. "Are you sure?" I sit up onto my knees and dive toward her. A squeal of giggles erupts as Alice runs in a wide circle away from the bed and back. "That can't be right. I think it's tomorrow."

She giggles and wrinkles her nose. "It's not tomorrow. Christmas is now!"

"Did you wake up the Lucy Princess?" A deep voice asks from the door.

Torin is standing there, shirtless and wearing the same pajama pants with dancing Christmas trees that he wears all season. Rubbing a towel against his wet hair, he drops his hands when I look up at him.

"Let's go." Alice bounces past, taking our hands. "There are presents! I saw them!"

"Alright, alright." Torin swings her up and sets her down in the hall. "Go on. *Farmor's* downstairs. I'll be down in a minute to see what Santa brought."

Alice dances out of view, and I saunter over to the doorway. "I think I like my present best," I tease, leaning up to kiss him lightly. "Merry Christmas, Sexy Santa."

"Oh, it's your fault I had to do that again this year, isn't it?" he says.

"Maybe," I say, as I move to slide past him, and he reaches for me.

A door down the hall opens and, in unspoken agreement, I let him pull me into my room. Torin closes the door halfway behind us, wrapping his arms around me. "I will never get tired of waking up with you nearby."

"Well, good because this fancy Christmas present you gave me suggests we're going to be spending a lot of mornings together."

"Mmm." He picks up my hand kissing each finger before holding it out to see his engagement ring resting there. "You do look gorgeous with my ring on your finger."

Footsteps walk past as he leans in kissing me lightly. "Careful," I say, putting on a teasing version of Ingrid's Swedish accent. "*This is a respectable place.*"

"If it's so respectable," he whispers, his lips brushing my ear, "what were you doing with a guest in your room so late last night?"

My jaw drops and I shake my head at him. "You're lucky I let you hang around."

"Oh, I know." He sets a light kiss to my lips and backs out into the hallway. "I'll meet you downstairs, okay?"

I nod and, as soon as he's gone, hurry back and don a pair of thick socks and a sweater over my tank top. Though my cute nightwear isn't inappropriate, it's not exactly Christmas trees dancing over flannel. Torin is the only thing keeping me warm right now.

Once I've got my thick, full-length leggings on, I descend the stairs. My smile is unfettered, listening to Alice and Wally laugh and play. "Merry Christmas, everyone."

I freeze at the bottom of the stairs.

Erik is by the Christmas tree.

"Merry Christmas, Lucy." He smiles up at me, and I try to respond in kind, but my lips won't cooperate. It becomes a battle to keep a glare off my face.

"What—" I almost ask what he's doing here, but it's his parents' house, and I'm sure they're glad he's home. "What are your Christmas plans?" I ask, amending my inappropriate question.

Erik rolls his eyes, laughter playing with his smirk as he sees through my attempt at propriety. "I'm only here for a little while, and then I'm headed back to Florida." Erik nods toward me and flicks his eyebrows up. "Can I talk to you?"

"I guess so." I look around, searching for a reason to stay, but both Wally and Ingrid are playing with Alice, and Torin is still upstairs. I sigh. There's no excuse for me not to go with him.

Erik gestures to the door, and as I follow, Torin finally appears on the stairs.

"Is everything all right?" Torin's eyes hide in worried shadows.

I nod. "It's fine. We'll just be right outside the door. Right?"

"Of course," Erik says, and I follow him outside. He sticks his hands in his pockets and looks out over the porch. "We weren't ever going to work out, were we?"

"Erik, I never meant—"

"I don't want to hear it. I just said I'm not okay with it. But I'm trying to put some things behind me."

"Is that an apology?" I'm not sure I'd recognize a nice word from him even if he spelled it out in perfume and flowers.

"God, no. I'm just trying to be transparent. I understand that you're with my brother now. So, just keep the kissing and touching down to a minimum when I'm around."

"Is that going to be a problem? Are you actually going to start visiting your family?"

He pauses long enough to reach up and tug at my ear, and I brush him off.

"Someone has convinced me that they might be worth getting to know again." He tugs my ear again.

"You know that used to annoy the heck out of me." I shake my head at him. "Probably because it made me feel like a little sister, instead of your girlfriend."

He smiles "I guess it fits . . . now."

"It does." I smile, and he wraps me in a hug, letting go when the door opens and Torin emerges.

"Everything still all right Lucy?" He slips a hand around my waist.

"Jeezum crow. I wasn't trying to maul her." Erik scoffs but I don't care. I lean into his grip enjoying the safety and happiness in his embrace. "I was apologizing."

I shoot him a look at the admission, but he doesn't look back. He bumps Torin's shoulder heavily as he walks past and into the house.

"It's snowing!" Alice flies from the entry hall onto the porch, ready to launch herself right into the snowy yard if Torin hadn't caught her. "Let's make angels, Daddy! And get kisses and make wishes and do all the snow things. Please, Daddy!"

"How can you say no to that little face?" I ask.

Torin glares at me. "You're no help."

I shrug happily and take Alice from his arms. "Come on, big girl. Let's go find your snow things and we'll make angels together."

"For mommy?" Alice asks.

"For mommy."

"Grandma?" Alice yells, running inside with laughter in her wake. "I need my snow boots!"

Torin catches me before I can pass the window to follow her. "Miss Lucy Almost-Nyström, I have a gift for you. But first I need you to kiss me."

"Oh? Is that why you sent Alice inside?" I push up on tiptoe and attempt to kiss him, but he turns away.

"Oh, darn. You missed. Let's try again." Torin loops my waist and lifts me up, my legs wrapping his waist. I cradle my arms around his head. "Torin Nyström. You are holding my heart, and I need to kiss you" I move my lips over his, and he groans happily. "Because otherwise I won't get my Christmas present," I whisper.

Torin laughs as he sets me down and pulls a small bag out from his back pocket. "Here, Merry Christmas, Lucy."

"Mmm, all of a sudden I'm debating. Will I like this better than the kissing?"

"You tell me." Torin grins and presses a kiss to my forehead, pulling me into his side as we walk toward the front door.

The thin pink pouch holds a silver snowflake pendant on a chain. Tiny diamonds stud the arms of the delicate snowflake. A new necklace to replace the one I lost last year as our relationship was getting started.

I can't breathe. I look up at him. "How did you know?"

"How did I know what?"

"How much this would mean to me." Tears spill past my eyelids, trailing hot tears down my cheeks.

"I didn't. I just figured if snowflake wishes brought us together, I want you to be able to keep wishing."

I brush the emotion away and lean up on tiptoe, offering him another kiss. "I'm going to need to kiss you a lot."

"I won't complain about that." He takes the necklace from my hand and clasps it around my neck. "You are the answer to all my wishes," he whispers.

I reach for it, finding it exactly where it's supposed to be.

"Tell me again how to say I love you in Swedish?"

His eyes are soft as he looks down at me. "*Jag älskar dig.*"

I smile, feeling the words work their way into my heart. "Tell me again."

His wide grin stretches across his face this time, and he leans down to kiss me. "*Jag älskar dig.*" He kisses my nose and runs his lips down to my jaw. "*Jag älskar dig.*" He works down my collar bone with tiny presses of his lips, pushing the snowflake pendant to the side, before placing a firm kiss where my pulse beats wildly.

"I love you," I breathe back to him.

Drawing his lips up my neck, he kisses my chin, stopping as he molds his lips lightly to mine. I can feel his smile with my eyes closed, and when I open them, I'm not cold anymore.

I pull back, examining the pleased look on his face. "What?"

He laughs and kisses my nose. "You're blushing."

Acknowledgments

I cannot express the appreciation I have for the amazing team of authors I have been working with in the Seasons of Sugar Creek series. Their support and imagination and genius has been a joy as we created this incredible community of characters, events, and locations. I am so grateful to be connected to them.

I'm not gonna lie, I had a bit of a breakdown writing this novel. I crashed and didn't know if I'd be able to complete it or any other novel. Thanks to deadlines and dear friends, a lot of chocolate and ice cream, I kept working. In all truth, this novel would not exist in a readable form if not for my dear friend Heidi Boyd. Her book was also published while I was completing this novel and is a wonderful women's fiction novel called Paint the Grass by H.R. Boyd it reminded me that the efforts we go through on a daily basis are nothing, if we aren't doing what we love.

My daughter, Allyson Osmond, as always is my first and last reader and editor. Many thanks for your suggestions, inspiration and your red pen. My husband has been my everything through this journey . . . and I do mean everything. There are days of frustration and missing me so much he wants me to quit but his support surpasses even the hard times. He has spent months picking up kids, grocery shopping, cleaning the house, making dinners, and working a full-time job so I can pursue my author career that together we hope will bless us both.

This book is dedicated to my grandmother and great grandmother, but their influence was felt most heavily through my mother and her deep love for her heritage. I have seen and been a Santa Lucia many years of my life, because of her. I have sat at the foot of my great grandmother's bed learning Swedish and playing with her *Swedish Dancing Dolls* (I highly suspect they had a different name than this but I loved them.) because my mother suggested it when I showed an interest in the language. I have baked in old kitchens next to my grandma in her wrap around full body apron watching her wrinkled hands create magic because my mother loved her mother and wanted me to know her joy. Their food, and love, and words, expressions, laughter, hugs, humor, style, grace, romance, and passion will live with me forever . . . because my mother kept our family together. Driving us across counties to visit her childhood home and share the memories that would shape our futures. I cannot thank you enough for the life and childhood you gave me and my siblings. Your joy and laughter and creativity shaped everything that I am. I love you.

Lastly, I need to thank the readers and fans that have loved my words enough to buy my books. You give me the strength to keep writing and the validation of knowing someone will enjoy my stories and ramblings. I love you all and cannot wait to send this book, and many more, out into the world.

Pronunciation Guide

Disclaimer: This is a very basic pronunciation guide designed by myself, a native English speaker, who loves the Swedish language but is by no means fluent or a linguist.
I did have a wonderful Swedish Great Grandmother whom I knew until she passed away while I was in my twenties, and who tried to teach me to speak her native language.
Plus, another Grandmother who spoke Swedish fluently and loved to teach us silly phrases like *du luktar som en get* – meaning: *you smell like a goat*.
Simply, I'm trying to help you hear the sounds that will make it easier to be familiar with the few, beloved Swedish words included in this novel.

Älskling	–EH-lsk-lēng	–darling
En söt	– In sut	– sweet one
En lite grann	– In leet gr-aw-n	– A little bit
Farfar	–FAAr-fAAr	–Grandpa (Father's father)
Morfar – MAWr-fAAr also means Grandpa (Mother's father)		
Farmor	– FAAr-mAWr	–Grandma(Father's mother)
Mormor – MAWr-mAWr – also means Grandma (Mother's mother)		
Försiktig	– Fur-shik-tig	– Careful or protected
(Such as "Careful with my heart." - *Försiktig med mitt hjärta*)		
Glad Lucia, mina älsklingar	– Gl-AWd Loo-sia mē-na EH-lsk-lēng-ahr	– Happy Lucia Day, my darlings
Ja	–Ya	– Yes
Jag älskar dig	– Ya-G-ĕls-kah day	– I love you
Mycket gott, sötnos.	– M-yeh-kit goat, sūt-nōs	– very good sweetie
Mitt hjärta	– Mēt hĕj-YAR-ta	– my heart
Nej	– Nay	– No
På Svenska	– Po-uh Svĕn-skuh	– In Swedish
Sankta Lucia	–Sawn-k-ta Loo-sia	– Santa Lucia
Sötnos	– Sut-nōs	– sweetheart or sweetie
Tack så mycket	– Talk so m-yeh-kit	– Thank you so much

Ingrid Nystrom's Pepparkakor Cookies

(Torin and the author's favorite)

- ¾ cup Shortening
- 1 cup Sugar
- 4 tablespoons Molasses
- 1 Egg, beaten
- 2 cups Flour
- 2 teaspoons Baking Soda
- 1 teaspoon each of Cloves, Cinnamon, and Ginger

Cream sugar and shortening together, add egg and molasses, blend well.

Add the spices to the flour and sift, then add it to the creamed mixture. Let cool for 1 hour in refrigerator covered in plastic wrap.

Then roll into balls the size of walnuts, roll each ball in sugar, place onto a cookie sheet, then smash with a flat-bottomed glass. Press one raisin in the center of each cookie.

Bake at 350 degrees F for 5-10 minutes until the edges are set and slightly more golden than the rest.

Sankta Lucia

Natten går tunga fjät runt gård och stuva.
Kring jord som sol förlät, skuggorna ruva.
Då i vårt mörka hus, stiger med tända ljus,
Sankta Lucia, Sankta Lucia.

Natten var stor och stum. Nu hör, det svingar,
I alla tysta rum, sus som av vingar.
Se på vår tröskel står vitkläd, med ljus i hår,
Sankta Lucia, Sankta Lucia.

"Mörkret skall flykta snart ur jordens dalar."
Så hon ett underbart ord till oss talar:
Dagen skall åter gry, stiga ur rosig sky.
Sankta Lucia, Sankta Lucia.

Santa Lucia

Night walks with a heavy step
round yard and hearth,
As the sun departs from earth,
shadows are brooding.
There in our dark house, walking
with lit candles,
Santa Lucia, Santa Lucia!

Night walks grand, yet silent,
now hear its gentle wings,
In every room so hushed,
whispering like wings.
Look, at our threshold stands,
white-clad with light in her hair,
Santa Lucia, Santa Lucia!

"Darkness shall take flight soon,
from earth's valleys."
So she speaks wonderful words to
us:
A new day will rise again from the
rosy sky.
Santa Lucia, Santa Lucia!

Sankta Lucia

Text: Arvid Rosen
Translation: Anne-Charlotte Harvey

Neopolitan Folk Tune
Lyrics and Music Arr: Hillary Sperry

Note from the author –

I arranged this when my children were young. I had one daughter playing viola and one playing violin (short lived but wonderful experiences.). I merged English and Swedish to help them learn the song in its original language, and used the spurts of English to keep my young kids paying attention.

It must have worked, because over a decade later, they still remember it.

The text and translations are credited on the music to the individuals who originally wrote and translated the song.

About the Author

I fell into romance writing with two of my best friends and couldn't be happier. I write every day and I love creating. So that's what I do. I create food, art, music, love, and especially books.

I love letting my imagination roam through new and familiar worlds. I love romance and adventure, ice cream, flowers, cheesecake, and I have yet to find a store-bought cake that is as good as mine.

More from Sugar Creek

One Last Christmas
BY CYNTHIA GUNDERSON

One Last Christmas

www.CindyGunderson.com

Chapter 1

I lifted my hand to knock on the door of the house I'd grown up in. I hesitated. *How had I ended up here again?* I shifted my weight on the doormat and set down my suitcase. It wasn't that I didn't want to see my mom and sister, but this wasn't the plan. I was supposed to be relaxing on a beach right now—not parked on my old cul-de-sac, prepped to move back home for a month.

I drew a deep breath and steeled myself, then rapped my knuckles on the worn wood. I inspected the planters next to the door and the rocking chair on the porch. This house looked exactly like I remembered it, but that wasn't a surprise. Mom was brilliant and creative...and also had zero desire to take on house projects. She threw herself full-tilt into work and theater projects and had time for little else. Especially now that I was gone and Megs was the only one at home.

Footsteps sounded inside, and before I could decide whether I was standing too close to the door, it flew open, and there was Mom. Her glasses were slightly askew, and a few curls that had escaped her hair clip were flying haphazardly around her ears. She smiled so widely I thought her face might split in two.

"Bobbi! You made it!" She threw her arms around me before I even had a chance to step inside.

"Hi, Mom." I grinned, not able to return the embrace because she had my arms in a vice grip. Sylvia DeBosse was short and slender, but her hugs were no joke. That woman had some serious strength locked inside her thin appendages.

"Here, let me help you." Mom dropped her arms and reached for my suitcase.

"It's okay, I've got it." I brushed her hands away and lifted the bag over the threshold. "I'll bring in the rest of my things tomorrow."

She nodded as she beamed at me. "I thought you wouldn't be here until after dinner."

I shrugged. "I got on the road a little earlier than I thought. But don't feel like you have to feed—"

Mom scoffed. "Of course, I'm going to feed you." She reached out and pushed the door closed, then walked past the sofa in the front living room. "Megs!" she called down the hall. "Your little sister's here!"

Megs tromped down the hallway. "Mom, what are you doing? You need to be at least six feet from her!"

I rolled my eyes. "Megs, you know I already finished quarantining, and my test came back negative." She looked at me skeptically. "You seriously think I'd show up here when I was contagious?"

Megs shrugged, and Mom made a point to step close and pat my shoulder. "Go ahead and get settled in your room. Come to the table whenever you're ready, honey."

I nodded, set my shoes on the mud rack, then lifted my suitcase—to avoid rolling snow-covered wheels on the wood floor—and carried it through the entry toward the hall on the left. I glanced longingly to the right where Megs' room was. It had its own private bathroom. I'd hoped to move in there during my senior year of high school, but Megs never moved out. That meant I was forever relegated to a room the size of a postage stamp with a bathroom across the hall.

I pushed the door open—my Olympic rings sticker still stuck proudly between the panels—and set my suitcase on the floor in the corner by the dresser. The zipper caught as I tried to open it, but it eventually gave way. I sat back on my knees and stared at my winter clothes, then glanced around the bedroom. I couldn't help but compare my old twin bed with the patchwork quilt and the four-and-a-half-star beachside resort I was supposed to be staying in.

I yanked out my sweaters and stacked them on the carpet. Sugar Creek was a lovely town—especially around the holidays—but it held nothing for me anymore. Besides Mom and Megs. I sighed. And Haley, but this wasn't the plan. Missing my graduation trip? Not the plan. Having to wait three weeks to move into my Los Angeles apartment? *Not the plan.*

Even though I'd had time to come to terms with this shift in my life trajectory, I still couldn't get over the ridiculousness of it. *How had my COVID test come back positive?* I didn't even have any symptoms when I took the test.

I stood, opened the larger middle drawer of my dresser, and plopped the sweaters inside. The airline and resort hadn't cared about my lack of cough or runny nose. They wanted proof in the form of a piece of paper, which I couldn't provide them. At least I'd gotten the hotel refunded after a few hours on hold. And the airline did give me flight credits. But there hadn't been an affordable option to rebook the trip so close to Christmas, and I wasn't going to be a jerk and ruin everyone else's trip just because I couldn't go.

I closed my eyes and exhaled slowly. It was fine. I could enjoy Christmas here with the family and pretend I didn't know that my two best friends from film school were sitting on a blissful white sand beach without me. I could muscle through until it was finally time to make my way to L.A.—hopefully with a shiny new internship at B25 Productions to show up for.

I reached into my back pocket and pulled out my phone, then swiped to my inbox. I'd already checked it three times today, but the workday still hadn't finished on the Pacific Coast. I scrolled through advertisements, clothing sale announcements, and student loan reminders and grimaced, then pulled off my jeans and slipped into my favorite fuzzy pajama pants.

"Can I help with anything?" I asked as I walked into the kitchen and straightened my oversized sweatshirt. Megs was sitting on a stool at the island, and Mom was pulling something out of the oven.

"Hi to you, too." Megs' heavily mascaraed eyes flashed with annoyance. It was just the invitation I needed.

"Oh, Meggie, it's so good to see you!" I ran to her and smashed my face against her cheek as I wrapped my arms around her shoulders.

"Ewww! Bobbi, get off me!" she groaned, but I could hear a smile breaking through her feigned disgust. I let her go with one final obnoxious squeeze, then backed away before she could smack me.

"You asked for it." I grinned and walked to the opposite side of the island, then rested my elbows on the countertop. "How are you?"

"Good." Megs rolled her eyes. "I started a new job."

"Oh yeah? Where at?"

"Sugar Creek Loop."

My eyes widened. "Are you one of the performers? For the Christmas train?" Somehow I knew Megs was not talking about being hired to take tickets or clean rail cars—that had never been her style. Which was why she was in her current predicament.

"Yep." She smiled proudly. "I auditioned in September and got one of the singing roles."

"That's great." I mustered as much excitement as I could after sitting in the car for five-and-a-half hours. It wasn't that I didn't feel genuine happiness for her and this new gig—I was thrilled she was working and doing something she loved. But how long was it going to last? They wouldn't have performers on the train after the holidays, and then what? We'd watched her go down this road many times before, and it never ended well.

Mom removed the tin foil from the top of the pan she'd pulled out of the oven. "I really went all out tonight, girls." She held her arms out dramatically. "Freezer lasagna. Ooooh!"

She turned with the foil from the top of the pan still in her hand. Gooey cheese dripped on the tile as she opened the fridge. "And bagged salad." She set the foil down on the counter, held the door open with her hip, then reached into the crisping drawer and pulled out a salad kit.

"Looks great, Mom." I wasn't being sarcastic. Store-bought or not, this was better than nine out of ten meals I'd eaten in my apartment lately.

Mom threw the salad at me. "Can you grab a bowl and toss that up?"

I nodded and walked to the cupboard, impressed that after two years away, I still remembered where everything was.

Mom stepped on the dripped cheese and muttered something under her breath, then reached for a paper towel to wipe it up. "Megs, you get the plates and fill a few glasses with water."

Megs slid her stool out from the counter and did as she was told. This all felt so familiar, it was almost jarring. Like I was living this moment in parallel worlds that had somehow collided into one moment in time.

I opened the plastic bag and dumped the shredded broccoli into the bowl, then added the packet of nuts and dried cranberries and tossed the whole thing with the sweet poppyseed dressing. I threw the empty bags in the trash and brought the bowl and tongs to the table, then took my seat between the two of them.

It was the same four-top table we'd always had. Three chairs—one on each side with the fourth edge being pressed up against the wall to give more room between the breakfast nook and the island. We hadn't needed four chairs since I was six years old.

Mom reached out and pulled one of each of our hands into hers. "It's so nice to have both of you girls here." She turned her attention to me. "I'm sorry your trip didn't work out."

I nodded and plastered a smile on my face so she couldn't see the very real disappointment on my face. The last thing I wanted was for her to think she came in second to friends or a tropical destination.

She gave our hands a final squeeze and let them go, then picked up the spatula on the table and cut herself a piece of lasagna.

My brow furrowed as I watched her transfer it to her plate. I scanned the family room and glanced at the empty railing leading down to the basement. "Where are all the costumes?"

Mom lifted her head in confusion with her fork halfway to her mouth.

I pointed to the bare countertops. "Normally you have stuff all over the place this time of year. Doesn't *White Christmas* open the second weekend in December?"

"It does." Mom nodded. "But—"

"Mom doesn't do that part anymore." Megs picked up the serving spoons and dished up her salad.

"What do you mean 'doesn't do that part?'"

"She doesn't do the costumes. She hired someone."

My eyes widened in surprise. "Really? When did that happen?"

Mom shrugged as if it were no big deal that after fifteen years of insisting she needed to do everything herself, she'd retracted her claws from a portion of the production.

"Last year," she answered finally, then blew on the glob of lasagna on her fork and put it in her mouth.

"Wow." I lifted the spatula. It was clear she didn't want to make a big deal of it, but I was stunned. "That's got to feel good. Not having to do it all yourself."

Mom nodded curtly.

I slid the piece of lasagna onto my plate. "What about the set?"

"Frank's doing that this year. He's putting it together in his outbuilding."

My fork froze halfway to my mouth. "Frank? As in...Mr. McGinnis?" He was my social studies teacher in middle school, and I swear, he'd always had a thing for mom. "Didn't he ask you out once?"

A blush rose to Mom's cheeks. "No—"

"He *totally* did." Megs grinned as she wiped marinara sauce from her lips. "Remember? After Bobbi's eighth grade graduation?"

"I have no idea." Mom looked flustered. "That was so long ago—"

"You turned him down. Said you didn't make it a habit to date your children's teachers," Megs continued.

"You didn't!" I gaped at her. "Poor Mr.—"

"Okay, that's enough." Mom was blushing furiously now. "Your dad and I had barely finalized our divorce. I wasn't in a good place."

I looked down at my plate. By 'barely,' she meant they finalized it over four years earlier. I guess time passed quickly when you were taking care of two little girls on your own.

"I still think he has a thing for you." Megs arched an eyebrow, and I snorted.

Mom flashed me a look, but I didn't miss the slight curve of her lips as she took another bite of lasagna.

We ate in comfortable silence until I noticed Mom glance up at Megs. I looked over and saw Megs give Mom an almost imperceptible shake of the head.

"What?" I asked, and the energy in the room tangibly shifted. "What's wrong?"

Mom sighed and nodded to Megs. "She needs to know."

"Know what?" My voice raised in pitch.

"I think we could've waited 'till tomorrow," Megs muttered, and my heart raced. *What news could be bad enough to warrant this kind of trepidation?* The two of them looked healthy, but maybe something was going on under the surface. The blood drained from my face as I sank into my seat. Was Mom—?

"You know the McNeils returned to Sugar Creek last year," Mom started, and I blinked in confusion. Mom had told me Ben's parents moved back from Colorado, but why would she be bringing them up?

Mom clasped her hands on the table nervously.

"Mom—"

"Ben's back," Megs spit out.

For a second, I forgot to breathe. Ben McNeil was back? *Here in Sugar Creek?*

Mom squeezed her eyes shut. "He moved back home at the beginning of November because..." She sucked in a breath, and when she turned her eyes to mine, they were shimmering with tears. "Bobbi, Corinne is sick."

I swallowed hard. Ben and I had gone skiing every Friday after school together during the season, and every other day he was either here at my house, or I was over at his. Corinne had been like a second mother to me.

"How sick?" My voice came out in a whisper.

Mom pursed her lips and shook her head as a tear spilled onto her cheek.

My breathing became shallow, and the kitchen suddenly felt stifling. Without saying a word, I pushed my chair back and stood, then rushed to my room.

Seasons of Sugar Creek: Winter

INN LOVE FOR CHRISTMAS is part of the SEASONS OF SUGAR CREEK series. The books do not need to be read in order. They are stand-alone stories that all take place in our imaginary small town in Vermont.

This book has been a joy to write and I'm so looking forward to more stories in this town. It feels like a real place to me and I have to remind myself that it's not on the map.

Feel free to enjoy Sugar Creek with us in all six books of the Winter season and watch for the upcoming seasons as well.

Seasons of Sugar Creek: Fall
Seasons of Sugar Creek: Summer
Seasons of Sugar Creek: Spring
Seasons of Sugar Creek: New Years